The Violent Season

BY *Robert Goulet*

The Violent Season

GEORGE BRAZILLER, NEW YORK, 1961

THIS BOOK IS FOR *PIERRETTE*
MY SEMAPHORE

"As long as that house stands we shall have bad luck."

"Tell you what you *could* do. What is it you call this thing where an old man marries a young girl, and you come out with horns and—"

"Charivari?"

"Yes, that's it."

Old Creole Days, by
George Washington Cable.

That was one hundred and fifty years ago in New Orleans. Today, in Quebec, charivaris still take place. The one in New Orleans was raised by men and the purpose was ridicule and the results satisfactory, however sad. Mine, in Quebec, is raised by women and the purpose is righteous and the results—that depends on what you believe in. In any case, when the women of Quebec Timberland rise in a charivari, it is for blood. And if it so happens that their God is better served this way, who will say that they did wrong? Not one among them, to be sure. Nor I, whose only task is to seek the substance of their soul in a mood as sincere as if their ultimate truth were my own reality.

R. G.

one

Monsieur Louis Dupre, stationmaster
of the one-man train depot in La Buche, had spent many
years craving for escapades hardly respectable for a man of
his position in this small, belfry-hearted community lost in
the wilds of Quebec timberland. He had a large family, was
a church warden, earned the highest salary in town. His wife
had the important post of treasurer of Les Dames de la Grâce.
He enjoyed the distinction of going to work dressed in a suit,
with shirt and tie, and was allowed a daily quota of two
bottles of ale at Lambert's after work. Yet he was an unhappy
little man, gnawed with frustration and mortally afraid of his
wife. In moments of loneliness he liked to compare his exist-

ence to a discarded train ticket stamped with pleasure-sounding places like Montreal, New York, Old Orchard: each one meant an old dream, all of them were punched *canceled*.

Then one day, a few years ago, it seemed that all of a sudden the least chaste of his secret desires would be satisfied at last. It was on a Wednesday evening. He had just left Lambert's tavern, when he found himself in a strange room. The door closed behind him. He stood shaking his head in wide-eyed incredulity—here he was, all alone with a beautiful young woman who seemed willing.

At first he supposed himself overcome by one of his dreams of lust from which he always awoke with a red face, carefully avoiding looking his wife and nine children in the eye. Then he decided that he was not really here, in this room; no, he was still at Lambert's listening to Maurice and Altar Boy who had treated him to an extra bottle of ale and were telling dirty stories. Only he wasn't at Lambert's, either. There were sounds of people walking barefoot, upstairs. A woman giggled in the next room. The front door opened, sending down the hall a wave of male voices that soon met with girls' whisperings.

Monsieur Dupré felt warm. A soft light shone at the head of the bed. He could see the young woman glide about with silent feet, elusive yet within reach, radiating that thrilling mystery of strangers about to be loved. All of his senses quickened, suddenly. He could no longer escape the reality of it. And be became tense with mingled fear and hunger, aware of himself on the point of plunging head-first into an embrace that both frightened and attracted him, and that he now wanted desperately to prolong, even before it started, if only to postpone for a while the remorse and the shame that would follow.

"Take off your coat," said the young woman.

"Of course, of course." His voice was brittle, high pitched. He was short, bald, had a long nose and wore thick glasses. With trembling hands he took off his jacket, and as if rummaging in the top of his desk for a lost label he began looking for a place to put it. His head was tilted over his right shoulder, a habit born of years of listening to the wireless buzzer and talking to people at the ticket window. When he had finally hung his jacket on the back of a chair, near the door, he removed the plastic cuffs fastened to his shirt sleeves by paper clips, and put them away in the pockets. Then he turned round and began to move toward the young woman by the bed, drawing courage, it seemed, from an unconscious mannerism of constantly adjusting his glasses on the bridge of his nose.

She had removed the top sheet and was folding it at the foot of the bed. As she bent over, his legs nearly touched her strong, full hips under the tightly draped skirt. Monsieur Dupré could not recall the day he had come so near young flesh. A sudden urge to feel took hold of him. With quivering fingers he reached to caress her, gently, just a bit for now.

But she straightened up, turned, and snapped: "Don't pinch."

His hand dropped. He felt that he was going to blush. His glasses bothered him terribly. At last he ventured: "You are so nice."

She was tall, but not as tall as his wife, so that he did not feel short beside her. Plump, pleasantly so, she had a full bosom that was unmistakably made of two individual parts, not a sloppy mass of flesh flopping up and down like his wife's. Her hair was black, streaming casually down the sides of an oval face striking for its pale complexion and large dark eyes. In them he thought he could detect now a flicker of boldness,

11

now a fleeting shadow of melancholy. She was lovely, he thought. And again he felt the urge to touch her, run his fingertips lightly over the skin of her neck, up and down her vein-marbled arms. "Oh, you are nice," he repeated, growing bold. "Very, very nice."

"How do you know?"

His small gray eyes flashed hunger. "I can tell."

"That is what they all say just before. But when it's over they don't say it again. They look sour and slam the door. Sometimes they even try to beat you, as if you had robbed them of something."

"Not me."

She smiled, then made a vague gesture of indifference.

"I will be good to you, even after," he insisted.

"Really!"

"Oh, you are only teasing."

"You don't look to me as if you needed much teasing."

"Let me kiss you. Just a little one."

She turned abruptly.

Monsieur Dupré stood watching as she took off her stockings, stepped out of her panties. The nearer he moved to her intimacy the more violently he hungered for her, yet the more disappointed he became, for the stronger his suspicion grew that somehow he was being fooled. That she had many admirers, he knew. Maurice had mentioned arranging for her to meet some of his friends. Presumably, she and the other girls who worked in this bead factory that belonged to Maurice felt lonely at night, new as they were in this small town whose men would not come back from the logging camps for another few weeks. An occasional escapade, then, was in the order of things. But why did she have to talk about other men just now? It did tend to make her sound like a prostitute, which, he knew, or at least wanted to believe, she was not at

12

all. Well, perhaps other men had paid to make love to her. Perhaps. But what an ugly thought to entertain at a time like this!

"What is your name?"

"They call me Lise."

"Lise! What a lovely name!" he mused aloud, more at ease now. A moment ago he had got the impression that she did not care for him, that she even despised him. But now her voice had no trace of resentment in it. She did not sound very friendly, true enough. But that was to be expected. After all, it was not easy for a young woman to let a perfect stranger make love to her just like that. She had to put up some kind of front. That boldness in her look was no doubt a disguise, a devilish way of hiding her prudery. Oh, she was a real teaser! he thought, tracing with hungry eyes every line of her young body under the clothes, as she deposited her stockings, then her panties, at the foot of the bed. There was a quiet grace about her, a delicate poise that told him she must be a well-brought-up young lady.

Indeed, Monsieur Dupré reflected, one could see that this lovely girl was no prostitute; although, to be sure, he would not know what a prostitute was like, since he had never slept with one. Oh, no! He was a respectable man, after all, which was probably the reason why Maurice had chosen him for her. She looked so much like a young lady educated in the sound traditions of our good French-Canadian Catholic families that he felt moved to ask: "Do you come from the city?"

She lay on the bed keeping her skirt and blouse on. As she did not seem to have heard his question, he repeated: "Do you mind if I ask where you come from?"

"The Orphanage in Trois-Rivières," she replied.

They heard a door open across the hall, a woman's voice, then a man's, arguing in urgent tones.

"Are there many girls in this house?" he asked.

"Quite a few."

"Maurice tells me the equipment is in the back room."

"That's right."

"I like this room of yours."

"I only work here. My room is near the Haymarket."

"I see."

There was a long silence, during which Monsieur Dupré looked back and forth from her skirt and blouse to her face, trying to attract her gaze and tell her silently: "Won't you please take them off, too, just for me?" But she kept staring at the ceiling as if he were not there. Finally he said: "I hear that you and Maurice are good friends."

"He's my boss."

"But—you know what I mean."

"I work for him. That's all."

He let out a sigh, as of relief. Now his mind was free to contemplate another meeting with her, possibly on that unclaimed mattress in the baggage room. The rush period at the depot would begin in the next few days; there would be plenty of excuses for coming home late. "Do you think that perhaps we could meet again after tonight?" he said. "Once in a while you might pay me a short visit at the depot. You see, I am the stationmaster here."

"Maurice told me."

"He didn't forget a thing, did he?"

"He never does."

Puzzled by this remark, he at once discarded it lest it spoil his pleasure. And he went on: "I was thinking: if you should find that you like me a little, I may be able to do things for you. Do you like train rides?"

"Sometimes."

"I could give you some tickets, free."

14

"I am not going anywhere."

"You might want to, someday."

"Please," she said. "It's getting late."

"You are right, Lise. Perfectly right," he said, wringing his hands in sudden panic at this abrupt reminder that if he wanted his pleasure he must take it now. He would have liked to go on talking a while. It was so much better when one took time. He removed his tie, put it neatly on top of his jacket. Then he began fumbling with the buttons of his shirt.

She was looking at him with an air that meant: "Look, Monsieur the stationmaster, you needn't go to all that trouble."

Somewhat coyly, he said: "Promise you will not tell anyone about this little moment of ours."

"Why should I tell?"

"I am rather well known here, you know. And then, there is my wife."

"I only work here. When I leave, I remember nothing."

"Good girl." Monsieur Dupré felt better, reassured. Gone were the doubts concerning the girl and this house. All of his faculties he could now concentrate on making her happy. If he succeeded in being a good lover, which he wanted so frantically to be, then the next few days and weeks and even months would look bright indeed. At last he would have a mistress! And this prospect made him smile, nervously, just as the nearness of his pleasure was making him giddy. It was only through conscious application that he could refrain from toying with his glasses. He did not want to remove them because he could hardly see without them; yet he was afraid they might hurt her cheeks. He took off his shirt; his gaze fell upon her underwear at the foot of the bed, it lingered there in intensely pleasurable contemplation.

"Couldn't you hurry a little?" she said.

15

Slowly, with an effort to look very seductive, he moved up to her along the edge of the bed. "You are such an impatient little thing." He tried a first caress, running his hand gently up her legs, slowly, then suddenly all the way up.

She kept staring at the ceiling. Her face was calm. His growing sensuality she took with passive, impersonal quietness. Then as he became bold her flesh began to quiver and the muscles and nerves in her limbs tightened.

Monsieur Dupré thought that he was making her happy. He relished the way her flesh reacted to his gentle manipulations. Every corner of her body revealed a new source of delight. His passion could wait no longer. He must have her now.

"Please hurry," she said, closing her eyes.

Now he took her, in a sudden blinding fit of passionate jerks and bounds that covered him with perspiration and made him gasp out little cries of endearment mingled with a sighing, pleading tenderness. He wanted this moment to last. He tried desperately to make it last. He held back. He raged against himself. But soon it was all over: the thing of an instant, thirty years of dreaming come to ripeness as enough drops of sweat to soil a used sheet.

When he had rolled over, gasping for breath, she pulled down her skirt and picked up her underwear and stockings.

"Are you happy, my little Lise?" he asked.

"Are you?"

"Of course, my lovely."

"Then tell Maurice about it, so he will be happy too. That is very important."

"Let's not talk about him."

"You must get up now and dress."

"Couldn't you let me have these as a souvenir?" he asked, his eyes riveted upon the panties she was pulling up under her skirt.

"Ask Maurice. He's the boss."

This made him get up quickly and reach for his clothes. He felt nervous again. Why was she so hard, so brutal, all of a sudden? There was a strange smile on her lips. He felt sure she was laughing at him.

"Tell me, Monsieur Dupré," she said. "What did Maurice say the girls are doing in this house?"

He stopped abruptly in the middle of knotting his tie. "Why?"

"Do you expect me to believe that you swallowed that tale of the rosary-bead factory?"

"But this *is* a rosary-bead factory, isn't it? I saw the machinery being delivered by truck at this very door."

"Those were gambling tables. I can ask our manager, Paula, to show them to you in the back room."

"Then all these girls . . . ?"

"Yes."

"And you?"

"Yes."

"No!"

"That's right. This is a brothel."

"I don't believe it."

"Go on. You knew it all along."

"I swear I didn't."

She laughed.

He rushed to the door in panic, knocking his glasses off his nose. Now he could not find his coat, could not even see where he was. Lise picked up his glasses and gave them to him. He fumbled a moment trying to put them on. Then he grabbed his coat and reached for the doorknob.

"I thought you were going to be good to me," she said. "Even after."

He turned. "Oh, I am sorry, my dear. You are perfectly

17

right. I ought to give you a little something, I suppose." He felt his pockets for his wallet. "I am afraid I have no money on me just now. Could I mail it to you?"

"Never mind. It's on the house. Maurice is giving samples these days."

He opened the door and peered down the hall.

"There is nothing to be afraid of," she said. "All our customers are solid respectable citizens, just like you, Monsieur the stationmaster."

He did not dare leave the room. "Won't you go up to the front and make sure nobody sees me?"

She laughed a loud, full-throated laugh.

"Please," Monsieur Dupré pleaded, wringing his hands in distress.

"You phony little man," she went on laughing.

Between her scorn and ridicule, and the empty hall stretching before him, he finally chose the latter. Throwing his coat over his head, he ran all the way to the front door and out of the house, like a robber fleeing in the rain.

Lise slammed the door shut. Then as the echo of her scornful laughter receded, she walked back to the bed and sat down, beaten.

It was no good. To have humiliated this customer did not make her feel better. The shame was still there, gnawing inside her like a burning ejaculation from the devil himself. She had been able to do her work without feeling at one time; but now, it was impossible. Each customer she must torture in order to shake the haunting guilt. And in the end it was not the customer, but she, who was left to battle the monstrosity of this sin.

She tidied up the bed a little. Then she left the room and went into the parlor for a good talk with Paula.

18

Paula was one of the most competent supervisors in the pro-
fession. She had worked in a number of establishments in
Montreal, from bawdy houses east of the Rue Bleury to the
great 620 Rue du Cardinal, which was shut down a few years
ago after a high government official died suddenly in one of
its plush boudoirs. Since then she had put her vast experience
at the service of a man named Maurice, who was now
setting up a chain of houses throughout the province. A big
blonde woman of about forty, she sported two magnificent
gold teeth, one at each end of her smile, and wore perfumes
imported from France. The girls looked up to her because of
her notorious past. They trusted her with confidences, even
money, and came to her for advice and encouragement.

As soon as Lise entered the parlor, Paula guessed from her
look that this was a case of fatigue. Before the girl had had time
to voice her complaints she made her sit on the couch, held
her hands and said, with sincere affection: "I know, honey;
what you need is a rest. That's easy to understand. And I
would be the happiest woman in the world if I could come to
you with a bundle and say: 'Here, honey, take this and go
spend a couple of weeks all by yourself in the Laurentians;
have fun, relax, take a lot of fresh air, sleep all day, and then
come back to work when your nerves are rested a little.' But I
can't do it, dearie, much as I would like to. Not at this time.
The jacks will be coming out of the camps any day now. I
need every girl in the house."

"I can't bear these men around here," Lise protested. "In
the city, at least, when a man comes to us he is open about it.
He doesn't pretend not to know he's in a brothel."

"A house of joy, honey," Paula corrected.

"I'm fed up."

"Now, calm down, dearie. Don't let your nerves get the best of you. I understand. When a girl has worked as hard as you have lately, she gets tired, and the first thing you know she begins to take things personally. But in this kind of work you've got to stay businesslike all along. You don't feel nothing. You don't think nothing. If a customer wants to be cheap, to hell with him! They're all the same anyway, you and I know that by now; they are always in a hurry to get in but they hate to get out. So let them be cheap. You and I are guardian angels to nobody. We're here to earn a decent living the best way we know how, that's all. Take it with a grain of salt, honey. It isn't you and me who invented sex and money and go around telling people what's right and what's wrong."

"I'm quitting just the same," Lise insisted.

Paula squeezed her hands. "Be reasonable, dearie. Don't walk out on us at a time like this. I hate to think how mad Maurice would be."

"My mind is made up."

"We have been open one month, now, paying salaries and taking practically nothing in. Our work so far has been public relations, giving out samples, making friends. But as soon as the loggers come back to town we'll be in full swing and the money will start coming in like you have never seen money in your life. Look, honey, we might even be able to arrange a raise for you."

"Thanks," said Lise, withdrawing her hands.

"I promise I'll talk to Maurice about it."

Lise shook her head. "I've been a whore long enough."

"Stop calling yourself a whore. That's the wrong attitude. Remember what Maurice said: we are not whores, but social workers."

Lise let out a sarcastic laugh.

Paula saw that she must use a different approach if she was to get results. Looking directly into Lise's eyes, then, she asked in a severe voice: "What's wrong?"

Lise shrugged her shoulders, hesitant to unburden herself.

"Come on, dearie," said Paula, growing motherly, "What's the matter?"

Lise lowered her head. Her long black hair streamed gently, undulating down into the white birth of her breasts. She blushed a little and bit her bottom lip, as if ashamed of herself. Finally she said: "I met someone . . ."

"Well!" exclaimed Paula. "When did *that* happen?"

"The first day we arrived here. I had gone out to look at the rapids. He was there."

How romantic! thought Paula, scornful.

Lise went on, "He's just a young fellow about my age, and very sick. He has only a short time to live. We want to be together now. I'm going to take him away somewhere."

"Now don't lose your head, honey. Things like that happen to all of us once in a while. But that's no reason to give up your career. It's not because a woman finds herself a lover that she must drop her husband."

"You don't understand, Paula. This is different. I love him. Why, he even reads poems to me—to me, can you imagine? It's the sort of thing I used to dream about when I was little. I know almost nothing about him, except that he has been in the seminary all his life and now his mother won't leave him alone a minute."

"Anything between the two of you?"

"Well, the first day, yes. He was so desperate. And I felt it was so nice to have it that way, for a change."

"Would it make you feel better," Paula said, "if I let you off tonight so that you can spend some time with him?"

"Not tonight. His mother is with him. But tomorrow,

maybe. There will be a meeting of Les Dames de la Grâce, and I suppose she will go, since she is the *présidente*."

Paula stood up abruptly. "Look here, honey; you're stepping on dangerous grounds. That association is the government in this town. If his mother is the *présidente* of it, you'd better not take chances. Something goes wrong between you and her, then all of us are in deep trouble."

"I'll be careful," Lise said. "I might want to come back after it's all over. You never know. But right now I'm ready to give up everything for him. For once in my life I have a chance to do something good and clean."

A lot of sentimental trash, Paula said to herself. "How long would you be away?" she asked.

"A few weeks."

Paula was silent for some minutes. Then she said: "I think you're making a mistake. But if you want to go I can't hold you here against your will. I won't promise to take you back, though. There's Maurice to consider in all this. And I'm afraid he won't like the idea at all."

"Could I get my money tonight?"

"Let's not rush through this, honey. We must think it over first. Tomorrow you might feel different about it."

"Part of it, at least?"

"Maybe. But I'll have to talk with Maurice."

"How much does he owe me, altogether?"

"Well, we can always try to figure it out."

But hardly had they begun adding up figures in Paula's patent-leather notebook, when footsteps on the sidewalk attracted their attention. Paula went to the window and peeped through the curtains.

It was a tall skinny man with one shoulder lower than the other. He came to a hesitant stop in front of the house, then began looking up, all the way up, as though studying the

22

architecture of a non-existent belfry on top of the roof, while from the corners of his eyes he glanced furtively up and down the street. Suddenly he made a dash for it, head down, shoulders hunched.

Paula turned to Lise. "Here is one for you. The beadle."

"Him again!"

"Do it for me, honey."

"He has had a dozen samples already," Lise protested.

"I know. But he's important to us."

They heard a loud, urgent knock at the door. Lise made a wry face. "Do it for me, honey," said Paula. "Then I'll see what I can do for you. Come now, cheer up, my pet. You're still my prettiest one."

two

La Buche is situated near one of the
largest and most beautiful rapids in the Quebec timberland.
Here the Saint Maurice river becomes a five-hundred-yard
stretch of turbulent water spraying clouds of silver-green mist
over pointed rocks along the foot of a high, wooded bank so
steep that the pine trees on it seem to grow one on top of
the other. At this time of the year, in April, the river below
and above the rapids is fully covered with logs, most of them
barkless and turning constantly as they float downstream,
glossy in the sun. The chute, too, is full to capacity. This is
a wooden channel-slide hanging from the bank above the
water through which the logs by-pass the rapids on their way

to the pulp and paper mills of Trois-Rivières, one hundred miles to the south. Many logs tip overboard and drop among the rocks, where they pile up in a jam that must be blown up with dynamite before it grows into a barrier. The funnel-like mouth of the chute, into which the logs are channeled between booms floating upstream, seems to be on the point of crashing down from the pressure of so much timber rushing on. Knock-knock-knock—a deep, fast beat as of a mechanical heart racing below the surface of the earth—is the sound the logs make as they hit the chute. It can be heard from one end of town to the other, just as can be smelled everywhere the sharp odor of wet bark, both carried to the folks by a light wind constantly blowing westward from the river to La Colline Sainte Marie.

Looking down from the top of this hill, you get the impression that La Buche is two separate towns sharing the strip of low land which stretches alongside the river. The larger part of it is bordered on the north by the shirt factory near the river, the Haymarket at the foot of the hills several blocks away, and on the east by the train station, whose rear platform and yard overlook the rapids across a ravine that is the ancient bed of the Saint Maurice. It looks like an overgrown logging camp in which the houses, all the same size, might have been built by the same person. Running parallel with the rapids are row after row of gable-roofed two-story dwellings, small, box-like, with a front porch large enough for a couple of rocking chairs. They all have a coal bin in the back and a galvanized iron stovepipe sticking out of the roof. Only the roofs and the fronts are shingled, the sides are planked, have two small windows one above the other, and the foundations show layers of logs weather-stripped with straw or old rags. These houses, or shacks, face one another across dirt roads edged with wooden sidewalks, roads so narrow that Monsieur le Curé's

Chevrolet can pass only by riding two wheels on one of the sidewalks, and a woman at a front window does not have to raise her voice to gossip with a neighbor across the way. Weather, time, the absence of men nine months of the year, have painted this part of La Buche the dull gray-brown of misery. Very little sunlight ever gets indoors.

But the rest of the town, to the south, presents a different view. It appears to have been planned with space in mind. There is a clean expansive look about the buildings. An air of everlasting solidity prevails. It is this section, indeed, which inspires some folks to say that while the lumberjacks set foot here before the priest, the priest has done very well catching up with them. Within three blocks stand the church, the presbytery, the Seminary and the Convent of the Ursulines, in the shape of a T; the Rue des Erables, with offices and shops; and the Rue des Pins, with its well-kept houses, both streets paved and lined with sidewalks made of octagonal slates. Except for the shirt factory, these are the only brick or stone buildings in La Buche. They are also the tallest ones, and all of them have a cross on the roof, so that at every hour of the day, from sunrise to sunset, the shadow of a cross moves slowly through the Place de l'Eglise.

To the left of this public square stands the Police-and-Fire House, a two-story building where a dozen police officers, who double as firemen, work and live downstairs, the upstairs being a jail whose windows offer a full view of the presbytery across the Place. There Monsieur le Curé lives in a massive fieldstone residence that has a veranda and a second-floor balcony from which he speaks to the crowd on special occasions. It is large and impressive, yet it looks small in comparison with the church. This is also a fieldstone construction, long, rectangular, with high windows and a gabled roof, a cross between a Gothic cathedral and a barn: its black iron doors are stately, somber-looking, and its belfry is a copper-sheathed bladelike tower that sparkles fiercely in the sun. The church is said to have cost nearly as much as all the other houses in town combined; the folks paid for it in cold cash, an achievement the women of La Buche are very proud of.

*　*　*

The whole countryside was echoing peals from the church bells, when Monsieur Dupré, around eight o'clock on the morning after his visit to the Red House, left home with his eldest daughter. They walked together as far as the Rue des Erables, where they kissed on the cheeks, then parted; he, on his way to the depot, she, on her way to church. At this hour, more than half the female population of La Buche was at work in the shirt factory; yet in a matter of minutes the dirt roads everywhere filled with women and children who, fresh from the breakfast table, fell into columns of four or five marching between rows of shacks, a formation they kept all the way to the Place de l'Eglise.

When Monsieur le Curé entered the church by the side door, a while later, he was pleased that so many of the faithful were showing up at this Special Mass. Two altar boys had just lit the candles on each side of the tabernacle. Monsieur Dupré's daughter sat at the organ and began playing pious music that buried the noises women and children made as they entered the pews. Then the bells stopped ringing.

Fulgence, the beadle, came out on the front step and waved the folks inside. Women and children who had gathered on the Place de l'Eglise broke off their gossip and came up the steps, where they queued to the fonts of Holy Water on the inner porch. He stared at them in a way that meant: "If you don't hurry, Monsieur le Curé will be angry again." They shuffled in a little faster. Out of the Police Station,

28

where he had spent the night, came Arthur, a tall, thin man in shabby clothes; he stood for a moment looking scornfully at the women, then after waving good morning to Fulgence he went on into the Rue des Erables. On reaching Lambert's tavern, he sat on the sidewalk with his back against the door and feet touching the curb. Women had to make a detour to avoid stepping on his legs, which brought him many a piercing glance of disapproval. He had taken a flask of gin out of his back pocket and was rapidly emptying it down his throat, his bloodshot eyes fixed upon Ti-Pit's store across the street.

All the shops were closed, except Ti-Pit's. His door was open, but he would serve no one until after Mass—Monsieur le Curé was very insistent on this point. A woman ventured to step across the sill, but Ti-Pit reminded her angrily that he was not going to break the rule for anybody. A mother who then happened to pass by with two children had difficulty dragging her young ones away from the window to which Ti-Pit's loud voice was attracting them. It was not wise to antagonize Ti-Pit, who was famous for cutting credit on those who poked their noses into his business, she began to explain, but was suddenly interrupted by exclamations of surprise rising from the square.

A bus was driving into the street between the church and the presbytery. Entering the Place de l'Eglise, the bus, painted bright red with black trimming around the windows and doors and much chrome everywhere, looked like an alien mechanical intrusion upon the quiet piety of the town. The queue to the fonts of Holy Water was broken up immediately; women and children ran down the steps; a crowd gathered on the square. Some of the women gazed at the bus in open-mouthed admiration, others looked proud as if they owned it, while children jumped about with exclamations of delight as if they were seeing Santa Claus in person. Then as the first surprise began

29

to wear off, and the women glimpsed the smiling face of Bernard Toupin at the wheel, wives and mothers agreed that it was a godsend; the bus would be able to transport their men back and forth from the camps much faster, more safely, than Bernard's old truck had. The bus drove into the Rue des Erables; more women came out of the church to see what the excitement was all about. Fulgence threw away his cigarette and went back angrily inside the church. A few women hurried after him, dragging their reluctant children and promising that there would be ample time to look at the bus after Mass. But the rest of them followed the vehicle with exclamations of wonder.

On both sides of the Rue des Erables people walked close to the store fronts, as though in fear the bus might run them over. Then as soon as it stopped in front of Ti-Pit's, women and children rushed in a wild scramble to be the first to see it at close range, touch it, feel it, talk to Bernard Toupin and perhaps get a ride. He opened the driver's window all the way. Questions came flying from everywhere. He did his best to answer them all, forgetting, at the same time, to turn off the engine, so that a cloud of black smoke began rising from the rear exhaust. It brought shouts of resentment from the women crowding there. The street and the Place de l'Eglise were rapidly taking on an atmosphere of festivity.

Then all of a sudden the church bells began ringing again, but much louder this time. Everybody looked toward the church.

There was Monsieur le Curé, out on the front step, with the alb and the stole on, ready for Mass. His round face was puffing with indignation, his red hair was wild, his fat arms were making all sorts of angry gestures at the crowd.

Immediately, the women dragged their children back inside the church. They hurried, with heads lowered, not daring to

30

speak above nervous whispers of self-reproach, blaming their children. In less than five minutes the Place de l'Eglise and the Rue des Erables were deserted. The bus went on puffing out smoke toward the church, where Monsieur le Curé let go with a flow of harsh words upon the congregation. Of all days, this was the one he and the beadle had chosen to go fishing: since fishing by the foot of the rapids was not good at this time, they would have to travel several miles upstream, which meant getting started early, and now this Special Mass would begin at least fifteen minutes late.

Bernard, meanwhile, was having a last look at himself in the rear-view mirror. His navy-blue suit looked neat, so did his new cap with the glossy visor, just like the ones he had seen on the bus drivers in Montreal. This uniform really gave class to his business, he reflected, as he tilted the mirror back in position and got up. He was short, heavy set, had a flat boyish face. Although in his late twenties, he looked no more than twenty-one or two, probably due to the eagerness that brightened up his small, shrewd eyes. Sitting at the wheel so much had caused his belly to grow somewhat prominent, but he could not be called a fat man, not by any means, he now told himself, while pulling his jacket neatly down around his waist. Or at least he was not as fat as Ti-Pit, to be sure! And with this pleasant thought in his mind, he pulled the hand-brake all the way, secure, and after checking the time by his watch, a gift from the grocer's wife, he turned off the engine and with a lighthearted swing of the arms he stepped down, across the sidewalk and into Ti-Pit's store.

"Good morning, Ti-Pit."

A large man with a sagging belly and a round head topped with a handful of grey hair which age had mercilessly trimmed like a Franciscan tonsure, Ti-Pit looked up from stacking cases of beer near the front door. He had a coarse face, blown up

31

with beer, and wore the sullen-sour expression of a man tormented by the twofold insecurity of needing to sell on credit in order to remain in business, and of having a wife twenty years his junior, an attractive young woman with a notorious past but to all appearances turned respectable. "Morning," he mumbled, more grumpy than usual.

"Well, what do you think of it?"

"Good-looking cart."

"Did you see that crowd go wild—"

"This beer is for Bechard," the grocer interrupted. "Twenty-four cases in all. And I have a few more things for you in the back. So why don't you start loading now while I do something else. There is more work here than I can handle this morning. And that lazy thing upstairs is in no hurry to give me a hand."

Bernard did not wish to get involved in a discussion concerning Ti-Pit's wife, so he immediately set out to carry the cases to his bus where he placed them under the back seats, while the grocer went behind the counter to sort out the orders. Ti-Pit's temper was running short. Whenever there was a Special Mass on weekdays all the women decided to do their shopping at the same time, immediately after Mass. The rush would start exactly when the delivery boy came to work, and all these orders had to go out before noon. If only his wife would come down and give him a hand! Here, four small orders he had put aside for her; one for the Seminary, one for Monsieur le Curé, one for the Convent, and a tiny one for the Bureau sisters. He picked up a broom from under the counter and knocked three times on the ceiling. No answer. He knocked again. No answer. "What the hell!" he mumbled, his face puffing up red in anger, and he gathered several small paper bags and began filling them up with peas, beans, sugar, flour and biscuits from the many-windowed drawers that lined the foot of the counter.

32

Bernard came back inside for another two cases of beer. He handed Ti-Pit a small book. "I'd appreciate it," he said, "if you would get your delivery boy to take this over to where I live. It's for a girl called Lise, who has a room next to mine. She asked me to buy it for her in Montreal."

"The Flowers of Evil" Ti-Pit read. "Holy Sacraments! What's that?"

"Verses."

"Sound's like pretty hot stuff." He opened it. "No pictures!" he exclaimed, disappointed. "But I'd better wrap it up well. Sure can't afford to have it lying around here, if you know what I mean."

"She wants it before six o'clock tonight," Bernard explained. "I promised I would get it to her this morning, but I won't have time now. That crowd held me back too long. You'd think Monsieur le Curé had decided to have a High Mass in my honor this morning."

"It's enough to make a man turn Protestant, the way they carry on with their Special Masses here and special meetings there. Hell, every time one of those association women misses her period, or Mother Superior lets out a fart, they sing a High Mass."

Bernard laughed. "What is this one for?"

"The charivari of '37, I guess," replied Ti-Pit, referring to the incidents that had rocked the town thirteen years before. Two young women living in a rooming house near the Haymarket had started a business of their own in order to supplement their meager pay from the shirt factory: at night they would entertain men in their rooms, for a fee, which proved so remunerative that after a few weeks they were able to leave their daytime job. But the boom did not last long. Word got around, Les Dames de la Grâce stepped in, a charivari was raised; the house was mobbed, set on fire, causing the death

33

of the two girls and five men trapped in the flames. "Not that I don't approve of closing down a brothel," he went on. "But it seems to me there are better ways of dealing with that sort of thing. Anyway, what is done is done. Only, I don't think this is anything to cheer about. And why in the hell they go on having a special Mass to celebrate the thing every year on the date it happened, that beats me."

Bernard agreed. "That's not having your sense of religion in the right place."

"And confidentially," said the grocer, lowering his voice, "word is getting around . . ." But now he held his tongue: his wife had just appeared at the door of the back room.

La Pitoune was a plump woman of about twenty-five with blond hair and an attractive look that was sometimes soft and gentle, sometimes bold. In her usual nonchalant manner, which she got from her father, Arthur, she came sliding in, as it were, along the edge of the counter. Ti-Pit had married her three years before, when he could no longer stand not to sleep with the pretty young slut who, in the year and a half that she worked for him, allowed him no more than a little feel under the skirt once in a while. It was well known in La Buche that from the age of sixteen until then, any young jack willing to give her a bag of Planters Peanuts or a box of Laura Secord Chocolates could roll her over in the ravine, or, when it was cold, in the hayloft above the stables at the Haymarket. But let any sharp tongue mention her past now, and that would mean the end of credit for a whole family. This morning she had put on a blue crepe dress under a red gabardine spring coat; her little red hat was brand new.

"Holy Sacraments!" Ti-Pit exclaimed. "What's the idea?"

"I'm going to church."

"But we got work to do."

34

"You should have asked me before I got into my Sunday's best."

"Look here." He moved to face her across the counter. "You've got four small orders, right here in front of you. Won't take you more than a couple of minutes. How about it?"

"Madame Dupré will be here any second now," she protested. "After Mass."

"There will be a rush then."

"Sorry," she said, with a shrug of the shoulders. And from her handbag she took a small mirror and admired her hat.

He thought of trying the diplomatic approach. It had worked before. So he cleared his throat, and with an effort to put on a winning smile he said: "That's a pretty little hat you're wearing."

"Thank you."

"When did you get it?"

"Yesterday."

"From Eaton's in Montreal?" he asked, knowing how proud she was of buying all her things through Eaton's catalogue.

"That's right. Cost a dollar nineteen."

"Wouldn't it look nice at Sunday High Mass?"

"Sure. But it's going to look just as nice this morning."

He let out a short sigh of helplessness. "All right, then. Do as you please." Then suddenly his rage got the better of him. "But I'm telling you . . ."

"What?"

"You're a bitch, see."

"Ti-Pit, take back those words."

"Like hell."

"I give you one more chance, Ti-Pit. Take back what you just said."

He leaned over the counter, breathing hard in her face. "A B-I-T-C-H, bitch, is that clear?"

35

"All right then. But don't you come back tonight begging for pea soup," she cried, using that precious word which belonged to their secret lovers' code—"pea soup," an expression he himself had introduced in the intimacy of their bed upstairs, born of the memory of the first time he had ventured a feverish hand up her legs while she sat on a bag of peas in the back room.

"For all I care about your pea soup, you know what you can do with it," he burst out in rage. "Bloody sour it is, anyway, after every jack in the valley has driveled in it."

"But you're pretty glad to have a nibble at it just the same, you big fat bully."

"Shut up," he screamed, defeated. He was going to say something else, but held back. It was no use. When she had something stuck in her head she didn't have it dangling from her behind, he muttered, and he continued to fill his paper bags, swearing to himself that a day would come when he would send that lazy bitch flying back to the hayloft where she belonged.

Bernard, who had preferred to stay on the sidewalk during this exchange, now came back inside for the rest of the order. La Pitoune was calmly prettying herself up in her compact mirror. Their eyes met. He caught the bold flicker he had learned to recognize.

"Good morning," she said.

"Good morning, Madame Leblanc," he replied politely.

"Good morning, Ti-Pit. Good morning, my dear. Morning young man," intoned Madame Dupré, who burst in at that moment. A tall, large woman with a prominent bust carried with pride, she walked stiffly, bearing her chin up with a determination and self-conscious dignity befitting her powerful position as treasurer of Les Dames de la Grâce. She had a severe face, never wore powder or lipstick, and her eyes sparkled from a passionate ambition which even her socially important position as the wife of the stationmaster could not fully satisfy.

Ti-Pit, without looking at her, mumbled a string of obscenities. Bernard returned her greetings and hurried back to work, this time carrying three cases instead of two. La Pitoune, behind the counter, said nothing; her face had suddenly taken on the expression of a beaten pup.

"Well, my dear, are you ready? Good gracious, what a pretty little hat!"

"He won't let me go to church," she whined.

Madame Dupré stiffened. She had adopted La Pitoune as a spiritual ward soon after her marriage to Ti-Pit. Not only was this important to one's credit with the grocer, but also, as her good sense told her, if she wanted to improve her position, she must associate herself with the feared but strong rather than with the loved but weak. So she directed Ti-Pit's wife's religious life with a zeal equaled only by the relentless severity with which she supervised her own family. To skip Mass on such an occasion was indeed unthinkable. "What's the meaning of this?" she snapped, turning to Ti-Pit. "Am I hearing right?"

"I reckon you are. Now, if you'll do us the favor of going on to church and leaving us alone, it will be very much appreciated I'm sure."

Madame Dupré smiled. It was not below her dignity to enjoy a good argument, especially when it involved the rights of a poor beaten wife like Ti-Pit's. And she was ready, having just primed herself through a good run-in with her husband for coming home late the night before. "So that's what we are all coming to, eh! Now our husbands won't let their wives do their religious duties. Well, I am sure we are going to have to do something about *that*."

"Look here, Madame, I don't go around poking my nose into your affairs, do I? So why don't you do the same, and everybody will be happy."

"It is my duty to see that our women are not taken advantage of."

"All he wants me to do is work and work," La Pitoune complained. "As if I hadn't done enough around here before he married me. Now he won't even let me go to church except on Sundays."

Ti-Pit threw his paper bags on the floor. "Shut up, you little liar. You haven't earned a bite of bread in this store since the day you hooked me."

"Don't worry, my dear," Madame Dupré told her. "Times have changed. We women mean to take care of ourselves from now on."

"Why don't you go home and take care of your nine brats and leave us to our work?" Ti-Pit said.

"You can't talk to me that way."

"Oh no? And what are you going to do about it? You're on my property, you know."

La Pitoune warned: "Ti-Pit, don't be rude." And Madame Dupré demanded an apology. "Right now."

"You're going to get one, all right. Up your fat bottom."

"Why! You brute!" Madame the treasurer blurted out, suddenly losing countenance and using language she was ordinarily careful to avoid outside her home. In an effort to pull herself together she walked stiffly to the front door and looked toward the church. It was still too early for her. She would never enter the church until everybody had sat down; it was a nice long walk up the center aisle to her pew in front.

Ti-Pit wiped his forehead. "Three sacks of peas," he said to Bernard, "two of sugar, and five gallons of molasses. Out there in the back room. I guess you know where to find them."

"Sure."

La Pitoune was watching Bernard's every move from the corner of her eye. After he had disappeared into the back room, she read the orders her husband had put aside for her. Then she picked out the one for Monsieur le Curé. At that moment Madame Dupré came back to the counter, in full possession of her fighting spirit once again. "I hear rumors," she began.

"Holy Sacraments!" cried Ti-Pit. "You still here!"

"Never mind your rudeness. I hear there is a house of sin in town, and, apparently, you, Ti-Pit Leblanc, are mixed up in it. Now what do you have to say for yourself?"

He was about to answer, when his wife put in: "Excuse me. I'll go and prepare Monsieur le Curé's order."

His eyes widened. A broad smile lit up his face. "Well, I'll be damned," he beamed. She had picked up a sheet of brown wrapping paper and a few bags. She really meant to give him a hand! "Go on, my pretty," he said, sending her off with a pinch at her round behind. "Give Monsieur le Curé the best we got." Then he turned to Madame Dupré, ready to fight with renewed vigor. "What was that you said about a brothel?"

"I said a house of sin."

"What's the difference?"

"As you like. The point is, your delivery boy was seen bringing merchandise to the Bureau sisters' Red House, and we know the girls in there don't make rosary beads, as we were told they would."

"Holy Sacraments!" Ti-Pit exclaimed in assumed surprise.

"We have observed the activities around that house for the last two weeks, and I'll have you know that what goes on in there is no laughing matter."

"You mean to tell me the Bureau sisters have rented out their house for a brothel? No, really. You're joking."

"The day those girls moved in, that very same night, one

of them threw a rock at the street light in front and blew it to pieces, just so we wouldn't see the men go in after dark."

"Don't believe it," said Ti-Pit.

"Well, I thought I'd warn you. Because, if it turns out that we were right after all, you know what is likely to happen to the house, to the people in there, and to those among us who do business with them."

Ti-Pit became serious. "Now look here . . ."

"One more thing . . ."

"Just a minute. I got something to say . . ."

"I haven't finished yet . . ."

In the back room, meanwhile, Bernard Toupin rounded up the sacks of peas and sugar and put them on a dolly which he pushed to the far end of the room where the molasses was. Then he climbed on top of a wooden box and reached for the one-gallon cans. He could hear the muffled footsteps of La Pitoune in the sawdust behind a stack of cartons.

She had already filled one bag with oatmeal and a second with pancake flour. Looking now for the soap that would complete Monsieur le Curé's order, she called out: "Any soap out there?"

"Yes," Bernard replied. "How many bars do you need?"

"Ten," she said, coming closer to him. "Did you have a good trip?"

"So, so."

"I missed you."

"I was only gone two days. Here you are." He handed her the bars of soap.

She put them on the floor. "Are you going to give me a ride soon?"

"Sure."

"Kind of independent this morning, aren't you?"

"I've got to get going early."

40

"I know," she said. Then after a pause, "But we got time, Bernie."

He looked down at her from atop the wooden box. "Not now. It's too risky. This is Thursday. I'll be seeing you tonight."

But didn't he know how much more she liked it when it was risky, especially after a row with her husband? "Come on, Bernie. We got time if you hurry."

He looked at her again, undecided, telling himself she would get him in trouble someday.

"Come down, Bernie. Don't make me wait like this. It's not fair."

"Oh, all right."

Hurriedly, she covered a low bank of cartons with the brown wrapping paper that she was going to use for Monsieur le Curé's order, and lay down on it, reaching for her skirt with hands trembling from the sudden desire that swept through her body.

"Hurry up. I'll be late for Mass."

"And I'm going to tell you something else," Ti-Pit was shouting. "A damn good thing it would be for this town if we had a brothel in it. Might make some of you lazy bitches appreciate your husbands a little more."

"Obviously, you know when the shoe fits you," Madame Dupré said.

"Shut up," Ti-Pit screamed. "You've got nothing to reproach my wife. Sure, she doesn't do as much work as she ought to. I know that. But as far as what you're trying to insinuate is concerned, she's changed, she's a clean woman now, and you know that yourself, otherwise you wouldn't be here now, would you."

Madame Dupré raised her eyebrows in disdain. Then turn-

ing her back to Ti-Pit she called out toward the back room:
"Coming, dear?"

"Yes, yes," was the muffled reply: "Coming."

*　　*　　*

Back at the wheel of his bus, Bernard Toupin fell a prey
to remorse. "So I did it again, damn it." It was hard to resist
La Pitoune. Yet he must, otherwise there was sure to be
trouble one of these days. If there was a scandal, didn't he
stand to lose much more than she did? "Next time I'm gonna
walk away, run." There was bound to be a last time, so why
not now. "Yes, that's it. Never again." The resolution was a
relief. Now he was free to enjoy the sensation of relaxed well-
being that his body always knew after a session with La
Pitoune.

But when he arrived at the train station, and saw La
Pitoune's father, Arthur, on the platform, recurring pangs of
guilt moved him to walk past him without a word. He went
directly into the depot, where Monsieur Dupré greeted him
with the mail for Camp Bechard.

Meanwhile Arthur got up and climbed into the bus and
made himself comfortable on the front seat. He had time to
take another long drink of gin before they returned.

Monsieur Dupré was asking: "How many passengers will
you carry?"

"Forty-eight seated. But I could squeeze in as many as
sixty."

"Must have cost a pretty penny. Is it new?"

"Only one year of service in Montreal."

"Congratulations, Bernard. You deserve it. I, for one, am
always pleased to see an honest young man get ahead. Good
luck."

"Thanks."

42

"Will you be able to make it back and forth in one day?"

"That is my schedule from now on. I'll be back in time for tonight's train," said Bernard, and he stepped inside the bus. Monsieur Dupré's reception had helped him recover his light-hearted pleasant manner. "Morning, Arthur. Like my new baby?"

"Too damn fancy for this neck of the woods," Arthur replied. Monsieur Dupré had turned toward the station. He called him back: "Hey, Louis. Don't you say hello to your old pal this morning?"

The other stopped still. Then toying nervously with his glasses he said: "You ought to be ashamed of yourself, Arthur. Drunk again. You could have waited at least until Mass was over."

"Did your wife give you another beating last night?"

"You just go on talking that way," warned the stationmaster, who usually hired Arthur as a helper during the rush in April and September, "and you'll find yourself out of a job."

"Did you get away with it?"

Monsieur Dupré turned pale.

"Where were you last night?" Arthur said.

"At Lambert's."

"I didn't see you."

"You were drunk, that's why," Monsieur Dupré said, searching for a clue as to whether or not Arthur knew about last night.

"Sorry, Louis. Didn't mean to upset you."

But Monsieur Dupré was not convinced. Without saying another word he walked away and into the station, where he sat at his desk, head between his hands, and for the nth time since last night he tried to remember if he had seen anyone come out of the red house in the dark.

43

Bernard had opened the driver's window and bent over to speak with a tall dignified middle-aged woman who stood there, short of breath from having run most of the way from her home in the Rue des Pins. She gave him a letter, saying: "It's for my son Paul."

"Sure, Madame Gauthier."

At the sound of this name, Arthur got up and looked, to make sure he had heard right. Then he sat down again, scorn on his face.

"When are you coming back?" she asked.

"Tonight for sure," Bernard replied.

"Please, don't forget. It is so very urgent."

"Don't worry, Madame. Everything is going to be all right." He was then going to inquire about her other son, Claude; but she abruptly turned round and walked away into the Rue des Pins. He put the letter in his pocket, and turned to Arthur. "Must be pretty serious. In all the years I have been servicing the camps this is the first time she ever gives me a letter for Paul."

Arthur said: "I can't stand the looks of her."

"Come now. Don't be so hard on the poor woman."

"She's the biggest bitch in town."

"A bit stuck-up maybe. But I think she's okay."

"I've known her a long time," Arthur said: "Way back, her old man and I used to chum around quite a bit. That was after he quit his job as first foreman for Bechard. Often we'd go out on the town together, or we'd go fishing and hunting, and sometimes we'd spend a couple of days up at the lake that used to belong to his folks. I remember one night we were coming back from there and he asked me to have supper with his family. I was pretty sober then, so I went, knowing I wouldn't make a disgrace of myself, if you know what I mean. We had a pretty good meal. But then what do you

44

suppose she wants us to do after we finished? She tells us to
kneel down and say the beads with her and the two kids
before she puts them to bed. What do you think of that?
Man, did I give her a piece of my mind! And he did the same,
he did."

Bernard Toupin shifted in first gear.

Ignoring the hint to get off, Arthur went on: "Now that I
look back, I feel kind of sorry for the fellow. He was really
stuck. And a nice guy he was, just a regular guy, even though
he had the best job any of us could hope for. Well, we
walked out of there fast, I'm telling you. Straight to Lambert's
we went, and all night he kept treating me, wouldn't take a
treat from me at all; he wanted to make up for what his wife
had done, he said. Can you imagine what the poor guy must
have gone through? Man, I'm telling you, if she didn't kill
him with the rosary, that's only because the beads weren't
tough enough. When a man is stuck with a woman like that
he's better off dead. The Lord must have taken pity on him
the night he died in that fire. That's what I've been saying
ever since. The Lord . . ."

Bernard Toupin cut him short. "So you don't like her. And
that's that. Now how about getting off?"

"Why should I?"

"Come on. Be a nice guy. I'll give you a ride some other
time."

"I'm coming with you."

"But what are you going to do up there?"

"Business."

"Oh, come on."

"I'm serious."

"Got the ten dollars on you?"

"You sure want to get this thing paid off in a hurry," Arthur
said, and he gave him the fare. "Here you are."

45

"No spitting on the floor," said Bernard. And they drove off.

After a short distance, the sound of the engine was buried under the loud humming of machines as they drove along the walls of the shirt factory. Then they made a right turn, and all they could hear was the fast beat of the logs in the chute. The river soon came into view at the end of the road: a vast expanse of logs glinting in the sun. Less than a hundred feet from the river bank a left turn led them into a narrow dirt road north to the camps. For a few miles they traveled along the edge of the river. They were silent, absorbed by the spectacle of the timber floating downstream.

After a while, Bernard Toupin said: "Well, tell me, Arthur; seriously, what are you going to do up north?"

"Business."

"Where did you get the ten dollars?"

"That was an advance on my commission," said Arthur. And taking a pack of cards out of his pockets, he explained: "See these, with my name on them? Well, for every man I give one to, if he goes to the brothel, I earn one buck."

"I don't get it."

"It's simple. Instead of passing these around when the men get in town, I go straight to the source. I come to the camps, distribute the cards, and give a little talk at the same time, if you know what I mean. That gives them time to build up an appetite."

"Do you realize what you are doing? This is not like getting drunk. It is serious. Hell, don't you remember what happened in '37?"

"But that won't happen again. This time there's a real organization behind the whole thing. You see how they convinced everybody they're setting up a rosary-bead factory in there, with equipment and all, and all this time it's a brothel with a gambling room in the back. Man, I'm telling you, these people know their business. And I'm going to let you in on a little secret. They've already got so many people involved that nobody will ever dare open his mouth."

"They won't get away with it. Not in La Buche."

"Why, man! They got this town sewed up tight," said Arthur. "As tight as the fly on his Eminence the Cardinal of Quebec." And he burst out laughing.

Bernard shuddered. He did not like lewd remarks about the priests or the church. "It ain't funny," he muttered.

Arthur went on laughing.

Bernard turned the visor upside down, looking for a Saint Christopher medal. "It ain't funny, Arthur," he said again. "It ain't funny at all."

They talked very little after this. Having forgotten to transfer his religious medal from the old truck, Bernard Toupin, driving very carefully, prayed the rest of the trip.

three

"*You know, Paul, what I like about* French-Canadians is their simplicity. You have no idea how inspiring it is for a city-bred fellow like me to see your people at close range, to live and work with them, feel the strength they have. These people have pure hearts. You can see it on their faces and in everything they do. All of us have to return to this way of life, someday, if we are to find peace of mind and solid moral values."

This was Israel speaking. A young man whom Paul Gauthier had befriended at the start of the season, he came from Montreal where his family owned a delicatessen on Van Horn Street. Upon graduation from college the previous year, he

49

had decided to go to Israel, but his family objected. They wanted him to stay in Montreal and become a doctor, or a lawyer if he preferred. They did not share his views on Zionism, would not give him one dollar toward traveling to Palestine. So he was now roughing it up at Bechard, hoping that one full season might bring enough money to carry out his plans. His name was Emmanuel Goldsmith, but the lumberjacks nicknamed him Israel because he always talked of Israel as his fatherland.

Short and of slight build, he had drooping shoulders, dark hair and brown eyes, a full mouth; his hands were white, delicate. City clothes had undoubtedly fitted him better than did the logger's outfit bought at Ti-Pit's store. He gave the impression that if he managed to stand up straight for any length of time it was thanks to the weight of his calked boots; his red shirt and green corduroy breeches were so large that even the most gentle breeze, out in the open air of the cutting line, made him look as though he were walking laboriously into a head wind. To the jacks he presented a perfect specimen of "green saplings from the city." He would not be talked into taking snuff, not even into smoking a pipe. He stuck to his city dandyism of cigarettes which he rolled himself, more as a measure of economy than as a concession to rough living. The men thought him a sissy, a penny pincher; in their opinion his nickname fitted him right, tight as bark on a tree.

Israel accepted his nickname graciously enough. That it sounded a faint note of anti-semitism he found no reason to resent. Rather, it seemed to him something to be proud of. While displaying sorrow over any form of anti-semitic treatment, he secretly thrilled at being reminded of his outcast state. Left alone, Israel looked sad, dejected; yet his expression would brighten up the moment a few loggers fell to showering him with ridicule. He did not smile nor weep then; his mouth

50

would take on a thin grin suggesting both suffering and delight. And he refused doggedly to see any evil behind the men's bantering. The more they tormented him, in fact, the readier he was to forgive them. His attitude was wholly incomprehensible to Paul Gauthier, who saw no great virtue in presenting the other cheek, especially with a smile. "But they don't mean any harm, Paul," Israel would explain, repeatedly, even after that nearly tragic incident which took place toward the end of his first week at Bechard.

It was after the evening meal. The camp, a double row of log cabins facing one another across a dirt road a quarter mile long, was domed with deepening darkness. Each cabin housed a complete gang of loggers, about forty, with their foreman. In Paul Gauthier's cabin, the one across the road from the kitchen and dining shack, oil lamps from rafters were casting high-yellow rays through the bluish smoke above the men now enjoying a few hours of recreation before sleep. The air was lively with talk. There were men playing cards in the center of the room, and next to them, over a barrel of sawdust, two jacks were matching strength in an Indian wrestling contest. A few tired loggers were lying on their bunks, snoring. Some were writing letters, others scanning the pages of a French edition of *Reader's Digest*. Now and then a burst of laughter came from the front of the room, where Red Mallet, a skinny good-natured scoundrel with flaming-red hair and great blue eyes, was telling dirty stories to the jacks gathered around him.

One of them, however, was not laughing. This was a stocky fellow named Salou, a newcomer, who carried his chest full forward, chin up, broad hands ready to curl into tight fists. Several times he had declared officially that he was willing to fight anybody, anytime, anywhere, anyhow. But nobody had picked up his challenge yet. He was itching with fight-hunger. His eyes kept shifting back to Israel and Paul Gauthier, who

51

were talking quietly on their bunks at the other end of the room.

Israel was telling Paul about Palestine. His decision to settle there had come from his belief concerning the future of mankind, namely, that all the ills of our decadent society, with its slums and machine-slave citizens, could be remedied by a world-wide return to a primitive existence such as agriculture or timbering, together with a rebirth of religious faith. He was convinced that the people of Israel, in obedience to some ancient mandate from the prophets, were now setting an example that the rest of humanity must follow in order to achieve peace and happiness on earth. "They are just like the French-Canadians," Israel concluded.

"Bullshit!" Salou muttered between his teeth. He started up in the direction of their bunks.

In his college days Israel had read *Maria Chapdelaine* and the novels of Mazo de la Roche. Hitchhiking to the Gaspé Peninsula on a summer vacation he had thrilled at the sight of so many roadside crosses and praying stations, the blissful quiet of little towns squatting at the foot of sparkling belfries. He had seen on television a drama based on the life of Pierre Radisson, and on a motion picture screen a documentary film depicting the rough but clean and simple life of French-Canadian lumberjacks. All of this had led him to conclude that the people of Quebec were living the great Israel experiment, though in somewhat less dramatic circumstances than did the Jews, a difference he was quick to explain as being the result of their not holding a mandate from the prophets. But no matter. For sheer simple living, these French-Canadians deserved to be looked up to.

Paul mumbled a vague word of interest. Lying on his bunk down below, he was listening less to the meaning of the words than to their sound, that reminded him of his

52

brother. In spite of an accent, Israel spoke a beautiful French, like Claude's; this was the French of educated people, it had the flavor of superior intelligence, which Paul admired with secret pride, as would a father who found in his son glorious achievements in those very fields where he himself had sacrificed his future for that of the child. A flood of memories swept across his vision, as he lay staring into Israel's mattress above. He was not aware that Salou had just moved to stand only a few bunks away, a smirk on his face.

Israel went on talking. His enthusiasm for the simple life among the lumberjacks had spread to embrace the spectacle of the men under the dim light of oil lamps inside the shack. They were the real people, so true to nature, so simple. No manners to spoil them. Nothing between them and nature. "That's what I call real people," he exclaimed, with a sweep of the arm over the whole cabin. "The salt of the earth!"

"Hey, Jew-boy, what are you trying to do, make fun of us jacks?" Salou cried at the top of his voice. He stood at the foot of Israel's bunk and from the corner of one eye he watched Paul down below.

"Leave the kid alone," Paul said.

"Try and make me."

Paul shrugged his shoulders, and turned away. Then Salou, smarting at the snub, cried: "Hey, Israel. Is it true what they say about the Jews?"

"What?"

"That you guys have the longest ones?"

Slowly, Paul Gauthier sat up on his bunk. Now there were whispers in every corner of the cabin. Games were interrupted. Red Mallet stopped short in the middle of a story. All the men looked up. A heavy silence was felt, intensified by Israel's nervous giggling sounds as he tried to laugh the whole thing off as a bad joke.

53

Salou said: "I even hear that you guys get it trimmed just like we do."

Israel made an effort to reply. "You mean circumcised?"

"Circumscribed, or whatever you call it, come on, show us. All of us jacks want to know if it's true."

Paul Gauthier jumped to his feet. A solid logger of thirty, he stood six foot four, with broad shoulders, a strong neck, a handsome face under a mop of yellow hair, tanned deep copper by thirteen years of snow-sun and high winds of the valley. Nobody had ever licked him. Few had ever tried. He had the quiet, confident bearing of a man respected for his strength and courage. And he was one of the best-liked foremen at Bechard. Here was a jack really worth giving the pox to, Salou seemed to think as he looked him up and down with a somber glow of defiance, feverish to do him in.

"Better go for a walk," Paul said. "Take some fresh air, fellow, and cool off a bit."

In reply Salou turned to Israel. "Come on, Jew-boy. Pull down your pants and let's have a look."

Israel crawled to the head of the bunk, fright twisting his face.

"Come on, or I'll drag you down here and do it myself," said Salou, and at the same time he raised one hand toward Israel's bunk and with the other struck Paul Gauthier in the chest. Paul reeled back and Salou went after him, raging. Men jumped from their bunks and formed a tight cordon around the center of the room. Salou was hitting Paul in the chest, then in the face. He fought like a man trained in boxing; his punches landed hard, accurate. Paul's face was cut, blood appeared before he had time to defend himself. The sight of blood sent Israel huddling against the wall; he looked on the point of vomiting. Stubbornly Paul groped for Salou with his large hands, trying to get hold of his opponent to crush the fight out of him. But Salou stepped back and went on hitting, his mouth twisted in a grin, his eyes glowing with excitement, as the men watched with gaping mouths and hungry eyes. Paul swung freely, but failed to land any telling blows on Salou. He was blinded by blood; each time he thought he could see Salou on his right the other shifted to the left, away, below the blows, only to come back swinging for the head. Paul's face jerked in pain at each punch, he rocked heavily on his long legs and at one point seemed about to drop to the floor. Salou thought he had him at last. He began to kick him in the legs, hit him in the belly, anything to bring him down. Paul was bending under the blows, but he kept his hands stretched up in a blind groping for Salou, who had uncovered his face when he dropped his arms to hit lower.

Suddenly Paul's hands made contact with Salou's throat. His opponent tried to wrench himself free, swung wildly but ineffectually. But as Paul, pale with fury, tightened his grip around the man's throat, Salou's arms dropped, stretched rigid; his knees stiffened, until he was standing on tip toes, hanging by the neck.

"Let go," the men cried. "Let go, Paul. You're killing him."

Salou's face was rapidly turning blue. His mouth opened, revealing the protruding, swollen tongue. Then the fury seemed to drain out of Paul and he let go. Salou dropped to the floor unconscious.

Immediately the cordon of men was broken up. Everybody rushed to Salou, while Paul walked to his bunk, where Israel handed him a handkerchief to wipe the blood off his face. One of the men ran outside. The next minute he was back with a bucketful of cold water. They threw it on Salou's head, slapped him on the cheeks, shook him by the shoulders to make him come to. Gradually he regained consciousness, began to breathe more easily. Several of the men helped him up to his legs.

Now it was Salou's turn.

"Balls a'roasting!" Red Mallet roared.

As if all of them had been waiting for this call, the men at once set out to give Salou the treatment usually handed out to braggart jacks. Paul tried to intervene, but it was useless. The men seized Salou and tied his hands behind his back, then pulled down his trousers and tore off his underwear. Red Mallet got up on the barrel of sawdust and took down one of the oil lamps hanging from the rafters. Using Salou's belt, a harness was fastened around the man's thighs, and the oil lamp was hooked to the buckle so as to hang secure between his legs. They tied his knees together with his braces, to prevent him from running while allowing him enough freedom to leap and bounce. Red Mallet adjusted the flame, not too low, not too high. Then they pulled and pushed Salou to the door of the cabin. They offered Israel the honor of kicking him off, but Israel declined. Red Mallet stepped behind Salou, and swung him a great kick smack in the buttocks, which sent him bouncing down the road naked as a fish from the waist down, the unshaded oil lamp roasting his sex.

Salou's screams could be heard all over the camp. Loggers came running out of the cabins to watch him leaping and bouncing while he yelled for help. The flame was licking his hair to singeing. Some of the men tapped him on the shoulder to encourage him. One of them turned the flame a little higher. Roars of laughter greeted him at every door. Red Mallet shouted: "Out of oil, Salou?" Someone advised him to urinate if he wanted to put out the fire. The more he screamed, the higher he bounced in the middle of the road, the louder the laughter grew. Finally, a kind soul shouted at him to go and jump in the river, which is exactly what he did, just in time to escape emasculation by roasting.

The next day, Salou packed up and left.

"The poor fellow didn't mean any harm," Israel said. "He only wanted to match strength with you, Paul, show off, so he used me as a pretext for a fight. People like that are not to be resented, but pitied instead."

"All right," Paul said. "Forget it. Let's get to work. At the rate you're going you'll never fill your quota."

They were at the cutting line beyond the hills half a mile from camp: a hole in the forest, a sort of pit walled in by trees, where hundreds of men sawed and trimmed and loaded logs onto horse-drawn flats that became a panting, leather-creaking conveyer belt constantly moving back and forth to the river. The forest was alive with the whacks of the axes, the swish-swish of the saws, the neighing of horses. Here and there a man stopped swinging to wipe his neck, or spit. A steady pace of work was maintained by the shouts of the foremen. The rhythm of it soon took hold of Israel. This was it, he thought: men working close to nature, with nature, just like the settlers in Israel. It was soul-lifting, conducive to clean religious living. And he did not fail to tell Paul about it on their way back to the camp at the end of the day.

Paul listened with a sort of amused, affectionate tolerance. Inasmuch as Israel filled in his heart the void created by the absence of his brother, it sometimes enabled him to pretend it was Claude himself speaking, so much alike did they sound in words and youthful idealism despite their different backgrounds and callings. At the same time, his big-brother instinct of protection was aroused by Israel's self-consciousness as a Jew, which Paul viewed as the main obstacle to the lad's getting on with the other jacks. "Now look here, Israel," he said. "Let me give you a tip. Try and forget that Jewish business for a while, will you. Remember, you're not in Palestine yet; you're still here with us in the thick of the woods and nobody here gives a damn about all that highfalutin' stuff you talk. Just try to be a regular guy like the rest of us. You'll see, it ain't too hard if you just start thinking a little less about yourself."

"I'll try," Israel laughed. Paul was right. He took himself too seriously.

After they had eaten, that night, Paul read him some of the poems Claude used to recite when the two brothers went vacationing by the lake in the summer. He had transcribed them by hand in a small notebook. "Yes," said Israel; the handwriting was pretty good. And Paul blushed a little in modest pride.

In the course of the season their friendship had grown into a warm exchange of favors. Israel's hands having a tendency to swell and chafe and bleed at the cutting line, Paul took over some of his work to fill his minimum quota; and if the manual on forestry presented pages too difficult for Paul, it was Israel's help that solved the problems, usually with simple arithmetic. After January, when Claude's letters suddenly ceased coming, and Paul's letters to his brother grew longer and more insistent on a reply, the point was often given special emphasis through Israel's advice with a word here, a different sentence structure there. It was the sort of friendship that does not suffer from differences of views. On the contrary, the very expression of their different convictions tended to bring them closer to each other.

One Sunday in March, the Curé of La Buche, as was his custom twice a month, came to camp Bechard to hear confessions and celebrate Mass in the dining shack. Afterwards he spent the afternoon visiting the cabins and drinking with the jacks.

"No wonder people here are so religious, with such a simple man as their priest," Israel declared.

"I have nothing against him," said Paul. "He was a jack himself at one time. A good friend of my father's."

Israel went on to tell how impressed he had been with the simple piety of La Buche folks during his few hours there last September: women and children on their way to church, mothers teaching their young ones how to cross themselves at Holy Water fonts. "What a beautiful sight!" he said.

A lot of sentimental nonsense, Paul thought. "Bah, you got it all wrong, Israel. You know nothing about us because you keep seeing us with the eyes of a foreigner. On your way back next month, stick around a while and have a good second look: then you might find out what really goes on in this timberland. You'll see—there ain't two logs truly alike. As far as I'm concerned, I don't go to church anymore. If other folks want to follow the priest, let them. I don't stick my nose in other people's business."

"But didn't you say your brother was going to be a priest?"

"That's different. Claude's always wanted to become a priest ever since he was little. If our father was alive today he would help him all he could. That's a matter of duty. Religion has nothing to do with it. I do what my father would have done."

"Does Claude know you don't go to church?"

"Of course."

"And what does he say?"

"We never discuss it."

"Tell me, Paul, why did you give it up?"

"Well," Paul said, after a moment's hesitation, "it's like this. When I was little I used to serve Mass every day of the week and twice on Sundays. The curé would give me a nickel each Mass, and it made my mother happy to see me in a white surplice. Later, when my kid brother came home one night

59

and said he had heard the call of God and he was going to become a priest when he grew up, why, all of us were happy to hear that. The next morning I went down by the rapids and felled a tall spruce. I trimmed it and used the wood to build a nice-looking altar for him. I set it up in his room, even made the chalice and the cross out of the same wood. We would take turns saying Mass and being altar boys. I remember"—Paul laughed—"for Mass wine we used apple cider, and mother made us a couple of surplices out of old bed sheets.

"Then one day," he continued, suddenly serious again, "a couple of years later, there was a big fire at a farm on the outskirts of town. Everybody wanted to see the fire, so my father took us along, my brother and me. When we got there I saw a little girl about my age caught in the door of the hayloft; the fire was all around her. We shouted to her to jump, but the poor kid was too frightened. I saw that she was going to burn alive right there, so I jerked myself free from my father's hand and I ran up to the side of the barn and tried to climb up to her. I might have made it, too, but then the crowd came after me and pulled me down by the legs. It seemed nobody would help the poor kid. They just stood there and watched with their dumb faces. She finally dropped in the flames. Even to this day when I'm alone in the woods at night I hear her screams calling after me. There was a priest from the Seminary, Father Boulanger it was, the same priest who takes care of my brother's soul right now; he came out of the crowd and made a sermon. 'God has sent this tragedy our way,' he said, 'in order to remind us that we are all sinners. We must return to God while there is time. For unless we do, most of us, sinners that we are, will spend eternity in flaming Hell. And that will be much worse than the terrible tortures this poor child has just suffered before our very eyes.'

60

"That's what he said. Or just about. Anyway, from that day on I began to figure things out for myself. If God was so cruel as to do a thing like that to a little girl, I figured, then I was not going to have any more to do with Him. And I was not going to have anything to do with any priest who talked that way either. That was the way I figured things out then, and that's the way I still feel today."

*   *   *

The men finally blew up the remaining log jams. Spring's last rush of timber went floating wild downstream.

About forty loggers, most of them belonging to Paul Gauthier's gang, had been given their final pay the previous night. They were now free to return home, or go down-river on the drive, or head for the taverns and brothels of Trois-Rivières and Quebec and Montreal where the trade was making ready for them. With the season drawing to a close, each day a small group like this was released, so as to provide an adequate number of men for the drive at the southern end of the river. But the best loggers remained at camp to wrap up the season. The foremen, including Paul, and the La Buche lumberjacks, were usually the last to leave. They made up the hard core of the true dyed-in-the-wool jacks; it was beneath their dignity to pack up before the boss had put the key in the door of the front office, which would be in another two to three weeks.

This morning, the customary send-off party was being held in the cabin in which Israel and Paul had spent the season. There were a barrel of beer and a barrel of ale, one paid for by the boss and the other by the men. The jacks did their best to put themselves in a condition not to feel the bumps on the road back home. Even Israel, who ordinarily would not have dared join the party without the protective company of Paul, as soon as he had finished packing, eagerly accepted a

61

mug of beer, then another, and another. He was feeling quite gay by the time Paul, returning to camp for lunch, appeared at the door.

"You bloody fool," Paul said, drawing him outside. "Do you realize what you're doing? Getting loaded on your way back home with more than two thousand dollars on you? Man, you're asking for trouble. And mind you, I won't be there to get you out of it this time." Against Israel's tipsy protestations that he was quite sober, he pulled him across the road. "Come on. You need food."

The bus was just then pulling to a stop in front of the dining shack. Bernard Toupin stepped down and, with an uneasy smile, handed Paul the letter from Madame Gauthier.

The handwriting brought a look of alarm to Paul's face. He hastened to tear open the envelope.

Bernard tried to sound a note of cheerfulness. "Well. Going home?"

Israel nodded yes.

"Then you'll have the honor of trying out my new bus."

"I'll be leaving, too," said Paul, his face set in an expression of mingled grief and anger.

"What's the matter?" Israel asked.

Paul showed him the note. 'Your brother is dying. Come home. Your mother.'

"Sorry I had to bring such bad news," said Bernard, glancing at it over Israel's shoulder.

"I'm sorry, Paul," Israel said.

Paul put the envelope in his pocket. Israel's words of sympathy irritated him. "Never mind," he snapped. He walked away at a fast, determined pace toward the office in the back of the dining hall.

"Too bad," Bernard commented. "He's close to his kid brother. Been a sort of father to him all these years since the old man died."

62

Israel didn't say anything. He felt unhappy for his friend and regretted the conventional remark he had made.

Men were bringing their bags and blankets inside the bus and dropping them on seats they wanted to reserve. Two drunken loggers carried cases of beer inside the cabin, where others hurried to help themselves, there being none left in the barrels. The air resounded with merrymaking: hoarse drunken voices laughing, singing. One tipsy jack stood urinating nonchalantly on a rear tire of the bus.

"Well, that's the way it goes, sometimes," Bernard Toupin said, with a shrug of peasant resignation in the face of calamity and death. "When you got to go, you go. There's not much anybody can do about it." And having delivered himself of this bit of philosophy, he crossed the road and entered the cabin.

Israel stood in the middle of the road not knowing what to do, until Red Mallet shouted from the door of the cabin. "Hey, Jew-boy, plenty of beer inside." Reluctantly, Israel went back to join the party.

About an hour later, Paul came out of the office with his final pay. Bowed with concern for his brother, he walked across the road barely lifting his boots, so that they dug on his trail two deep ruts, mud-lipped. A couple of jacks were lying drunk across the front door of the cabin. Paul lifted his feet carefully over them, and went inside, directly to his bunk.

The party was reaching the peak of confusion and tipsy gaiety. Drunken jacks lay on bunks or on the floor, while a steady traffic was being maintained to and from the privies in the back. The ceiling was a cloud of smoke and the air smelled of beer and tobacco and sharp masculine sweat. Someone had brought from the kitchen a pot of black coffee and put it on the stove. A group sat playing poker on a bunk near the front of the room. Bernard watched the game over their shoulders, his eyes hungry and sad—so much money being

63

wasted on gambling! Here and there men were finishing their packing while still sober enough to know what they were doing.

But the largest group of all, and also the liveliest, was made up of a few dozen men gathered around Arthur. Holding a bottle of beer in one hand and a pack of calling cards in the other, he was telling them in his husky, gin-toned voice about the women at the brothel; they were of the highest caliber of beauty and skill in the delicate art of sin, their performance had that refinement which you could find only in the best whorehouses in Montreal, if you could find it anywhere at all. Better still, there was a money-back guarantee of satisfaction.

Israel sat alone near the stove, alternating between a long drink from a bottle of beer and a long stare at the card Arthur had given him. Incredible! he was thinking. A brothel in La Buche? Surely they must have had to bring girls from the cities.

A few feet away, Red was about to answer a ten-dollar bet in a round of Indian wrestling. His opponent, a serious-looking fellow who would never have challenged Red if he had not drunk too much, sat facing him across an empty beer barrel. Now they grasped each other's right hand above the ten dollar bill. The challenger braced himself, ready to pull as hard as he could, while Red watched with a mischievous look. With clenched teeth, locking hands tight, they waited for the signal. "Go." The challenger gave a twist of the wrist, pulled down, a little further down. Red fought him hard, or so it seemed from the strained look on his face. But then, suddenly, as his hand was almost touching the table in defeat, he tightened his buttocks, lifted one leg and let out an ample blast. This broke down the challenger's effort. Red swung his hand back, to win. And before the fellow had time to recover from this surprise Red had grabbed the money and

64

held it triumphantly for everyone to see. The other protested: it wasn't fair! But Red's reply was a more formidable explosion. The men roared with laughter.

Paul, during this time, seemed unaware of what was going on around him. From under the bunk he had pulled out a large bag which he was filling with personal effects kept on shelves above the head of his bunk. His face expressed no emotion. His eyes, however, usually clear and glowing in simple-hearted goodness, had a dull look now, the look of a man lost in a sudden sorrow. Absently he threw into the bag sets of winter underwear, three pairs of breeches, shirts, socks, toilet articles. There were books: on arithmetic, logging, forestry, the manufacture of pulp and paper, one manual of grammar and a pocket-size dictionary. Then came the notebook of poems. But the sight of it aroused no emotion in him. This object which connected his life so intimately with Claude's, this notebook, had no meaning now. Memories of his brother, along with the power to feel, were sinking deep into the hidden recesses of his heart, buried under the weight of that terrifying mystery with which the very mention of the word, death, overwhelmed him.

It was the same sensation he had experienced at the side of his father's coffin. He and Claude had not been allowed to see their father before embalmment, only their mother had. Then after the body was brought home the sons had asked once again to see their father, but their mother had said no. That night, while friends and relatives were eating in the kitchen, the brothers had stolen downstairs, barefooted, to see for themselves. The coffin was closed. They tried to push the lid open, but the screws had been been driven in tight; they could not open it to look inside.

Then suddenly Paul had seen death in a new way, a terror no longer identified in his mind with a skeleton painted white

65

on black wax-cloth, but an abyss into which his father had sunk, was still disappearing, an endless bottom that pulled the father away and left the son to grip desperately a handful of earth and wilted flowers to soothe his anguish. The unshakable silence of it, the void of it that you could not throw your arms around and crush to a cry of farewell, this was the mystery, the terror. That you could not fight death with your body in a man-to-man combat to the finish, that you could not strangle it to a whispered explanation—this was what made him rage inside. Death had locked and sealed the coffin, pervaded his life with a haunting fear of the very name.

When they lowered the coffin into the grave, he had stood there dry-eyed after the last shovel of earth was thrown at the face of his father; they had had to drag him away. After that, in his grief against which he could only fight with a child's rage, he had sworn that never again would he let death strike in the same manner. Next time he would be prepared for it, he would struggle with it. Even if death won in the end, he would have put up a fight like a man.

But now, it was happening all over again! Would he come home again to a closed coffin? Mechanically he took the roll of bank notes from his pocket. Trying to concentrate on what he was doing, he unrolled the bills flat on the bunk, counted them, put them neatly inside the money belt under his shirt. Then he threaded his way toward the back door, careful not to be noticed by the tipsy jacks around him. A long walk by himself was what he needed now.

But Israel, running after him, called: "Hey, Paul!"

The men looked up. "Where do you think you're going?"

"Come back here."

"Join the party."

"Don't run away, Paul."

"Hey, men," Red shouted. "Big Paul is here."

"You ought to know better," Paul said to Israel. "Now look what you've done."

"I want to come with you," Israel said, grasping his arm.

"Let me alone," Paul said, turning on him in anger. "Can't you understand that a man wants to be alone sometimes?"

Hurt by Paul's attitude, Israel retreated unhappily to his bunk.

Red offered Paul a bottle of beer. "Here, don't be a party-pooper."

"You know I don't drink," Paul snapped.

"Have one just the same."

A small group gathered at the door. They would not let him go out. One of them tried to pull him to the center of the room. Paul jerked his arm free.

Israel shouted at the top of his voice: "Paul says he wants to be alone. So why don't you guys leave him alone."

"Shut up," Red shouted back. "He's big enough to take care of himself."

From the other end of the room, where Bernard had told the men the bad news, five or six of the more sober jacks came to Paul with grave expressions on their faces. They began to tell him that they felt sorry, maybe everything would be all right when he got back home.

Paul changed his mind abruptly. Reluctant as he was to stay, he dreaded even more having to tell them in detail why he must return home. Besides, it was easier to join the party than to have to stand the fruitless sympathy of others. He went to the potbelly stove and poured himself a mugful of black coffee.

Red jumped on top of the beer barrel and threw up his arms. "Hear me, men. Ye good knights of the most high and celebrated order of the axe and the saw. Hear me!"

All over the room loggers turned their drunken eyes to him
—never a dull moment with Red!

"Do ye hear me, ye?"

"Come on, Red."

"Then hear this, ye. Our most noble knight here, Big Paul,
is returning to his most esteemed kingdom in the flower-
filled gardens of La Buche, and . . ."

"Cut out the bullshit."

"And I say to ye all: our most noble knight here, Big Paul,
is walking out without giving us the case of beer he owes us
as winner of the tree-cutting contest. Now . . ."

"All right, Red," Paul said. "Here's five dollars. I'm sorry.
I had forgotten." He gave the money to Bernard.

"Hurrah for the champion!" the men thundered. "Hurrah!"

Then Paul, forcing himself to smile, took Red's place on
the beer barrel and made ready to perform the traditional
ritual that went with the title he had earned. Red gave him
a bottle of beer. He held it between his hands, slowly brought
it up to his mouth; he took a solid grip with his teeth around
the cap, bit it off, and finished with a long pull at the bottle.
The men rubbed elbows, straining their eyes to watch him
through the haze of smoke. Now Paul took the cap between
thumb and forefinger, held it high above his head, so that all
could see it well. Then slowly, without a trace of effort on his
face, he folded the cap neatly into a half-moon, folded it again,
in half. He put it between his teeth, chewed the edges in,
rounded one corner. Again he held it up to the men. It looked
like a dime.

"Hurrah!"

He forced the cap inside the bottle, and took another long
drink.

"Hurrah!"

He held the bottle high above his head.

"Hurrah!"

"Now?"

"Now!" Paul echoed, and at the same time he threw the bottle against the door of the privies, where it smashed to pieces.

"Hurrah!" the men shouted once more, and they went back to their drinking.

Feeling that his duty was now performed in full, Paul again tried to leave by the back door. But he did not get very far. The men crowded around him, blocking his way. He pushed them away as gently as he could, told them he wanted to be left alone. Someone was pulling his sleeve. He turned around. "What, Arthur?" he asked, looking into the man's bloodshot eyes.

"I want to ask you a little favor."

Anticipating a demand for money, Paul pulled out a dollar bill. But Arthur refused. "Then what do you want?"

"Here, take this," Arthur said, handing him one of his cards. If Paul, with his prestige among the men, were to accept it in front of the others, what a cinch it would be to convince the rest! "How would you like to get yourself a nice bit of fun back in town?"

"Nonsense," Paul snapped, and gave him back the card.

"But you can't do that to me, Paul; me, an old friend of your dad's."

"My father was never a friend of yours."

"Well, maybe you're right about that, and maybe you're not. But tell me this. What's wrong with the brothel? What have you got against it?"

"I'm not interested. That's all."

"A young man like you, strong, good-looking; you ought to be ashamed of yourself. Or maybe you plan to get there first and don't want the others to know. Is that it?"

69

"You'll never find me in a brothel. The day I have to pay for it I'll be too old to do it anyway."

"That's right," echoed Bernard. "Men of our age ought to be able to get it free."

Arthur turned to Bernard. "I wouldn't talk so smart if I was you. Don't think I don't know whose needle you've been threading all this time. You better shut up, man, or else it's going to cost you plenty, and you won't have no needle to thread no more."

Bernard turned pale and walked quietly away to the front door, then to his bus.

"Bernard is right," Paul said. "There's something wrong with a man who has to pay a woman to sleep with him. No, sir. Not for me. Any man who can't get a woman without paying for it is not a man, that's what I say." He tried to leave them, when Arthur, pointing a finger at him, shouted: "Now look who's talking. By Christ, his old man himself died in a brothel. Yes, that's true. That's where his old man gave up the ghost. I was there, saw it with my own two eyes, I did."

"How's that?" Paul said quietly.

"In the charivari of '37. I was there. I was one of those who found him, right under one of the beds, naked, not even a religious medal on him."

"Don't say things like that about my father, Arthur. That's not true and you know it." Paul still spoke softly, but there was a dangerous glint in his eyes.

"I saw the whole thing, I tell you. Naked like a mortal sin he was."

"Take back what you said, Arthur."

"I shit on you."

"Take back what you said about my father," Paul repeated. But Arthur sneered: "Maybe that's why you don't want to go to the brothel now. Is that it?"

70

The next moment Paul had grabbed the old drunk by the throat and lifted him off his feet, shaking him like a rag doll. He was barely aware of the men around him shouting to let go, pulling at his arms in an attempt to loose his grip. Then suddenly he let Arthur fall to the floor, and stood towering above him, staring at his own empty hands.

Something had broken loose inside him, cutting short the rage and the urge to kill. It was an image, a face, Arthur's face, younger, coming from the deep past of that night years ago, when, through the balusters of the staircase, Paul had seen Arthur kneeling alone at the side of his father's coffin. And now he remembered: he, of all the mourners, was the only one who had wept.

"He must be telling the truth," Paul muttered, dimly aware of the men huddled around Arthur's prostrate form. He heard Israel say something, but the voice sounded far off. His mind, his whole body felt numb, as he turned away still muttering to himself: "So that's how it was."

In the bus back to La Buche, later that afternoon, Israel sat next to Paul and tried to get him to say something, anything, in the hope that speaking about his grief might make it easier to bear. But his friend remained indifferent to his questions.

Paul could think of nothing but his brother's illness and the shame of his father's destruction. The news of Claude's imminent death, then Arthur's revelation—these two shocking disclosures, striking in rapid succession, had stunned him. Now he was unable to distinguish one blow from the other; the two had blended inextricably to produce in him the certainty that his life from now on would never be the same. Now he would no longer have a brother to be a father to, no longer have a father to remember with fond respect. Until today the responsibility of Claude's future had given his life a direction, a purpose; the memory of his father had helped keep alive a deep sense of personal dignity. As long as he had these as central points in his life, he had been free of the torments of shame and guilt. His simple soul had fed on a simple morality, and he had known dignity.

But now all of that was gone, leaving him naked to the futility and shame of tomorrow.

And tomorrow was now, this sudden inescapable reality. Without his brother to look after, what was there for him to live and work for? And in his father's testament, what was there for him but the guarantee that he had no right to illusions of dignity? The very blood in his veins, it seemed to him now, had the color of shame.

four

After putting his cane on the sill Claude Gauthier drew the curtains apart. The windowpane reflected a long emaciated face the color of clay, deep-set eyes too large, too dark, a glossy forehead, hollow temples streaked with darkening veins, black hair unruly and dry that did not seem to belong to the head. This was death, alien yet intimate. Claude surrendered to it as he would to a terror inescapable but friendly. He leaned his hot forehead against the glass, and now his cheeks; it was soothing. When he withdrew, the pane was clouded with vapor from his burning lungs. With the palm of his hands he wiped the glass clean. Then he moved back a little, steadied himself on his cane, and drew the curtains apart all the way.

Once again, as he had done that morning and twice a day during the past month, he fell to gazing up and down the Rue des Erables and the Rue des Pins. The late afternoon crowd of women and children entering and leaving the shops, people he knew too well to see them clearly, enveloped as they were in the fog of his habit of watching them every day, moved before him as in a dream. In this way he followed the coming of springtime, in the daily lengthening of shadows, in the observation that the narrow gravel paths in the seminary gardens seemed a little dryer, then in the sudden discovery of a young delicate blade of grass peeping through the blankets of pebbles. He also noticed that many sidewalk slates had tilted out of position; another few days of alternating frost and thaw would make them dangerous to walk on, so that very soon the men would begin to remove them, level the bed of sand underneath, repair the broken curbs, and then the slates would be laid back even and neat, ready for another year of wear. His gaze wandered across the Place de l'Eglise, where the doors of the church, even from where he stood, showed patches of dried-off paint and streaks of rust running down from the hinges. In a few days Monsieur le Curé would stand in the center of the square to supervise, pipe in hand, the annual springtime repainting of the doors, the belfry and the cross. In a few days! The thought of it caused him to imagine the hearse moving slowly up the Rue des Erables, the hearse that carried this body of his followed by mourners dressed in black, some of them with large white handkerchiefs in hands, all heads lowered in grief. But just when he tried to identify the mourners, the cortege suddenly vanished under the advancing shadow of the belfry.

"Claude!"

Under the spell of his vision he did not hear his mother,

who had just come out of the kitchen at the sound of his cane hitting the floor. "Are you all right?" she asked.

He steadied himself.

"You shouldn't stand there so long. You will get tired again."

"I'm all right."

"Maybe you ought to go up to your room and lie down a while."

"I feel fine," he said. "May I open the window?"

"It's still too early. Next week maybe, if the mild weather keeps up."

Next week, next week, it was always next week, he thought.

"Do you want to go up now?"

"In a little while."

She went back into the kitchen. Moments later he heard a sigh, then a low-voiced recitation of Aves that blended with the noise of dishes being washed. He had won a reprieve.

Now he saw the Bureau sisters come out of their house across the street. Two little old women always dressed in long black coats, they carried their beads and recited the Rosary wherever they went. Every day at this hour they would come scuttling around the corner and up the Rue des Erables to church, where they did the Stations of the Cross and dropped fifty cents in the alms box. But instead of turning into the Rue des Erables, presently they crossed the street in front of the Gauthier home and kept walking on the Rue des Pins. Claude suddenly remembered that this was Thursday, and it occurred to him that the Bureau sisters were probably on their way to a meeting of Les Dames de la Grâce in the auditorium of the seminary. His mother had not yet told him that she would attend. She had insisted on staying home with him the last two Thursday nights, and for that reason Lise had not come.

75

He was still thinking about this, wishing that his mother might attend the meeting, when he heard footsteps coming from the right on this side of the street. He recognized the hesitant pace of Doctor Gendron's gait. But it was too early for the doctor to pick up his mail at the train station; he would usually pass by after Mademoiselle Serval, the woman with a "past," had left the telephone office across the street from the Convent of the Ursulines and entered her apartment on the second floor of the Bureau sisters' home. Someone must have been taken ill, Claude reflected. The footsteps were growing near. They sent to his mind a picture of the old doctor's kind face, the dark eyes full of warmth and compassion, the white hair and moustache that reminded him of his father. He could still hear the gentle yet firm tone of his voice, that same voice which only a few weeks ago had announced to his mother that there was no hope for a cure. And now he saw him. Suddenly, as if by force of habit, the old doctor stopped and looked. Their eyes met. The doctor smiled with an air that seemed to say: "I am sorry, boy. I did all I could," and disappeared down the street.

Claude wished that his mother would ask Dr. Gendron in for a visit once in a while, even though there was no hope. The old man always had a good story to tell of the days he and Claude's father used to go fishing and hunting together. Some of those stories Claude began to recall, but the tender melancholy into which they led him soon found an echo in the deep quiet that he felt now descending upon the center of town. He watched the clerk pull down the steel curtain across the front of the Liquor Commission store. A woman with arms full of groceries walked out of Ti-Pit's. In small groups of four and five the salesgirls from the five-and-ten store came out on the sidewalk across the street from Lambert's tavern. His old classmates filed out into the seminary garden to stroll in pious meditation along the narrow paths. Father Boulanger would join them any moment now. Not a sound came from the sidewalk slates. Silence everywhere. Claude wished that he could open the window, to listen to the thumping of the logs in the chute. The silence pressed against his temples, a heavy oppressive stillness as if he were being buried alive.

His mother came out of the kitchen. "What is the matter, Claude? You have been standing there for almost one hour. And you don't even answer when I call."

Slowly he managed to control his fear, pull himself together —he must be more careful next time, must train himself to dispel those hallucinations before it was too late.

"You had better come upstairs."

"It's too early."

"I have to go to the meeting tonight," she announced. "So you must come to bed now."

This helped him feel better. But as he had not seen Monsieur Dupré pass by, which meant that the bus had not yet arrived at the station, he asked again to be allowed to stay at the window, "just a little while longer."

"You are not being reasonable, Claude."

"Do you really think Paul will come home tonight?"

"I wrote to him. I have done my duty. Now let us hope he does his."

"I want to wait for him."

"It would only tire you."

"Give me another fifteen minutes, please. Maybe the bus is just coming in at the station now. You go and get ready. I will be in bed before you leave, I promise."

"And what if you have another spell?"

His mother was standing at the foot of the stairs, holding an apron in her hands. He saw her blue housedress, the one that she wore every day and that had become for him the symbol of confinement, closed windows, intolerable solicitude. He saw her strong shoulders, the shoulders that were permanently held back in a posture of authority and unbreakable endurance. And he saw the fine golden chain that held a cross lying secure upon the slope of her breasts. But he did not want to look in her eyes. He must do all he could to avoid a scene. For a scene might bring on a spell, and that would make her change her mind about going to the meeting.

"You come to bed now and I will give you a pill," she insisted.

Sighing, he nodded yes. Then he began laboriously walking toward her. She started to help him. He stopped abruptly, tense all over. "Please, mother. Please, don't," he snapped.

She stopped, a look of pained surprise on her face.

In a lower tone of voice, he said: "You must leave me alone, Mother."

"I am only trying to help you."

"I know, I know," he said wearily.

"Then come," she insisted, and she put her arm around his shoulders. "Don't tire yourself, my son. Come."

He reacted almost unconsciously, as to a physical pain. Gripping his cane with both hands he cried: "Please, mother. Please leave me alone. Alone."

She stepped back, stunned by this sudden revolt. For a second she looked as if she might begin to cry. But she controlled herself. Then her face grew tender, full of pity. "How sick you are, my boy! How terribly sick! And you won't even let your poor mother help you."

Claude continued to grip his cane in an effort to repress the flow of violent emotions that surged in him. It was not only his mother's coercive solicitude and constant watch over him that he resented. It was also this false pity of hers, which prevented him from telling her the truth, what had happened in the past weeks with Lise, the change in his life. How could he speak frankly with her, the way she continued to nurse him and to pretend that he would soon be cured while all the time she fretted about the details of his funeral, like sending the furniture slipcovers to the cleaners and bringing his photograph to Father Boulanger. The way she imposed upon him the burden of hope even though she herself had none, forced him to hope when he did not seek it, when, in fact, he feared hope more than death itself. Why must she go on pretending and lying even after the doctor had rendered his final verdict; why did she have to go on talking about his future as a priest when all the time she knew that he was aware of the plans she had already made for herself: to quit her post as president of Les Dames de la Grâce, sell the house and enter the convent?

All that false pity, that solicitude, he could no longer bear. Truth! He needed truth between them, truth between himself and Father Boulanger, as much as he needed air in his rotting lungs. Why couldn't she see it? Why couldn't she see that her constant pretending was the worst of his tortures? Once a man was doomed and he accepted the fact, the least people could do for him was to let him face it his own way. A sentence of death was a final statement of truth, of truth so overpowering and blinding that it made you loathe nothing so violently as a lie. He was resigned. He knew how he wanted to die. All he needed from her was a moment of tolerance, not pity, a moment of truth, so that he might tell her about the great beautiful change that had taken place in his life, just as he had once run to her lap and wept with joy at the sudden discovery that he wanted to become a priest. He was resolved to speak to her, no matter what. He would tell her everything, at once.

79

But when he finally did look up, she was no longer standing there. He listened. Those were her footsteps above. She was in her bedroom now, changing.

A long sigh of relief flowed from his lips. Yes, he had avoided a scene. But it was only temporary. Like the end itself, truth would have to come out someday, soon. If only Paul would come! If only he could see Lise tonight!

Suddenly, he felt a sharp pain in the back of his head. The long moment of intense repression was having its effect. Unless he went to bed, he would have another spell. He started walking toward the staircase, which he managed to climb with the help of his cane only after an exhausting effort.

At the head of the stairs he straightened, struggling for air. His mother was standing there waiting for him. "*Now* you are being *reasonable*," she said kindly.

She had put on her black dress with the mandarin collar. She looked well, invincible in her uniform of lieutenant to God. He could not repress a sudden feeling of bitterness at the sight of her healthy, dignified piety. It was as though she had sided with God against him.

She said: "I'll leave the front door unlocked in case your brother comes home while I am at the meeting. Then you won't have to get out of bed."

He lowered his eyes as he passed by her on his way to his room down the hall.

"Shall I ask Father Boulanger to come tomorrow morning?"

"I am always ready for communion," he replied.

"Then I will tell him to come," she said, going down the stairs.

Weary, depressed and out of breath, Claude opened his bedroom door and walked in. Then he closed the door with a bang, for he knew that she would not leave the house until she was sure he was in his room. He leaned against the door, listening to her footsteps on the sidewalk slates. This is wrong, he said to himself. I must not let her and Father Boulanger drive me to bitterness. When he could no longer hear her footsteps, he crossed over to the window and opened it.

A cool breeze was blowing from across the river. It felt good on his face, through his hair. The sky was blue-gray, with long streaks of crimson above the far end of town. The air had the good smell of wet bark. He took several deep breaths. His gaze wandered over the tight-knitted quilt of loggers' shacks, and he saw the Red House with the closed shutters where Lise worked. Going by the alley that began half a block down on the Rue des Pins he could walk there in very little time, if only he had the strength. Ah, if only Paul could come now! Through him he might get word to Lise that his mother had gone to the meeting!

His lungs could no longer take the cool air, and he began to cough. It was a weak cough, but it was followed by a stronger one, then by another that hurt. His heart began to beat rapidly, and with the pain in his chest came a string of coughs cascading out of his gaping mouth and shaking his head so violently that he lost consciousness.

When he came to, he was aware of his hands gripping the window sill. A dull weight pressed on the top of his head, his temples ached, and there was numbness at the back of his neck. He knew that he must get his head on the pillow, for this was the beginning of another spell.

But first the window had to be shut. His mother must not find it open when she returned. He reached out to close it, only to be shaken by another spell of coughing. He put his handkerchief to his lips, to catch the blood, but the coughing shook him so violently that the handkerchief dropped to the floor. Darkness closed in on him. His room was getting smaller, his bed larger, further away and now closer and

81

smaller; the little altar in the corner kept coming in and out of focus; he could not look up at the ceiling without feeling his knees folding. Sliding against the wall, and guiding himself with his fingertips on the wallpaper, he inched toward the bed. Then throwing his arms around his chest in an anguishing need to still the beating of his heart and crush the burning walls of his chest, still coughing and spitting blood, he fell upon the bed, crying out in despair: "No! Not now. No. No. Oh, Paul! Lise!" In a short while his moans grew weaker. He drifted into exhaustion, sleep.

* * *

The Rue des Pins and the Rue des Erables had taken on their Thursday evening look. Women and young girls and children were coming from all parts of town to the seminary where the meeting would begin in about one hour. Madame Gauthier, going in the opposite direction, kept to the middle of the sidewalk, walking with her usual air of determination and self-confidence. She smiled, kindly, as she returned the respectful greetings which women and young girls sent her way from each side of the street. Not one of them suspected in the least that behind this smile there raged a tormenting battle between the urge to return to her son's bedside at once, and the decision to answer the call of duty and visit Mademoiselle Serval, who had telephoned and insisted on seeing her about an important matter which required immediate consideration at tonight's meeting of Les Dames de la Grâce. She even waved a gracious hand here, gave a pleasant word there, creating in everyone the impression that all was well at home, and that the rapids might flood the town and still their Madame la Présidente would not look alarmed.

Actually, it was always this way with Madame Gauthier: nobody ever knew how she felt, what preyed on her mind.

So much so that some of her enemies, few though they were, liked to say that her heart was as hard as a dry log and that there was more pride in her than in Lucifer. Around the stalls at the Haymarket of a Saturday morning, along the counter at Ti-Pit's, or wherever professional gossips got together for a quick session, she would be whisperedly referred to as "The Lady," in mocking allusion to the degrading circumstances of her husband's death. These had shocked them all far less, however, than the fact that she did not weep at the funeral and never mentioned his name after that day. Such quiet in grief was not easy to understand.

Madame Dupré, who openly praised her and always supported her policies at meetings of the association, secretly resented her for holding an office which she righteously believed ought to have come to her instead, to her, the dutiful wife of an honorable hard-working man, father of nine children; the least act of insubordination in her daughters would drive her to come down on them in wrathful punishment for behaving in a manner that she called "stuck-up like La Gauthier." The stationmaster's wife, in her bitter envy and frustrated ambition, never considered the fact that Madame Gauthier had been elected to her post, true as it may be that her most active supporter was Father Boulanger, the chaplain of the association, and that his support alone was enough to win the election.

Whatever Father Boulanger's motives were in backing Madame Gauthier, however, there were many valid reasons for wanting her in that post. She was an educated woman: in fact, she was probably the only woman in La Buche who had gone to school until the age of sixteen. More than any other woman in town she could spare the time, since she did not need to work for a living and had no small children at home: after the death of her husband she had been able to support herself entirely on a small income from the uncle who had brought her up in Trois-Rivières. These two factors, while of some value in getting her elected, were also the basis of resentment from the women of the town. But there were other causes for envy, such as the fact that she had never worked in the shirt factory. And then she owned her own house, which meant that she did not have to bear the nasty curses from the Bureau sisters, who were landladies to nearly half the population and whose rents few people ever paid on time. Nor did she ever gossip—Oh, no, she was too much of a "lady" for that, too damn "stuck-up." But perhaps the most difficult thing of all to take, for it was no doubt what hurt the women most, was the cruel truth that Madame Gauthier did not look in the least like the wife of a La Buche lumberjack, although her husband had spent most of his life in the camps up north.

By the age of forty-five the average woman of La Buche had borne more than half a dozen children, some of them between shifts at the shirt factory; she looked haggard and thin and her shoulders were round from hard work and poor food. Her skin was glossy and tight from the bitter cold of long winters, and her voice coarse from shouting after the children at home when she was not wrangling with Ti-Pit for another week of credit. But Madame Gauthier had a handsome face, the soft rosy complexion of a well-fed nun; her body was slim and her back was strong because she had borne only two children; she had fine white hair, the voice and gracious manners of a convent-bred lady.

When she met a mother on the street she would inquire about the health of the children, and seldom failed to ask when the father or husband was expected back from the camps. Never would she mention the illness of her own son, let alone complain of the frustrations of being a widow and the mother of a son who did not go to church. She was thrifty, did not need to depend on money from the camp, so she had no reason to charge at Ti-Pit's, and as a result had no cause for complaining about him.

For all of these reasons, gossip was inevitable indeed. It seldom rose above a whisper, however, nor did it prevent even the most malicious of gossip-mongers from openly praising her virtues of piety and cleanliness and fortitude and good manners. Not to show her respect in public would have amounted to near blasphemy. In this regard Madame Gauthier stood on an equal footing with Monsieur le Curé, with whom she was rumored not to see eye to eye on many things. But that did not really matter, since she was on the best of terms with Father Boulanger, who, as some would say, wielded much more power behind the scenes than most people thought he did, that old crafty Jesuit!

But, as a matter of truth, Madame Gauthier was not the person of strength and pride and self-confidence which the women in town judged her to be. At bottom she was tormented by shame. Her husband's death had filled her life with a bitter feeling of unworthiness that only grew the more haunting as it was never given an outlet of expression and was fed, moreover, by Paul's outrageous refusal to go to church. The work she did for Les Dames de la Grâce had helped a little at the beginning, but what had really saved her from nervous collapse was her girl-like love of Jesus Christ. The son of God was so vivid and real a part of her religious life that often she would converse with Him in the dark of her living room while her son Claude slept upstairs. With Him she made a pact, whereby if He were to choose Claude as one of his priests, she, in return, would retire to the Convent of the Ursulines on the day of his first Mass: this, in a way, would atone for the sins of her husband and of Paul. Claude

85

had already announced his vocation years before, and had showed no sign of a change of mind since. But she felt that she needed a more formal announcement, as a proof that Jesus Christ had agreed to her offer. And this had come, one day, when Father Boulanger himself, the spiritual director of the seminarists, came to tell her that in his opinion Claude would make one of the best priests that La Buche had ever had the honor of presenting to his Excellency the Bishop of Trois-Rivières. From that time on she had lived only for the day of his first Mass.

Then came this illness. Had Jesus Christ suddenly forgotten about their understanding? No, it couldn't be. Surely the Lord was not going to let her down at this point. She waited, a prey to her ancient shame. It is no wonder, then, that when Claude's illness made it clear that he would never become a priest, she readily accepted Father Boulanger's promise that the boy, because of his exemplary virtuous youth, would surely go straight to heaven the day of his death. Indeed, she reasoned, this was a variation of her long-standing arrangement with Jesus Christ. Yes, Jesus Christ was still on her side. What greater proof! Now the sins of her husband and of her son Paul would be redeemed by the death of Claude. And she would retire to the Convent. Could there be greater glory than to be chosen the mother of a saint? At times it seemed almost too good and glorious to be true. It was as Father Boulanger would say, when he declared that some of us, poor blind humans, are often unable to see the work of God around us, close to us, among us, that sanctity is a living thing, and that we only need to open our eyes a little to find it at our elbows. Indeed! Father Boulanger was a learned priest, he was a Jesuit and he had studied in Rome and seen the Pope in person. He was able to understand such things.

Thus Madame Gauthier would reflect, sometimes. But there were times, like today, when she would suddenly be gripped with a terrible dread lest the will of Jesus Christ be thwarted again. What if Claude were to die in a fit of rebellion against his pains, without her or Father Boulanger at his bedside to make sure he received the Host? Worse still, what if he were to die now, at this very moment, when she was out visiting a woman with a "past"? And with only his sinful brother at his bedside?

"Good evening, Madame Gauthier," said a man passing by.

It was Monsieur De Blois, a thin little clerk at the office of the light company. His wife was expecting a baby, and though in a hurry to get home from work he took time to greet Madame la Présidente. "How is your son today?"

"Much better, thank you. How is Madame De Blois?"

"I think this is the great day, Madame."

"I do hope all goes well. And please let me know if it is a boy or a girl," said Madame Gauthier, as she would have to send baby clothes through the association.

"I certainly will, Madame. Good evening," Monsieur De Blois said, and bowed respectfully before proceeding on his way.

Madame Gauthier followed him with her eyes for a while; it took her mind off Claude's condition. It also helped soothe the disquiet of finding herself rapidly approaching the Bureau sisters' house, where the light was on at the window upstairs. It was not easy for a woman of Madame Gauthier's virtue and position to call on a woman with Mademoiselle Serval's past. A certain period of self-conditioning was needed, for the caller to summon up all her reserve of forgiveness and tolerance. And this was precisely what Madame Gauthier was about to achieve in her delicate soul, when her attention was suddenly attracted to the train depot at the end of the Rue des Pins.

The bus had just arrived. A crowd was gathering. Lumber-jacks got off sleepily, stretched their legs, walked around to relax their muscles. Monsieur Dupré was all over the place, waving his arms busily in the air, shouting at the men to hurry, the train had waited long enough. Some of the men were carrying their bags and rolled-up blankets to the train. There were bright colored shirts everywhere in the crowd now, as many of the men just stood there trying to decide whether to go on south or stay in La Buche for an overnight spree. A small group began singing with drunken voices:

> Auprès de ma blonde, qu'il fait bon, fait bon, fait bon!
> Auprès de ma blonde, qu'il fait bon dormir!

There were many exchanges of bold looks between the men and the factory girls, who shuffled through the crowd with large bright eyes full of desire for one of those bronze-faced jacks to give them a quick tumble where the ground was dry in the ravine.

From where she stood, Madame Gauthier could see the head of her son Paul towering above the crowd. She sighed in relief. At least people could not say he was not doing his duty toward his brother. She had left him a note—he was not to go upstairs and disturb Claude, but wait for her return, and if something went wrong he must get in touch with her at the meeting; then in case he had had a change of soul, lately, he knew where to find his rosary of better days: it was still there in that tea cup on a shelf in the kitchen. She saw Paul leave the crowd. He was coming her way.

She turned into the path in front of the Bureau sisters' house. The gravel was soft between high hedges of haw-thornes. At the end of the path she began climbing the nar-row staircase. But she stopped halfway up, hesitant. For a second it seemed that Mademoiselle Serval's notorious past was going to swerve her from her purpose.

The striking feature of Mademoiselle Serval's past was that nobody knew exactly what it consisted of. There were a few well-founded doubts about her virtue, to be sure. But the label was mainly the product of an assumption in the minds of the people. For this reason, it sounded much more appalling than if the tall spinster had been caught one night near the rapids with her skirt in the air and a panting jack on top of her. It surrounded her with an aura of spicy wickedness that would remain with her until the day she died or left town, even after.

She had come from Montreal some fifteen years back, to take charge of the telephone office, and soon after moving into her present apartment she had openly challenged the townspeople by entertaining a week-end guest from out of town. This was bold, shocking. And it had given the folks a lot to talk about—Who did she think she was to scandalize their children like that? And not even the decency to say that he was her cousin or something of the sort! Why, she needed a good lesson. And she had sure come to the right place to learn a thing or two about morals!

Aware of the gossips through the telephone wires and the cold glances shot at her on the street, Mademoiselle Serval had then thought that the best way to silence them all was to hit the folks with a double blow. The following Sunday she had made a formal appearance at High Mass, with her lover. The rest of that day, and all week long, the town resounded with cries of charivari. As had once been the fate of another loose woman in La Buche some fifty years before, the wicked spinster would be dragged out of her apartment, stripped naked in the Place de l'Eglise; they would lapidate her with chunks of coal until her body turned black, the color of her soul, and then they would throw her in the rapids to drown and be carried down to hell where she belonged. The charivari had been called off, however, when her lover failed to return the next week end, and ever after that.

Vividly remembering these events, while reciting Ave after Ave for the salvation of the poor spinster's soul and for the courage and humility without which she could never speak to her like a true Christian, Madame Gauthier continued up the stairs and finally knocked at the door.

Mademoiselle Serval opened at once. She was wearing a pink satin robe. "Come in, Madame la Présidente," she said.

"Were you not expecting me?"

"Of course. Oh! I'm sorry I am not ready yet. I just came home a few minutes ago."

As Madame Gauthier walked in, Mademoiselle Serval led her into a small living room furnished simply but cozily. The lighting was low, intimate. A strong perfume filled the air. The floor was covered from wall to wall with a blue carpet. And there were cushions on the couch and on the armchairs, great big cushions covered with pink satin and looking soft and comfortable. "Decidedly!" Madame Gauthier thought, "This woman still leads a double life."

She was saying: "I hope you will forgive me for asking you to come so early. With all your problems at home, it isn't fair."

"Well, I am here now. What is it you wanted to see me about?"

"Please, Madame, help yourself while I change into something else," Mademoiselle Serval said, indicating the pot of fresh coffee next to a plate of home-made cookies on a low table in front of the couch. And she went into her bedroom, leaving the door open.

Such a display of kindness made Madame Gauthier relent a little. "Very well," she said. "But please hurry." Then with the air of a woman afraid to soil a new dress on dirty furniture, she chose the chair that seemed the least comfortable, and sat down on the edge of it. "This must be the room where she committed all her week-end sins," she thought. "Oh, my Lord, please help me forget all that. Let me be tolerant and forgiving. Ah, but this perfume, and all this pink!"

"Do you like my cookies?" Mademoiselle Serval said.

Madame Gauthier picked one up with her fingertips and took a tiny bite; then without tasting it she replied yes, they were very good.

"I made so many of them that I would gladly give you some for your son Claude. I don't suppose you have much time for baking, these days."

"That is very kind of you, Mademoiselle. But Claude is not allowed sweets."

"Too bad. How is he feeling, by the way?"

"Much better, thank you."

"Have you heard about Madame De Blois? He is there now, you know, Doctor Gendron. I took the call. This is his second visit today. And it is beginning to look like a difficult delivery."

"Poor woman!" Madame Gauthier said, and added that she hoped and prayed that all might go well.

Mademoiselle Serval then began talking about large families, Ti-Pit's high prices, and those gossip-mongers who listened in on the wires all day long. Madame Gauthier sat stiff, listening with one ear while praying God to help her trust this woman whom she could not make out in the least. On the telephone this afternoon she had sounded frightened; now she seemed relaxed, carefree. And that familiarity! And the nerve she had, to offer some of *her* cookies for Claude! Ah, it was not easy to be tolerant and forgiving!

Mademoiselle Serval was now on the subject of her apartment. Yes, it was nice, and she liked it. After all the years she had spent fixing it, she was beginning to feel at home here. As for what it looked like when she first moved in, well, she

91

was not going to talk about *that*. The less said, the better. But there was the problem of the rent. "Would you believe it, Madame. In the last ten years it has more than tripled. And each year they keep adding another ten dollars. If it weren't for the law that protects me they would throw me out on the street. Now, what am I going to do when they increase it again May first? Truly, Madame, I have reached the limit."

"Taxes are very high."

"But the sisters have so much money."

"That is what people say."

"And where do you think all their money will go after they die?"

"Why, Mademoiselle. I was under the impression that you were a devout churchgoer."

There followed a long silence. Finally Mademoiselle Serval appeared from her bedroom. She was wearing a plain gray dress, buttoned high. Madame Gauthier took a long searching look at her. For the first time she noticed that the spinster suffered from a rather pronounced nervous tick: her large brown eyes, it seemed, could not stay fixed on anything very long; they kept looking left and right, giving her an air of fear that belied the poise and lighthearted tone of her voice and manners. It struck Madame Gauthier suddenly that Mademoiselle Serval was more jittery now than a moment ago. She seemed undecided as to whether she ought to sit down or remain standing. "I should have been more tolerant. The poor woman is disturbed. Now I can see it. Oh, why was I so mistrustful?" Madame Gauthier said to herself. Then in a warm voice she asked: "Well, what is it?"

"I suppose you have heard the latest about me?"

"I am not interested in gossip, Mademoiselle."

"Rumors are going around that a man visits me at night. They say it is the new man in town, you know, the one who owns the rosary-bead factory."

"Do these rumors reflect the truth?"

"Of course not."

"Are you sure?"

"You must trust me, Madame. Please, believe me."

"Go on."

"I would like you to take me to the meeting tonight, so that I may challenge them to come out openly and prove what they say against me. You see, Madame, the point is, that rosary-bead factory is not really a place where they make beads for rosaries. That man runs a brothel in there."

"What!" Madame Gauthier stood up.

"A brothel, Madame."

"You mean, a house of sin!"

"If you prefer."

"Oh, dear, dear. But are you sure?"

"That's another thing I want to do at the meeting. I will tell all I know about it."

"Of course, of course," Madame Gauthier repeated absently.

Mademoiselle Serval tried to soften the blow a little. "I am sorry that I had to tell you such terrible news at a time like this, with your son so ill and all that. But I felt it was my duty to try and do something."

"Where did you get your information?"

"At the switchboard."

"I see. Well, I suppose you did right in listening, this time."

"A lot of men are coming in from the camps this week end, and all of next week. I thought something ought to be done now."

"Indeed."

"A charivari might force the owners to close down."

"But we can't risk it," Madame Gauthier protested. "After all, as you know yourself, charivaris are nearly always fatal to someone."

"I did not mean to refer to . . ."

"To what?"

Mademoiselle Serval hesitated. "Well . . ."

"If that is what you are thinking about, Mademoiselle. I must remind you that Monsieur Gauthier died doing his duty, *putting out the fire.*"

Mademoiselle Serval lowered her eyes in a show of genuine regret. And it moved Madame Gauthier to reprimand herself for having lost her temper. "Let us go to Father Boulanger, at once," she said.

Mademoiselle Serval went to her room. A moment later she came back wearing a light coat a shade darker than her dress.

"You can tell me the rest on the way," said Madame Gauthier rising from her chair. As they were descending the stairs she stopped suddenly. "But that house of sin happens to belong to the Bureau sisters!" she exclaimed.

"That is right," said Mademoiselle Serval.

Madame Gauthier looked at her searchingly. "I know that the sisters and you do not get along. You are not doing all this in revenge, are you?"

"Even if I did, Madame. Don't you think I would still be doing my duty?"

Such frankness left Madame Gauthier utterly speechless. They reached the sidewalk in silence, and started up the Rue des Erables. Women and young girls stared in surprise, puzzled at the sight of Mademoiselle walking stiff and confident with Madame la Présidente. After a short distance, Mademoiselle Serval began telling Madame Gauthier all that she knew about the house of sin. There was a thin smile of satisfaction on her face. But Madame Gauthier did not see it, for she kept looking ahead while listening, and praying in silence: "Lord, forgive me for being so mistrustful. I ought to have been more charitable toward this poor woman who has sinned so much in the past but who wants to serve you faithfully now like the rest of us. Forgive me, Lord. And thank you for reminding me, through her, of the sins in my own family. Help me, Lord. Help me to master thy enemies. Advise me and Father Boulanger on the wisest action to take in this terrible calamity that has befallen us. And please see if there is something that Thou might do about my son Paul. Now that my little Claude is on his way to Thee, please see if Thou could not consider the poor soul of his brother. Thou hast brought Mademoiselle Serval back to Thy Fold. Please, Lord, do the same for my Paul!"

* * *

Claude became conscious of the darkness around him. His head hurt, his back and legs were wet with perspiration. Now he knew that he was lying in bed, under the blankets. His throat felt dry, his lips tasted blood. He opened his eyes: a faint light filtered in through the shuttered window. But the window was shut! He remembered suddenly that he had failed to close it. What time was it? Had he slept all night? He reached for the lamp on the bedside table and switched on the light.

"Hello," said Lise.

He rubbed his eyes, unbelieving.

"No, you are not dreaming, Claude. I am here."

"Lise!" He sat up. He took her hands and kissed them passionately. "Oh, Lise! I didn't think you would ever come again."

"I waited until I saw your mother on her way to the meeting."

He ran his fingers up her arms, shoulders, into her hair. "Let me look at you."

95

She leaned closer, her dark eyes glowing.

"You haven't changed," he whispered happily.

"I wanted to come before."

"I know."

"But your mother . . ."

"Every night," he said, "I watched you go to work, from my window here. If mother had not been downstairs I would have called out to you. Tonight I was going to send Paul with a message." Then, after a pause to catch his breath, he asked: "But where is Paul? Have you seen him?"

"No."

"But I am sure he is here. I saw him just a moment ago, standing at the door and telling me to take it easy and go back to sleep. It was he who closed the window. I remember now. I could not have dreamed all that, could I? Has the bus arrived yet?"

"It's in front of Ti-Pit's."

"Then Paul must be home."

"Maybe you were dreaming, Claude."

Exhausted, he lay back on the pillows. His respiration was hoarse from speaking so fast, with so much excitement. "Maybe you are right," he said, after a while. "I must have been dreaming again. It is so hard to tell the difference, these days."

Lise reached to pull the blankets over his chest. "What happened?" she cried, alarmed. The front of his nightshirt was bloodstained.

"That's nothing," he said, drawing his robe over it. "It's not as bad as it looks, really."

"You had a hemorrhage?"

"Yes, but I am used to it."

She stood up, speechless, not daring to ask for details.

"Don't worry," he pleaded.

"At least, let me get you a clean shirt."

"Don't bother. If mother finds out that I have changed, she will make a scene. You might get me a glass of water instead, if you want."

On the point of crying, she turned abruptly, walked out of the room and across the hall into the bathroom.

Claude took two pills out of a bottle in the drawer of the bedside table. A small parcel was next to the lamp. He felt it with his fingers. A book! Perhaps he had been dreaming about Paul, but now there was no doubting that he was fully awake. He could smell Lise's perfume in every breath of air, hear the gurgling sound of water. He felt acutely the dull ache in his head, the throbbing at his temples; the dryness inside his throat was like a knot. Yet all of this was good in a way; it made him feel alive. Lise came back into the room with the glass of water. How good the water tasted, how cool, how real. He followed every movement of her hands as she unwrapped the parcel. He could almost feel her young, vital flesh as she moved. And once again he knew in all his limbs that feverish desire which had been the only reality that mattered in these past weeks, a reality even more acute than the burning tentacles that gnawed at his wasting body. "Sit here, Lise," he said. "Close to me."

She did as he asked, then gave him the book.

"Baudelaire!"

And she explained that she had asked Bernard Toupin to bring a book of poems from Montreal, any book of poems; she did not know what sort these were, she hoped he would like them.

His death-shadowed face was all lit up with rapture. "Baudelaire!"

She lowered her eyes, reluctant to believe that she could actually give him so much pleasure and joy. She had reacted

97

the same way to his transports the first time she gave herself to him. For a moment she almost succeeded in making herself believe that she was not a whore, while she watched Claude turning the pages of the book, slowly, running his fingers down the edge of each page in a delight that was almost sensual. All these years he had wanted to read Baudelaire, but had been able to do it in hiding only, for this was a forbidden poet. He now read her a line here, a complete poem there. In each passage they found an echo of their deep, desperate longing for a time and place all for themselves, invitations to exotic lands the poet seemed to have written specifically for them. And when they came to the line, "J'ai plus de souvenirs que si j'avais mille ans," Claude paused, and looking deeply into her eyes he said: "This is what I want to be able to tell myself. It's the only way to go. The only way."

Lise threw her arms around him. "That is the way it will be, my darling. From now on you will live, really live. I will give you so much to take away, so much." And he held her close to him, already tasting the bitter flavor of his last hours. The book of poems dropped to the floor. They did not pick it up.

Later, they talked about their plans: where they would go, how, and when. Claude had decided on the lake, the one his great-grandfather had discovered and given the family name to. It was in the mountains south of La Buche, only a few hours' drive. When he was a little boy, he had gone there with his brother and father on fishing trips that lasted sometimes as long as three weeks. And after that he had returned often with Paul, to hunt. It was a beautiful wild lake. Nobody else ever went there. The pines grew down to the very edge of the water; at night you went to sleep lulled by their gentle rustling. The two brothers had felled a few trees and put up an open shack, in which three persons, even four, could sleep. "We will be all alone," Claude went on. "Or maybe we could ask Paul to bring a friend. Mother, and Father Boulanger, will be out of our lives. We will live in the open where we belong. No more walls, no more closed windows. The air is always pure and cool on the lake. We will fish and eat the fish we catch. We will sleep on the ground, just as when we were children. And in the morning we will wash ourselves in the water of the lake."

"When can we leave?" said Lise.

"As soon as Paul is home. He will rent a car and drive us."

"But when do you think he will come?"

"Tomorrow, the latest. And he will not refuse me this favor. Paul is a good man. You will like him."

"Does he know about us?"

"I don't think he received my letters."

"What about your mother, and Father Boulanger?"

"It is the same as always. But they will not be able to keep me here, if Paul is willing to come with us."

Suddenly Lise felt chilled, and she knew with a dreadful certainty that what they were talking about, what they looked forward to so eagerly, would never happen.

"Darling, you are trembling," Claude said, gathering her in his arms again.

"Oh, Claude, I'm so afraid," she whispered, clinging to him.

"Don't worry," said Claude. "Everything is going to be all right."

They worked out a system of signals. "On your way to work tomorrow," he explained; "you stop on the porch and look at this window. If I wave with two hands it will mean that Paul is here and we can leave tomorrow night. He would then go and pick you up at work. If I wave with one hand only it will mean that he has not arrived yet. In that case you wait for my signal the day after tomorrow. He will have come home by then, I am sure."

"One thing," said Lise. "I had planned on quitting tonight, after they give me the rest of what they owe me. I may not be there tomorrow."

"I could send Paul to your rooming house."

After a moment's reflection, Lise said: "All right, do that, then." And she took out of her handbag an envelope that contained two hundred dollars. "I would feel better if you kept this here," she said. "It's not safe where I live."

They put the money inside the book, and the book under the mattress. And again they became silent, each absorbed in finding in the other's gaze a reflection of overwhelming desire. The window hung a shimmering pane of crimson twilight. Rapid footsteps died away in the distance. The rumble of the rapids could be heard as though part of the silence, and the silence was alive with their restless yearning. Lise stood up abruptly. "I must go," she said. "Your mother will be back soon."

"Don't go now," Claude said, imploring. He took her hands. Lise looked at him compassionately. "Not tonight, darling."

"I want you."

"But . . ."

"Don't you?" he insisted, leading her hands under the blankets.

"Yes, but . . ." the touch of him sent a last spasm of struggle through her flesh. "Claude, Claude," she whispered as her hands caressed him. She stared into the death of his face with a clear, bold, desperate passion.

He turned out the light, and removed the bloodstained nightshirt. Down his arms, legs, back, there flowed a sensation of strength that dulled the pains, quickened the beat of

100

his heart, as he waited for her to undress and slip under the covers.

"My love." He kissed her eyes, her lips, her breasts. "Oh, my love." Through his fevered hands he could feel her cool flesh flowing into him, life-giving.

And she received him, open to all of him that she hungered for, all that she needed so desperately to help her forget. To give, to give. Oh, gladly would she give all of herself, gladly die that he might live. She had no words to tell him this, only her lingering kisses, the quivering of her flesh, until at last he took her, in a final swoon of desperate yearning.

*　　*　　*

"Our little Claude is a saint, Madame," Father Boulanger was saying. "You must not lose courage when he becomes impatient and irritable. He is also a human being. He will have many more moments of weakness. Ah, I know: perhaps it sounds cruel that I should be talking to you this way, you, his loving mother. But think of the Virgin Mary. Consider how much she must have suffered at the foot of the cross; her son Jesus was in greater pain than at any other moment in His life, and yet there was nothing she could do to help Him, nothing." His voice was warm, convincing.

A short and fragile-looking old priest with downy white hair, a pale complexion and deep blue eyes that could look either mild with the glow of mystical contemplation or bright and alert with the logic of the Jesuit, he spoke in a low tone, soul-to-soul, and with his head tilted gently to the side of the person he talked to, accompanying his words with graceful motions of the hands, as though to mold the thoughts and put them in their proper place inside the mind of his listener. When he did not wish to be interrupted he would simply raise a forefinger in a gesture that meant: "Not now, please.

101

If you don't mind." And after a short pause he would go on, as he did now, explaining how Claude's illness in its last stages might drive the sick boy to rebellion, might change his saintly resignation to cries of revolt, even blasphemy.

For the third time in the last fifteen minutes Mademoiselle Serval, who was walking on his right, tried to get his attention in the hope of changing the subject of conversation. But once again the delicate forefinger rose to remind her that the matter of the Little Saint of La Buche was more important than whatever she may have come here to discuss. She tried to signal Madame Gauthier, who walked on the other side of the old priest, but Claude's mother would not be disturbed out of the head-bent submission in which she was listening to the wise words from the learned man of God.

The three of them were strolling up and down a gravel path that stretched across one end of the seminary garden along a high wrought-iron fence covered with ivy springtime green. A gentle breeze from the river cooled the air, that seemed to quiver with the deep rumble from the rapids. There were several black-robed youths walking meditatively along the other paths of the garden, in an atmosphere pervaded with pious tranquillity. At the far end stood the great massive shape of the seminary, silhouetted dark against broad beams of reddish light that the setting sun, from under the horizon, shot in a wide fan into the sky. Lights were on at the basement windows on each side of the auditorium entrance, where women and young girls and children kept arriving in increasing numbers. From the auditorium there came now and then the sounds of suppressed giggles, shouts of angry mothers calling their children to order. But these sounds hardly disturbed the still, hushed quiet of the garden, to which Mademoiselle Serval seemed to listen with growing restlessness, more acutely aware of its time-marking stillness than of the voice of Father Boulanger.

102

"Indeed, Madame," he was saying. "Claude will suffer other moments of weakness like the one you say he had this afternoon. He might even become frantic. 'Father, Father, do not forsake me!' You see, even Jesus Himself was weak at the end. For although He was the son of God, He was also a man of flesh and bones. And at the moment of death, my dear Madame, man is truly at his weakest. Faith is never so difficult to hold as then. Yet, it is at that very instant that the just must earn his place in heaven, through a solemn act of faith. 'I deliver my soul into Thy hands!' This is the supreme act of faith, the one that really counts."

Mademoiselle Serval watched the young seminarians leave the garden on their way to the front entrance to the seminary on the Rue des Pins. She saw a group of women gather round Madame Dupré at the auditorium door, obviously wondering why Madame la Présidente and the chaplain would not come to open the meeting. Mademoiselle Serval was determined to try once more to put in a word about the house of sin. She slowed down, to force the old priest and Madame Gauthier to notice that she was not listening. But the other two went on ahead as if she were not there. They turned into the path that cut across the middle of the garden. All of a sudden the old priest stopped. Mademoiselle Serval hastened to catch up with them. But just as she was about to speak, Father Boulanger spread wide his arms, and with an expression of pure ecstasy lighting up his pale old face he pointed to the ground and said: "It was here, Madame, on this very spot; I remember, on an evening very much like this one, with the sky fiery as it is now. We had been walking in silence for a while and I was marveling at the peaceful music of our rapids, marveling how soothing it was for the soul, how much nearer to God these rapids made us feel; and he was gazing into the

103

distance above that fence as if he were seeing someone or hearing something very special from there. His beautiful young eyes were all aglow. How I remember! Suddenly he turned to me and cried out, feverishly, 'Listen, Father! That is the voice of God we hear from the bottom of the rapids. The voice of the Last Judgment. Do you hear? Do you hear the rumble? That is the rumble of the Last Judgment. Now I know what I will preach about when I become a priest. All my life, Father, I will preach about the Last Judgment, Eternity!' "

The voice of the old priest broke from the surge of emotions which the memory of that moment in Claude's life had released in him. He gazed at the ground with eyes full of melancholy tenderness. Madame Gauthier could not take her own eyes off the spot of ground; great tears of joy and sorrow ran freely down her cheeks. Even Mademoiselle Serval was moved. And she looked down, too, as if to find there the truth beneath all the rumors she had heard about the Little Saint of La Buche. But all she could see was two paths crossing each other at a right angle, some pebbles, scattered blades of grass.

At last the old priest pulled himself together. With a gentle tilt of the head toward Madame Gauthier, he concluded: "So you see, Madame. Claude does not really belong to you or me. He belongs to God. He always has. You gave him his body. I took care of his soul. Like Joseph and Mary, we are the instruments of God's Divine Will. We have been chosen to perform a very special duty. If at times our task appears difficult, even cruel, we must accept it as Jesus accepted His cross. And we must be grateful."

"You are right," Madame Gauthier sighed, and she dried her tears.

At that moment, Madame Dupré's heavy steps on the gravel made them all look up at the same time. Large and heavy and forceful she came, with an assumed air of joviality. Her strong masculine voice rang loud and boisterous. "Well, what's holding up the meeting, Father? It is past seven, Madame la Présidente!" Then to Mademoiselle Serval: "What are *you* doing here?"

The spinster looked pleadingly to Madame Gauthier, who, suddenly remembering the purpose of their visit, turned to Father Boulanger and whispered in his ear.

"Dear, dear!" exclaimed the old priest, shocked. "What now!"

"I'd like to know what it's all about," said Madame Dupré, resentful of the secret exchange. "Are you bringing us special news, Mademoiselle. Something about the rosary-bead factory, maybe? I hear you have been listening in on the wires quite a lot lately. Or do you get your information more directly, person-to-person, say?"

Mademoiselle Serval turned pale. But Madame Gauthier came to her rescue. "Now, now, Madame Dupré, we must not be uncharitable to one another. Let's forget the past. There is work to do. We need to stand united."

And Father Boulanger echoed: "We must remain calm. This is a matter of utmost importance."

"You have guessed right, Madame Dupré," said Madame Gauthier. "It seems that there is a house of sin in our dear La Buche. But I will vouch personally for Mademoiselle Serval. She has nothing to do with it."

After a cold look of disdain at the spinster, Madame Dupré declared: "We have known about it for some time. And I have a feeling the members expect some sort of action, tonight. What are we going to do?"

"Nothing," said Father Boulanger. "This is a problem for Monsieur le Curé to solve. I will go and telephone the presbytery. Suppose you come with me, Madame Gauthier. There is something I want to show you at the same time."

105

Mademoiselle Serval looked alarmed. Madame Dupré's hostility toward her made her wish that Madame Gauthier would stay to support her speech to the members.

To the treasurer, Madame la Présidente said: "Go and open the meeting with the usual prayers. Then wait for Father Boulanger and me. Do not allow any discussion about this house of sin."

Madame Dupré said yes, she would do as in the last two meetings. Quite pleased now, she managed to smile affably at Mademoiselle Serval.

"If we take too long," the chaplain suggested, "say the beads."

"And you might say one decade for my son Claude."

"We will do that," said Madame Dupré, anxious to agree to everything, and secretly wishing that Madame Gauthier might not come back at all, so that she might once again stand up as president for the entire meeting. Although she was convinced that Mademoiselle Serval was mixed up in this house-of-sin affair, she was glad that she had come to say all she knew about it. She was not concerned with why the slim sinner might want to do such a thing, but only with her own opportunity to show the women of La Buche what true leadership was. She drew Mademoiselle Serval aside and said in a tone of secret confidence: "Now, you are going to tell me everything you know, everything."

Father Boulanger and Madame Gauthier walked up the concrete path that led to the front doors of the seminary. Here, at the foot of tall white columns, stood a number of young seminarians enjoying a last smoke before going in for their evening studies. At the sight of Father Boulanger and Madame Gauthier two of them rushed to open the heavy wrought-iron doors. With one of them Father Boulanger left word that he would not be available for spiritual consultation this evening, while Madame Gauthier smiled affectionately at the other, whom she recognized as one of Claude's classmates. Then they went inside.

All the way through the large entrance hall they did not say a word. They entered a long, dark corridor with many doors on each side. The sound of their footsteps on the marble floor filled the air. Madame Gauthier took out her rosary and began saying the beads; Father Boulanger took out his pipe and lit it.

At the foot of the stairs, he said: "You must not worry, Madame. Monsieur le Curé will be able to handle this situation, I am sure. The matter of Claude is more important now."

She nodded agreement, as she always did with Father Boulanger. They continued up to his office on the third floor. Madame Gauthier walked slightly behind the old priest, her head bent, her lips moving in prayer. Nothing in her countenance at this moment suggested that she possessed those qualities of leadership which had made her direct the affairs of Les Dames de la Grâce so efficiently in the past ten years. Rather, she looked like a young girl on her way up the aisle to receive First Communion. Father Boulanger only needed to look deeply into her eyes, and at once the woman in her, the leader in her, even the mother in her, would vanish: she became the young girl who had vowed to wear on her finger the ring of nunnery, and her will to action would dissolve into a swoonlike transport that lifted her to the highest peak of mystical abandon. This had taken place in the garden a moment before. And now it was happening again, with perhaps greater intensity, for, added to the presence of the old priest, was the atmosphere of these walls, this austere quiet, this soul-soothing odor of piety which pervaded every breath of air, the shimmering presence of Him that veiled the front of

107

the altar as, passing in front of the open doors of the chapel, she genuflected a moment before going on. This moment was a preview of all those years she would spend in the secure beatitude of a nun's life. It brought to her face a look of sweet ecstasy, which remained there lingering like a remembered caress from Jesus Himself, as she entered Father Boulanger's office and sat down in the large armchair in front of his desk, the chair that she knew almost as well as any piece of furniture in her own house.

This was the room that had been tabernacle to her most secret thoughts for so many years. It was here that she always came to confession, kneeling on the prie-dieu upholstered in red velvet which she was secretly convinced had once belonged to a cardinal, or at least a bishop. She felt pleasurably weak and humble here, yet secure, in this atmosphere of divine knowledge. The walls were lined with books from floor to ceiling, large thick books bound in black leather and showing titles imprinted with gold, all those books that contained the mysterious and awe-inspiring knowledge of Our Mother the Church, Jesus, and the Holy Ghost, and which Father Boulanger was said not to read any more since he already knew their contents by heart. Even the strong masculine scent of Canadian pipe tobacco had a flavor of inspiration: it moved her to imagine stately learned bishops and Princes of the Church in pipe-smoking seminars on dogmas that they alone were permitted and able to discuss. And behind the desk, those three large windows overlooking the entire town! They presented a view of the sky footed with tree tops, a vast expanse of soul-lifting void, so that with the solemn voice of Father Boulanger in her ears she needed only to look out those windows to know a wonderful close-to-God feeling. Here indeed she felt pure, and so much closer to her convent life of tomorrow that she little cared for the problems of Les Dames de la Grâce.

108

That is why she said nothing when, presently, Father Boulanger came out of his bedroom and announced: "I have just called Monsieur le Vicaire Martin. He is on his way to the rapids now to get Monsieur le Curé. So, I don't think we ought to worry too much. Once Monsieur le Curé talks to the members everything will be under control, and that will give us time to investigate." He then sat behind his desk, and opened the top drawer from which he took out a large scrapbook.

Madame Gauthier sat up in her chair.

Clipped to the cover of the scrapbook was Claude's portrait which she had given him the previous week. Father Boulanger put it in a large envelope and gave it back to her. At the same time he showed her a small reproduction of it, and asked: "Do you like it?"

Yes. The printer had done his work well. Only she did not know what to say about the cloud-like effect of grey-black around the head. And the blank space for the date at the bottom sent a pang to her heart.

"I received a thousand of them this afternoon," the old priest said. "You know, ever since I have used Claude as an example of resignation to suffering and death, in my sermons here and at the orphanage in Trois-Rivières, the children have been asking for his portrait. Tomorrow I will begin to distribute these. A little six-year-old boy came to me the other day with an envelope he wanted me to deliver to Claude. I opened it and found a letter in which this poor little orphan was asking Claude to ask God to send him a father and a mother as soon as he arrived in heaven. Here it is," he added, and handed the letter to Madame Gauthier.

But she did not take it. "I would rather let Claude read it first."

"I will bring it to him tomorrow," he said. Then he flipped the pages of the book to the last entry in what was a daily chronicle of observations on Claude, to be used for the biography he would write on the Little Saint of La Buche. And he asked: "Did you notice anything unusual, today?"

"He has become so distant," she replied. "He will not look me in the eye. I don't know what is happening to him, Father."

"No allusions to his pains, or perhaps his death?"

"No, Father. He seems to be daydreaming most of the time, as if he were meditating."

The old priest hastened to make a note of this, explaining that Claude was undoubtedly entering the first stage of contemplation. "You see, his irritability and impatience are caused by the fever, and also by the pains in his chest. Now, as he is nearing the kingdom of heaven, most of his time is spent in contemplation of his future life of beatitude, so that when the pains do shake him abruptly out of this state, naturally he becomes annoyed. As you can see, it is very simple to understand. Now, what we must look for are signs of rebellion."

"I wish I could tell you more. But this is all I have noticed today," said Claude's mother, while Father Boulanger completed his notes. Then it seemed that all of a sudden she could not control herself any longer. It was as if something lodged deep inside her had suddenly forced itself up through the pressure of resignation and sacrifice, something that was more powerful than her spirit of grace, more urgently demanding to be heard. Tears of misery rolled down her cheeks as she said: "Forgive me, Father. But sometimes I feel that I must have done something very evil in my life to deserve this. After all, Claude is my son. I am still his mother. And now he is becoming such a stranger to me. Can't he go to heaven and still remain my little boy?"

Father Boulanger came to stand next to her and put his hand on her shoulder: "Think of the Virgin Mary, my dear

110

Madame. You suffer in your mother's heart now, but you are a good woman and you have done no evil. That is why God makes you suffer, as Jesus made His mother suffer, whom He loved like a dutiful son. Remember that God always punishes those whom He loves the most."

"I am sorry, Father. I was weak," she said, drying her tears and getting up.

At the door, he announced: "I will come tomorrow morning."

"Claude will be ready."

"Perhaps you ought to go to him at once. That would be better than to attend the meeting. I will go there myself and see what I can do."

They went downstairs in silence. Then as they walked out the front door she asked: "Have you talked to Mother Superior?"

"Not yet. But I will, tomorrow. Now would you like me to take care of the matter of your resignation?"

"I did not intend to resign until . . ."

"I know. But perhaps you should do it now. I would rather not see you involved in this new problem. And besides, you may need to stay home all the time from now on."

After a moment of reflection, she said: "Very well, Father."

"God be with you," said the old priest, with a kind smile. Then he walked away toward the entrance of the auditorium.

Madame Gauthier continued down the Rue des Pins, thinking of her son Claude. There was joy in her heart. But there was also a deep aching sorrow that she did not know how to soothe except in prayers asking God to give her strength to bear her cross.

five

The short moment of love which La
Pitoune had had with Bernard in the back room that morning was a mere side-dish in the feast of her infidelities. The main course, the one that she counted on to satisfy her healthy appetite, consisted of a regular Thursday evening rendezvous with her lover, again in the back room, but lasting at least half an hour and garnished with the luxury of a bed made of several bags of peas piled up against the doors. This secret escapade was the most important event in her week, and she always prepared for it as if that night were the first or might be the last. Nothing else in her life received so much loving care, was planned with more feverish application and awaited with greater eagerness.

At six o'clock sharp, two hours earlier than usual, her husband would lock the front door. Then he would count his cash hurriedly, and rush upstairs to a quick meal which was always ready on time on Thursday. Since this was the night of the weekly meeting of Les Dames de la Grâce, which his wife attended in the company of Madame Dupré who would call for her shortly after seven, it was agreed that it might as well be Ti-Pit's weekly night out also—a few beers with the men at Lambert's tavern, followed by a session of gin rummy at the Police-and-Fire House. By about six-twenty, tonight, he had finished eating and put on his black corduroy jacket, ready to leave.

From the bathroom where his wife was having a warm bath—a woman of her position in the community simply must bathe and dress up for a meeting of Les Dames de la Grâce—came the usual last-minute reminder: "Ti-Pit, don't forget the bags!"

"All right."

"And lock the front door."

"Yes."

"And the trap door."

"Yes."

"Are you going now?"

"When you see horseface Dupré, tell her to go to hell, will you."

"Ti-Pit!"

"All right. So I'll tell her myself next time."

He went downstairs, to stack the bags against the doors. This was to avoid a repetition of the burglary which had taken place last September when the town was full of tipsy loggers on their way to the camps. And he was glad to do it, even though it cost considerable labor and sweat, what with his enormous belly, his short arms, and the fear of splitting

114

his trousers when he bent down. He still had a lot of steam to work out of himself after that argument with Madame Dupré in the morning; it had been on his mind all day. With each bag he threw against the doors he muttered to himself how he would like to throw that one smack at her big arse. This helped a little. And as he kept working and sweating, so soon after his meal, the continuous bending down and lifting began to affect his bowels, so that he now paused, braced himself, and sent out a deep roaring blast, with the comment, "Run after that one, horseface!"

Now he felt better, and he returned to work with a lighter heart. The bags were heavy enough, but it had to be done. With loggers all over town tonight you could not be too cautious. When he had finished, he wiped the sweat off his forehead and the back of his neck. He was tired, out of breath. But he felt at peace, confident. He went to see if the key to the trap door was in the cash drawer. It was. Then he walked out the front door, made sure the lock was on, and started across the street toward Lambert's, smacking his lips in anticipation of the cool bottle of ale awaiting him.

From the bathroom window, upstairs, La Pitoune watched him enter the tavern. She giggled, thinking of how her husband had so diligently prepared the bed upon which she was about to deceive him again. It was no small part of her Thursday night pleasure. Standing in the bathtub, while the water gurgled down the drain, she finished drying herself, her hands lingering caressingly here and there. She had read in a magazine that there was nothing like a warm bath to condition a person for the act of love-making. It was one of the most important discoveries in her life. By the time Bernard made his appearance she would be more than ready for him.

The very air of the room after a bath was a source of excitement, with its cloud of silken steam that clung warm and

115

sensuous to every pore of her body. And there was her special Thursday night soap, which she now put back into its ivory box and slipped under the tub; she had sent for it through Eaton's catalogue, and it cost so much money that if Ti-Pit found out about it he would surely have a fit. But it was worth it, worth every cent of it! Its perfume was so exotic that each time she stepped out of the tub, smelling a deep long breath of it, her imagination would flatter her with visions of herself as a great mistress of antiquity lying languorous amidst deep pink cushions while naked young slaves caressed her from head to toe.

The vision still lingered in her mind, as she rubbed the mirror clean of steam and looked fondly at her body—she was lovely. A little plump, but Bernard liked her that way. Her flesh was firm, everywhere, and her Thursday night soap gave her skin a soft, exciting feeling. Indeed she was lovely, much too lovely for that big fat brute of a Ti-Pit, who always took his pleasure without bothering about hers. Bernard was a lucky fellow. If she were a man, she would be thrilled to death to have such a woman to make love to. There were not many women in La Buche who were as good looking as she was. And there was no danger of being put in the family way, since her ovaries did not function properly, according to Doctor Gendron. Ti-Pit claimed it was because she had had too much of it in her ravine-hayloft days. Well, let him say what he wanted.

She went into the bedroom, where she put on a dark woolen smock that she tied with a bow on her belly. Then she gathered and placed neatly together at the foot of the bed the underwear and high-buttoned black dress that she would have to get into hurriedly after Bernard had left. She put on a pair of stockings, rolled them up to her knees, slipped into her shoes, and went downstairs, carrying her husband's shaving mirror, which she hung from the ceiling behind the door at the end of the counter. By tilting it at a certain angle she was able to observe the front of the store from where the bags were piled up against the doors.

It was still daylight; Bernard was due any moment now. She went to the cash drawer, picked up the key, and going into the back room, unlocked the trap door, lifted it, and listened. Bernard was late. Much good it did to have given him that beautiful watch! She listened again. Still not a sound of him. She began pacing up and down between the walls of cartons and sacks of grain and flour and sugar, pausing finally to cover the top bags with a sheet of brown wrapping paper; it made her think of more pleasant things than his being late. After a few more minutes of waiting she went back to the trap door and this time she listened with her ear glued to the floor. Still not a sound of his footsteps coming up the alley. All this waiting intensified her desire. So much so, that she now had to sit on top of the wall of bags to control the trembling in her knees. She felt cold, with only her smock on, and cuddled her breasts within the fold of her arms.

A sudden noise at the front door made her look up, surprised, into the mirror. And there she saw him, rattling the doorknob and peering through the glass. Without thinking of her scanty attire she ran all the way to the front door in sudden hope mingling with dread. Her hands trembled. She fumbled with the lock a long moment before finally succeeding in releasing it.

He walked in, smiling: "Hullo."

"Bernie! What happened?"

"Nothing."

"But this is Thursday."

He bit his bottom lip. "God, I forgot all about it."

"How could you, Bernie?"

117

"I'm sorry." His fingers toyed with a sheet of paper sticking out of his shirt pocket.

"Well, come on, then," she said, and she grabbed his free hand and led him toward the back room.

But halfway there he stopped and said: "Look, I guess we had better forget about it tonight. It's sort of late, don't you think?"

"You made me wait long enough already. We still have time if you hurry. Come."

"It's just that . . . Well, actually, I was only coming in to bring this order for Bechard tomorrow morning." He was red in the face and looked down at the floor.

"What's wrong, Bernie?" she cried, her voice at the breaking point.

"I guess you and I had better talk things over a little."

"Talk things over! What things?"

"Let me get rid of this paper, first. My bus is outside and Ti-Pit will know I am here. So I need an excuse, don't I?" He walked to the counter where he put the slip of paper on the spike. "I am going to take part of this order with me tonight, so Ti-Pit will know I had a good reason for being here," he added. Then he got the dolly and went into the back room without saying another word.

"So that's what it is," she muttered. "Now that he has had his fun this morning, he thinks he's going to let me dry up like an old hen tonight. Well, we are going to see about that, my boy." She planted herself solidly near the door at the end of the counter.

He climbed up a pile of cartons and reached for cans of cooking oil on a shelf hanging from the ceiling. Now that he did not have to talk to her face to face, he felt a little braver. "You know, baby, I've been doing a lot of thinking lately about you, I mean us. You know what I mean."

"No, I don't know what you mean."

"Well, I've been thinking that maybe you and me have been carrying on a little too much. Now don't get me wrong. It's not that I don't like it. But you know how it is. Like this morning, for instance. That was *really* asking for trouble."

"We've done it before."

"I know. But someone's bound to find out one of these days, and when that happens—God, it will be too late."

"Nobody knows," she snapped. "What are you talking about? That's not what's on your mind. You're getting a big head, that's what's wrong. Now that you got your new bus, you want to play stuck-up, I suppose. So Ti-Pit's wife's not good enough for you, is she?"

"Your father knows."

"So what!"

"It's bad business, darling."

"Don't darling me."

"He's bound to spill out the whole story, one of these days. When he's drunk, he doesn't know what he's doing."

"You don't know my father. He may be a drunkard, but he is not the kind who will sell his daughter out. No sir. You are wrong there. Dad would never hurt me."

"That's what you think. Why, only this afternoon he practically spilled out the whole story in front of the men at Bechard. He got me so embarrassed I didn't know where to put myself. Do you know what he said to me? 'I know whose needle you've been threading all along!' That's what he said."

She seemed to consider this a moment. Then she said: "Maybe he knows something I don't know?"

"What do you mean?"

"You know full well what I mean. Do you think you'd want to give me the brush-off now, if you didn't have another woman waiting for you somewhere else? That's it. I guess

119

there's some young factory slut waiting for you right now, now that you got your new bus and there's plenty of room in it to mess around. Come on, tell the truth. Dad was right, wasn't he?"

"Don't be jealous."

"Me, jealous!" she cried, in pained indignation.

"Not so loud," he said, pushing the loaded dolly around to where she stood.

She began to shout at the top of her voice. "You got a bloody nerve, you."

He dropped the load and came up to her. "Look here; let's not have a scene. The door is open and they will hear us out on the street. Let's try to settle this in a friendly way, like nice people. All right?"

"So now you want to be nice about it!" she raged. "After I take a warm bath and make Ti-Pit put up the bags for us, and I sit here waiting for you all this time, you come here and say you want to call it quits."

"Not so loud."

"After all I did for you. All the times I risked my neck."

"Please, they'll hear us all the way up the church."

"That's it. All you worry about is what people will say. But what about me? Where do *I* fit in?"

He came closer, tried to take her in his arms to quiet her.

"Don't touch me," she pushed him off. "Get out, you coward."

"Come, now."

"Go. Go and get your pin sharpened by some filthy slut in the ravine."

"Don't talk like that."

"Go to the brothel then. See if they'll stretch it for you. Go on. Go to the brothel."

Hurriedly he grabbed the handles of the dolly and pushed

120

the load past her, up to the front of the store. There he stopped abruptly, unstrapped the watch from his wrist, and with an uneasy air of sorrow on his face he put it on the counter.

"Get out," she cried. "And shut the door."

Once outside, he glanced up and down the street. He was in the clear, except for a few loggers walking into Lambert's across the street. He quickly pushed the dolly to his bus and hurried to put everything, oil cans and dolly, behind the driver's seat. Then he switched on the engine and drove off.

At last! It was all over. Now he would drive around the block once, maybe twice, to relax a little before going to Lambert's for a few beers. He felt sorry about his watch, but it was worth losing it to get that load off his chest. First thing tomorrow morning he must go to confession, a general confession this time. When you drove a brand new bus and your business was on the point of booming, it was good luck to start fresh, with a clean soul, a firm decision not to mess around with married women any more.

La Pitoune, meanwhile, was standing in the doorway at the end of the counter, gazing blindly into the darkening emptiness of the front room. She shivered as though an icy gust of wind were blowing through her smock. She began moving about rapidly. She went to the trap door and locked it, put the key back into the cash drawer, removed the wrapping paper from the pile of bags, doing all these things mechanically, from force of habit as if nothing unusual had happened. But her mind was in a turmoil. She could not accept the fact that Bernard had left her. No, it was too fantastic to be true. It was only a joke. He was teasing her, would go around the block once, then come right back, just as he had done one night a few months ago. She began to giggle uncontrollably, her whole body shaking so she had to lean against the counter in an effort to control herself. Suddenly she felt something cold against her hand on the counter: it was his wrist watch.

A fit of rage seized her. She grabbed the wrist watch and threw it over the counter. It landed with a click against the glass window of a box of biscuits. She went after it, this time to hurl it more violently. The watch hit the door frame and ricocheted into the back room.

"The swine. The filthy swine!"

She ran behind the counter, looking left and right for something to throw, anything to break or smash to pieces. In the semi-darkness her eyes caught the gleam of a steel blade on a shelf. She grabbed the knife and ran into the back room. Like a mad murderess she leapt upon the pile of bags and plunged the knife into one of them, the top middle one, stabbing away at it, again and again, until a long deep gash was opened. The peas surged out and cascaded on the floor around her feet.

"The swine. The filthy pot-bellied swine, no better than Ti-Pit. The big, fat-headed, pot-bellied bugger of a swine. I could kill him," she cried, and she struck again with the knife at another bag, raging and kicking away at the peas spilling out upon her. The more she kicked and cursed the more violent her rage grew. Then she started to stamp on the peas, grinding them under her heels, as if she would mash every last one of them to powder, kicking and grinding like one demented, until suddenly she slipped, and fell flat on her behind, the hard peas stinging her tender buttocks.

"Jesus Mary, that hurts!"

The shock of her fall drained her clean of rage, and now a wave of helplessness swept over her; her eyes filled with tears of self-pity. "Jesus Mary, what have I done?" she wailed, rubbing her aching buttocks while a river of peas kept cascading down upon her shoulders, her back, even under her smock, little cold peas running between her breasts, her legs. Crushed with self-pity, she sobbed like a little girl, sniffling, smearing the tears all over her face with the back of her hand, biting at the ends of her tumbled blond hair. "After all I did for him," she wailed. "Even stealing from my own husband to buy him a nice watch. Poor Ti-Pit. Jesus Mary. It isn't fair. Now what am I going to do?"

She was not angry at Bernard any more. On the contrary, she now wanted him more feverishly than ever before. Oh, how she would love him now, if only he would come back. She would give him all she had, all of her, as if it were for the first time, so much good loving she would give him that never would he think of leaving her again.

"Is anyone in?"

"What!" Startled, she stopped crying. Her body stiffened to attention.

"Say. Is anybody here?" A man was calling at the front door.

La Pitoune jumped to her feet. "Just a minute!" She shook the peas out of her smock, wiped her face on her sleeves and ran her hands through her disordered hair. Then she hurried to the doorway and peered in the front room.

Standing at the counter was Israel. "Are you open for business?"

"Who could he be?" she wondered, intrigued by his polite accent. She stepped forward along the counter, studying his face.

Noticing her smock, and her eyes red and swollen, Israel felt the need to apologize. "The door was open, so I walked in," he said. "But if you are closed I will come back tomorrow morning."

She walked up to him for a closer look. "Ah, now I remember!" she exclaimed suddenly. "You were here last fall, weren't you?"

Flattered, Israel smiled yes.

"What can I do for you, sir?" she said; but before he had

123

time to reply, she added: "But you don't have to say it. I remember. A shirt like the one you have on now. It comes from here, doesn't it? You see, Madame Leblanc has a very good memory, sometimes."

"Thank you," Israel said. "But what I really need is a couple of handkerchiefs." The beer and the bumpy ride had made him ill in the bus; his two handkerchiefs were soiled.

She took a box from a shelf and, still standing on the same side of the counter as her customer, displayed a wide assortment of what he wanted. And at the same time she winked at him.

Israel was confused by this sudden cordiality. Ill at ease, he shifted his weight from one foot to the other.

She was saying: "I never forget a face, especially when people are nice and polite like you. Did you like it at Bechard?"

"It was interesting."

"Was it cold?"

"Very. What sort of winter did you have here?"

"Very cold."

"I see. Well, I guess I'll take two of these, the white ones, if you please."

"I thought so," she said. "A real gentleman's handkerchief, hey!"

He smiled to conceal his embarrassment at her familiarity. He found it difficult to meet her bold gaze, and lowered his eyes to the counter.

La Pitoune tightened the belt of her smock, and extended one leg slightly so that the smock fell away from her thigh. Suggestively she ran her hands over her hips.

Israel looked up, blushing, then looked away guiltily. "You don't need to wrap them up," he mumbled. "How much?"

But she insisted on wrapping the handkerchiefs, "Are you going to stay in La Buche long?"

124

"A few days, I suppose," he replied, aware that his face was burning, his body trembling. "Please, you don't have to wrap them up."

"I only want to be nice to you. That's all."

He swallowed hard.

"Would you like to do me a little favor?"

"How much do I owe you?"

"Don't be in such a hurry. I like fellows who are nice and polite like you. What is your name?"

"They call me Israel."

"Israel!" she said softly, holding his gaze riveted to hers. "Oh, I like that." She gave him the parcel. "Would you like to come to the back room for a short while? I had a little accident just before you came in. Spilled a bag of peas on the floor. How about giving me a hand before my husband comes back? If he finds out, he is going to beat me again."

Suspicious, wishing he had the courage to bolt from the store, yet lacking the will to leave, he followed her. She handed him a small bag and took one for herself, and they began shoveling the peas into them. After a while her silence began to make him nervous and apprehensive again. She fetched a broom and a dustpan, told him to hold the pan for her while she swept the powdered peas into it. As she swept, the front of her smock kept opening and closing, each time revealing a full leg with the stocking rolled up to the knee. Her perfume and the good smell of a young woman's body filled every breath of air that he breathed.

Israel straightened up, and the dustpan dropped to the floor, He wanted to go. Yet he wanted to stay.

She stepped close to him, loosening her belt so that he could see the swell of her half-revealed breasts. Embarrassed, in fact frightened, Israel wet his parched lips with his tongue.

"I just had a nice bath," she whispered.

125

Finally he was able to mutter: "Are we through with the peas?"

"Don't think about that, now." She put her hand on his arm.

"I'd better be on my way."

"Israel," she begged hoarsely, and seizing his hand she slipped it feverishly under her smock. "Be nice to me. I want you." And with the violence of her pent-up desire she threw herself upon him, kissing him and pressing all her body against his.

Israel felt himself reeling, breaking against the thrust of her passion. "Not now," he moaned, "it is not right," and with a last desperate effort he pulled free of her.

"Maybe we could meet some other time," he said, hardly able to control his voice, his face flaming with guilt and desire. "I will stay in La Buche a few days."

Suddenly she said: "What time is it?"

"I don't know."

She rushed to the door, to see how dark it was outside. Then she came back behind the counter and telephoned Madame Dupré. To the child who answered she left a message that Madame Dupré was not to call for Madame Leblanc tonight: Madame Lebanc was busy, would come to the meeting late. Then after hanging up she said to Israel: "Meet me in about fifteen minutes, when it gets a bit darker, in back of the train depot. You go there and just walk around as if to take the air or look at the rapids, and I'll see you. Go now. My husband will be coming out of the tavern across the street; I'm not supposed to be in here at this hour. Will you come?"

Mutely, he nodded.

She walked him to the door. Her lustful eyes full of bright hope, she squeezed his hand. "Will you be good to me?"

Oh, my God, he thought, why am I saying yes?

126

six

Lambert's tavern was the only drink-
ing house in La Buche. But it was large enough for the town,
even in the busy periods of September and April: the long
narrow room could accommodate several hundred men. It was
lighted with electric bulbs inside wire-netting guards close to
the ceiling high above the trajectory of flying beer bottles.
The bar stood against the rear wall facing the entrance across
a jungle of round tables and chairs made of metal, unbreakable. Back of it was displayed Lambert's own symbol of
logging; two axes crossed on a logger's shirt with sleeves rolled
decoratively around the handles; the axes were nailed to the
wall with giant spikes to insure their not being snatched off

127

in the heat of a brawl. Lambert was very proud of this em-
blem; he liked to stand in front of it with his head between
the axes and his arms spread out to lean on the bar. A tall,
broad-shouldered ex-logger usually dressed in a jack's shirt
and corduroy breeches under the white apron, he wore constantly on his round face a hearty smile of joviality. He had
a keen eye for business, a sense of humor rich in good-natured
coarseness, and he only discussed with his customers things
about which he was sure to be in agreement with them.

As soon as Ti-Pit appeared at the door, Lambert ordered
one of his waiters to bring two bottles of ale to his favorite
table, near the bar. Then he joined his friend the grocer, who
was still out of breath and sweating.

"Evening, Pit. Did you put up the bags?"

"Sure did."

"Good. And how's the wife?"

"Same as ever. Does nothing all day and spends all night
in the bathtub."

"That's women for you."

"Split between the legs and split in the head."

"You said it."

"They fill the bottom crack with soap and perfume. And
their hole up there is so full of rosary-beads they rattle with
Aves each time you ask them to shake their arse a little and
get to work."

"Bloody nuisance, if you ask me."

"It ain't Catholic."

"Times have changed. A woman ain't a woman no more."

"But it's all our fault, Lambert. I said it before, and I say
it again: give women the right to vote, and they'll vote you
right out of bed."

"Well, I'm glad I never got hooked."

"Marriage ain't worth a fart."

128

"Take Dupré, for instance."

"Poor Louis."

"Poor Louis."

"To yours."

"To yours."

They touched glasses, and drank to each other's health. One of the waiters had come over to tell his boss that he was wanted at a table in front. Lambert gave Ti-Pit a tap on the shoulders. "See you later."

Ti-Pit sat back in his chair. Then he carefully lifted his large belly to make it rest comfortably on his lap, and went on drinking long gulps of the cool, refreshing, rich-flavored "Devil's Brew," as he called it. God created women, and the Devil created beer to keep men from messing around with God's creation: great idea! Ah, there was no place like Lambert's after a day of hard work!

The tavern was indeed becoming a lively place. Men kept arriving in increasing numbers. Most of them sat at tables on the right and ordered draft beer which they drank with great thirst as they exchanged the latest news and jokes while their wives were out at the meeting of Les Dames de la Grâce. These were the regular Thursday night customers, who sometimes made the place seem as crowded as on the wild days of late September and April. Loggers, also, were coming in, but they sat on the left side of the room, for the atmosphere was not yet lively enough to promote a free-for-all mingling with the townsmen. About five or six of them, all in need of a shave and haircut, took a table next to Ti-Pit's, and banging their fists called for beer. A few more joined them after a while, and they drew two tables together to accommodate the newcomers.

The cloud of blue-yellow smoke grew thick; the sharp odor of Canadian tobacco so permeated the air that Ti-Pit could

129

taste it in each gulp of ale. When the voices of the men at the next table rose with laughter, he began casting looks of mistrust at those loggers. It was one one of them, or at least one like them, who had broken into his back room the previous autumn! He kept one ear open for what they were saying.

Red Mallet had just joined them and begun to tell about his conquest of a young factory girl in the ravine by the rapids. Amidst exclamations of wonder and curiosity from the others, he was dwelling upon details with a relish and art of embellishment that made the escapade sound like some forbidden dream of lust. And when he reached the moment of exquisite pleasure he braced himself for an imitation of the sounds the girl had made under the stimulant of his sex. He let out a series of panting swoons, rhythmic and alternating with full-throated noises that increased in intensity to climax, finally, in a long sigh of contentment.

This was greeted by a fresh outburst of laughter. Some of the men stared at Red with gaping mouths, others fell to gazing at their beer with dreamy eyes full of desire, or chuckled in fond admiration of the storyteller.

"Just a lot of lumberjack bluff," said Ti-Pit, with a scornful nod toward Red. Though he could enjoy a dirty joke as well as the next fellow, he objected to a man's boasting of his amorous conquests. "What decent girl could ever go for you."

"Hey, you, big fart," Red Mallet shouted. "Mind your words."

Ti-Pit flushed in sudden anger, but Red only grinned.

"All right, pop. I apologize," he said. "Nobody's a bigger fart than me."

Everybody laughed. Waiters brought another round, and the jacks resumed telling stories, while lone drinkers from nearby tables joined them. More men kept coming in the front

130

door. The tobacco smoke grew thicker, the smell of beer and sweat and pipe-juice grew sharper.

At a table near the front of the room, meanwhile, Monsieur Dupré was talking with Maurice and Altar Boy. To judge from the way he toyed with his glasses on the bridge of his nose, this was not a very friendly chat.

"I don't like the looks of it, I tell you," he was saying. "After I left that place last night someone followed me all the way home. And now I can't walk in here without you fellows waiting for me." He went on complaining that he had been fooled; he was not going to stand for all this spying around.

Maurice and Altar Boy listened without interrupting him, apparently not satisfied yet that their guest was mellow enough to talk business on their own terms. A mild-mannered man of about forty, dressed in the gray-striped suit of a man-about-town, Maurice had a pleasant smile that brought out the fine line of his thin moustache, and his dark hair was combed neat with brilliantine. He was leaning back leisurely in his chair. His dark eyes, cool, alert, did not leave the stationmaster's face, while he pointed a forefinger at the glasses on the table, which Altar Boy obediently made sure to keep full to the brim. After a first bottle drunk in rapid long gulps, the stationmaster seemed to gain courage, and the tone of his voice grew slightly defiant. "You have even hired Arthur to spy on me," he declared. "This morning he came to the depot and started teasing."

"What did he say?" asked Maurice.

"Enough to make it clear that he knows where I was last night."

"Do you think he might try to blackmail you?"

"If he does, he won't get very far."

131

Maurice turned to his assistant. "Perhaps you had better look after Arthur, so he doesn't bother our friend here."

"Yes, boss," said Altar Boy, a giant of a fellow with dark curly hair and a young face bashed in like a prize-fighter's. He had enormous hands, so striking in their powerful big-bonedness that when he grabbed a bottle to fill Monsieur Dupré's glass the little stationmaster shuddered and hastened to drink submissively.

"Now, Monsieur Dupré, do you feel more at ease?"

"What do you want from me?"

Maurice said: "Tomorrow and Saturday there will be a lot of men coming in from the camps. And most of them will want to go on south. Now I want them to stay right here in La Buche and have a bit of fun and try their luck at my tables. So, your job is to make sure no train comes here tomorrow or Saturday, no train 'till next week."

"But I can't do that."

"Didn't you telephone Trois-Rivières that you were ready for the rush schedule, one train each day for the next three weeks?"

"But you don't understand. The Trois-Rivières office knows the camps are beginning to close down this week end. If I change the order, they'll think something is wrong and they'll check with Bechard."

"They won't do that before next week, and it's this week-end trade that I want. You just telephone the cancellation tomorrow morning, and everything is going to be fine."

"I can't. I won't do it."

"In that case, I suppose you'll have to pay your fee for last night."

"Oh, with pleasure," said Monsieur Dupré, suddenly hopeful and relieved. "How much, please?"

"Ten dollars."

"Right now, gentlemen, right now," he mumbled, as he brought out a ten-dollar bill. "Here you are."

Maurice pushed the bill back to him. "Will your wife be home tomorrow?"

"Why, of course."

"Then leave it with her. One of my girls will collect in person."

Monsieur Dupré jumped to his feet. "You filthy swine."

Altar Boy slapped his back, hard and full, so that the little stationmaster, turning white, sank back in his chair.

Getting up, Maurice said: "Don't lose your temper, you two."

"You filthy blackmailers," Monsieur Dupré screamed. "You are going to make me lose my job."

Maurice gave him a tap on the shoulder. "Take the night to think it over. We will be in to see you first thing tomorrow morning. Good luck!" Then to Altar Boy, "Come on. Let's get back to the house. I have a feeling we are going to be busy tonight."

Monsieur Dupré went after them, pleading. "Wait a minute. Maybe we could find something a bit easier to do, no?"

But they paid no attention to him. At the door, Altar Boy said: "Now what about skinny Serval, boss?"

"We'll take care of her later. Let's go."

Through the haze of tobacco smoke that veiled the front window Monsieur Dupré watched them walk away up the street. An expression of acute distress settled on his face. He fell to staring blindly into his glass of beer. Two or three times he shuddered from head to toe, as if suddenly plunged in an ice-cold bath. Incoherent thoughts began swirling madly in his head; thoughts of his wife's wrath, train schedules, memories of the night before, dark sinister plans of murderous revenge. His eyes moist with raging impotence, he gazed at

133

the merry crowd of carefree drinkers. He could not face it any longer. In a burst of feverish haste he picked up his ten-dollar bill and walked out of the place, so fast that Lambert, who had noticed that Maurice and Altar Boy had left, and was now on his way to treat Monsieur Dupré to a free beer, arrived in the front of the room only to see the frightened figure of the little stationmaster disappear hurriedly up the street.

Lambert returned to the bar, but without the jovial smile on his face. He had agreed with Maurice to introduce him to certain people in La Buche in return for a small percentage of the business in the Red House. But he had also warned Maurice that he would not tolerate excessive pressure upon his best customers. Like everything else, blackmail was all right, so long as it was done in moderation.

Now he told one of his waiters to prepare an order of ten cases of beer for the Red House; they were to be placed in his car parked in the alley back of the tavern. He would deliver them in person right away.

It was then that Bernard Toupin came in. On catching sight of him, Ti-Pit called him over with a great show of friendship. A few bottles always had this effect on him. He was generally what could be called a good drunk; nasty and belligerent when sober, he tended to grow mellow after a few bottles, and only when he had reached a high pitch of intoxication, which he had not done yet, would his nastiness return. "Sit down, Bernie. Have a drink."

Bernard sat down. But he did not take the glass of beer which Ti-Pit pushed before him. His hands trembled too much, from a sudden return of his old superstitions which seemed to torment him even more acutely now that he had broken off with La Pitoune. Ti-Pit's mood of tipsy friendliness sounded weirdly false to him; he felt sure the deceived husband had learned the truth.

134

"I saw your bus in front of the store," Ti-Pit was saying. "Did the wife take good care of you?"

Bernard cleared his throat. "She did."

"Did you have a big order?"

"Big enough. I took about half of it already."

"Did she help you any?"

"Yes."

"But she was mad, I suppose?"

"No. She was not mad."

Ti-Pit looked disappointed. "Well, anyway, I'm glad she came down and shook her arse a little. She ain't a bad girl when she don't want to be. Maybe she's having a turn of soul, hey?"

"You never know, with women," Bernard sighed. And at the same time he turned toward Red's table in a move designed to tell Ti-Pit that he was less interested in his wife than in the lewd stories coming from there.

This, Ti-Pit resented. "Hey, there," he called out. "Can't you keep your filthy jokes to yourself?"

Interrupted in the middle of a story, Red turned to Ti-Pit and, with an air of wounded pride, challenged him to repeat the insult. The drunken loggers at his table started getting up, ready for a brawl. Bernard, relieved, hurried away to the front of the room where he had just seen Israel enter.

Ti-Pit was shouting: "We can't hear ourselves think in here, with all your hollering and cheap jokes fit for the pigs. Shut up, will you."

Red jumped on top of the table and motioned his companions back to their seats. "Never mind, men. I'll handle this alone." Then in a very gentle voice he asked Ti-Pit: "How would you like to kiss my arse?"

"Say that again!"

"Kiss my arse."

Ti-Pit grabbed a bottle and started toward Red, panting

with rage. The men stared at him with great expectant eyes. Grinning, Red turned round and presented his behind, as Ti-Pit, approaching the table, drew the bottle back above his head and swung to strike on the very spot where he had been invited to deposit a kiss. But at that instant Red let out a powerful blast. Ti-Pit's hand stopped in mid-air.

Then all of a sudden, as the men burst out laughing, the incident took an unexpected turn. A look of joy flashed on Ti-Pit's face. He stared at Red with a great childlike thrill. The bottle dropped from his hand. He bent forward, and pressing with his hands on his knees he returned Red's greetings with a louder and longer explosion that shook his large body. This was greeted by a wave of loud applause, a fresh outburst of mirthful laughter. Ti-Pit, his carefree tipsiness swiftly returning under the stimulant of such good-natured coarseness, went on to challenge Red to a duel of windiness.

Red picked up the challenge with a graceful bow of the head. One of the waiters was told to bring the equipment that all taverns in the region kept on hand for such occasions. The drunken loggers drew their chairs away, into a wide circle that now grew larger as men from other tables joined the party. A table was placed in the center, and on top of it a bottle with a small Union Jack stuck in the cork. Ti-Pit and Red took their positions, back to back across the table, and pulled down their pants. One of the loggers smashed an empty bottle on the floor, as their signal. And now they went at it: Ti-Pit first, then Red, each taking his turn, forcing and blowing out as much wind as he could. Whoever made the flag wave the highest would be the winner. More men joined the circle. The waiters started collecting bets. There wasn't a sound to be heard in the tavern besides the panting of the contestants, the sudden explosions, the outbursts of applause, the words of encouragement. All eyes shifted back and forth between the

136

behinds of the contestants and the little flag that had not yet
been raised high enough to suggest that the windy fellows were
able to blow with greater force than a gentle breeze. But
they went on struggling, and panting, and puffing, and the
smell added to the fun. Finally, Ti-Pit, slapping his knees and
bending low for more power, let out a violent gust of wind
that made the Union Jack wave gently erect atop the beer
bottle, an achievement which Red, windless and exhausted,
readily conceded he could not beat. There followed a mad
scramble with the waiters and the drunken loggers anxious to
collect their winnings. Red and Ti-Pit went to the bar for a
quick glass to each other's health.

"You're a real jack," said Ti-Pit, beaming.

"Last time I lost was in Quebec five years ago. I've got to
hand it to you, fatty, you're a real champion."

"You don't sound too bad yourself," Ti-Pit said.

Then a group of loggers gathered around him. They tried
to talk him into joining them in the brothel, but he refused.
They insisted, saying they would take care of his fee as a token
of their admiration for his spectacular windiness. Still he refused, although he thanked them all in a tipsy outpouring of
affection from his big heart. He hadn't felt so happy in a long
time. He was so happy that his tired blinking eyes were moist
with emotion when, amidst the swelling wave of hurrahs and
handclapping for the champion, he threaded his way through
the noisy crowd and upturned tables and chairs and walked
out.

Now he would go to the Police-Fire House for his game of
gin rummy. Oh, what fun a man could have when there was
no woman around! Drowsy, and weeping inside with happiness, he went on up the Rue des Erables, careless of the
increasing narrowness of the sidewalk.

Little concerned with what had just taken place, Israel and

Bernard were sitting over a glass of beer, absorbed in an exchange of confidences that made them look like old bosom friends.

Israel was saying: "How would you feel if a woman you thought was a symbol of virtue were suddenly to make a pass at you? What would you do?"

"I couldn't say. It never happened to me."

"I was shocked."

"Maybe that's normal."

"To think that less than a year ago, when I first saw her behind that counter, so polite, working so hard to help her husband . . ."

"Who's that?" interrupted Bernard.

"If I tell you, will you promise to keep it between us?"

"Sure."

"You know that woman across the street, La Pitoune?"

Suddenly on his guard, Bernard said: "Sure, I know her, like everybody else in town."

"When I was in the store just now she tried to make me."

"You're kidding!"

"See, it shocks you, too. You didn't expect that, did you?"

"Did you let her?"

"I managed to get away in time."

"You saw that big man walk out of here just now?" Bernard said. "That's her husband. If I were you, I wouldn't mess around."

"Don't worry. I won't."

"If I were you I'd get out of town first thing tomorrow. Take my word, it's not healthy to mess around with that kind of people."

"I told you I wasn't having any of it."

"Well, see that you don't," Bernard said with sudden bitterness. "She's a bitch."

138

And now it was Israel's turn to be confused. "What's the matter? Why are you so worked up all of a sudden?"

"Never mind," snapped Bernard. He shoved back his chair and stalked out of the room.

Israel sat there gazing at his beer with mouth wide open. He sensed Bernard's sudden jealousy. Why? He could only conclude that Bernard resented any foreigner having anything to do with a local woman, especially if the foreigner happened to be a Jew. Yes, that must be it, Israel thought. Gentile hostility took so many forms.

"Hey, Jew-boy, what do you look so sad for on a night like this?" Red Mallet shouted, at the head of a group of tipsy jacks walking out of the tavern. "Come along. There's lots of fun where we're going."

Making an effort to smile, Israel joined them.

seven

A short distance past the train depot
on the Rue des Sapins, Paul Gauthier turned right on a dirt
road leading to a narrow footbridge over the rails. For an hour
he had been wandering aimlessly through the town; now he
wanted to go and sit near the river. Ahead walked a girl with
her jack. The evening air was cool; it smelled of thawing earth
and wet bark, and was alive with the deep rumble from the
rapids on the left, where, hugging the rocks, thin clouds of
green-silver spray hung gently rolling beneath the lowering
dusk. Further left, a vast expanse of logs floated calmly toward
the chute that footed the darkening pines across the river.
And now the ravine came in full view beyond the footbridge.
A small valley, it lay parallel with the river between the tracks

141

and a wall of earth topped with boulders placed there as a protection against flash floods. The brush was thick, and in spots grew tall enough to hide a man even of Paul's height.

Paul quickened his pace, drawn by the beat of logs in the chute. The sound of his calked boots biting hard into the wooden planks of the footbridge caused the lovers ahead to stop suddenly and look back with the air of people caught in the act; swiftly, they glided into a more secluded spot. Paul entered a pathway that cut across the ravine to the very edge of the rapids. He could feel the presence of lovers in the shrubs, and restless he hastened on ahead. Through the thickening dusk he could see the end of the path, a passageway between boulders on the earth bank, beyond which lay a narrow strip of rocky beach where one could feel alone. He had reached the bottom of the ravine and was about to stride on up the opposite slope, when suddenly he heard the sound of a woman's voice calling his name in a tone of hushed urgency.

It was La Pitoune with her blond head peeping out of the brush. "Hey, Paul, come over here."

At first the wish to be alone held him back.

"Come and keep me company for a while."

The sudden prospect of an old friend's confidence decided him.

She led him to a glade surrounded with thick shrubs. He remembered those summer nights, years back, when on this same ground they used to make love with the raw hunger of puppies never satisfied until the dish was empty. They had had a full time of it and been able to part without bitterness.

"What's the matter, Paul? You look so depressed," she said, as they sat on a strip of wrapping paper which she had unfolded on the damp earth.

He stretched his long legs, so that his feet reached out among pebbles that the last flood had left behind. "You don't

142

look too cheerful yourself," he said. "What are you doing here?"

"Just waiting," she replied with assumed nonchalance, although inwardly she was still raging at Israel's failure to keep his tryst with her. Toying with the buttons of her black dress she asked: "I suppose you have seen your brother?"

"I have."

"They tell me he is feeling poorly these days."

"That's a mild way of putting it," he said.

From the bus, earlier, he had gone directly to his mother's house. On entering Claude's room he had been struck to the heart with what he found: the boy lay sprawled on the bed, a look of agonizing pain twisting his face, a streak of blood caking at the mouth. Paul had moved Claude to a more comfortable position under the blankets, and after washing off the blood and closing the window he had carried his bag to his own bedroom and walked out of the house, haunted by the gasping respiration from his brother's room. He did not know where he was going, but in his feeling of futility and defeat he felt himself drawn to the brothel where he might experience the shame of his father, and forget for a moment the awesome look of death on his brother's face. At the same time, the thought of going to the brothel was repugnant to him, and resolutely he set his course in the opposite direction.

"The boy is finished," he said now, despondently.

"I'm sorry," said La Pitoune. "But maybe it is better this way, seeing how sick he is."

"Maybe."

"I suppose the good Lord wants him back early."

"Maybe," Paul repeated absently, gazing at the wall of boulders.

After a moment's silence, she asked: "Did you have a good season?"

"Fair."

143

"Going back in September?"

"Can't plan that far ahead any more. Even tomorrow looks like a lifetime from tonight."

They relapsed into silence again. There was a faint rustling sound in the brush behind them; a girl started giggling, then suddenly stopped, as if a hand had been put over her mouth.

La Pitoune, gazing dreamily at the ground, said softly: "Things haven't changed much."

"In the old days we used to be more careful choosing our spots."

"Why do you say in the old days? It really wasn't so long ago."

"It seems that way," Paul said. Then he asked: "Who are you waiting for?"

"Somebody," she said vaguely, shrugging her shoulders.

"Who?"

"What do you care?"

"So you are fooling Ti-Pit? I thought you had become a good wife."

"I was a good girl for a long time. It's only last winter that it finally got to be too much for me. A woman can't go on forever without a bit of fun once in a while, you know."

"What's wrong with your husband?"

"You guess."

"Did you really give it a good try?"

"Downways, upways, sideways, backways, frontways, no matter how we try, there is always his fat belly in the way. In the beginning he used to make an effort to accommodate me a little, but now he just doesn't care. In all the time we've slept together, he never made me get my pleasure once. Now, that's not fair, is it?"

"I reckon it must be tough."

"If you only knew what I went through those first two

144

years. The good Lord can't say I didn't try hard to be a good wife. Oh, Paul, I just don't know what to do with myself."

"Cheer up. We can't both of us be depressed at the same time."

"Do you suppose there is something wrong with me?"

"You like men, that's all."

"But it's beginning to worry me, Paul. Sometimes I feel I'm not normal. I want a man so bad I almost go out of my mind. If I don't have it when I want it I sort of go to pieces, I want to break things, I even feel that I could kill."

"You should try to control yourself."

"I can't. That's the trouble."

Paul shrugged. "Some people call it vice. As far as I'm concerned, it's only another trick of Fate. Some women are born for a man, others for God and the beads. It's in your blood."

"But I never felt this way before I got married. I mean I never felt it was a vice."

"You were younger then. That makes all the difference. Everything you do when you are young is a dream."

La Pitoune sighed. "The good Lord is not always easy to understand, is He?"

"I guess not. The good Lord wants the boy back early, so He takes the boy early. Do you think He's going to ask *my* permission first? Like hell. What does the good Lord care about the way I feel about it? Someone up there is having a good joke on us down here; maybe because we're simple lumberjacks and don't have the brains to figure things out for ourselves. I don't know."

Paul picked up a pebble and threw it above the earth bank ahead. They waited for the sound it would make as it hit the water. But they heard nothing, only the low rumble from the rapids and the fast beat from the chute.

145

La Pitoune grew melancholy. "Remember how you used to be so free, and all the fun we used to have together, right here?"

"Claude was not dying then," Paul said, his eyes suddenly moist. He picked up another pebble, a larger one, and threw it hard toward the river. She watched the clean arc that it drew into the thickening dust above the wall of boulders. Then they heard the faint knock, and roll, of its landing on the rocky beach. There followed a long silence, peopled with the rustling sounds from the brush around them. La Pitoune fell to gazing at the ground, a dreamy expression on her face; while Paul, restless, picked up a handful of pebbles.

"Sometimes I wish we had never split up," she said.

He started juggling the pebbles.

"You were my best, Paul," she went on. "It has never been as good with anybody else. You remember the night we did it 'till the sun came up from behind the trees across the river? And how we did it again, to say good morning to the sun the same way we had said goodnight to the moon the night before. You said you didn't want to make the sun jealous of the moon on account of us."

He rubbed the pebbles between his hands.

"I'll never forget that night," she went on. "Sometimes when I feel lonely in bed I make a little prayer to ask the good Lord to make me dream about it. It's worked, a couple of times, but not often enough." She paused, and looked at him fondly. "And now we're here again." She waited a moment. Then as he remained silent, she asked: "Are you listening, Paul?"

"I got a lot of troubles on my mind."

She moved close to him. "Just a moment ago you said you wished we were young again. Maybe if we tried a little?"

He stood up, clenching the handful of pebbles. "I got too much on my mind."

"You haven't forgotten, have you, Paul?"

"No, I haven't," he said, hurling the handful of pebbles high over the wall of boulders.

This time she did not wait for the sound of their landing. She hastened to add, almost pleading: "Then let me help you a little, Paul. We're both sad tonight. We ought to try and help each other. No?"

Suddenly there was an outburst of cursing and hollering from behind the boulders. Looking up, they saw Monsieur le Curé appear at the end of the passageway. Shaking an angry fist toward the ravine, he shouted at the top of his voice: "Hey, you, out there. Keep your blasted pebbles to yourselves. For the love of green horse, isn't it enough to go on offending the Lord like a bunch of pigs? Now you want to kill your priest into the bargain!"

La Pitoune jumped to her feet.

"Keep still," Paul said, pulling her down beside him.

From one end of the ravine to the other the brush came alive with rustling sounds. The lovers behind Paul and La Pitoune made a dash for the pathway. A girl giggled. Nearby a man swore. A lanky logger glided fast in front of Paul; he was red in the face and his hands fumbled with his fly. Then came a young girl, all flushed and looking frightened, struggling through the shrubs to get out of there fast and at the same time slip her panties up under her skirt. Several pairs of lovers converged upon the pathway, hurrying toward the safety of the footbridge. Hushed giggles, bursts of nervous laughter rose from the deep of the ravine. In the brush some couples lay quietly waiting for the storm to abate. But there were others, to judge from the crackling branches, who went back to their pleasure with renewed zest and thrill, as though to prove a belief popular in timberland—ah, fornication is never so delicious as when enjoyed in the shadow of the belfry!

And this was probably what Monsieur le Curé suspected,

147

standing there shaking an angry fist over the ravine. This lively rustling brush was driving him to the peak of wrathful indignation. As if to castigate the whole countryside from the pulpit, he burst out again: "So go on, you pigs. Forrr-nicate. All of you down there, forrr-nicate all you can. You are only digging your own graves, while the Lord is watching. Mark my words: the Lord is watching every one of you dirty pigs, at this very instant. The good Lord is WATCHING! So, go on, then. Forrr-nicate. I have done my duty by the Lord. By green horse, I have."

"I must get away," La Pitoune said. "If he finds me here—"

"Stay where you are," said Paul. "I'll go and try to quiet him down. At the rate he's going he will have a stroke." Then he walked off into the brush toward the path leading to the bank.

At that moment, after a last sweeping gesture of condemnation over the ravine, Monsieur le Curé stepped down from the wall of boulders and, puffing out curses of doom and swearing by "green horse" that he would soon flood this brush clean of all these shameful forrr-nicators, he went back to Fulgence on the beach, and told him to round up their things, he had had enough for the day. He then sat down on a large rock, knees apart, panting, and tried to drown his smoldering wrath under long gulps of beer. There was only one bottle left. His fishing rod had been knocked out of his hands; it was now floating gently downstream towards the paper mills of Trois-Rivières.

"Ach, but they are going to pay for it, the pigs," he swore to himself. "And plenty."

Quick-tempered though he was, Monsieur le Curé might not have flown into such a rage, had this incident occurred at any other time. A succession of petty problems had kept him home until five o'clock, ruining the one day on which he had

148

counted for a restful outing of his favorite sport. And then a few minutes before the shower of pebbles, his vicar Father Martin had come to deliver Father Boulanger's message that the Curé was urgently needed at the meeting of Les Dames de la Grâce. Above all this, in truth, he had not known a moment of peace since the new Cardinal of Montreal, two weeks ago, had conferred with his arch enemy, Father Boulanger the Jesuit. He was convinced that these two, in league with the Bishop of Trois-Rivières had entered upon a secret pact designed to drive him out of his parish, so that they might apply to La Buche the reforms which his Eminence was bent on instituting throughout Quebec. This, indeed, preyed heavily on his mind. But there was something else contributing to his acute irritability; it had to do with these shameful goings-on in the ravine. A while ago he had received a letter from the foundling home in Trois-Rivières informing him that once again last year the community of La Buche had outdone all the other towns of the valley in contributing illegitimate babies to the home, and warning him that if the same thing happened this year, he would be forced to double his already large share of funds needed to maintain the foundling home. It was in view of the gravity of this situation that on the previous Sunday he had delivered one of his most severe admonitions to the women of the town. But to what end? On the very first night the loggers were back in La Buche, the whole festival of fornication was beginning all over again.

"It stinks of sin. I can smell it from here. After all the years I worked to build this parish, now the dirty pigs are going to drive it into bankruptcy with their shameful forrrnication," he said to himself, as his anger gradually dissolved into sorrowful depression. At the bottom of his heart he was truly grieved. The blame could not really be laid on the women of La Buche. Most of them were at the meeting now, mothers

149

and daughters. It was these factory girls, lying with loggers from the south who took their fun between a bus ride and a train trip. And worse still, for this was like an act of Divine Vengeance, most of these poor girls came from the orphanage and the foundling home, where they had been shipped after being conceived in this very ravine.

"Never mind the worms, Fulgence. Get the line, and the hooks. They cost money. And let's get away from here."

Just then Paul appeared at the passageway. "What's the matter, Monsieur le Curé?"

"Pretty soon a priest will need the protection of a regiment of Zouaves, if he is going to go on serving the Lord in these parts."

"Did you get hit?"

"No. But I lost my rod."

"And two quarts of beer," Fulgence put in.

"Sorry about that. But I'm quite willing to pay for the damages."

"So it was you!"

"I didn't know you were here."

Monsieur le Curé turned to his beadle. "How much did the rod cost, Fulgence?"

"Twenty-two bucks."

Paul opened his shirt and reached inside his money-belt, as the priest added: "Plus the beer, that makes it twenty-two fifty. And you might as well add another two-fifty for the annoyance. So, let's make it twenty-five altogether."

Paul counted out the money. Monsieur le Curé stuffed the bills under his soutane, and said: "Good, my boy. Bills paid promptly keep people friendly. Hurry up, Fulgence, I'm hungry."

The beadle hastened to put everything inside the basket,

150

while Paul and the rotund Curé walked toward the passage-way.

The damages now recovered, Monsieur le Curé seemed to be drifting into a more pleasant mood. He was glad to see Paul, whose soul he had never despaired of returning to the good Lord. After a while he said: "What about your Easter duties, this year?"

"I thought it was understood we would never talk about that," Paul replied.

"You can't blame me for trying, can you?"

"Not any more than you can blame me for reminding you of our agreement."

"That is what I like about you, my boy. You are frank. I don't know if you know where you stand. But it is clear to me that you know where I stand."

"Fine," Paul smiled. "So let's leave it at that, Monsieur le Curé."

As they stopped to wait for Fulgence, the priest added: "By the way, did you see him, how is he feeling tonight?"

"He is finished."

"I don't suppose anything I might say would be of any help."

"No. There's been enough priest stuff in his life."

"Now don't get nasty, Paul. It's tough enough as it is," Monsieur le Curé said in a sudden outburst of deep feeling. "Don't hold me responsible for everything the Lord does. After all, when I traded the axe for this robe, it was only to help my fellow men suffer a little less. I am no believer in miracles, you know. I do the best I can, the rest is in the hands of God. And each day I pray that He knows what He is doing. I am not the best of priests, but then maybe that's the way the Lord wants me."

"All right," said Paul. "Forget it." And Fulgence having

151

joined them, they began crossing the ravine. Not a word was said until they reached the footbridge, where Fulgence asked Monsieur le Curé: "Did you say we were going to eat, first?"

"Sure," replied the priest. "Let that foxy Jesuit sweat it out a bit. Then we'll see how well he can manage when I'm not there to tell him what to do. Good night, Paul."

"Good night, Monsieur le Curé."

As Monsieur le Curé and Fulgence walked up the Rue des Pins toward the presbytery, Paul stood gazing into the ravine below.

There, in the dark of the brush, La Pitoune was probably waiting. He was tempted to go back to her. The desire for her was still there; beneath his refusal a moment ago he had sensed a rebirth of his old passion for her. He could still take her as in the past. Yet he could not.

Abruptly, he left the footbridge and started down the dirt road toward the Rue des Sapins. It was not the need for sex that was driving him there. It was something else, the feeling that he was bound to end up in the brothel, just like his father. Just like his father, that was the essence of it. His father had let him down. Now he would revenge himself by going through the same ritual. Turning into the Rue des Sapins, he had the almost physical sensation that his legs were actually leading him to the brothel, no matter how much he might fight against it.

Soon, he found himself across the street from the Red House. Light footsteps came up suddenly from the dark of the alley that ran from the side of the brothel to a few houses down the street from his mother's on the Rue des Pins. A girl dressed in a skirt and sweater came out of the alley; she stopped, looked around, saw him, then abruptly she went up the steps and knocked at the door three times. A moment later the door opened. Her long black hair glided swiftly into a

152

world of pink light. Paul crossed the street and knocked at the door.

In the dark of a porch across the way, La Pitoune stood watching. She had followed Paul, and now her frustrated hunger had released the dark powers of rage inside her once more. Once more she was possessed with that uncontrollable urge to crush and smother and destroy. She could not bear to see him go inside that house. She must do something, quick. She started up the street toward the seminary, hurrying to get there before the meeting ended.

Paul saw her shadow moving wild along the row of porches, and for a moment he thought of going after her. Anything would be better than this senseless impulse to visit the brothel. What was he doing here, anyway? Was it merely curiosity, or some secret desire to feel closer to his father through the vicarious knowledge of an experience his father had known in his last moments? Or was this only an excuse so that he might hide from the awful fact of death. When the door opened he did not know what to do, or what to say.

Paula, golden blonde and wearing a blue dress, held the door half-open. "What can I do for you?"

In a voice made harsh by self-consciousness, he replied: "You know what I want."

"Who sent you?"

He thought a moment, then said: "Arthur."

She opened the door all the way.

He stepped into a long corridor full of pink light. On his left a staircase spiraled up to the second floor. Both sides of the corridor had many bedroom doors, closed.

"In here, if you please," said Paula, opening the first one on his right.

He entered a small parlor about the size of the living room in his mother's house. The floor was covered with a thick

153

carpet. Conscious of his calked boots, he stepped lightly onto it. The room had an atmosphere of warm intimacy, dimly lit by a glass chandelier whose red bulbs were covered with shades the color of flesh. A jukebox stood in one corner, and along the wall facing the entrance was a long couch between end tables. One window gave out on the street, and the other, behind the couch, would undoubtedly open out on the alley that ran along the side of the house; both were shut, and curtained. The room was warm, redolent with perfume. He could hear faint footsteps upstairs.

"Won't you sit down, please," Paula suggested in the correct French of educated people. She was standing in the doorway. Tall and strongly built, she had broad hips, full breasts half-exposed in the low front of her dress. The light told him that she wore nothing underneath. There was a thick coat of make-up on her face, but it did not hide the wrinkles, the dark circles around the eyes. She was looking at him with an air of mingled surprise and admiration, as if she had never seen a man so tall and strong looking. He could feel the blood hot in his face, as he returned her gaze, then lowered his eyes.

Aware of his uneasiness, and anxious to make him feel at home, she said with a suggestive wink: "What is your pleasure?"

"A woman," he blurted out.

She walked casually over to the window on the right and began straightening the folds of the curtain. "For the night?"

"I don't think so."

"It is only fifty dollars."

"I will not stay the night."

"In that case," she said, "it will be ten dollars."

He reached inside his money belt and brought out a ten-dollar bill. She came up to him and took the money. Her eyes, which to this moment had worn a vague look of aloof correctness, became full of warmth and her speech and manner grew less formal. "Are you sure it will be enough," she said. "You look quite hungry to me, big boy. What's your name?"

"Paul."

"Well! You and I ought to get on famously. Mine is Paula."

"It's hot in here."

"That's because you're hungry, my big Paul," she explained, and squeezing his arm in affectionate familiarity she added: "What you need is a full night to cool down. After a long winter at camp, that's only natural. You don't expect to get it out of you in one short instant, do you?"

"I won't stay the night," he repeated.

She paused, expecting her silence to win him over. But he shook his head obstinately. She stepped close to him, so that he began to feel, against his will, the magnetic pull of her body. Her skin was very white, and mingling with the perfume in the air now came the strong scent of her flesh.

"You are such a hunk of a man," she said; "I should really charge you double. But I will give you a break tonight because I know you are hungry. Next time you come, though, try to be less in a hurry and spend the night. You won't regret it. Our girls are very nice, you'll see." Then she stepped back and, cupping her hands around her mouth, she shouted down the corridor: "Come on, girls."

Paul sat down benumbed, lost. Things were happening so fast. He was startled by the change taking place in him. The shame and the disgrace were less acute, somehow. The thought of his father still lingered on his mind, but dimly. And he was not so sure any more that he would never make love to a woman like Paula. Yet there was still a part of him that wanted out. He even considered a moment the idea of offering her another ten dollars if she would let him go without laughing at him. But it was too late now.

155

The girls were beginning to file into the room. Three, four, five, six, wearing two-piece bathing suits of black satin. Silently, ceremoniously, they formed a half circle facing him; while Paula went to the jukebox, from there she could supervise the proceedings and at the same time peep outside through an open fold in the curtains.

Now was the time for him to choose. All the girls looked the same age, about twenty, and they seemed well fed and not at all tired as he had vaguely expected them to appear. The first one on his right was looking at his boots. The one next to her was chewing gum and gazing at the ceiling in a pose of boredom. When he met the glance of the third one, she looked frightened and lowered her eyes. Next was a tall one, with long hair dyed red, who winked and turned round to give him a view of her behind and profile and then stood still, expectant. He looked quickly at the other two on his left; one glanced at him casually, the other seemed to be waiting for his inspection with urgency and hunger, and determined to be chosen, for she met his glance with a sudden full bump-and-grind motion of the pelvis and said: "Hi, handsome!"

Paul felt himself sweating with embarrassment and indecision. Paula was sliding the nickel-slot of the jukebox in and out; click, in; click, out; click, in; click, out. When he looked at her, she lifted an eyebrow. "Well, what is your pleasure?" she said, continuing to play with the money slot. The mechanical sound seemed to intensify the silence of the girls, whose looks he felt bearing down upon him now as if *he* had become the object of inspection. The girl on his right looked up from his boots to his face; he saw in her stare a cold hostility. The one next to her began making loud saliva-noises as she chewed her gum. Over the shoulder of the girl immediately in front he saw a lanky jack pass by on his way out. A door banged open somewhere down the corridor, a man burst out swearing in a loud drunken voice, men's voices rose to quiet him down, then the door was slammed shut. In the tense stillness that followed he could hear his own heart beating fast. The tall red-headed girl let out a sigh of impatience. Then the eager one on his right made another suggestive motion with her pelvis to attract him, and when she had succeeded, she told him in silent articulation with her lips: "Come on, handsome, make up your mind."

But he could not decide. All the girls began shifting their weight from one leg to the other. Paula quickened the pace of sliding in, out, in, out, the nickel slot. The impatient motions of the girls released a sharp smell of perspiration to mingle with the stifling perfume. Almost on the verge of panic, he tried to look from one to the other, to make a decision. Then, all of a sudden, his gaze met the eyes of the girl who had looked frightened a moment ago; she did not lower her eyes now; they were full of bitter disgust.

"No." He stood up.

The girls reacted with expressions of indignation, shrugs of indifference, giggles and sniffs of disgust.

"All right, girls," Paula said in a quiet voice; "that will be all for now."

Then just as they had come in, they left, in single file, ceremoniously. But once in the corridor they fell to whispering among themselves. Paula called back the one who chewed gum; "Marie, see if Lise is ready."

"She don't want to work."

"Tell her to come here right away."

"She's bucking, I told you."

"Marie, do as I say," Paula insisted. Then she came back into the parlor. "You should have told me you were fussy," she said. "Now, if you'll wait a minute, maybe I'll get you the girl you really want."

157

"It's no use."

"Sit down and relax a while," she said, going to the juke-box and putting a nickel in the slot. "What do you want to hear?"

"Nothing."

She made a selection. And then she went back to the door where Marie had just appeared.

"What did she say?"

"Just like I told you: she's bucking. Still has all her clothes on."

"Never mind," said Paula. "I'll talk to her later."

From the jukebox came the first notes of a mellow senti-mental waltz. Paula went to the machine and adjusted the sound very low. Then she closed the door and planted herself solidly before him. "What's the matter?"

"I guess I really didn't feel like it in the first place."

"Would you like to try your luck in the back, first?"

"I don't gamble."

"Barbotte is easy. And Maurice will take good care of you."

"I want to get out of here," Paul snapped, unable to hide his annoyance with himself.

In a voice heavy with repressed impatience, she said: "Now look here, big boy. You just gave me ten dollars. And I know you didn't come here just to say your beads. So, make it easy on us, will you; be a regular fellow and tell us what you want."

"I don't know," he stammered. "I suppose I only wanted to see what it was like." The words came out of him against his will. Only after he had spoken did he realize how faithfully they expressed his hidden desire, and how shameful that desire was. Now he knew that he had invited more humiliation from Paula. He sat down, resigned to bear all the insults that he felt she was justified in pouring over him.

But Paula did not react this way. Her manner suddenly be-

158

came one of gentle, affectionate scolding; so the words struck with greater impact than if she had shouted at the top of her voice. Like a mother reprimanding her son, she said: "You know, big Paul, this is not very nice for a man your age. The girls are here to do a job, earn a living. And it isn't the best kind of work a woman can hope for. Don't you think it's a bit unfair for you to just drop in like this and have a look as if this were a circus or a peep show? I don't know what pleasure a man could find in that. I suppose there are some people who get some sort of satisfaction out of watching other people sin. But, truly, I didn't think you were that kind of man."

He stared at his boots, smarting under the sting of her words. He had never suspected that paid women could feel, or speak this way.

Paula was aware that her performance was winning him over. She was an expert with the green ones; experience had taught her that when every means of seduction had failed, the trick of shaming them a little always produced results. Now she waited for him to make the next move. Silence after the sermon was the usual finishing touch.

At last he stood up, as from the momentum of a sudden important decision, and asked: "A cigarette?"

She stepped up to him, slowly, offering her body: "Are you sure it's a cigarette you want right now?"

"All right," he sighed. "You come with me then."

She threw her arms around his neck like a little girl bursting with love, gave him a big hug and planted a warm moist kiss on his mouth. "I knew it. I knew it all along," she laughed softly, seductively.

A wave of relief swept through his body. Gone was the acute anguish of indecision, the fear of ridicule. He felt as though he were about to buy from her body a sort of redemption from shame and disgrace.

159

"You're such a good-looking hunk of man I don't mind making a special," Paula said. Then she went to the door and called Marie to tell her to take over for a while.

He followed her to the end of the corridor. The last door on the left was open, and inside he could see the girls sitting there, waiting. Paula went in for a short and heated exchange with Lise, whom he recognized as the girl he had seen enter the house a few minutes before he did. He could hear from beyond the next door a low rumble of men's voices, silence, the rolling of dice, and again men's voices. Paula came back, looking annoyed, but this did not prevent her from smiling as she opened the door on the right for him.

The room was as small as a cell, and as bare—a cell that reeked of perfume. Near the bed was a table with a newspaper on it. A chair, a washbasin, and above the bed a small black-and-gold crucifix completed the meager fixtures.

Paula picked up the newspaper and spread it on the foot of the bed, explaining: "With this, here, you won't need to take off your boots. And we will try not to dirty the sheets too much. You can imagine what it would amount to if we had to change them each time. So, be careful, my big Paul; Maurice is very fussy about these things."

At that moment they heard an outbreak of men's voices and footsteps, immediately followed by Marie's call: "All the girls in front. Come on, girls."

Hurriedly, Paula picked up the washbasin and walked out of the room, leaving the door open.

The corridor was bustling with the noisy chatter of girls answering the call to work. From the sound of the activities in the front room Paul gathered that a number of men had come together. Going over to the doorway, he was brought to a sudden stop by the laughing voice of Red Mallet sounding off above the others. And now he saw in the room across the corridor the girl named Lise, sitting with head lowered

160

in thought. He wondered what could have happened to make her quit so suddenly: remorse, illness, a better house somewhere else? At that moment she must have felt the weight of his stare, for she got up and after glancing at him moved to another corner of the room where he could not see her. But in this short glance, furtive and resentful, he saw such an expression of distress that he was moved to a sudden feeling of pity for the girl, as though her misery were the result of some wrongdoing on his part. He was tempted to go and offer help, but all of this suddenly vanished from his mind when he saw Israel pass by on the way to the gambling room. He ducked behind the door.

He was still there when Paula came back, a moment later, with the washbasin full of water. After closing the door, she announced: "The rush is on. And we don't have enough girls. So we'll have to be quick about it."

How efficient she is, he thought with disgust.

"Come over here, big Paul, and pull down your pants. I'm going to wash you."

He did as she asked, without hesitation and feeling no emotions deeper than a mild shyness and a sort of amused tolerance. Even the fact that his sex was not ready did not worry him.

She said: "Now I'm going to tell you a little secret. I'm not supposed to be here. My job is in the front. But as I told you before, a woman doesn't mind making a special for a good-looking man like you. Only, I hope you remember it before you leave. It helps sometimes to make a little extra on the side, if you get what I mean. So try to remember your friend Paula, all right?"

He nodded yes.

"Anyway, I can tell a gentleman when I see one. So I know you'll do things right."

The mild soap, the lukewarm water and the gentle manipu-

161

lation were having their effect. "Well, now, that's the spirit!" Paula exclaimed. "Come on." And she went to the bed to lie on her back, pulling up her skirt and folding it neatly under. "Come on, big Paul."

What am I doing here! he thought as he moved mechanically toward the bed, hating the woman who lay there awaiting him, hating himself even more.

It was all a trick, shameful to the end, played by the one who offered on the one who paid. And he was now going to pay, just as his father had paid. In a surge of bitterness and anguish he lay down beside her.

"Now, that's better," she sighed.

He went into her strong, raging. And she took him with simulated sounds of delight designed to let him know how much pleasure he was giving her. But it sounded false to him, and he kept driving his sex into her with increasing passion, a passion born of his wanting desperately to smother the falsehood of her womanness with the power of his maleness. She told him he was good. She whispered in his neck that she was making a special. She told him that she was ready to come, now, although she never came for anybody else, and she licked his ears to prove how much pleasure he was giving her. But the more she insisted he was good, the more violently he assaulted her, as if he would force her to yield the truth that he knew had been denied to his father. With hatred, with revenge, with despair, he smothered her in a wild embrace that caused her to become silent, as though shocked, to seek him, rise to him, take him, and now, in a deep dark void, now, now, in an endless swoon, to come, silently and fully to come, mastered by the raging maleness of him, the terrifying power of his craving for an instant of truth.

eight

Long before the proceedings got
under way at the meeting of Les Dames de la Grâce, it became
obvious that the auditorium would not be large enough. Word
of scandalous revelations to be made at the meeting had spread
through the town. By half past seven there were at least five
hundred women crowded into the room, many accompanied
by their children, with those who could not find seats standing
in the aisles and along the wall in the rear.

Now it was time for Madame Dupré to open the meeting.
The tension in the air was all she could have wished for, en-
dowing her acting presidency with an aura of expectation that
gave her a thrilling sensation of power. Ponderous, her proud

bosom cleaving the way, she advanced slowly through the crowd at the door. Close on her heels came Mademoiselle Serval, stiff-backed, tight-lipped, furtively eyeing the crowd. They walked down the center aisle spreading behind them a widening silence. By the time they reached the front, and went up the five steps to the stage, the entire gathering had hushed itself to a tense quiet.

In the center of the stage, near the footlights, stood a pulpit archivolted with a blue banner on which LES DAMES DE LA GRÂCE was printed in flaming red letters. Behind the pulpit a half-dozen chairs had been placed in a semicircle. Madame Dupré motioned Mademoiselle Serval to one of them. Then she planted herself solid, solemn, under the banner, to gaze at her audience with stern authority, as if on the point of reprimanding all of her nine children and her husband to boot. Her gaze suddenly dropped upon the Bureau sisters, who sat surrounded by empty chairs in the front row. Shunned by all as if they carried a contagious disease, the two old women in black, accustomed though they were to being scorned, appeared deeply disturbed by this display of contempt. They also seemed puzzled by the whispers now reaching their ears. And the presence of Mademoiselle Serval on the stage offended them. But Madame Dupré gave them no cause for relief. Three years before, the sisters had refused to rent their red house to the Duprés on the ground that they had too many children. "Now, at last, I'm going to get even with you," her hard stare seemed to say to them. And the distressed sisters lowered their eyes to the rosary beads that were cascading fast through trembling fingers on their laps. Not a sound rose from the floor. All eyes were fixed upon the pulpit.

Madame Dupré crossed her hands on her stomach in a posture of grave announcement. Then in a strong masculine voice she began: "Women of La Buche, I thank you for coming here

164

tonight in such large numbers. I thank you on behalf of our chaplain, Father Boulanger; I thank you on behalf of the entire population of La Buche, here and at the camps; and I say to you, mothers, we are proud of you, all of you, seeing how religiously you have answered the call to duty. So, I thank you all.

"Now, women of La Buche, I know that all of you are anxious to get on with the matter of the new threat to our welfare that has struck our beloved town lately. I know. And I, for one, am anxious to see what we are going to do about it. But first, I must tell you: Father Boulanger and Madame Gauthier have begged me to wait. At this moment they are trying to get hold of Monsieur le Curé, and the three of them should be here shortly. Meanwhile, they have begged me to open this meeting with a recitation of one decade of the Rosary, to ask God forgiveness for our sins, and to ask God to guide us in this hour of great danger. After that, we will proceed with a reading of my report on last week's bingo, and if we still have time we will vote on the question of our pilgrimage to Saint Anne de Beaupré this summer. So, let's all kneel down, now."

Whispers of disappointment rose from the assembly. The Bureau sisters helped each other to kneel down. There was a general stir on the floor. Amidst sighs of resignation, the rustling of skirts and the grating of chair legs against wood, the entire gathering went down on their knees. A few children insisted on standing up; their mothers pulled them down by the elbows. Several young girls in the side aisles stared angrily at Madame Dupré for making them dirty their Sunday best on the soiled floor.

Madame Dupré waited for complete stillness. Then in a voice sonorous and lofty she entoned: "We are now going to ask God to forgive our sins. And we are also going to thank

God for showing us, once again, the miraculous workings of His Divine Providence. As all of you may see, we are privileged in having among us, tonight, a woman whose conversion to a life of virtue nobody will doubt. All of us know what her past was. But do we know what her future will be? Nay, what her present life is like, inside her repentant soul? No, we don't know how merciful God has been to her. Merciful to her, and to us all at the same time. For I say to you, women of La Buche: Mademoiselle Serval, here, has come to this meeting in order to expose the terrible scandal that has befallen our pious town. God has sent her here tonight in order that she might do her share of work, in order that she might join us in ridding our town of the sins imported here by the devil himself; and, women of La Buche, in order that we might accept her as one of us from now on, as one whose virtue is forever beyond reproach. So, let us do our duty right now. Let us begin by inviting her to lead us in this prayer. Let us demonstrate to God that we recognize a virtuous soul when we see one. Yes, indeed, women of La Buche, let us ask Mademoiselle Serval to call the *Aves*, and let us pray as we have never prayed before."

Madame Dupré then turned to Mademoiselle Serval. The slim spinster, overcome by this lofty introduction, was quite pale. When she reached the pulpit, in front of which Madame Dupré knelt down, she kept her eyes up at the banner overhead. She had to clear her throat several times before finally being able to utter the first *Ave*, in a voice trembling and weak.

But just then she was interrupted by a sudden burst of activity in the front row. It was the Bureau sisters getting up. A current of distraction traveled through the mass of women. The two old figures in black began tottering up the center aisle, clenching their beads as they mumbled disapproval.

166

Madame Dupré lost no time getting back to the pulpit, where she waved Mademoiselle Serval to the side. Then in a voice hoarse with indignation she addressed the two sisters: "God will punish you for that."

The sisters stopped and turned. The younger one, in a shrill voice full of wounded dignity, replied: "We are not going to pray with her beside us. No, Madame. We respect God too much for that."

All over the room women stood up, hushing one another to silence. Then, as the sisters turned back up the aisle toward the door, Madame Dupré stepped to the very edge of the stage and cried out: "With all your money, and your houses, you will never buy your way into the good Lord's heaven. Come back here, pray with us. You have a lot to ask forgiveness for."

But the sisters went on, one leading the other by the hand, both shaking their heads in stubborn protest. And now the entire assembly stood up with a rising murmur of indignation.

Madame Dupré shouted: "Silence! Women of La Buche, hear me!"

She obtained a heavy, tense quiet. Then she went on addressing the two sisters: "What is the matter, Mesdemoiselles Bureau? Are you afraid to face the truth? Why don't you stay here and tell us what kind of business you rent your house for? Or don't we know enough already, eh, women of La Buche?"

"Yes, yes! That's right," burst out here and there from the floor, where everyone flashed angry looks upon the Bureau sisters now nearing the back of the room. The women standing there drew aside to let them pass. A clearing was made through the crowd. And at the end of this clearing, in the doorway, there suddenly appeared La Pitoune, flushed, panting, a fierce look in her eyes.

Madame Dupré was saying: "Now, women of La Buche, what more proof do we need that these two old misers are willing to do business with the devil himself? Look at them go away. They are guilty. And they know it. Isn't it enough they rob us with their outrageous rents? Now they want to ruin our men into the bargain!"

All as one the women echoed her feelings of indignation: "That's right. Yes, yes, quite true."

La Pitoune stalked to the center aisle, where she planted herself, legs apart, arms akimbo, while all around her women were crying out, working themselves up to a frenzy of indignation under the leadership of Madame Dupré, who now had to shout at the top of her voice in order to be heard.

"Now I ask you, women of La Buche, how long are we going to stand for this sort of thing? Are we going to tolerate a house of sin in this town?"

"Charivari!" burst out La Pitoune, dominating the assembly with this fierce call sounded in a stentorian tone. And from the four corners of the room came the echoes.

"Down with the brothel!"

"Charivari!"

"Charivari!" La Pitoune shouted once again, with fire in her eyes, as she started down the center aisle toward the stage.

Madame Dupré, afraid of losing control over the assembly, banged on the pulpit and demanded silence. There was a continuous loud grating of chairs against the floor, now accompanied by insistent, rhythmic tapping of feet, clapping of hands and shouts of "Charivari," "Down with the brothel," "Charivari!"

In the uproar, few women noticed that Father Boulanger was now trying to make his way through the crowded entrance where the Bureau sisters had stopped, frozen with terror at the sound of Charivari. One of the sisters tried to say something to him, but her voice broke and she fell to sobbing in her handkerchief. The other then led her away by the hand, while Father Boulanger, shaking his head in dismay, pleaded with the crowd to let him through. Slowly he reached the center aisle; the deafening uproar made him cover his ears with his hands. And as he went down toward the stage, women turned to look after his venerable white head, the sight of which was powerless to calm them now.

On the stage Madame Dupré said to La Pitoune: "You have made a mess of the whole thing. I will never control them now."

"You wanted action?" said the other. "So you have it. Now let's make the best of it. That brothel has got to be closed down, even if I have to do it myself, all alone."

Behind them, seated in the dark of the backstage, Mademoiselle Serval was surveying the scene, a thin smile of satisfaction on her face.

"Charivari!"

"Down with the brothel!"

About two thirds of the assembly were on their feet, angrily demanding quick action, tonight, now; there were cries of "protect our husbands and our sons," shrieking voices calling for a fire, the fire that kills all sin and drives away the devil as it had in the charivari of '37. The rest of the women remained seated, or moved to front rows when they saw Father Boulanger waving his arms over the footlights to enjoin attention. Out of respect for their chaplain, some of them seemed willing to hear what he had to say. In the wild hope that this small audience might gradually shame the others to quiet, the old priest began to speak, in deep tones of urgent appeal.

"My dear ladies! This is no time to raise a charivari. At this very moment one of our beloved sons is being called back to his Creator. Think of our little Claude, the dear son of your

169

beloved *présidente*; he may not last the night. Please, my dear ladies, let us remain calm and orderly. Let us respect the dying."

But these remarks did not make a favorable impression upon the few who had to crane their necks to hear him. The women began to complain aloud that they had not come here to listen to a sermon. They resented his mention of the sick boy as if it were a fraud—if he wanted an excuse to prevent the charivari, he had better dig for a better one than the Gauthier boy's illness!

Father Boulanger countered by raising his voice to high tones of religious eloquence. A charivari would not solve the problem. Sin was not destroyed by fire or noise or public protest against it. Sin was destroyed by vigilance, prayers. If there was a house of sin in La Buche, Monsieur Le Curé would find out where it was and would close it down immediately. That was vigilance. As for prayers, that would have to come now, at this very instant. They must kneel down, all of them, and pray with him. They must pray that the Good Lord continue to show them the Divine Mercy He had showed them in the past. In spite of all the sins of the people of La Buche, there was a saint in this town. The dying little Claude Gauthier was a living example of the Good Lord's Divine Mercy. Were they going to be blind to that? Were all of these good Christian mothers going to offend the Lord by raising a charivari just when their little saint was in his last moments of virtuous life among them? No, this must not happen. They must kneel down with him now, and offer prayers of thanks to the Good Lord. "Now," he said, and repeated, "Now," before it was too late.

But by the time he finished speaking, all the women had stood up. And his last words were drowned by clamoring

170

voices that stormed from the four corners of the auditorium.
"Charivari!"

The women did not want a sermon. The hour of praying
was past. Their faces, ravaged by toil, malnutrition and a long
severe winter, showed the one hysterical emotion that raged
inside each and every one of them. Theirs was a primitive
war cry, the war cry, spontaneous and fierce, of self-defense
against the threat which a brothel held out to their reclaiming
of their men after long months of cruel abstinence. Such a
frenzy could not be tamed by sermons or prayers. Only a fire
would calm them down at this point, for their instinct told
them irrevocably that only a fire could purge the sin, slay
their common enemy. "Fire!"

"But my good Christian mothers," Father Boulanger cried
out, again and again, now pleading, now scolding. His deep,
warm voice, so effective in the quiet intimacy of his office
or the confessional, hardly reached the front rows. He had
sent a second message to the presbytery, but now he began to
despair of obtaining calm before Monsieur le Curé arrived. He
demanded attention with his hands, he lifted his arms above
his head in a gesture of arresting command, he crossed his
fingers on his chest in a pose of intense praying, he raised
his voice until it broke, he tried everything. But still they
would not listen to him.

"Charivari!" they shouted.

And the uproar, feeding upon itself, continued with growing
intensity. The confusion nearly reached the point of panic,
as mothers, anxious to take their children home, converged
hastily toward the doors, where a crowd stood hesitating between going to the brothel at once and waiting for the rest of
the assembly to join them. Some got up on chairs and tried to
make speeches, but others pulled them down by the skirts. All
over the room women kept punching the air with fists shaking

171

in indignation. The older ones, less energetic, expressed their anger by shuffling chairs against the floor, or stamping hard with their feet; dust rose; the air was heavy with the strong reek of unbathed women's flesh. A group of young girls flocked to the front of the room in answer to a call from La Pitoune. Bending over the footlights, and shouting in shrill tones of fierce vengeance, she exhorted them to action through the argument that unless they drove the whores out of town immediately there would not be one clean jack left for any one of them to marry. The girls listened with gaping mouths, eyes bright with excitement.

Finally, after so many attempts to speak, each one defeated by a fresh outburst of shouting from the floor, Father Boulanger turned his back to the assembly. His old narrow shoulders drooped; he was overcome with distress. From Madame Dupré he demanded an explanation.

"But it isn't my fault," she said. "It's the Bureau sisters who started it."

"What are we going to do now?"

Her reply was a shrug of the shoulders. She was tempted to step down among the crowd and lead them all to the brothel at once. In her reckless hunger for power she was ready to do anything. But the very confusion on the floor held her back. She was afraid, not of the consequences of a charivari, but rather of another failure to regain her position of leadership.

Getting no help from her, Father Boulanger went to La Pitoune and bluntly planted himself between her and her audience. Not to be outdone, La Pitoune stepped aside and then jumped down from the stage. Her young audience followed her to the right, where she went on with her speech as if there had been no interruption. Father Boulanger then went to Mademoiselle Serval, whom he ordered, gently but decisively, to her knees, facing the crowd. He knelt down beside her. Together they began reciting the rosary at the top of their voices.

The uproar had reached its peak of loudness and confusion. At the doors a fight nearly broke out between the group who wanted to run to the brothel at once and another group who insisted that they wait until all were ready to go together. Many returned to their seats, exhausted. Some stood looking lost in the midst of the tumult. Others gazed with faces drawn in deep sadness. Here and there a lonely widow pulled out her beads, horrified at these goings-on that recalled so vividly the charivari of '37. A few women followed Father Boulanger's lead and knelt down in the front of the room where they could pray with him and Mademoiselle Serval. Others walked out in protest. The floor noises began to subside. Gradually the shouting dissolved into a loud conversation. For the first time since the call to Charivari was sounded by La Pitoune, the assembly seemed on the point of coming to order. Now the voice of Father Boulanger calling the Aves could be heard distinctly above the murmur from the floor.

Suddenly, a stir traveled through the crowd. The whispering grew abruptly louder, more intense. In the back of the room a woman shouted that it was true, he was coming now, Monsieur le Curé. And indeed, seconds later, the short rotund priest appeared at the doors.

"Women of La Buche, silence, please!" Madame Dupré shouted. Father Boulanger got up. La Pitoune cut short her speech; with a wave of the hand she enjoined her young audience to keep still for the time being. Mademoiselle Serval went back to her chair in the dark of the backstage.

Flap, flap, came Monsieur le Curé, striding down the center aisle in his fishing boots and his soutane tucked in at the crotch. His puffy red face had a streak of mustard at the

173

mouth. He looked neither left nor right, grumbling that things had gone too far; they wouldn't let him fish in peace, now they wouldn't even let him finish his supper. He swung his arms with dogged vigor, as though beating a path for himself through a thick brush. On the stage, he exchanged a few words with Madame Dupré. As for Father Boulanger, he let out at his face a long, deep-chested belch of contempt. Then he turned to the assembly, and setting his hands firmly on his hips he asked in his loud boisterous voice: "Have you finished?"

Silence fell at once.

"I could hear you all the way from the presbytery. For the love of green horse, what are you trying to do: wake up the dead?"

The only sound from the floor was the rapid breathing of his listeners.

"So maybe there is a brothel in town," Monsieur le Curé went on. "Maybe. And what of it? You know full well that if you give me a chance I'm going to close it down as soon as possible. Don't you have faith in your Curé? Did I ever let you down?" He paused for a reaction, but nobody spoke up.

"All right then. So let's behave like decent Christians. Let's cut out this nonsense. If I can't close the brothel down myself, then you go ahead and raise your charivari. But not before I tell you to. And if you must do it, this time I won't tolerate any fire. Clear?"

A wave of meek surrender ran over the rows of faces. Every woman looked as if she were cowering before her angry jack set for a good beating.

Monsieur le Curé went on bullying them. "Now, when I leave this room it will be to go straight to that house. And I don't want any of you to follow me there. You stay right here, get a bingo going, do whatever you want; but keep quiet. To-

174

morrow morning at eight there will be a Mass, and I want to see every one of you in church. Monsieur le Vicaire will officiate, and your chaplain here will deliver the sermon. After that, there will be another session of letter-writing in the presbytery, for those of you who want to get a word out to your men at the camp. Monsieur le Vicaire will take care of you." Then he turned to Father Boulanger and said: "Did you get that, Father?"

"Indeed, at eight tomorrow," replied the old priest.

"Now, Madame Dupré, do you have anything in mind to keep them busy for a while?"

"I have a report on last week's bingo."

"We might hold elections," Father Boulanger suggested; "Madame Gauthier is resigning, you know."

"Is she?" exclaimed Madame Dupré, with a show of being terribly sorry to hear this.

"Well, do what you want, as long as you keep this meeting in order," said Monsieur le Curé. And then without another word he stepped down from the stage and, as rapidly as he had come in, walked up the center aisle to the doors.

All the women stood up, from force of habit. His appearance on the stage had been so short, so forceful, that many of them only now began to realize he had spoken to them. The loud whispering began all over again. They turned to one another with eyes full of the question, "Well, what do you think of that?" Smarting under the outrageous bullying, all of them, feeling as women do after a sudden thrashing at the hands of their men, they were now ready to burst out into another uproar of indignation.

But this time Madame Dupré was quick to sense the danger. While she could still dominate the noise from the floor, she announced that elections would be held at once, for a new Madame la Présidente and a new Treasurer.

A burst of cheers filled the room. It was a nervous reaction. Had La Pitoune suddenly sounded another call to charivari, all the women would have picked up the call and the uproar would have started again. The women cheered because their aroused natures needed an outlet. Most of them cared little for elections; they had not given the matter a thought for the last ten years or so. Just as they had been willing to pray a moment ago, so now they were willing to vote and listen to speeches, or play bingo; they were willing to do anything, so long as they kept busy. In the heart of every one of them was one thought, the brothel; one wish, to burn as many whores as they could; and one conviction, that they would have to raise their charivari, for since Monsieur le Curé had not closed down the brothel in the past two weeks he was not going to do it tonight.

The meeting ended about an hour later. Madame Dupré was elected the new *présidente*, and La Pitoune the new treasurer. Father Boulanger managed to announce that tomorrow morning's Mass would be sung for the dying Little Saint of La Buche. Then he went home, to meditate on the sermon he must deliver for the occasion. The women left the auditorium calmly, but their faces looked more set and grave than before the meeting. Some of them went to Lambert's tavern to pick up their husbands. Others went directly to their homes, avoiding the usual gossip-stops on the way.

Madame Dupré and La Pitoune were the last to leave. After making a rendezvous with Mademoiselle Serval for tomorrow morning before Mass, they walked together to the sidewalk of the Rue des Pins. The assembly had voted in favor of the pilgrimage to Sainte Anne de Beaupré in July, but left it to Madame la Présidente and the Treasurer to work out the details of transportation: by train, or by bus. But the two women did not discuss this now. They congratulated each other warmly. La Pitoune ventured to ask Madame la Présidente what she contemplated doing in the event Monsieur le Curé failed to close the brothel tonight. Madame Dupré suggested waiting a few days. But La Pitoune preferred to pass to action at once, reasoning that the women were so worked up now that they could never wait that long.

"At any rate," said Madame Dupré. "Now that we are leading the association, we are going to act firmly."

"That's right," agreed the other. "Action is what we need. And action is what we are going to get."

Then on this strong note of agreement they said good night.

nine

For a long moment after Paul had
taken her with such fierce passion, Paula lay subdued, mellow, telling him softly how good he was, how fully he had
given her the true pleasure that a woman feels when she
holds a real man inside her. But soon she was telling him
just as softly, how lucky he was to have found a woman of
her understanding and generosity on his first visit to a house
of joy. For that kind of woman, an experienced woman like
herself, a man paid extra.

Paul lay beside her in a twilight mood of lassitude. The act
of raw carnality had dulled the edge of his anguish, and now
he felt only melancholy, a sadness that pervaded all thoughts

179

of his father and of himself and even of Paula. Mechanically he reached for his money belt and gave his companion another ten-dollar bill.

Paula quickly got out of bed. "Thank you, handsome," she said. "I was right. You're a real gentleman."

"You don't need to thank me."

She smiled. And tidying her skirt and hair she said: "You must look me up next time you come to Montreal. I'll always be glad to make a special for a gentleman like you. Wait here a minute, while I get a pencil and a piece of paper to give you my address." She hurried out of the room, leaving the door open.

The place hummed with activity. He could hear rapid footsteps in the corridor and up and down the stairs, the opening and closing of doors, the voices of girls, and of men, laughing and joking in the parlor. From behind the closed door of the back room came the sound of dice being rolled on felted wood, and the outbursts of the players. Paul thought of Israel, who was now gambling his money away. He sat up, intending to go and pull him away from the gambling tables. The thought of Israel made him think of Claude, and he started to leave the room, determined to go home to his brother immediately. At the door, however, he came to an abrupt stop, hearing Lise's voice in the room across the corridor. The door was open sufficiently for him to see that two men were with her.

"I want my money," she was pleading between sobs.

Maurice was shaking his fist at her. "You won't get one more penny from me," he said, "if you don't get back to work right away."

"But you owe it to me."

"Do as the boss says," Altar Boy snapped. And Maurice added: "Any other night would have been all right. But to walk out on us at a time like this! No, you won't get away with it."

Stamping the floor in helpless rage, Lise cried: "Give me my money. I need it."

With one swift backhanded blow that struck her on the shoulder, Altar Boy sent her staggering back to slump in a chair against the wall, where she fell into a fit of convulsive weeping, her face buried in her hands. Then the two men, with growing anger, stepped up to her, shouting both at once: "Get back to work."

At that moment Paula came rushing in to announce: "Monsieur le Curé is here."

Without taking his eyes off Lise, Maurice said: "Show him upstairs, to 32."

"That's taken. How about the small one in the attic?"

"That will do," said Maurice. "Bring him a bottle of beer. I'll be with him in a minute."

"Fine," said Paula. Then turning round she saw Paul in the doorway of his room. "I'll be right back," she told him; "but you had better keep that door closed." And she hurried on to Monsieur le Curé who was waiting impatiently at the front door.

Paul did not move.

Altar Boy, who had just caught sight of him, repeated Paula's words, but in a tone of rough command: "You heard what the lady said. Get back in there and shut that door."

"You come and close it yourself."

Altar Boy started up to answer the challenge, but Maurice held him back in time to avoid a clash. "Here. Keep your eye on her, while I talk with the Curé. And don't let her get away before I come back," he said. Then to Paul, politely: "I would advise you to leave now, if you don't mind."

"I'll get out of here when I'm sure this girl is safe."

181

"No harm will come to her."

"You don't expect me to take your word for it, do you?"

"It's none of your business anyway."

"Maybe so. But since I happen to be here now, you'd better tell your friend to lay off."

Maurice turned to Altar Boy. "You heard what the man said." Then he looked at Paul, as if to say: "Are you satisfied?"

"All right, boss, all right," Altar Boy said. Maurice went on his way down the corridor without another word.

Lise had jumped to her feet in sudden fright at the prospect of being left alone with Altar Boy. And it was this terrified expression on her face that Paul had caught. The sight of helplessness and of cruelty always had the same effect on him: indignation, a quick tightening of every muscle and nerve in his giant body. As he would pick up a fallen bird and tenderly nurse it back to flight, as he had risen to protect Israel from Salou's bullying, so now he would fight, unthinking and fierce, to protect Lise.

Altar Boy, casting a sneer of contempt at Paul, closed the door slowly, while saying to Lise in a tone of kindness that belied the lecherous gleam in his eyes: "Here, sit down. You and me are going to have a little talk."

Unable to see what happened next, Paul stepped up to the closed door. He heard confused sounds of a struggle: muffled cries and harsh breathing, a chair being knocked over, then a long, tense silence, pierced, suddenly, by a shrill call for "Help!" which was immediately stifled, then again silence. Paul kicked the door open and stepped inside.

Altar Boy was holding Lise smothered against the wall under the weight of his enormous body. One of his large hands was on her mouth, while with the other he was savagely plowing up under her skirt, as he muttered about teaching her a lesson: no little slut like her was going to play stuck-up

182

and make them lose money and get away with it. Not so long as Altar Boy here was around. Sandwiched between his body and the wall, Lise was vainly trying to fight back.

Paul grabbed Altar Boy from behind, and in a tremendous burst of strength jerked him off the ground, away from Lise. Then he stood solid behind him, with his powerful arms locked tight around the man's neck, and he pressed his forearms in against the throat, so that Altar Boy, caught by surprise and struggling for breath, soon became helpless. Lise dropped to the floor, exhausted, too frightened to move.

"Go now," Paul cried. "Hurry up!"

She stared at the two men in dumb terror.

"Get out now. Get out, girl. I'm holding him."

Slowly she picked herself up, and moved toward the door.

"Hurry up," Paul shouted. He tightened his grip around Altar Boy's neck, determined to hold on until the man was fully subdued. Suddenly he was aware of a sharp pain in the right ankle, where Altar Boy had just managed to kick him with a vicious heel. Paul brought his feet together, lifted the man a few inches off the ground, and carried him to the wall, where he pressed all his weight against him. But in doing so he had brought his arms down to below the man's shoulders. Altar Boy, his neck free, hit him so hard with the back of his head that Paul's eyes closed from the pain and blood streaked from his nose. Then he felt a sudden cutting pain below the ribs. He let go, folding at the waist, struggling for breath. Altar Boy quickly turned round and began to swing with both fists. The blows landed on the back of Paul's neck and on his shoulders. He tried to reach for the man's legs, but was knee-kicked in the face, so hard that his whole body straightened up. Then Altar Boy, getting a clear opening, struck out at him. Paul put up one hand and stopped the rushing fist in mid-air, pulling the arm down and twisting it back until Altar

183

Boy was forced to his knees. Paul struck him on the side of the head with his free hand. The blow sent Altar Boy's body slumping unconscious to the floor.

Paul did not wait to see if the man would get up again. He grabbed Lise by the hand and ran out of the room with her. The corridor was crowded with loggers and girls attracted there by the struggle. He pushed them aside, and still holding the girl's hand ran out the front door with her.

On the sidewalk, she said: "This way," indicating the right. And they ran towards the river.

"Where do you live?" he asked, when they had slackened their pace at the end of the block.

"Down by the Haymarket."

"I'm taking you home."

His head was on fire. There was blood all over his face, in his mouth. She was white, panting even more violently than he. They walked in silence, without looking at each other, all the way up to the Haymarket. He did not begin to feel the pains in his face until they had reached the house where she lived.

Then Lise said: "I wish I could do something, you are bleeding so much."

"Never mind," he said, fumbling in his pockets for a handkerchief.

Their eyes met. She began to cry.

"You will be safe now," he said, holding the handkerchief to his nose.

She seemed to want to say something, but the words stuck in her throat.

"Your name is Lise?"

She nodded.

"Mine's Paul."

She squeezed his hand in gratitude, then went up the steps and into the house.

184

Paul walked away, in the direction of his mother's house. The pains were less acute now. He felt only a general ache throughout his body. The cool air felt good. He walked slowly, aware of the sound of his calked boots on the wooden sidewalks. The fight and the escape had happened so fast, that were it not for his aching body and the taste of blood in his mouth, he might have thought it had been only a nightmare. As he walked, it all came back to him, every moment spent in the brothel, and the memory of Lise in terror and in tears, superimposed on the image of Claude's face ravaged by impending death, caused him such distress that tears began streaming down his face, choking him with grief.

Sin and shame seemed trivial indeed now, when contrasted with the misery that he sensed must be the cause of it all. Only when a man was in great distress could he do what he himself had done, what his father had done before him. Paul did not know what had made his father suffer so that he had had to seek relief in vice; he only knew that he must have suffered a great deal; his sin then, like his death, were to be viewed more with pity than condemnation. And not only his father's sin, but also the sins of Paula and the sins of Lise and his own, the sins of the whole of Timberland. And in that moment of compassion and understanding he felt as if he were embracing all misery-beaten wretches of this earth, wherever they might be. As long as others lived in darkness and unhappiness, he could not feel clean and virtuous as pious people do after praying for the sins of others. He felt sinful and caught in the same trap as his father and Paula and Lise and all the rest of them. There was between the world of sin and himself a bond stronger than his fleeting dream of dignity.

*   *   *

The first thing Madame Gauthier did on arriving home was to look for Paul. She called out his name several times,

185

careful not to raise her voice and wake up Claude. Getting no reply downstairs, she went up to his room. There she found his bag was on the floor near the bed. Thinking that he might be with his brother, she went to the door of Claude's room and listened. But all she could hear was the boy's hoarse breathing. The thought that Paul had gone out of the house and left his sick brother alone shocked her. She opened the door.

The light showed Claude alone, reading in bed. The window was open. Not to startle him, she rattled the doorknob a little. He looked up. She pushed the door wide open and walked in.

"Why aren't you asleep?" she inquired in a voice that betrayed her annoyance.

"I slept a little," he replied. Then while she went to the window he hastened to hide his Baudelaire under the mattress and pull the blankets over his bloodstained shirt.

She asked: "Did you take your sleeping pills?"

"Yes, mother."

"Maybe I should give you two more," she said, going over to the bedside table to pick up the glass. In the light of the lamp she noticed that his cheeks were flushed. "Did you have a spell while I was out?"

His face flushed. "Just a mild one, mother," he said. "I wish you would open my window."

"And where was your brother then?"

"So he is home!"

"You mean, you didn't hear or see him come in?"

"I thought I had."

"His bag is in his room."

"Great!" Claude exclaimed. "Don't bother with the pills, mother. I am going to wait up for him."

"Oh, no, you won't," she said. And going into the bathroom

186

across the hall she added: "You take these pills and go right back to sleep."

"Please, let me stay up. Now that Paul is back I don't want to sleep until I can talk with him."

She began to fill the glass with water. What was that strong alien odor pervading the bathroom? It was perfume, a woman's perfume! Could a woman have come into her house while she was out? Incredible! No, she did not want to believe what this perfume persisted in telling her must have taken place. Then all of a sudden she knew why Paul was not home. That was it! He had brought a woman into his mother's house and then walked out with her, leaving his sick brother alone. There could be no other explanation. Only he could do a thing so shameful. Only he could be so lacking in respect for his mother and his sick brother. It amounted to an outright profanation of her home, this very house where a saintly boy was dying and where the Good Lord visited in the form of the Holy Host. "Oh, no!" she moaned; as if she hadn't been through enough already, now this must happen on top of it all. Would there ever be an end to her misery? Her eyes filled with tears, and the sight of her tears in the mirror made her weep even more.

"Please, mother, forget about those pills," Claude said, when she came back to his room. "I don't want Paul to find me in bed."

She said: "Try to be reasonable. Go to sleep now, and tomorrow morning you can talk as much as you like with your brother. Here, take these."

The look of ill-disguised distress on her face, her moist eyes moved him to a compromise. "Very well," he said, "I will stay in bed. But I won't take the pills."

Madame Gauthier felt too distraught to insist further. She put out the light.

"Please, mother," Claude said softly, "when Paul comes home, please tell him to come up."

"I will not," she replied. "He and I have a lot to talk about. You can see him in the morning."

In a sudden cry of impatience he said: "But I must talk with Paul now, tonight."

"What sort of secret do you two have that can't wait 'till morning?"

Exhausted, he sank deep under the blankets. "You wouldn't understand, mother," he said with a sigh of despair.

"Try to sleep now. Goodnight."

Madame Gauthier crossed into the bathroom once again in the sudden hope that her sense of smell might have deceived her. But no. That evil perfume was still there. Not only had Paul profaned her house; her saintly Claude was now hiding things from her as well, sharing with his brother some secret which she had failed to detect through her vigilant intercepting of their mail. And what kind of secret might it be? she wondered, with a pang of alarm, on her way downstairs. What sort of influence on Claude could such a sinful person as Paul ever hold? Hadn't she suffered enough already? Hadn't she seen enough evil in her wretched life? Now that the hour of redemption was approaching, now that her little saint was about to bring a ray of purity and grace into her life, must all of her dreams of sanctity be shattered by his brother's wickedness. The sins of the fathers, she thought in anguish. O God, when would there finally be a day without sin, when would her life be at last secure from evil? She sat down in a dark corner of the living room, to wait for Paul.

As was her habit in sessions of sweet self-pity and religious meditation, Madame Gauthier said her beads. But her thoughts soon drifted away from the *Aves* that streamed fast and rhythmic from her lips. She thought of her married life,

188

of what it had amounted to: a purgatory on earth. It had held very few moments of happiness, and these had lost their beauty very early, for so much evil had followed. And all because she had said "No" to God, "Yes" to a man named Gauthier. Instead of being wedded to Jesus, as she had always dreamed of, she was wedded to a sinner who turned their first years of conjugal life into ugliness and sin so appalling that she could not recall those years, even now, without a quiver of repugnance running through her flesh. To think that she had given her body to that man for three full years, several times a week when he was home from camps, for the sole purpose of gratifying his base sexual needs! Ah, how he had taken advantage of her innocence! All the while, thinking she was doing her duty as a good Catholic wife, she had shared with him an existence of shameful degradation. To the very day of her death she would remember with bitterness how sinful and lowly she had felt in the confessional where, by the grace of God's mercy, the priest finally made her see what kind of brute her husband was and what abominable sins she had committed in his arms. But by then it was already too late. Two months later she had given birth to Paul. It was no wonder, then, she often reflected afterwards, that this first son of hers, a child of sin, was growing up in the exact image of his father. Conceived in sin, he lived in sin, and would no doubt die in sin, like his father. He was the living substance of her punishment. And if she could bear it, it was only through having Claude as a consolation, as a reminder that, after all, her life had not been entirely sinful. She had wanted a second child in order to make up to the Good Lord. Claude had been conceived in grace, in the true chaste Catholic way. To have him she had done her duty as a Catholic wife only once, and strictly in the manner and spirit of conceiving for the greater glory of God on earth. She had indeed done no

189

more than what the priest had told her was right. And as a reward God had given her a little saint.

But now, what had happened to her little Claude? Was he drawing away from her? From God? Oh, that Father Boulanger might be right and that this change in him might be caused only by the progress of the disease! Oh, that God might keep him in His Fold to the very last moment! That God might not allow Paul's influence to ruin his brother! That God might soon bring all this misery to an end and enable her to go to the convent at last!

Thus pleading, and praying, Madame Gauthier left the living room and went upstairs into Paul's room. In response to a sudden impulse she removed from his bed the sheets and blankets, and pillow slip; if she could not prevent him from sleeping in her house, she could at least see to it that he did not profane her linen with his sinful body. She took the bedclothes into her own room and locked them inside the linen closet.

Now was the hour when she usually changed into her garb of penitence. She took off her black dress with the mandarin collar. It made her think of Les Dames de la Grâce, but she swiftly chased the thought from her mind, for this, too, reeked of evil, what with the matter of the brothel which they must be discussing at this moment! She hastened to take out of the closet a long robe of rough black linen she had made several years ago; it was lined with abrasive material, the bottom hem was full of stones, and the seams were made of hairy string. Every night she wore it to bed, and she often slept in it on the floor. She put out the ceiling light, and continued to undress in the glow from the bedside lamp; this light was not bright enough to arouse her sense of modesty, yet strong enough to enable her to examine the marks of the garb on her naked body. Her knees, hips, shoulders and thighs had large patches of chafed skin where the rough cloth rubbed with every move she made. The sight of these wounds caused her to say softly: "Dear Jesus, see how hard I try to become worthy of Thee!" These were the wounds that she hoped might help expiate the sins of her husband and of her son, the wounds that she prayed might make her worthy of becoming the mother of the Little Saint of La Buche, prepare her for the austere life of the nunnery. Still, they were only minor. The wounds that really counted, for they hurt the most, were those inflicted upon her breasts and belly. "You will suffer the most in that part of your flesh with which you have sinned the most," she had repeated to herself, at the time of sewing small pieces of sandpaper where the cloth would rub against those areas of her body that she had allowed her husband to ravish so outrageously. Her breasts and her belly bled every night from the excessive irritation.

She noticed that the blood from last night had dried, coating the wounds with a protective scab, and she hastened to put on the garb. Then she dropped to her knees and prayed: "Lord, make me worthy of Thee. Make me worthy of being the mother of a little saint. Make me worthy of the nunnery!" Her fervor soon rose to a passionate plea. She threw herself on the bed, and rolled her body on it, pressing and rubbing her breasts and belly upon the abrasive cloth, until the pain became such that from deep in her throat came a long swooning cry of anguish: "O, my dear, sweet Jesus, am I worthy of Thee now?"

For a long moment after that she lay sprawled on her back with arms outstretched, in mystical abandon that brightened her tear-ravaged face with a glow as of joy.

Meanwhile, Paul had come home. In his state of acute depression he did no more than shrug his shoulders at the atmosphere of intense gloom that pervaded the house. The

191

sound of Claude's laborious respiration, mingled with the moanful praying from his mother's room, seemed part of that misery of life he felt so acutely. Walking softly, he went into the bathroom, and began to wash the blood from his face, careful not to make any noise to attract his mother's attention; as long as she prayed he would not have to face her and be drawn into one of her interminable scenes. There would be time enough for that tomorrow, he reflected, putting cold compresses on his nose and over the cut in his right eyebrow. His upper lip, cut inside, still bled a little. Tomorrow he would have to see Doctor Gendron about his nose; it felt as if it was broken, and the pain, when he touched it, shot up to the top of his head. He would go to bed and try to sleep.

On his way to his room he stopped suddenly at the sight of light at the bottom of Claude's door. He then heard his name being called out softly from inside. He went in.

"Come closer so I can have a good look at you." Claude's voice trembled from the strain of breathing and the excitement of seeing his brother.

Trying to smile, Paul walked quietly to the side of the bed: "How are you, boy?"

"But you are hurt! What happened?"

"I had a scrap at the tavern."

Claude sighed, and said with affection: "You'll never change."

"How do you feel. Do you have much pain?"

"Sometimes. How do I look?"

With an effort to sound casual, Paul replied: "You'll live."

Claude let out a chuckle of disbelief. "Well, this is it, Paul. I've known it for a long time."

"Come on, now. Don't talk like that."

"I don't mind, really. You get used to everything, even

death. Only, I do wish it could come soon. It's getting to be such an awful mess."

Paul began to move away, but Claude grabbed his hands. "Sit down a minute. I have so much to tell you."

"Take it easy, boy."

"I want you to do me a favor."

"Anything you say."

"You've got to get me out of here," Claude pleaded. "I don't want to die in this room. Let's go to the lake. Tomorrow."

"But. . . ."

"You have no idea what I have gone through with mother and Father Boulanger around me all the time. They are choking me with their prayers and talk of God. I can't take it any more. They will not even let me die in peace." Then after a pause for breath, he said: "I know what you are thinking, Paul. But that is not what happened. No, I have not lost my faith. I still believe in God. Only, they won't let me die alone, the way I want to."

Paul raised a hand for him to speak more slowly, not to get excited. But Claude was bent on unburdening himself. "You see; I have had much time to think, lately. And I have figured out a few things by myself. At least I think I have. When you know that you are going to die soon you begin to see things a different way. You don't feel like praying as much as you used to. You think less about that, somehow, and more about what is going to happen to you when it is all over. The hereafter becomes awfully important. You worry a lot about it because you don't know what awaits you on the other side of the river. And believe me, Paul, that is the worst part of it, the worst. You can't face it. So you begin imagining things. And first thing you know you are living again the best moments of your life, all the things you like to remember. And

193

you end up wishing that the hereafter were made of just that, the best moments of your life on earth."

Paul said: "And to think that all these years I was so sure you would become a priest."

"I might have, if I had not taken ill and had a chance to really figure things out by myself. But there is something else I must tell you. It has had a lot to do with the way I feel now. I met a girl, and now it seems as if I have led all of my true life in just these few weeks. I am so happy. I wish I could make you understand what I mean."

"I think I know," Paul said.

Claude went on: "Then you understand why I want her to come to the lake with us. It's my last chance."

"But you are not strong enough to take the trip."

"I am. I tell you I am."

"Mother will never let you."

"I will talk to her tomorrow."

Seeing that no argument would make him change his mind, Paul said: "All right, boy. I'll get Lambert's car tomorrow and buy the food and get things ready. But you must make your own arrangements with mother."

"I will," said Claude.

Paul got up. "Now you'd better get some sleep. I'll be in to see you first thing in the morning."

"I knew I could count on you," said Claude, smiling.

His smile went straight to Paul's heart. The light of joy on the face of death made him turn to the door, and he left the room, as Claude drifted swiftly into his most restful sleep in weeks.

Outside, in the dark of the hall, their mother stood waiting, gloomily impressive in her garb of penitence, blocking the way to Paul's bedroom. His expression of intense grief, even the cuts and bruises on his face as he walked up to her, failed to break her countenance to so little as a start of compassionate tenderness, a flicker of concern.

"Sorry I woke you up, mother," he said.

She flashed at him a cold look of hostility. "You brought a woman here while I was out," she said.

"I did not."

"You have profaned my house," she insisted.

"I came here to see my brother. That's all."

"How dare you lie to me like this? You brought a woman here. And I know it."

"Please go back to bed, mother. We are both tired. We'll talk tomorrow," he said kindly, but firmly. And he tried to move past her.

She stood still. "Kneel down. Ask forgiveness."

"I have nothing to ask forgiveness for. Now let me go to my room."

"On your knees."

"Would you rather I slept outside?"

"So that's it! One scandal in one night isn't enough for you, I suppose. After the whole town has seen you out with a woman while your brother is on his deathbed, now you want everybody to think that you mother won't let you sleep home?"

"You are going to wake up Claude."

"Much you care about your poor sick brother and me. I ask you, are you going to ask forgiveness or not?"

He looked at her, with an air of saying he would do anything to stop her from unloading her misery upon him, anything she asked him, anything but kneel down.

She waited.

Abruptly he turned away and started down the hall toward the stairs.

"Paul," she whispered tensely.

195

He stopped, hesitated a moment, then retraced his steps. She stepped aside to let him pass.

"Paul," she whispered again, as he walked into his room.

He turned to look at her, and saw that her eyes were filled with tears. "Paul," she pleaded, "kneel down and ask forgiveness, please, for me, your mother?"

He wanted to drop to his knees, give up, crawl in final surrender. But at the last moment something held him back, something stronger than his despair. "No," he said, slowly, emphatically, "no, no."

"Just like your father. Just like him you are," she cried, shaken with sobbing. And she turned away and hastily crossed herself again and again, pleading: "Lord, have mercy on us. Oh, Good Lord, have mercy on us."

Outside, in the hall, she clung desperately to the doorknob, unwilling to face her defeat that was also the defeat of the Good Lord, torn to anguish that this son of hers, her own flesh and blood, refused still, against the dying of his brother, against the tears of his mother, to humble himself and ask forgiveness, to repent. "No. Oh, no. No," she moaned softly.

He could hear her lament, feel her suffering through the closed door, and it tore at his heart. He had denied her, his mother, in response to something in himself that was more powerful than ties of blood. All this misery he was causing her, against his will, against his acute yearning for a fleeting embrace of tenderness. Helpless, he began to weep, fully and freely, as he had not wept since he was a little child.

The door opened, and looking up he saw his mother again, her face set stonily against him. "Get yourself a black suit," she said. "Otherwise, I will not allow you at the funeral." Paul shuddered. "And see the doctor about your face. You look like a murderer." And she slammed the door after her.

The cruelty of her remarks, together with the sight of

196

his bed stripped bare, was the last drop. It set seething in him a dark rage that cut short the helplessness and the tears.

He flung the window open and stood staring defiantly into the shimmering darkness blanketing the town below. And the rage, a good rage, sent currents of new life through his body.

Let her make her peace with the Good Lord, he thought. I will never crawl before Him. And aloud he said: "I must do something for the boy. I must get him out of here. Tomorrow, before it's too late."

ten

Against his better judgment, Israel had tried his luck at the gambling tables and lost fifty dollars. He decided to call it quits. Besides it was getting late and he had to find a place to sleep for the night. He asked Paula if she would let him have a bed, empty that is.

"Empty!" But would you rent a bed empty for five dollars when you could get fifty for the same bed with a lovely girl in it? Why, young man, it was a matter of simple arithmetic, and she could tell he looked bright enough to understand that. Now, if he could be persuaded to try and find out for himself how reasonable the price was, and how good the girls . . . "No!" Well, in that case he might try the rooming houses,

199

near the Haymarket, if he cared to. He would! Fine. No hard feelings. And good luck!

He inquired at several doors, only to be told that all the rooms had been rented to other transient loggers. Further down the road he saw a vacancy sign in a window. He rang the bell. The landlady answered at once, but she looked at him suspiciously and before he had time to open his mouth she declared: "Sorry. All my vacancies are reserved." With a shrug of puzzlement, Israel continued to the end of the road, toward the shirt factory. There he caught sight of a drunken logger entering a house that had a light burning on the porch. He recognized him as one of the men who had ridden on the bus from Camp Bechard that afternoon. Israel went over to the house and knocked at the door. But he had no luck here either. The landlady gave him a hard look of distrust and a flat "No, monsieur. I just rented the last one. Goodnight." With growing despair of finding a place, he set out to cover the town, searching the dark for a "Chambre à louer" card in a window; while his heart ached that these people resented him so, these very people he thought so highly of.

The reason, as a matter of truth, was simply that Israel looked too sober. The landladies usually kept a few rooms vacant until after Lambert's was closed; at that late hour some drunken loggers were bound to come reeling in, which often meant double rent and even a little extra out of the drunk's pockets when the lights were out and the snoring loud enough. But Israel, unaware of this, could only surmise that the landladies mistrusted him because of his looks. This unpleasant suspicion was later strengthened when he met with the same treatment at the door of a private home near the river. There was a "Chambre à louer" card pinned to the doorframe; yet the woman refused to let him in.

There now seemed to be nothing left to do but go to

Lambert's and kill a few hours. There, at least, the atmosphere was more friendly. But just as he stepped inside, one of the waiters told him that the tavern was closing. Israel asked where would be a safe place to sleep.

"In jail," said the waiter, adding that it was not so bad as it sounded. He might even find himself with a lot of gay company before the night was over.

At the Police-and-Fire House, he was greeted with the kind of welcome usually given stray loggers in La Buche. He had a choice: to be booked on a charge of vagrancy, or pay four dollars for a mattress. Choosing the latter, he dropped the four dollars where they indicated, into a pool on the card table around which sat Ti-Pit and three police-firemen. Then one of them led him upstairs, where two cells, both empty, stood one at each end of the room. On the floor between the cells were a dozen thin mattresses, several of them occupied by snoring loggers. Israel was directed to take one next to Arthur, who lay asleep with mouth twitching as from pain under the glaring ceiling light. He lay down and tried to sleep.

But he could not keep his eyes shut. The bright light, the loud snoring, the convulsive sleep of Arthur next to him and the voices of the card players downstairs kept him awake. Besides he was feeling wretched. It was not only that he bitterly regretted having followed Red Mallet to the brothel. Almost everything he had experienced since he had arrived in La Buche contradicted his beliefs about these people. He had thought them simple, close to nature, essentially fine and even noble. But what was the truth? He had to admit they were just as mean and corrupt as the people in the big cities.

Suddenly Arthur sat up on his mattress, uttering incoherent threats and pleadings, his hands stretched before him, now in a gesture of begging, now in motions of strangling some imaginary person rising out of the floor, while there flashed in

201

his bloodshot eyes a gleam of murderous violence. Then just as suddenly he slumped back into sleep, moaning: "You can't do that to me. Oh, no! You won't get away with this. You can't treat people that way. Oh, no!"

Israel moved away to the far edge of his own mattress. He heard a car driving fast up the Rue des Erables. He wished that he were in it now, on his way to Montreal and the travel agent for his ticket to Palestine.

*   *   *

When Mademoiselle Serval came back to her apartment from the Seminary auditorium, she was alarmed to find Maurice and his henchman, Altar Boy, in the living room.

"You must have left in a hurry," said Maurice. "Your door was not even locked."

Too frightened to speak, she stood there a moment gripping her handbag, biting her lips. Then in sudden panic she dashed to the door.

But not fast enough. Altar Boy moved swiftly to block her escape. "Take it easy, Skinny. The boss wants to talk to you."

"Let me go. Let me out of here," she cried, hitting him on the chest.

He gave her a push that sent her reeling into the living room and tumbling on the couch. This act of violence seemed to shock her out of her panic. She looked up at Maurice, who stood staring at her across the coffee table. Then she saw Altar Boy at the door, his face was cut and swollen and crisscrossed with strips of blood-stained adhesive tape. Once again her eyes fell to rolling wildly in their orbits.

In a calm voice, Maurice asked: "Why did you do it, Skinny?"

She stared at him in terror.

"I had promised to take good care of you," he went on,

referring to a cash pay-off for the help she had given him in setting up his operation.

Actually, she had done little beyond leading him to the right people. This was precisely what he had expected from her when he first maneuvered himself into her quiet, lonely life, a few months back. At that time, he had decided on La Buche as his next venture; but he knew nobody here and nobody knew him, so he needed as a starting point a person who could give him information on people he would have to deal with. In places like La Buche the person best equipped to render this service is usually the telephone operator. Maurice had moved with all the skill and experience of years of shady activities in Montreal. Mademoiselle Serval, after a few secret week ends in the city where he made her feel wonderfully young and pretty again, became his partner.

She sent him to Fulgence the beadle, whose side line it was to rent the Bureau sisters' house. A gambling spot? No, he could see nothing very wrong with the idea, so long as he could come in for a cut of the business. And later, when it developed that the gambling house also offered sex for sale, he was easily persuaded, with the inducement of guaranteed free privileges to his heart's content, that there was indeed much more to the institution of brotheling than usually meets the eye of prudish backward minds. By this time, Mademoiselle Serval's secret week ends to the city had ended, and this made her acutely sensitive to the brothel part of Maurice's operation.

She protested, claiming it had not been discussed in the original plans, she would not have cooperated if she had known. Maurice had made it clear that her work was finished, the pay would come later when business could afford it. Oh, yes? Well, they would hear from her again. She would talk, spill out the truth! She was too smart to do a thing like that, Maurice told her; and anyway, who would be so dumb as to believe she had nothing to do with it, after people had seen him come up to her flat? She had better consider that. If she was as smart as he knew she was, she would keep her mouth shut!

"I guess you aren't so smart as I thought you were," Maurice said now. "Look at the mess you've put yourself in. If you had kept your big trap shut, everything would have been all right, for you, and for us. What in the hell could have made you do a thing like that, I'll never know."

"Getting late, boss," said Altar Boy.

Finally she spoke up: "I had to do it. I just had to."

"Why?"

To save her own skin. It was as simple as that. Too many people knew about his visits here. And there was charivari in the air. She had to clear herself. Anyway, she owed him nothing, did she? He had taken her for a good long ride. He had used her all he could.

Altar Boy interrupted her: "What did I tell you, boss. There's more spite than meat in that skinny bitch."

"Keep quiet."

"After all I did for you," she went on, "you brush me off like an old rag and expect me to take the rap. Well, you can do what you want. I'm not going to let this town raise a charivari against me because of you. I have to protect myself."

Maurice said: "We're going to have to take you with us."

"Where?"

"Out in the country, so you don't arouse the women more than they are already."

Quite pale now, and trembling, she looked at him imploringly, as if to remind him of the few good nights they had shared together. She pleaded with nervous eyes, tried to smile in impotent but desperate seductiveness: "Oh, Maurice, please."

204

He said to Altar Boy: "I'll get the car. Don't do anything foolish."

"O.K. boss."

Then, as Maurice walked out, Altar Boy advanced toward her. She stepped back in fear, as far back as the perfumed pink curtains of her window. He grabbed her, with one hand on her mouth to silence her, and with the other around her waist to lift her, and this way he carried her out of the flat, and closed the door after putting out the light.

Frantic, she struggled to breathe, as Altar Boy carried her down the steps. She felt that she was going to faint. Then in a flash she knew this was death, the end, and her body grew stiff with apprehension. Down on the path, Altar Boy hid himself and his charge by the hawthornes. A flower tickled her cheeks. He jerked her head to the other side, for the car was coming to the curb and he needed to change his grip in order to carry her more easily. At that moment she caught sight of the older Bureau sister staring out the window at her with an expression of idiotic delight. She made a last desperate move for air, for life. But the grip tightened round her body, and on her mouth. The door of the car was flung open. She tried to scream. Darkness hit suddenly with a sharp cutting pain at the back of her head. Then numbness and void.

Seconds later, the automobile, which Maurice had borrowed from Lambert, turned sharply into the Rue des Erables, narrowly missing Doctor Gendron, who was crossing the street on his way to the De Blois' home where he hoped that this time, his third call, he would be able to deliver the mother with her baby.

*　　*　　*

Lise had just entered her room, when the landlady rapped on the door, ordering angrily: "Open up."

She was a plump widow with a silver-birch complexion and a hard look. Her drunken husband had drowned on the drive—good riddance—leaving enough insurance money to buy this house from the Bureau sisters. She charged according to the time of the year, the day of the week, the circumstances of the roomers. Five percent of her total income went into a box marked A HOME FOR THE VIRGINS OF MARY; this was for continued good luck, she would emphasize to a handful of admirers on the steps of the church after Sunday High Mass, when she had dropped the weekly installment in full view of an impressed parish. And it was no small contribution, her half-dozen rooms were always rented, sometimes by the hour on market days, and she derived an additional income from not wearing panties in September and April when the town was full of transient hot-blooded jacks. The waiters at Lambert's had been heard to recommend that the customer insist on her holding the tips of his ears very tight when he was on top of her, this being the only way to make sure she did not clean his pockets at the critical instant of sweet rapture. Gossips insisted that Bernard Toupin had been able to save enough for a new bus only after she granted him a special low rent, almost nothing, they said, in return for an occasional tumble during the lean winter months. From Lise she had been getting three times the highest rent ever paid for her room. But tonight's meeting of Les Dames de la Grâce had convinced her that, good though the money was, it still was not worth the risk of having her property be the target of a charivari. There was now a price on the heads of those rosary-bead factory girls and the neighbors knew that one of them lived here. It would be all over town by tomorrow noon. To evict the whore would not be easy, however. The rent was paid one week in advance, the girl was quiet and didn't bother anybody; it was late in the night. Since there was no excuse,

206

then, the landlady sensed that she could only press her order with a show of genuine indignation.

"You are leaving this house of mine tonight, right away," she announced, as soon as Lise opened the door.

Still shaken from Altar Boy's attack, Lise could only stare with an open mouth.

"I'm giving you five minutes."

"But you can't," Lise protested.

"There's no but. You heard me. Now pack up your things and get out."

Lise's large brown eyes suddenly flashed a fierce look of rebellion. She had gone through enough troubles for one night. It wasn't this wicked bundle of fat who was going to push her around at this hour. In a firm voice she said: "I will leave tomorrow. Good night." Then she slammed the door at the landlady's nose.

"Tomorrow, hey! Wait a minute. Open that door, you filthy slut. This is a respectable house. Open up, I said."

But Lise remained silent inside her room.

"Ah! So you think you're pretty smart and can lock yourself up in there! But wait. You've fooled me long enough, you cheap skinny whore. This is a respectable house, I'll have you know. I'm going to get you out of here, and quick. Where's my key?"

Panting in wrathful indignation, and swearing to uphold the respectability of her house, the landlady scuttled down the stairs in a flurry of rustling skirts.

The noise had aroused the roomers from sleep. Angry voices were heard from the rooms up and down the hall.

"Shut up."

"Don't throw her out."

"Go back to bed."

"Send her in here. I'll make room for her."

207

"Quiet."

Light appeared at the bottom of the doors. A sleepy jack, naked from the waist down, came out of his room for a peek down the staircase. Bernard, too, stepped out in the hall. He had not had a moment's peace since Israel's news about La Pitoune, for whom he now hungered with a passion that was not without hatred. As soon as the landlady returned upstairs, he was quick to offer his services. "Can I be of any help?"

"Stick around," the landlady told him. Then she thrust the key into the hole. A quick twist released the lock. She burst inside, followed by Bernard.

Lise was standing arms akimbo against the foot of the bed, her long black hair streaming wildly down her pale face.

"Well, are you getting out?" asked the landlady.

Lise stood firm, determined to defend herself.

The landlady screamed: "Or am I going to drag you out by the short hairs?"

"Please," Bernard intervened.

She turned upon him a look of dismay. "Why, Bernard, you, of all people! Do you mean to stick up for this whore, against me?"

"Of course not," he assured her. This was not what he meant. He only wanted to see if this affair could not be settled in a nice, friendly way, to the satisfaction of everyone, naturally. It was too late. Everybody wanted to get back to sleep.

"That's right," a man shouted from the next room. "Shut up and go back to bed."

"Quiet, goddamn it!"

These protests from the roomers fanned the landlady's wrath. Now this filthy slut was going to make her lose them all. Stepping up to her with one arm poised to strike, she shouted at the top of her voice: "Get out. OUT. OUT!"

Bernard pulled her back and held her still a moment. "Now,

208

now. Let's not fly at each other's throat," he said. That was not the way out. Of course he understood, and he didn't blame the landlady a bit. She ought to have been told what this girl did for a living. True enough. And now that she had found out, she was in her right, nobody said she didn't have a right to keep her house respectable. No doubt about that. But still, that was no reason to throw the girl out in the middle of the night. Besides, it was chilly outside. Now, if the landlady would only calm down a little, maybe they could find a solution to all this. Would she be satisfied, for instance, if the girl's trunk were carried out of the house tonight, as a guarantee that she would leave first thing in the morning? "I'll gladly take it outside myself, right now."

The landlady screwed up her eyes in hard pondering of this compromise.

"All right," Lise put in. "I will pack up, now, if that's what you want. But I'm coming back for the night."

"Sounds reasonable enough," Bernard commented.

Finally, after a long silence to emphasize her reluctance, the landlady nodded agreement with a sour curl of her lips. But her parting words made it plain that she would keep the advance-rent money, because of the risk in letting this "filthy whore stay in my house one more minute." Then she went back downstairs. The next minute she had closeted herself in the kitchen to telephone Lambert's tavern that she would have a vacant room starting tomorrow.

On the sidewalk, about fifteen minutes later, Bernard asked Lise if she knew where to put the trunk for the night, that is, until she could find herself another room.

"Could we take it to the depot?" she said. "I would check it in the morning."

"How about where you work?"

"I quit. And I'm leaving town tomorrow."

"Ah! Where to?"

"I don't know yet."

He tied the trunk between the opened front doors of the bus. Lise sat down behind the driver's seat. They would go around by the long way, he announced, to avoid bumpy roads where the trunk might be shaken loose and fall off.

The road stretched narrow and dark between sidewalks that were spotted with discs of light from porcelain-shaded bulbs overhead. Faint yellow lights could be seen at the windows of most houses on both sides of the road; they showed women sewing or mending, a mother saying her beads with a circle of children at her feet. About halfway toward the haymarket, Lise asked Bernard to slow down a little. She could see Claude's window above the layer of roofs on the right. His light was on. Was he reading their poems? Her thoughts embraced him in a surge of tenderness that swept away the wretchedness of being thrown out on the street. She was back in his arms and every fiber of her body quivered from the reliving of their embrace.

"What are you looking at, out there?" Bernard asked abruptly.

"Oh, nothing."

Moving restlessly on his seat he tried to catch her eye in the rear-view mirror, but she continued to gaze dreamily into the night. The sky was clear, full of stars, and the pattern of the treetops footing the horizon was a vast ribbon of torn lace. The droning sound of the engine made her feel sleepy, but at the same time she was aware of a growing apprehension. There was something about Bernard's silence, the way he was looking at her in the mirror, that frightened her. "Where are we now?" she asked.

"Getting there," he replied.

The window was veiled with dew. She cleared a spot with the palm of her hand. "The ravine!" she exclaimed.

"Don't worry," he said. "It's all right." He seemed cross. With her? With himself? "I'm sorry I cause you so much trouble," she said. "You must be tired, after all the driving you did today."

"That's all right."

It then occurred to her that perhaps he was cross because she had not yet paid him for the book of poems. She hastened to offer him a five-dollar bill, with apologies for not having done so earlier.

"Keep it."

She insisted, asked how much he wanted for this ride. He pushed aside the money. Then with exaggerated movements he adjusted his trousers that were beginning to feel tight.

Lise sat back. His attitude puzzled her. He had always been kind to her. They had often talked and joked on the stair landing when they chanced to meet on their way in or out of the house. Not once had he tried to take advantage of her. He, and that fellow Paul who had rescued her from Altar Boy, were the only two men in this town to be kind to her and show her some respect although they knew what she did for a living. Then why this sudden change? she wondered, more disturbed by it than by the landlady's insults.

The next moment, as she caught sight of his eyes in the rear-view mirror, she felt that she was wrong. He was smiling at her. She smiled back, moved to friendliness by the guilt of her lack of faith in him. She could not help saying: "You are a good man, Bernard."

"That's what they all say."

"For a second just now I thought you were turning against me, like the landlady."

"You can't blame her, can you. After all, a whore is a whore, and messing around with one of them is dangerous in this town."

A nervous giggle escaped her. As though to reassure herself, she said: "You have quite a sense of humor."

"That's what they all say."

Their eyes met again in the rear-view mirror. No, she wasn't wrong. That wide-eyed stare—how often she had seen it in the eyes of a customer who was going to be rough with her. A shudder of fright shook her whole body. The muscles of her thighs stiffened. She got up, panicky, to go to the door.

Bernard slammed the brakes on. The sudden stop threw her off balance and she reeled back up the aisle, grabbing at the back of the seats for support. Her fingers slipped; she fell on her back, knocking her head on the floor. There was pain, dulled by an instant of darkness. When she opened her eyes again he was standing at her feet.

"Don't."

"Come on."

"Don't, Bernard."

"What is it to you, anyway?"

"Please, don't."

Bernard was on his knees now, trying to force her legs apart. She tore at his hair and kicked out at him, trying to slide away from him on her back. But now he was pressing down on her with all his weight. He grabbed her wrists and twisted her hands off the seat support she was gripping, then stretched her arms at full length above her head. Helpless, she felt that she could struggle no more, she should give in, it would hurt less, when the image of Claude flashed back in her mind. Tears filled her eyes. She felt the veins of Bernard's neck swelling against her mouth, and suddenly, in a burst of savage resentment, she bit him. With a scream of pain, he released

212

her and in that moment she scrambled to her feet and ran to the back of the bus. But there was no way of escape. Enraged, Bernard came after her, chasing her from seat to seat and pulling her down again and again, only to fail each time as she fought and scratched and bit for her life, while his panting curses and her agonized cries mingled with the droning of the engine and the hollow knock of the logs in the chute. He knew it was bad luck for him to be doing this in his new bus. He would go to confession in the morning. Hell! This was just one more mortal sin, and not so serious; she was only a whore.

Now they were in the front of the bus again and he was finally mastering her on the rubber-matted floor. Her long black hair mopped the dirt at the foot of the trunk, her hands groped desperately to tear at him, until in a last desperate jerk of revulsion she pulled free of him enough to bring her knee up against his crotch, with all the last frenzied strength she could muster. Bernard staggered up, then dropped on the driver's seat with a groan.

The next second she had climbed on top of the trunk. There was just enough space to get through. She jumped down, landing on the side of the road. Pulling down her skirt, she looked around for a place to hide. A few hundred feet ahead was the depot. Behind her started the path that led to the ravine beyond the footbridge. The few houses across the road showed no sign of life. She started toward the depot.

But hardly had she gone a few feet when she stopped, and turned, at the sound of her trunk landing with a crash on the road. Bernard stood on the steps. "There's a dolly out there on the platform," he shouted. "Better not come back to the house tonight. Bloody whore!" And he slammed the doors shut.

As the sound of the engine receded in the night, Lise

walked on to the depot. She could feel the coolness of the breeze on her cheeks still wet with tears. It was almost like an unexpected act of kindness from a stranger's hands. Her whole body responded with a sobbing fit of wretchedness. Not since her orphanage days had she wept so freely. Yet, there was a measure of gladness in her heart, and mingled with her sobs was the name of Claude uttered in tones of yearning tenderness. She dried her tears and shook her head in the affirmative, as though Claude was there before her and she was reassuring him that yes, she would be brave, she had fought for him and for her, for them, for tomorrow, and the day after tomorrow.

When she had wheeled the dolly with her trunk onto the platform of the depot, it occurred to Lise that she ought to pencil a note: hold until tomorrow, or something of the sort. She was about to do this, when suddenly a sharp beam of light startled her. She looked up, and stared, terrified, into the headlights of a car.

The lights went out immediately. Lise ran off the platform, as Maurice and Altar Boy stepped down from the car. She ran all the way to the corner of the Rue des Pins and the Rue des Erables, sure that they were running after her. She turned into the alley near Claude's home, where she stopped for a backward look. The two men were talking animatedly on the platform. Relieved, she started running again, up the alley. The echo of her steps told her that everything was all right now, she was not being followed. Yet she went on running all the way to the end of the alley, where the brothel appeared suddenly on her right.

She turned left, ran on to the first corner. Then she turned right and did not slow down until two blocks up. She was gasping for breath; a fog of dizziness blurred everything in sight. When she was able to breathe more easily, she saw that

214

she was standing only a short distance from Bernard's bus parked in front of the rooming house. She set out in the direction of the ravine, which she could see now, beyond the Haymarket. A warped sidewalk plank made her trip. She fell to her knees, but quickly picked herself up and hastened on.

A short distance further, there suddenly loomed before her the black figure of a man. He was walking in her direction. It was a priest.

It was indeed Monsieur le Curé, who had been striding the steam of anger out of his system for the last hour. He had covered the town several times since leaving Maurice and Altar Boy. Their refusal to cooperate had thrown him into indignation. He was now nearing that stage where his fits of rage usually became fits of depression and melancholy. At the sight of Lise, whom he recognized instantly as one of Maurice's girls, he opened wide his arms. "Where are you going, daughter?"

She threw herself weeping into his embrace, and for a long moment they held each other. He patted her back gently. A heart-rending cry escaped her. "Why are they so cruel?"

His gaze, as distressed as her heart, was filled with sadness as he took in the dark mass of Timberland in the near distance. The man in him, the priest under the robe, could find no word to soothe her grief.

"Oh, why, Father. Why are they so cruel?"

All he could do was to continue patting her gently on the back, very gently, until she grew calm again, and withdrew from his arms. Their eyes met. His look was deep, kind. Hers told him of a wretchedness that tore at his heart, so that he shared it as if it were his own doing. "You need help, daughter."

She shook her head.

215

"It is cold. Have you no place to sleep?"

She shrugged her shoulders.

"The church is locked at this hour. But we could make room for you at the presbytery."

Again she shook her head.

Then he said: "There is a small corner sheltered from the wind on the right hand side of the last building, there, at the Haymarket. You will find some straw on the floor. Go there now, daughter. And cover yourself up with this." He unbuttoned his soutane and gave it to her.

Without another word, they parted. He took the road back to the presbytery. She walked slowly to the Haymarket.

*   *   *

Paul, still standing at his window, kept repeating to himself: "Tomorrow I must speak with the doctor. I've got to do something for the boy. Get him out of here, away from Mother . . . and death," he muttered.

His room had become an echo chamber for Claude's laborious respiration, struggling, it seemed, to keep up with the fast beat of the logs in the chute. He heard a car driving away from the depot. Scattered strains of drunken melancholy singing lingered down a distant road. He went to bed, closed his eyes and tried to sleep.

Suddenly the night's stillness was pierced by a woman's shrieks. They came from the older of the Bureau sisters. She had not ceased crying and whimpering since the call to charivari had been sounded, and the memory of her seeing Mademoiselle Serval being carried off by Altar Boy, precipitated the attack. She had flung open the windows of her bedroom and screamed: "Open the gates, Saint Peter. Open the gates." Her sister hurried to pull her away and close the window. Now the poor creature lay on her bed, shaken with trembling, and could

216

not stop repeating like a maniac's litany: "The Good Lord is mad at us. Open the gates, Saint Peter. Don't let the Good Lord stay mad at us. Open the gates. The Good Lord is mad at us, mad at us, mad at us . . ."

eleven

Madame Gauthier wrenched herself
out of sleep in a fit of anguish. She was perspiring heavily, and
the garb of penitence clung coarse-wet to her skin. Fragments
of an oppressive dream lingered in her mind. She sat up,
searching the morning of her room with eyes frightened and
wild.

A brilliant April sunrise was drying the windowpanes of dew.
It shot through the muslin curtains full beams of brightness
that slanted across her vision and poured shimmering pools
of light on the floor, on the bed.

So she was in bed, not on the floor! She recalled dragging
herself sleepily onto the bed after hours of lying on the hard

wood. And now her drowsy brain burst to wakefulness with the sudden return of her nightmare. "No," she uttered in panic, "No, no!" Her hands rose to shield her eyes. Paul was strangling her son Claude. The scene, so terrifying in its raw brutality, made her whole body shudder. The more she fought to dispel the vision, the more awesome and vivid it became; she could almost feel Paul's murderous hands tightening around her own throat. She fell back on the pillows, gasping for breath while her shrieks of agony resounded all over the house.

They soon woke Paul out of a light sleep already interrupted many times during the night by the pains in his face. He jumped out of bed and quickly went to his brother's room, his heart pounding from the sudden dread lest Claude might have taken a turn for the worse.

But no! Thank goodness! The boy was still fighting it out. In the clear light of morning Paul could see him on his back, sleeping as though in unconscious refusal to be aroused by his mother's hysterics. The blankets had slipped down below the chest, exposing the bloodstained nightshirt. Paul started to pull the blankets back up to the boy's chin, then changed his mind, lest the weight of them make his breathing even more difficult. Gently, he covered the bloodstains with the top sheet. Then he hurried across the hall and into his mother's room without knocking.

"What's the matter?" he said, less concerned than annoyed.

The question silenced her abruptly. She raised herself on her elbows and turned upon him a look full of pained surprise. He had never seen her so wretched. Her beautiful white hair streamed wild across her face; some of it stuck to her chin where tears had accumulated in the deeper wrinkles, and she was biting a long strand like a little girl weeping angrily. She looked pale and shrinking beneath the garb of penitence that

220

was a great shapeless mass of brown cloth bristling in the hard sunlight. From the bottom of it dangled, over the edge of the bed, two white feet showing streaks of dried blood at the ankles. "What's the matter?" Paul asked again, but less harshly this time.

She let out a long wailing sound, and threw herself face-down upon the pillows. Her head sank into a patch of grey where tears had stained the cloth. She rocked her cheeks in it with an almost sensual intensity.

"For heaven's sake, mother, get hold of yourself."

"No, no," she wailed. Her cross was too heavy. She couldn't bear it anymore. Wasn't it enough to have given up her little Claude? Why must the Good Lord go on torturing her this way? To haunt her sleep with such atrocious dreams! But there was a limit to what a mother's heart could endure. Could He not see that? He, in His great wisdom and knowledge of all secrets in His children's hearts, could He not see that she had suffered enough? Her heart was full to the brim, like the Lord's cup in the Garden of Gethsemane. "Pity, O Lord, pity; just a little pity!"

"Everything is going to be all right," Paul said, coming over to the foot of the bed.

She protested with a fresh outburst, blamed him for her misery. If he had not brought a woman here last night she would not be having such a nightmare. God was punishing her on account of him. His soul was black with sin and he still refused to humble himself—O, the torments of a mother when she had a sinner for a son!

He reached over to touch her.

"Don't," she screamed, drawing away from him.

"I'm going to talk with Doctor Gendron, see what can be done for the boy."

She calmed down at once. Then quickly she got up, shaking

221

the hair from her face and drying the tears with the back of her hands.

"There might still be a chance," Paul explained.

She faced him across the bed. "You'll do nothing of the kind."

"But we must try all we can."

"Are you accusing your mother of not doing her duty?"

"Of course not."

"Then you let *me* be the judge of what is good for Claude," she snapped, with sudden composure. She opened the door of her closet near the window, adding: "Claude's life is in the hands of the Almighty. If you really mean to do something for him, start by going to confession, and pray that God might give you back your faith. Then you could offer prayers for your brother's soul." A moment's silence followed, while she brought out her dark dress with the mandarin collar and placed it neatly at the foot of her bed. Then she said: "Father Boulanger will be here shortly. Shall I say that you asked to see him?"

"No," he said.

"Leave your mother's room. I must dress to receive the Lord."

Paul walked out, and went downstairs, into the kitchen, where he sat down with a sigh. "By Christ, she's going mad," he muttered: "really mad!" To refuse a doctor at a time like this was a thing no mother in her sane mind would ever do.

But what he termed madness, seemed to his mother a stroke of divine lucidity. Adjusting her dress in the mirror, she congratulated herself on having once again upheld God's Will against the efforts of impious medicine to thwart it. She had been vigilant, had seen clearly into the scheming mind of her sin-ridden Paul.

The abrupt transition from screams of agony to perfect calm

seemed to Paul to show an advanced state of insanity—why, the asylum in Quebec was full of people who went from one extreme mood to another, just like that.

She had shed tears, but in a moment of weakness, she now confessed to God. And this was followed by a long prayer of gratitude, for He had deigned to rescue her from rebellion.

Claude's breathing, which could be heard all over the house, led Paul to exclaim suddenly: "And what about the boy?" He began pacing up and down the length of the kitchen, tormented by the urgency he felt to help Claude, and the certainty of his mother's refusal.

Those long gasping breaths, she, too, could hear them, even from inside the linen closet where she had gone to fetch a pair of clean sheets for Claude's bed. And she listened to them intently, as if she were tracing with her eyes on the wall the graphic pattern of ascending whistling sounds, followed by descending sighs that sank into a long moaning; secretly, she compared today's rhythm with yesterday's, and told herself, as though to quiet down a latent wish: no, there was no sign of any coma yet.

Paul began to prepare his breakfast, toast and coffee, which he felt no appetite for, and which he did not think he could eat anyway because of the cuts and the swelling inside his mouth. But he must do something. The death-laden atmosphere of the house was insufferable. He looked at the clock; it was barely seven. It was at least another hour before he could knock at Doctor Gendron's door.

"Time to wake up!" Madame Gauthier announced with surprising gentleness, as she entered her son's room. "Father Boulanger will be here any minute." She went to the window and drew the curtains aside to let in a bit of sunlight, then came back to the bed, where she spoke to Claude in that strained whisper of old folks who, of a Sunday afternoon by

223

the graveside, commune with the dead. "Can you hear me, my little one?"

A faint stir traveled down the length of the sheet that lay molding his emaciated body as faithfully as would a shroud. His eyelids fluttered, but on the point of awakening, he sighed back into sleep.

"Claude, wake up now," she whispered. But he did not move. Might this indeed be the final coma? She looked closely.

The few strings of life left in him seemed to have recoiled overnight into his chest and throat, where they were now being stretched to the snapping point. With each breath, his chest rose and swelled as if to burst and his ribs quivered from the strain. There would come then a moment of stillness, a suspension of being, it seemed, deepened by the sound of cartilage twisting in the back of his mouth. And suddenly the air would come out of his body in a great gush, followed by a slow deflation, as his chest sank back under the sheet. Another moment of stillness. It seemed an eternity before his chest would rise again. Yet his face was calm. The morning light falling on his face gave his features an air of eternal repose sensed in the profiles of ancient saints immortalized in bas-reliefs. Only his mouth seemed alive, though the lips were dry, and gray, suggesting a desperate, insatiate thirst. Now and then a wrinkling furrow of strain would draw his eyebrows together until they nearly touched above the bridge of his nose. This was the only sign of pain that she could see.

How simple it would be if he could just pass on, now, without awakening! she thought. He had suffered long enough. His place in paradise was well earned. There was now so little life left in him. He was ready and waiting for the Good Lord. Maybe his soul had already risen to heaven.

She dropped to her knees and prayed God to take him away now. She was resigned. She wanted it, demanded it.

224

No sooner had she expressed this desire, however, than she was seized with a feeling of remorse. What right had she to tell God to take her son now? Why, this was rebellion! Once again she was weakening under the burden of her cross. O, Lord, would she be able to bear it to the end? Then as though in answer to this cry of despair, Father Boulanger's kind words of encouragement rang in her ears. She must be brave. The mother of a saint must show herself worthy of her divine calling. As her sacrifice was great, so her courage must reach the sublime.

She rose to her feet, and bent over her son. The warm voice of Father Boulanger was all she could hear. "Think of the Virgin Mary at the foot of the cross. It is not for her son, but for the son of God, that she is weeping!" A great wave of tender pity swelled her mother's heart. Her eyes filled with tears, blurring her vision of Claude. She was weeping for her little saint now. Never before had she known a sense of worthiness so great. Her rapturous transport was such that in the dread of seeing it shattered she could only extend onto Claude's shoulder a hand trembling violently—so violently, in fact, that the sick boy woke up immediately.

"Paul, Paul, where is Paul?" he cried, and started to sit up.

Gently, yet forcefully, she held him down on his back. "Easy, my little one."

"What time is it?"

"Time for communion."

"Is it late?"

"Yes."

"But Paul," he began, but could not go on. His lungs failed him; he struggled for air.

She looked searchingly into his face.

He lay back, exhausted, and fell to gazing at the window, at the closet, at the bottom of the door. Then he seemed to wake up fully. He asked for his brother again. And again what time it was.

She kept looking at him as if she had never seen him before. What was the meaning of all this? It was so unlike him to ask repeatedly what time it was when he awoke, and to insist on seeing his brother before having received Holy Communion.

He must be delirious, she thought. In a trembling voice she asked: "How do you feel?"

"All right," he replied. "But I would feel much better if Paul were here, and I could get up."

"This is it," she thought. The beginning of the end. He couldn't even feel his pains. A sure sign of delirium. There was no time to waste. "Come," she said; "let me change your bed. Father Boulanger is on his way."

He lifted himself onto the pillows. The sheet slipped down. She smothered a cry at the sight of the bloodstains.

"Don't worry," said Claude. "It is not so bad as it looks."

She thought: "The poor thing is not rational. That hemorrhage is what did it." And she smiled at him a little, with that air of awkward solicitude and ill-disguised suspicion that the soft-hearted bestow upon the insane. "You stay right where you are. I'll get you a clean nightshirt."

"Wake up Paul at the same time," he said.

In her room, Madame Gauthier became very busy. She pulled out of a chest of drawers, where it was wrapped in silk paper, his best nightshirt, the one his fellow seminarians had given him at Christmas. Then she gathered odd pieces of white linen to dress his bedside table as an altar. She replaced the candles in the candlesticks with new longer ones, white as a lily, the flower of chastity. Her room was full of vibrant sunlight. Oh, it would be a beautiful day, after all! She felt like crying, so happy did she feel: to think of all that joy and glory that awaited him in paradise!

But a moment later, on entering Claude's bedroom, she was seized with panic at the sight of him. He was standing stark naked in front of the closet, leaning with one hand against the door while with the other he showed her a pair of old socks. And on his face was a strained look of indignation. "What have you done with all my clothes?" he demanded to know.

She could barely make it to the bedside table to unload the linen and the candlesticks. "I . . . I took them to the cleaners," she stammered.

He knew this was a lie. His clothes had gone the way of his portrait: to Father Boulanger. She had emptied his closet while he was asleep. Now he needed his boots and breeches and a shirt, in order to leave with Paul and Lise. "I won't take Communion unless you get my clothes back," he said.

She sat on the edge of the bed, crossing herself.

"You want me to die with nothing on? That wouldn't be pretty, would it? Not very becoming for a saint!"

She crossed herself again, and again. Never had such words come out of his saintly lips. She could not believe her ears. This was not her little Claude standing there carrying on like this; his soul must have risen to heaven, and the devil was now entering his body. She had heard of saints being possessed of evil spirits just before dying. Was this the kind of delirium the Good Lord had reserved for her son?

"You think I have gone out of my mind," he panted, his voice hoarse with rage. "But you are mistaken. I know what I am doing. I need my clothes. And you will get them for me as soon as Father Boulanger comes in." He wanted to say more, but lacked the breath. His hands began to beat the air, as if a cloud of darkness had just lowered before his eyes. He took one step toward the bed. A mumbling sound came out of him. He dropped to his knees, and holding his chest as if to crush it he folded at the waist and rolled over at her feet, unconscious.

227

Madame Gauthier could only stare at her son with pain and horror. When she tried to help him back to his feet her hands froze as if she were touching the devil himself. All the bones of his body were visible; they seemed to have grown twice their size and length, and his skin was drawn tight, with large patches of grey-purple here and there. In a frenzy of agitation she pulled the blankets off the bed and changed the sheets. Claude's breathing grew louder, but at the same time it became slow and more regular. She thought of calling Paul to help put him to bed. But on second thought she decided against it; there were enough evil spirits in this room already. Finally, with much hesitation, she picked the boy up in her arms. How incredibly light he was. It sent a flood of tender memories through her mind—he weighed no more than when he was a little boy! Carefully she put him down on the bed, where she dressed him in his best nightshirt. Then she dropped to her knees and wept and prayed, burying her face in her hands.

After a while, Claude began to moan. He opened his eyes a little, slowly, as if awakening from a long night of sleep. He felt a heavy stillness around him. There was the sound of his mother weeping. He thought she was downstairs. His body felt numb all over. He heard himself cough. It did not hurt.

She looked up.

The sight of his mother suddenly brought the scene back to his mind, and with it came a sense of helplessness bordering on despair. He had so much wanted to tell her gently and avoid a scene, leave her without bitterness. What had made him burst out like that? And all the strength he had tried to save was now spent. If only she would not weep so! "I am sorry, mother," he said. "I'm so sorry." And he stroked her hair tenderly, wiped her tears with the sheet and then with his hands and asked if she forgave him. Of course, she forgave him, she cried, kissing his hands and helping him to dry her

228

own tears. She gazed fondly at him, then at his hands, those beautiful long white hands that were shaped to present the Host so delicately. She swallowed her sobs and gave a big, full-mouthed kiss on his fingers, mumbling little words of endearment just as when he was her little boy. She even called him "My little Poupou."

So intense an exchange of passionate feelings was more than his condition could cope with. He coughed. It looked like the beginning of another spell. But she quickly helped him out of it by tapping him on the back, until he could breathe again. Then he slumped down on the mattress, thoroughly exhausted.

"Rest, now," she said. "Don't be sad. Father Boulanger is coming with the Holy Communion. Try to receive the Good Lord with gladness in your heart."

She might have gone on. But he could no longer hear her now. He lay staring glassy-eyed at the ceiling in a state of deathlike torpor. She proceeded to dress up the bedside table as an altar, that everything might be ready when Father Boulanger arrived. She worked fast, moved, as she was, by a rebirth of enthusiasm. There was no doubt about it now: he had made that awful scene in a moment of delirium. This was obvious by the way he had become her little saintly boy again as soon as the fever had left his brain while he lay unconscious on the floor. There would be other scenes of this kind, she reasoned; but so long as between the spells he reverted to his old self, as he was now, so long as the Good Lord granted these moments of respite, she would be able to battle the evil spirits that entered his body when his soul sank into stupor. "Oh, thank you, Good Lord."

Thus regaining her composure, and lucidity, Madame Gauthier picked up the old sheets and the soiled nightshirt, rolled them into a bundle, and left the room.

On her way downstairs she felt something hard in the bundle under her arms. But a knock at the door prevented her from satisfying her curiosity on the spot. Paul walked out of the kitchen toward the front door. She called him back, afraid he might insult the venerable old priest. Without taking time to dispose of the soiled linen she hastened to the door and opened it.

A pale youth dressed in a surplice and carrying a lantern walked in. He was followed by Father Boulanger, also dressed in a surplice, and wearing a purple stole; he carried the pyx high before him, and his white head was lowered in silent communion with the Eucharist. Madame Gauthier dropped to her knees and shifted the bundle of linen out of the way. The object she had felt before dropped on the floor—a book! Father Boulanger was the first to see it. Then, as Madame Gauthier quickly reached down and picked it up, he read the title. Madame Gauthier uttered a little cry of horror when she saw what the book was. Paul was watching the scene from the kitchen door. The priest cast a meaningful glance toward him, designed to let the mother know clearly what sort of sinner this other son of hers was. Then, as though to soften the blow, he sighed mournfully: "You see, that's the kind of corruption going on in our logging camps nowadays. And no wonder, with Monsieur le Curé visiting the camps only twice a month."

Madame Gauthier nodded respectfully and hastened to throw the book down on a nearby chair.

Then the venerable old Jesuit asked Madame Gauthier how "Our Little Saint" was doing this morning.

"Very poorly," replied the mother.

"Ah!"

"He just made an awful scene."

"Like yesterday?" inquired the priest, his head tilted toward her like a doctor listening for symptoms.

"Oh, worse, Father, much worse," she said. And she went on to tell him what had happened. Two or three times he nodded knowingly. Then at the end of her report he lifted his finger: enough, his diagnosis was made. He cleared his throat, indicating that he was now ready to go up there and see for himself, then he motioned the pale youth up ahead to Claude's room.

As soon as they had reached the second floor, Madame Gauthier stood up.

"Flowers of Evil!"

Now they flashed back in her mind, those flaming-red letters. She had a vision of naked women with fire-red skin lying in poses of sin under Claude's bed. And the devil himself was there, too, poking the mattress with his three-pronged spear. Naked women pulled at his sheets and blankets and extended long lecherous arms around the sides of the bed to tease him down to their evil pleasures.

"How dare you!" she turned to Paul. "How dare you!"

What the hell is wrong now? thought Paul. What kind of crazy idea did that old monkey put in her head? He walked up to her.

Pointing a finger at the book she cried: "You put that evil thing under your brother's mattress?"

He shrugged his shoulders.

"Did you?"

"Maybe."

"Confess that you did."

"Yes, I did."

"To tempt your poor sick brother."

"Yes, mother," he repeated, realizing that to admit the crime would lead to less disastrous a scene than to plead innocent. He reached for the book. At least he would have a glimpse at what kind of book it was.

"Don't," she cried, standing firm between him and the chair.

At that moment their attention was distracted by rapid footsteps down the stairs. It was the surpliced youth, even paler now than a moment ago. He mumbled something about a most important errand, and hurried out of the house.

And now came Father Boulanger, looking very grave. "You were right, my dear Madame," he announced. "It *is* delirium, the very thing we discussed yesterday. So we will try not to contradict him. Now he wants his clothes. He ought to have them."

"If you say so, Father."

"It will make things easier for him and for all of us."

Paul, who could bear no more of this, abruptly headed for the door.

"I say, young man," Father Boulanger called him back. "There will be a special Mass for our little Claude this morning. What a great day of glory and joy, for all of us, if you took advantage of this occasion and made a public return to the faith of your fathers!"

"Listen, both of you," Paul snapped, "don't burn the bark before you fell the tree. The boy isn't dead yet." Then he stalked out of the house.

Madame Gauthier nearly fainted in the arms of her confessor.

But he was quick to comfort her. "Be brave, Madame," he said. "For every sinner on earth, there is in heaven a saint praying for his conversion. Have faith. Your Paul will return to us someday. His brother will see to that, Up There."

*   *   *

At this same hour, the presbytery was being turned into a tabernacle of terror. Monsieur le Curé was indeed having one

232

of his fits. He refused breakfast, drank three quarts of ale before seven o'clock, ordered everybody out of his sight and threatened to send his maid to the asylum, his beadle to jail, his vicar back to the bishop. And he would do it, he swore, by green horse he would; let anyone open his mouth and they would soon find out how far they could ride on his good nature. The whole building resounded with his thunderous wrath. The floor boards in his office crackled as he paced up and down, puffing at every step, his soutane unbuttoned. He drove his hands deep inside the pockets of his baggy trousers and he fanned his sides with his elbows. Each time he turned to retrace his steps the soutane would rise gently floating around his enormous body as if he were executing a pirouette. Now and again he stopped abruptly in the center of the room, or at the window, then shaking a fist toward the Seminary above the roofs of the town he swore at the top of his voice: "O, my Jesuit!"

It was one of his "bad moments," the maid Alice commented in tearful resignation. And she hurriedly carried the bowl of Sarazin-pancake batter outside on the back porch, where she felt less in danger than in the kitchen. Ah, if only he had not been so stubborn and had taken her advice, none of this would be happening now, she wailed, while whipping the batter fast in an unconscious effort to master her fear! Didn't she know, and hadn't she warned him again and again, that it would never do to allow a house of sin in La Buche.

She was right, the beadle agreed readily, meekly. His bad shoulder was lower than ever this morning. He had taken off his shoes and was roaming silently through the house in search of a place to hide, for he was in the grip of mortal fear of being called to explain why he had dragged his Curé into this filthy business in the first place. In a sudden excess of guilt-induced zeal, he rushed out of the presbytery and across the street and into the church where he began to ring the bells, half an hour

233

ahead of time. This brought a fresh outburst from Monsieur le Curé, who flung his window open and shouted across the Place de l'Eglise: "Stop, you idiot, stop that!" Fulgence had no choice but to run into the sacristy for refuge.

Moments later, women and children appeared up the Rue des Erables on their way to church. They had rushed out of their homes at the first peal of the bells, for they remembered yesterday's sermon and did not want to delay the beginning of Mass once again. At the sound of Monsieur le Curé's wrathful imprecations sailing across the Place de l'Eglise, they moved to within hearing distance of his window, where they listened hungrily for details while pretending to talk about the weather.

Israel, rubbing the sleep out of his eyes, came out of the Police-and-Fire House and crossed the square to a listening post near one of the Holy-Water fonts on the porch of the church. He signaled Arthur to join him, but the latter, who was just then stepping out on the sidewalk, saw nobody, heard nothing; he went on toward Lambert's with wide-eyed concentration and unsteady legs.

More women were arriving on the square. Word soon got around that Alice had been kicked out of her kitchen, so a handful of spinsters felt duty bound to sympathize with her on the back porch. They tried to find out what was wrong, but were quickly rebuffed for asking disrespectful questions. They ended up dipping their fingers into the batter, to taste it —she could make such good Sarazin pancakes. Ah, soutane or no soutane, men were all alike, ungrateful bullies! After a while the bells began to ring again. Israel inquired from the beadle what was the cause of it all. "Mind your own business," was Fulgence's reply. La Pitoune and Madame Dupré soon made their appearance in the crowd, both giving themselves an air of importance and scanning the presbytery with a look

234

that meant: "Wait 'till he hears what *we* have to tell *him*."
The Place was nearly full of women and children shuffling
about while rumors of all sorts circulated freely among them.
The beadle kept pulling at the bell rope with one hand, while
with the other he waved the crowd inside the church.

Now Monsieur le Curé appeared at his window. A hush of
expectation swept over the crowd; heads were raised, children
slapped to quiet. There came a moment's silence between two
peals of the bells, and now everbody heard clearly that
unorthodox exhortation for which Monsieur le Curé, to this
day, is notoriously remembered in La Buche: "What do you
think this is? Christmas in Bethlehem? The good God doesn't
sleep outdoors in April. So get in there, all of you. Get inside
that church and pray, PRAY!"

Shocked, women and children promptly shoved one another
into the church, then with downcast eyes they moved along
the aisles and into the benches where they knelt down; while
Fulgence, free to use his two arms, pulled at the ropes with a
zeal and vigor that sent the calls from the belfry ringing far
beyond the Colline Sainte-Marie.

Monsieur le Curé's anger began to subside. The spectacle
of mass obedience to his command was giving him a sense of
power that tempered his obsessive mistrust of Father Boulanger, which had increased to alarming proportions overnight.
As soon as the last women and children had disappeared inside
the church, he closed his window. Then turning his back to the
Seminary he sat at his desk and uncapped a fourth bottle of
ale. Feeling more in control of his faculties, he would try
now once again to see clearly into this grave situation.

The problem that confronted him was not easy to solve.
Maurice had bluntly refused to close the brothel, no authority
in town could be prevailed upon to apply effective pressure.
Les Dames de la Grâce were threatening to raise a charivari,

235

which meant possible bloodshed, headlines in the Quebec and Montreal newspapers, a terrible scandal, in short, precisely what the Bishop of Trois-Rivières and the Cardinal of Montreal could use as a pretext finally to take this parish away from him. Never had his contented existence been put in greater jeopardy. He was convinced that Father Boulanger had a hand in these developments. It was obvious, he reasoned, that the old Jesuit had talked Mademoiselle Serval into spilling out all she knew. There was something about last night's meeting that smelled of Jesuit intrigue: the way the old fox had knelt beside her on the stage, and the way he had spoken to the assembly, giving them a sweet talk about the sick Gauthier boy instead of whipping them to quiet with a stiff sermon. It was as clear as rapids water. Father Boulanger was promoting a charivari. That old foxy Jesuit was still after his soutane.

Reasoning along these lines, however, Monsieur le Curé was getting nowhere near a solution to his problem. He was moving, in fact, in the very direction that had led to his spectacular outburst of wrath. It was as if he sensed that the problem could not be solved, and fearing its calamitous consequences he could bear his anxiety more easily by putting the blame on his old enemy than by squarely facing up to his own failure and trying to find means of warding off the oncoming disaster.

The truth, if it must be faced, was not pleasant. As it happened, Monsieur le Curé had indeed allowed the brothel to operate without interferenc. Such behavior in a country priest might appear incredible. But even more fantastic was the fact that he had acted in absolute good faith. He honestly believed that a house of sin would help cut down the number of illegitimate children. In his scale of values the welfare of his flock rated above the strict letter of the Catechism. Between a few dozen mortal sins, committed, besides, by out-of-town

236

loggers, and a few dozen illegitimate babies to be cared for at the Trois-Rivières foundling home out of the parish funds, the choice was clear; he must decide in favor of that which cost less in the long run. Moreover, the money thus saved indirectly would, in turn, be put at the service of the parish, which needed it badly, if only to organize the factory girls into a society of The Virgins of Mary. He had hoped that such a society, in conjunction with the house of sin, might finally put an end to the goings-on in the ravine. With factory girls at meetings of the Virgins of Mary, and the transient loggers left to their filthy business inside the house of sin, one could certainly expect results beneficial to the entire community.

It is not surprising, then, that Monsieur le Curé was so upset when he realized that his bold policies were about to drag him down in ruin. He loved his parish dearly. These lumberjacks were "my people." No other priest would have done for them what he had done. Another Curé would have drained the parish clean and sent the money to the Bishop or the Cardinal, or gambled it on the stock market and lost everything; while he—why, look at this beautiful church, and the plans he had for a youth center to house The Virgins of Mary and the Crusaders of the Holy Eucharist. In another five years the parish funds would finance the building of chapels at the camps up north; and there were a lot of other things he was planning to do for his parishioners. But now, with the old Jesuit throwing the axe into his garden, all of this would be lost. It was a downright shame.

This train of thought, together with the ale, was gradually leading Monsieur le Curé away from another outburst and into a mood of melancholy that soon made him see his problem in a different light. He was vaguely aware that he had raged against his old enemy with a violence proportionate to his own ignorance of precisely what Father Boulanger had in mind, that is to say, how he intended to maneuver through the events of today. To be sure, the old Jesuit was ultimately after his soutane, and a charivari would insure victory for him. Nevertheless, how was he going to promote the charivari openly and yet escape the risk of being blamed for it afterwards?

"I need time," Monsieur le Curé reflected aloud. "I need time to see what his next move will be. I might yet be able to beat him to the punch."

This was a sobering idea. It suggested a battle of wits which, were he to win it, would not only save the day for him but also put an end to Father Boulanger's career in La Buche. Who said a country Curé didn't have the brains to handle a Jesuit?

"Alice, bring my breakfast. I'm hungry."

The door opened. But it was for Madame Dupré and La Pitoune. Against Alice's entreaties to please not go in now, they burst inside and planted themselves in front of Monsieur le Curé's desk, and, before he could open his mouth, announced flatly:

"Mademoiselle Serval is dead."

"Well!" exclaimed Monsieur le Curé, standing up.

"We went through her apartment. She did not sleep there last night."

"Those awful men from the house of sin must have kidnaped her."

"And we want to know what you intend to do about it," Madame Dupré concluded, in a manner clearly indicating that she meant to exercise the powers of her new post. "Are you going to help us find her body?"

"Now, please, ladies, give me time to think. Please. I call for my breakfast and look what I get. What are you trying to do to your Curé? You don't let me eat my dinner; you

238

don't let me eat my breakfast; and now you order me to get out and comb the woods for Mademoiselle Serval's body. How do you know she is dead in the first place? Come, sit down. And don't talk to your Curé as if he were an old nun."

Madame Dupré's reaction was a toss of the head in disdain. She sat down stiffly on the edge of the chair, as became her position. But La Pitoune lowered her gaze and sat with a submissive air. Her self-confidence was greatly affected by the fact that Monsieur le Curé was her confessor. There was a long silence, during which the priest finished buttoning up his soutane and then put the empty quarts of ale on the floor behind his desk. Finally he asked: "What makes you feel so sure that something has happened to her?"

"That's what everybody is saying," Madame Dupré replied.

"So you have told everybody already?"

"A few people."

"What are you trying to do, arouse the whole town?"

"We need action."

"Brains is what you need."

Madame Dupré swallowed hard, her jaw set with obstinate firmness, while La Pitoune squirmed on her chair.

"If it is a charivari that you want, you are certainly going about it the right way," Monsieur le Curé went on. "Yet your job is to prevent this sort of thing. It's your duty to make sure nobody interferes with my work. I thought I had made this quite clear to you last night."

"There are certain things we can't control," Madame Dupré said. "After all, we are not the ones who killed her."

"Maybe nobody did. That's the point. You are jumping to conclusions too fast. How do we know she did not leave town last night to spend a few days in the city? She might even be going back to her old habits; who knows?"

"I doubt it," said Madame Dupré. "After what she did for

the whole town at last night's meeting, we all know she has reformed for good."

"Much you women know about who's reformed, and who's not, and for how long!"

La Pitoune felt that she was blushing, and that both Monsieur le Curé and Madame Dupré were aware of it. To hide her embarrassment she began speaking very fast: "Anyway, it's those men who did her in. No doubt about that. They kidnaped her because of what she did last night, probably threw her body in the river. They are quite capable of a thing like that, you know. It gives me the shivers just to think of it."

"Never mind, dearie, we'll get to the bottom of this. We're not going to just stand by and do nothing while one of us is being killed for having done her duty."

"That's right," echoed Monsieur le Curé. And he stood up to escort them out. "You are not going to just stand by and do nothing. You are going to go out on the square right after Mass and spread word around that Mademoiselle Serval left for Grand-Mère in the middle of the night. That's my order to you, ladies. I want you to tell everybody that I drove her there myself, in my car; she was sick, appendicitis or something of the sort, you invent some kind of disease, three, four kinds, so that, while everybody tries to figure out what she has, nobody will be saying she got killed. Understand?"

Reluctantly, Madame Dupré nodded that she did. Then both she and La Pitoune seemed to want to say something else, but Monsieur le Curé cut them short. "Good day, ladies. Don't forget." Then he gently, but firmly, shut the door in their faces.

And he immediately sent for Fulgence, who walked in seconds later looking frightened and expecting the worst. "I am going to give you a chance to make up for the mess you've put me in," the priest announced, to the intense relief of the

240

beadle. And he proceeded to list his instructions. About half a mile south of La Buche, where the rapids widen and are so shallow that the logs have to bypass them through a second chute, there is a wall of boulders and rocks that stands combing the river all the way across. Now, did he remember, a few years back, that drunken logger who drowned trying to jump the rapids by moonlight, and his canoe and body were found stuck between those rocks? So he did! Well, if he went there now, and had a good look, he might find Mademoiselle Serval's body.

Fulgence made a wry face.

"But first," Monsieur le Curé went on, "I want you to go to her apartment. Talk to the Bureau sisters. Find out if they heard anything unusual last night. If Maurice did get her out of the way, the chances are he threw her body in the river thinking it would turn up in Grand-Mère or Trois-Rivières. Another thing: stop at Lambert's and have him spread word around that Mademoiselle Serval is in Grand-Mère Hospital; I drove her there myself, last night. Then if you find anything in the water, come right back, so we can hide it until the women have quieted down a little. We need time. Hurry up. On your way."

*   *   *

Claude had just finished his confession. It had been informal, Father Boulanger dispensing with the opening and closing prayers out of regard for the delirious state of the penitent. Claude had to confess only his outburst of wrath over the missing clothes. He then recited the Act of Contrition, while the old priest blessed him with Absolution. And now came the Holy Sacrament.

The surpliced youth walked into the room carrying the paten. He was white as a shroud, filled with awe by the solemnity of the occasion. Madame Gauthier followed with Claude's corduroy breeches, red-and-black shirt, and boots, which she displayed at the foot of the bed, smiling at her son with an air of forgiveness, as if to say that she yielded to his extravagant fancies only because she knew these were caused by his illness. The youth moved to stand facing Father Boulanger across the bed, where, from the corner of one eye he watched the blessed fingers dip ceremoniously into the pyx, while with the other he glanced furtively at Claude, the Saint of La Buche whose picture he carried in his wallet and whose last moments he had the honor to witness. What luck, to hear his last words so as to be able to repeat them to his classmates with the silencing authority of having got them "with my own ears." The exciting anticipation of such glory made him tremble so much that when the time came to present the paten he struck Claude on the chin with it. Now Father Boulanger, holding the Host between thumb and forefinger, moved to deposit It on the tip of Claude's tongue. There followed an instant of profound suspense; Claude seemed unable to swallow the Holy Wafer. He coughed, choking; the Host was expelled to the very edge of his lips. He held it there a moment, until it had begun to melt into soft dough; then he tried again to swallow, and this time he succeeded. Father Boulanger nodded with satisfaction and Madame Gauthier sighed with a thankful heart.

The ceremony ended, Madame Gauthier and the pale youth drew back with grave faces, and left the room, while Father Boulanger knelt down, and taking Claude's hands in his, asked: "How do you feel now, son?"

"Fine," Claude said calmly. His eyes did not shift from the clothes on the foot of the bed. From their presence here he seemed to draw a satisfaction that mellowed his resentment. The certainty that he would leave his room in a matter of hours caused him to feel tolerant in a detached sort of way. "Father," he began, "there is something I want to tell you."

But the old priest made a quick gesture that meant: "Do not exert yourself." He was scrutinizing the boy's face for signs of incipient lucidity. He had hoped for an instant of clear consciousness, a last soul-to-soul communion between them. He spoke of the Kingdom of Heaven, the reward for having suffered so much and accepted death so resignedly. "It will not be long now, son. The spirit of Heaven is already in you. I see you smile. Tell me, are you happy?"

"I am thinking about the Kingdom of Heaven," said Claude.

"What do you see?"

"I am embracing her, Father. Oh, how I love her!"

"You can now see her in all her heavenly splendor, can't you?"

"Oh, how I will love her, to the last breath of the last moment!"

"*Ad Vitam Aeternam,*" Father Boulanger echoed in a solemn voice. Then after making the sign of benediction over him, he added: "*Deo Gratias.*"

There followed a moment's silence, after which Claude fixed his gaze straight into the eyes of his confessor and declared: "We will never see each other again, Father."

The old priest bent down for a close look into the boy's face. "What makes you say such things, son? Have you heard voices? Did you have a vision? Tell me."

"I am leaving this afternoon."

Father Boulanger reached for a glass of water and offered it to him. Claude shook his head in refusal. Then raising his voice the priest asked: "Can you hear me, son? Can you see me?"

Claude nodded yes.

But the old priest would not dare believe his ears. Was the

243

Saint of La Buche, his own little saint, prophesying the hour of his death? "*Ad Majorem Dei Gloriam*," Father Boulanger uttered, and he crossed himself again and again with feverish haste, as if in shock before a sudden vision of Jesus Himself.

Claude's gaze had wandered back to his clothes. In a dreamy voice he said: "It is only in the past few weeks that I have begun to know what life is. I am in love, Father. Lise is her name. She will come away with me this afternoon. With her I am going to live my life all over again, just the two of us at the lake, in the little time there is left."

Father Boulanger stepped back to verify the intensity of the dreamy stare. There was no doubt in his mind now that the boy was sinking into delirium again. "Look at me, son. Look at me," he implored.

But Claude kept looking at his clothes, seeing the end of today beyond them. And he kept talking about Lise, and about the lake, reeling out the details of their being together before sunset. He did not seem to hear the urgent pleas that he relax, try to sleep, think of nothing else now but the Kingdom of Heaven. Father Boulanger reached to feel the glossy forehead: the fever was rising. Then as Claude went on talking, his old shoulders slumped in helplessness. There was nothing left to do but draw a great solemn sign of benediction over the bed. After which he slipped from the room without a sound.

Downstairs, he found Madame Gauthier and the youth on their knees in the living room. They stood up at once, alerted by the grave look on his face. "Our little one is still delirious," he announced, heading for the door. "But for a moment just now he was conscious enough to declare that he would no longer be with us after tonight. Truly, I don't know what we ought to understand by this. It may be that we shall witness an event of great importance. I think I will now have to revise my sermon for this morning. Come, child. We must be on our way. Be brave, my good woman. And pray that the Lord inspire his poor servant to a sermon worthy of the great events in store for all of us today. Have faith, my good woman."

Once alone, Madame Gauthier turned those words over and over again in her mind. One second she fell prey to grief, but the next moment she knew a sense of relief that it would all be over soon. And this relief brought along a sweet emotion of inner glory. At last, it would happen the way she had always prayed it might happen! Now she would recite a whole Rosary in gratitude, up there, at the bedside of her little saintly one.

She had gone only a few steps, however, when the thought vanished instantly from her mind at the sight of the evil book on the chair. She picked it up. A flurry of bills went sailing down to scatter around her feet. Hardly conscious of what she was doing, she dropped to her knees and gathered the money, intending to throw it in the garbage pail where it belonged with the evil book and everything else that came from the sacrilegious hands of Paul. The very feel of these bills aroused her to spasms of revulsion, shook her whole body with shivers as from contact with a living thing impure, hell-skinned. She hurried toward the kitchen. But a sudden impulse of curiosity brought her to a standstill in the doorway, and frenziedly she began to count the bills. Her pale wrinkled face grew hot from her mingled feelings of shame and sinfulness. She stopped counting, crossed herself, and went over to the garbage pail and lifted the lid. But at that moment, her curiosity again returned to assault her scruples, and with such force that this time she could not resist its urgent demands. As if to escape the piercing stare of her Guardian Angel, she hid herself inside the pantry, where she resumed counting the money in the faint light from the half-shut door.

Two hundred dollars! Her hands trembled uncontrollably. She counted again, and once more. Two hundred dollars! "Oh,

245

Lord. That could buy two hundred Low Masses, or twenty High Masses at ten dollars each! I must give it all to Father Boulanger."

The calculation and the decision came to her without effort. The impact of such a providential inspiration cleansed her soul of shame and sinfulness, moved her to exclamations of joyful gratitude. "Oh, Lord. Thank you, Lord!" She slipped the bills into the parting of her breasts below the golden cross that hung at the end of a chain from her neck. Then she returned into the sunlight of the living room, where she sat in her corner next to the window, to listen for possible changes in Claude's respiration. Ah, she felt much better now!

But not for long. A number of puzzling questions arose all at once to torment her. Why had Paul given so much money to Claude? Did it have any connection with their alleged secret? What sort of diabolical scheme was there brewing in the black soul of that sinner? What would Father Boulanger do when she brought him all this money? Would he accept it, if she told him whom it came from? Could a sinner's money be put to the service of the Good Lord, really? Perhaps it would be safer to pretend it came from somebody else? But who? And this would be a lie. Would such a lie be a mortal sin, then, or just a venial sin? The amount of money being so great, perhaps it would be a mortal sin. But considering the purpose of the lie, could it not be called a venial sin only? After all, for two hundred Low Masses, or twenty High Masses . . .

As she pondered these questions, finding no ready answer to any one of them, Madame Gauthier grew aware of a slight change in Claude's breathing. It was more rapid, she thought, and she also detected the muffled sounds of hesitant footsteps overhead. She hastened to his room.

Claude had got out of bed and put on his shirt and breeches

246

and heavy woolen socks. With the support of his cane he was walking slowly back and forth between the window and the door, testing the flexibility of his knees and ankles and straining his eyes as though to pierce a curtain of fog lowered across his vision.

"Poor boy," she sighed.

He went on as if his mother were not there. At the window he stopped for a breath of air. Then he started back toward the door, where she stood watching him with that same look of tender solicitude that had come to her face when she first discovered he was delirious.

"Where are you going, my son?"

"To the lake, mother."

She shook her head in sadness.

He said: "Didn't Father Boulanger tell you about it?"

"Poor boy."

He tried to stand steady without his cane. A faint smile parted his lips. "I am doing well, don't you think?"

"My poor little boy," she sighed again.

She went back downstairs with a heavy heart, pained that he could not recognize her any more. He had used the word mother, but in his look she had read that he could not see her clearly. Father Boulanger was right, then; perhaps he had regained consciousness only long enough to announce that this was his last day, and now he would remain delirious until the end. If only he had asked for his seminarian's uniform instead of hunting clothes! It was only fitting that at the hour of death one be dressed in the clothes of one's dreams. She had even hoped that Father Boulanger might obtain special permission to dress him in a real soutane when it was all over. Ah, death had cruel ways, it cared little about the looks of the saintly ones. To think that her Claude would face His Creator in hunting clothes, of all things!

No sooner had Madame Gauthier uttered this thought to herself than, in a flash of intuition, she knew all about the secret between Paul and Claude.

"The lake! He thinks he is going to hunt at the lake. Last night they must have talked about it, as they always do when Paul comes back from camp, and now the fever is keeping the idea fixed in his poor sick head. I should have known; they always say delirious people keep repeating the last thing that was on their mind when they were conscious. Now I know. That sinner Paul wants to take my boy away. And he means to use this money to do it. It is the curse of their father. *That's* what it is. Oh, Lord. I must do something."

More firmly now than before, she was convinced that she must take the money to her confessor. Perhaps the wise man of God would suggest additional means of preventing Paul from carrying out his evil plans.

Only, she would have to lie, and that would not be easy. It was not the sin of it that tormented her at this point, but rather the fear of not being able to invent a lie convincing enough. For a woman who could not remember the last time she had consciously told a lie, this was a great problem indeed.

* * *

Monsieur Dupré was not eager to go to work this morning. Maurice's demands and threats had not left his mind since he woke up. Considered in this bright daylight and with a sober head, the order to cancel all week-end trains seemed even more preposterous than it had after three quarts of ale in the smoky air of the tavern. And the threats far more terrifying. Also, the hour for a reply was drawing near. But that reply would have to be the same as last night's, however hard he tried changing it to satisfy the blackmailers.

So, for one step toward the train depot, Monsieur Dupré

wanted to take ten in the direction of Lambert's, but the tavern was not open yet. He wished that he could go fishing for the day, or simply hide in the woods behind La Colline Sainte-Marie. But his wife would find out that he was not at work, and his absence from the cage might be as difficult to explain as his presence in the rosary-bead factory two nights ago. He thought of joining the crowd of women going to Mass, but since he was only a respectable churchgoer and not a pious man, his concentration in prayers would not be sufficiently intense to enable him to forget his problem. Thus he continued down the Rue des Pins, talking to himself, adjusting his glasses at every other step. And he did the next best thing to running away, he made great decisions.

"One of these days I am going to put my foot down," he muttered, stamping the sidewalk slates in emphasis. He would make sure that from now on his word was law. The mess he was in today would not have come up if he had been man enough to wear the pants in his own house. From now on he would; they could be sure of that. Strength, will power, courage, to fight for his due, that's what was needed.

"It's all a matter of who wears the pants in a marriage, young man," he declared to Bernard Toupin, who stood waiting for him on the platform of the depot. "The wife, Monsieur le Curé, or the husband. And if you want my advice, don't ever get married before you have got this thing settled once and for all."

Bernard received this unusual morning salutation with a sort of amused tolerance. "I agree, Monsieur Dupré," he said. It was a smart piece of advice. But since he did not like to say anything against the priests, he preferred to limit the conflict to a question of size between the husband and wife. And, in this respect, he was confident that Monsieur Dupré's unfortunate predicament would never happen to him. "Why, it

249

would take a pretty big woman to wear the pants of a man my size, don't you think?"

"Good for you," the stationmaster said wrily. Then pointing to a trunk near the door, he was quick to add: "In that case I don't suppose it will hurt you any to give me a hand with this."

"Always glad to be of service," said Bernard, going to fetch the dolly at the end of the platform.

Monsieur Dupré examined the trunk, looking for a tag of destination. "Good heavens! Do they expect me to guess where it is going? As if I didn't have enough troubles of my own."

"It belongs to a girl I know," Bernard said. "I carried it here last night. Sort of gave her a hand with it."

"Always ready to help people, aren't you. Well, I guess that's why you are so successful."

Bernard smiled in a show of simple modesty. "She will probably come by today and write out a tag for it."

"Let's weigh it, anyway."

They tilted the trunk onto the dolly and wheeled it inside the depot to the scale. "What did she put in it, soaked logs?" exclaimed Monsieur Dupré. It weighed one hundred and forty pounds.

"Here," said Bernard, "let's stand it against the wall, so it won't be too far from the loading platform."

The matter of the trunk now out of the way, Monsieur Dupré went to his desk inside the cage and began sorting out the mail for the camps. His hands were shaking. Letters kept slipping between his fingers.

"Too much work," said Bernard at the ticket window. "Why don't you get Arthur to come in and help you, now that the rush is on?"

The stationmaster shook his head: it was not work that

250

upset him. He had problems, terrible problems. "If you don't put your foot down, you get into trouble, deep trouble. Remember that, young man," he said. Then he began to tell him a thing or two about getting married in La Buche.

As he saw it, citing his own marriage as an example, Monsieur le Curé's views on family planning were the source of all the evil, the cause of all his trouble. Nine children, nine! And still Monsieur le Curé would not permit the Duprés to use those you-know-whats. And why? Because the station-master earned the highest salary in town, and, according to Monsieur le Curé, this meant he must also produce the largest family in town, just to set a good example for the rest. "Now, do you call that fair? I don't."

Bernard nodded agreement.

"What do you do, when the highest salary in town is not enough to support the nine children and the wife, let alone have a couple more kids? What do you do then?"

"Make a knot in it, I suppose," Bernard suggested.

"Ah! But that's not easy, young man. At my age, and with the strong healthy woman I have as a wife. But, anyway, you give it a try. You do your best. You start keeping away from the wife, go to bed later at night, sometimes you even sleep with your pants on. In other words, you try everything, even coming home drunk. But then what happens? It's the wife who can't take it. She gets mad; nagging, nagging, nagging. The moment you set foot in the house she raises hell. Home life becomes intolerable. What do you do next? You try to forget your troubles, naturally. So you take an extra quart with the boys at Lambert's, you let yourself go a little, if you get what I mean, and the first thing you know, man, you are in trouble way above your ears. And then it's too late. Ah, I've got problems. And all because I wasn't man enough to set my foot down and say to Monsieur le Curé: 'Here, it's about time we started using those English you-know-whats. We have earned them, good heavens.' "

Thinking that the trouble was an unexpected pregnancy, Bernard was anxious to put in a word of encouragement. "Bah!" he said: "I don't suppose one more or less will make much difference."

"What! Don't ever say that, young man. You don't know my wife. Just to hear you would be enough to put her in the family way again. Oh, thank heavens, no," Monsieur Dupré exclaimed, and let out a long sigh of relief. Then in a self-consoling tone of voice he added: "And thank heavens she got elected last night. That ought to keep her busy for a while."

"What elections?" asked Bernard.

"Didn't you hear about it? Madame Gauthier resigned. So now it's my wife who is the boss over there."

"And who is the new treasurer?"

"La Pitoune, of course."

Bernard grinned sourly. "Have you got my mail ready?"

"In a moment."

"Give me what you have there. I'll pick up the rest later."

"What's the rush, all of a sudden?"

"I just remembered that I forgot something at Ti-Pit's."

"Take your time," said Monsieur Dupré. But Bernard grabbed the bundle of mail and hurried outside.

This sudden departure left the stationmaster somewhat puzzled. But more disquieting, it made him realize abruptly that he was all alone in the depot. His desk was stacked with paperwork. On the rear platform rose piles of yesterday's shipments that must be processed today. It was a few minutes past nine o'clock. In four, perhaps three, hours from now, Maurice and Altar Boy would surely come for his reply. His old fears returned to haunt the quiet of the cage, moved him to imagine that he could see the two men arriving on the front platform even now. He ran to the door.

The bus was driving off.

"Hey, Bernard," he called. "If you see Arthur downtown tell him to come up to work. If he's sober, that is."

Bernard opened the driver's window: "But what if he's not?"

"Tell him to come anyway. Too much work here for one man all alone."

"O.K.," Bernard waved. Then he drove off in the direction of the Rue des Erables.

Monsieur Dupré turned back inside the depot. Determined to concentrate on the work on his desk so as to forget about Maurice and Altar Boy, he walked rapidly toward the cage, keeping his head down as people do when moving to a set purpose. But about the middle of the room he came to a sudden stop. His hands shot up to his glasses. He looked again, in the hope that he had not seen right.

Running across the floor almost to his feet were drops of blood. He followed their trail with eyes widening in terror and saw that they led in the direction of the trunk. Curious, and frightened, he went over to the trunk and saw that there was blood at the bottom end, now almost dry. He studied the lock and was relieved that there was no key. Now he had a good reason not to open it. But hardly had he mumbled this to himself when he realized that he was no longer standing by the trunk but was rummaging the baggage room for a crowbar. He found it near the coal bucket, and ran back with it into the waiting room, where he worked in feverish haste to pry the lock loose. Now and then he glanced fearfully at the door and at the windows. The phone rang, but he paid no attention to it. He went on pulling and lifting and jerking with the crowbar until the lock was finally torn off. Then he braced himself with arms stretched out to the upper corners of the trunk and, in a last effort, succeeded in sliding the halves apart. With a cry of horror he let the top slam closed again and ran to the cage where the phone was still ringing. Oh, my God! There was a corpse in the trunk and the corpse was Mademoiselle Serval, with her poor body twisted and broken to fill the narrow space. He shuddered. He could still feel those terrible empty eyes staring at him.

"Hello, hello!"

"What's going on out there, Louis?"

"Who is this?"

"It's me, Fulgence."

"Oh, my God!"

"What's the matter? It takes you an hour to answer the phone. And now you sound half-dead."

"Troubles, Fulgence. Terrible troubles."

"You too! The presbytery is all upside down this morning. Monsieur le Curé got up in one of his moods. But what's wrong out there, anyway?"

"I can't tell you just now."

"Serious?"

"You had better come over."

"Wait a minute. I have a message for you."

"Tell me later."

"But this is important."

"All right. What is it?"

"Now listen carefully, Louis. This is very important. If anybody comes to you during the day and asks if you saw Mademoiselle Serval, Monsieur le Curé wants you to say that she left for Grand-Mère in the middle of the night. She is in the hospital out there, very sick. Got that?"

Monsieur Dupré was silent.

"Are you listening, Louis?"

In a breaking voice Monsieur Dupré said: "Is this a joke, Fulgence?"

"No, sir. There is a lot more than I can tell you right now."

"I know that."

"What's that you said?"

"I said, come over here right away. I need help."

"As soon as I can. But in the meantime don't forget what I just told you."

Monsieur Dupré hung up. Then carefully avoiding looking at the trunk he walked swiftly across the waiting room and out onto the front platform. He would not go back inside until Arthur reported for work.

twelve

The Mass had just ended when

Bernard Toupin parked in front of Ti-Pit's. Women were crowding into the store. It was the wrong moment to try and get La Pitoune into the back room. Bernard decided to wait 'till after the rush. He crossed the street and walked into Lambert's.

The tavern was empty, except for Arthur and Israel at a table near the bar. Bernard could hear Arthur's gin-hoarse voice from the entrance: he was speaking as if the place were packed with loggers come here for the sole purpose of hearing him speak. "You have to be pretty low to pull a trick like that on people," he was saying. "I ride that stinking new bus one

257

full day to go and fish some customers for them. I spend a couple of hours making a speech to the jacks. I practically get strangled to death. And when I come back here and try to collect my commission, what do you suppose they do? They pull the trick on me. Sit, here, Bernard. You were right, I never should have gotten mixed up with those city-slickers. Wait 'till you hear what they did to me. Sit here."

Bernard took a chair next to Israel. The memory of last night's talk about La Pitoune caused them to eye each other suspiciously. Israel ordered a round of beer, but Bernard refused, saying he did not want a drink just before starting out for the camps. As for Arthur, his mickey of gin was still half-full. Leaning on his elbows on the edge of the table, he went on: "First of all, I never did trust those two fellows. When they asked me to work for them I said to myself: 'Look here, Arthur, better be careful. You're dealing with a couple of sharpies, here. These city-slickers can be smooth. Use your brains, Arthur,' I said to myself. And that's just what I did. I told them: 'Listen, gentlemen; I'm not going to pay to get those cards printed. And you'll have to take care of my expenses back and forth to the camps. That's only fair, isn't it?' 'Fine,' they said, 'don't worry about a thing, Arthur. We'll take good care of you.' But I didn't trust them. What I did was this: I counted all the cards I gave out, and I made sure to remember the faces of all the fellows I gave a card to. That was easy enough. I never forget a face. Then last night I hid under the porch out there and watched the fellows go in; fifteen of them went in, fifteen of the ones I had given a card to. To make sure I was making no mistake, I waited there until every one of them came out again. It was fifteen all right. That meant fifteen bucks for my commission, see. But when I went inside to collect, they let me have it." Arthur paused to take another drink of gin.

258

" 'Paula here will take care of you,' they said. 'We're in a hurry.' So what do you think happened. Paula takes me to the back room and says: 'Come on, Arthur, open up!' So I say to her: 'Now look here, sister, I didn't come here for a piece of fun. It's my commission I want. Let's have it. Fifteen bucks.' 'What are you talking about?' she says. 'Why, you couldn't get a piece of fun even if you tried.' And, man, did I get mad! 'That's what *you* think,' I said. 'Well, you just wait a second, sister, and I'm going to show you that Arthur here hasn't got a cardinal's little finger where he ought to have a real man's pride.' That's what I said to her. I was so mad. I didn't care about my fifteen bucks anymore. The bitch was laughing at me. 'What do you call this?' she said. 'Wait a minute, sister,' I said, and I went on trying. I tried, and I tried, and I tried. But I guess I was too drunk. But I wasn't too drunk to ask for my fifteen bucks."

The front door opened and Paul Gauthier walked in. Israel and Bernard watched him walk to the bar and begin talking with Lambert, while Arthur went on with his story.

" 'Fifteen bucks!' she says. 'What are you talking about? Nobody owes you fifteen bucks any more. You just got paid,' she says. 'What do you mean?' I said, 'I just got paid?' And she says: 'Just what I said. The boss gave you ten bucks already.' I told her that was expense money, but she says: 'No, sir. That was an advance on your commission,' she says. What could I do? 'All right, sister,' I said, 'but how about my other five bucks? Ten bucks out of fifteen leaves five, don't it?' 'That's right,' she says, 'but you just got paid in goods. And I gave you a special price on top of it. One minute is ten bucks, you know that yourself. For you I charged only five. Now what are you kicking about?' she says. I said to her: 'Are you serious, Paula? Do you really mean to pull a cheap trick like that on me, Arthur, after all the work I've done for you girls

259

in here? Do you really mean to do that to me, Paula?' I said. And she says, 'Is it my fault if you have a caramel between your legs? I did my best. Now leave me alone. I have work to do,' she says, and walks out on me."

Arthur banged an angry fist on the table. "They won't get away with it," he said. "I'll get my revenge. It's not the money part of it that burns me, it's the other thing, the way that bitch laughed at me. Now, I don't mind insults. But I won't stand for this. No, sir. I may be a drunk, but I still have a bit of pride left in me. And the bitch who attacks me there is done for, I assure you. Wait 'till I get hold of Maurice and Altar Boy."

Bernard chuckled. Israel saw in Arthur's bloodshot eyes that same look of somber wrath which had so frightened him the night before. This man, he felt, could commit some violent act, even murder, in a moment of obsession intensified by drink. Bernard was now trying to quiet Arthur down by telling him to go to work at the depot where Monsieur Dupré was waiting for him. Israel was quick to suggest that this was indeed a good idea, the best way, in fact, to forget his troubles. Arthur countered by insisting that the only way to forget the insult was to get his hands on those city-slickers—oh, would he love to give that bitch Paula a good licking! And again he banged the table in emphasis. Bernard, who feared disclosures dangerous to himself when Arthur was in such a state, brought up the question of money to be earned at the depot. Arthur began to show signs of giving in; the mickey of gin was getting low. Israel got up, walked over to the bar for a word with Paul.

Lambert was telling Paul why he could not promise to rent him the car. "If only you had come half an hour ago," he said. "I might have been able to do it. But they just called to say they need it 'till the end of the afternoon."

260

"About what time?" Paul inquired.

"I have no idea," said Lambert. Then leaning over the bar he explained confidentially: "If you ask me, I'd say they smell trouble and want to lie low for a while. Looks to me like they are moving out for a few days, just long enough to let things simmer down a bit."

Paul said: "I'll come back this afternoon around four or five."

"Do that. If they bring it back by then, I'll be glad to let you use it."

"Would you like to drive to Montreal with me this afternoon?" Paul said, turning to Israel.

"I don't know," Israel pondered.

"Think about it," said Paul. "I'll see you later." Then as he headed for the door, Israel said: "Wait." And they left the tavern together.

The Rue des Erables was crowded as on market days. Women came out of the stores carrying bags of food and utensils under one arm, while with the other they pulled angrily at strings of recalcitrant children at their heels. The air was vibrant with news, rumors, charivari hunger. Out of Lambert's, Arthur now came navigating laboriously through the crowd, his tall, gin-languid body wavering from left to right as though he were riding the rapids standing up in a canoe. Women stepped out of his way, anxious to avoid rubbing elbows with him. Children were running in and out of the hardware store where they bought themselves something to make noise with. A large canvas sign fresh-painted in red letters hung floating above the entrance:

"CHARIVARI SPECIAL"
Pie plates–pots–pans–cookie sheets
Hit Them–They Ring Loud
10 cents each–3 for 25

261

And on the sidewalks were displayed washtubs full of ladles, pie plates, dough rollers, all sorts of kitchen utensils. The five-and-ten store also was featuring Charivari Specials: mops, brooms, toys that let out shrill sounds, first-aid supplies in the event the demonstration took a bad turn. Ti-Pit's store was the only one that did not advertise a Charivari Special in the windows or on the sidewalk; but the crowd already knew that this was the place to buy old fruits and vegetables.

As Paul and Israel weaved through the crowd, women here and there pointed a finger at the giant Gauthier son, drew other women's attention to him, the brother of the Little Saint of La Buche. There were many who shook their heads in sad protest that the saintly one must die while the sinner went on living. And that skinny jack with him, didn't he look odd?

Israel had visited the church earlier expecting to hear a sermon by Monsieur le Curé, but instead he had listened to Father Boulanger announce solemnly that the sick Gauthier boy had just predicted the hour of his death: he was offering his life for the sins of La Buche. Events of great importance would take place before the end of the day. Should the Little Saint's prediction come true, then everybody would know for sure that he had gone straight to heaven.

"I never knew that your brother was a saintly man," Israel said, when they had reached the corner of the Rue des Pins where the crowd was less noisy and they could finally hear each other. "You should have been in church to hear what the priest said about him."

"Nonsense," Paul snapped. "My brother is just a plain boy who is sick and nobody will do anything for him. Naturally he resigns himself. What else can he do? And now everybody thinks he is a saint. But Father Boulanger will have to fish himself a saint out of heaven if he wants one. I'm taking the boy to Montreal this afternoon, to get him cured."

"But," Israel exclaimed, "I thought he was too ill."

"The doctor tells me that a friend of his in Montreal can operate and save the boy," Paul explained. "Only my mother has to sign permission, first. He has asked her once already, and she has refused. She won't do it unless that confessor of hers says it's all right. So I'm going to talk with the priest now, to make sure he tells her to sign. We ought to be on our way by the end of the afternoon. Are you coming?"

"I'd like to," Israel replied. "But somehow I think I should stay here and see what happens. I'd like to win back some of the money I lost last night."

"You had better keep away from that place, especially today."

"Why today especially?"

"Look, Israel, I've worried about you long enough. If you don't want to take my advice, suit yourself."

Israel said: "I'll be at Lambert's later this afternoon, I'll watch for you."

"See you then," Paul said, and he continued up the Rue des Pins toward the Seminary. Israel turned back in the direction of the crowd.

*　　*　　*

La Pitoune was working in the back room. Seated on a wooden crate, with her legs stretched onto the rims of two washtubs full of vegetables, and her skirt tucked up for greater freedom of movement, she was sorting potatoes, picking out the bad ones which she dropped in a pail between her legs. She must work fast; Ti-Pit was restless for the pailfuls; dozens of women were asking for them in the front room.

How warm it was. Running drops of perspiration tickled the nape of her neck. Her hair felt sticky and wet at the temples. "What a life!" she sighed. She wanted to be out

263

on the streets where everybody was talking about the charivari and Father Boulanger's sermon, not here, sorting out these rotten potatoes. What a disgrace, to be doing this kind of work on the morning after her election as Treasurer of Les Dames de la Grâce! And it was all her fault: all because she had suddenly resolved to become a good wife again. Resolutions, resolutions! But what was the point of resolutions if nobody helped you keep them? Why didn't Ti-Pit let her stay in the front room, at least, where she might hear the latest and know what was brewing? Ah, the pot-bellied swine! That's how he appreciated his wife's good resolutions! What angered her the most was the fact that this sale on rotten vegetables was her idea in the first place.

"Let me give you a hand," said Bernard, suddenly appearing at the door.

She looked up. "Get out. Out with you."

Slowly he walked up to her, while she threatened to throw a potato at him.

"I only came to congratulate you, Madame the Treasurer," Bernard grinned. "Now, is this the way to greet your old friend Bernie?"

"All right. So laugh at me. Have fun."

"I'm not laughing at you. Frankly, the joke is on me. I want to apologize for last night. Be nice to your old Bernie, Pitoune. I'm sorry."

She looked suspiciously at him. He had stepped around one of the washtubs to stand near her. Abruptly, she stood up, and carried her pailful of potatoes to the front room. When she returned, a moment later, her manner was calm, confident. To see Bernard on the wooden crate sorting the potatoes helped soothe her wounded pride.

She squatted next to him on the crate and they began working together. "Forgive me, Pitoune?" he whispered.

264

Her pride forced her to say nothing, and this thrilled him even more than if she had thrown her arms around him. "I'm not the only one who did wrong last night."

She frowned. He tried a first gentle caress down her spine. From the front room came Ti-Pit's voice: "Got another one ready, sweetie?"

"Coming," she replied. She grabbed the pail between Bernard's legs and took it quickly to the front. He had almost filled up another by the time she came back.

Bernard rose from the crate and tried to throw his arms around her. La Pitoune turned her back to him, her blond hair lightly whipping his chin, and stood facing a high bank of cartons. His arms were around her shoulders, his body pressed against her. She leaned her face against the hard surface of a carton, and a long shudder escaped her, as he worked his hands around her waist and began gently stroking her belly. His lips touched the nape of her neck. "Oh, Bernie," she moaned, melting in his hands, "I was going to be a good wife from now on."

"And I was going to go to confession this morning," he said.

"You come back to me only because I can help you and your business."

"And you take me back because you can't do without me."

She turned. "We are two of the same kind, Bernie."

"That's why we should stick together. No?"

He began to take her.

"Not now."

Her husband's voice was heard again calling for a pailful of potatoes. She wriggled herself out of Bernard's arms.

"Tonight?"

"Yes."

*　　*　　*

As soon as the beadle appeared at the depot, Monsieur Dupré, in a rush of fearful agitation, showed him the contents of the trunk. Fulgence let out a cry of horror. It was a long moment before he could find the strength to say: "Did you call the police, Louis?"

"Not yet," Monsieur Dupré answered, with a sigh of help-lessness. "I was going to, but he would not let me," he explained, pointing to Arthur, who was on his knees scrubbing the floor clean of bloodstains.

"Good. We must hide it," said Fulgence. "I am sure this is how Monsieur le Curé would want to see this thing handled. 'Above all,' he said to me: 'make sure nobody finds out what happened, if anything wrong did happen.' That's what he said when I left."

"But where?" asked Monsieur Dupré, fingering his eye-glasses nervously.

"Why not the baggage room?" Fulgence suggested.

Monsieur Dupré looked to Arthur for an opinion. Arthur scratched his head in silence, as if he was weighing the idea. Suddenly his eyes lit up with a cunning gleam. "The trouble with the baggage room," he said, "it's going to stink like hell. No windows. And I have a lot of work to do in there the rest of the day. Besides, there is no lock on the door. Why not the coal shack?" he suggested, as if it were an after-thought.

Yes, Monsieur Dupré and Fulgence agreed, that should do the trick. They lifted the trunk onto the dolly, and wheeled it over the tracks and across the yard. At last, Monsieur Dupré thought to himself, he would be able to work in peace for a while, now that the trunk was out of sight.

The coal shack was a boxlike construction with an opening for a feed-in chute in the upper part of the front wall. It con-

266

tained two compartments, one for kerosene drums and the other for coal, with a seven-foot partition between them. On the coal side, at ground level, was a wicket through which the coal was shoveled out. The opposite wall had a wide door lifted by counterweights hooked to a rope. After taking out two drums in order to make room for the trunk, Arthur cut the rope down to a few strings. "We shall see what we shall see," he muttered as he worked. In his mind there was a doubt as to who the murderers were. When they came for the trunk he would be ready for them.

Monsieur Dupré's shoulders drooped as if he was drained of all courage and strength. Fulgence walked back to the depot with him and tried to cheer him up a little.

"Everything is happening to me today," Monsieur Dupré sighed. "I don't know what to do. Keeping this trunk here is going to make me an accomplice, I suppose."

"Don't worry, Louis," Fulgence said. "It's hidden, at least. I'll tell the Curé."

But what about those two? Monsieur Dupré thought. I'll have to deal with them. He shivered, thinking of the impending visit of Maurice and Altar Boy.

"Everything is going to be all right. Don't let yourself get so upset. Monsieur le Curé will be so glad to hear that the body is hidden."

A ray of hope shone on the face of the stationmaster. "Listen, Fulgence, don't forget to tell him what I'm doing for him now. The chances I take, and all that. Make sure he knows I'm trying to help him out, will you."

At the coal shack, meanwhile, Arthur decided to try the wicket for size. Sliding down the coal pile feet first, he was able to pass through easily after a few wiggles of the hips. Just large enough for him, yet small enough to prevent Maurice and Altar Boy from escaping through it. A broad grin parted his lips. His bloodshot eyes gleamed. "Fine!"

thirteen

Monsieur le Curé reacted to Father Boulanger's sermon the way one receives intelligence that one's enemy has just overstepped the limits of prudence by a stroke as bold as it is fraught with dangers. He was surprised, but delighted. He did not relax his alertness. Immediately after Mass he sent Alice on reconnaissance through the crowded Place de l'Eglise and Rue des Erables, to gather what effect the sermon had upon the restless women.

As Monsieur le Curé saw it, Father Boulanger's remarks about the dying Gauthier boy meant clearly that the old Jesuit intended no action to prevent a charivari, but that, instead, he planned to encourage one, in the hope that the

269

uprising might be turned to his own advantage. In this respect, Monsieur le Curé's earlier suspicions were confirmed. What did surprise him, however, was the bold idea of planting in the minds of the women a direct connection between the charivari and the imminent death of the Gauthier boy. Monsieur le Curé had often sampled the old Jesuit's cunning, the keenness of it had sometimes disturbed his secular soul with fear, and envy, and he had long ago adopted the attitude of expecting the wildest strokes of intrigue from the enemy camp, so that he would not be caught by surprise; yet he had never imagined the old Jesuit capable of a scheme so fantastic as this one. To announce from the pulpit that the dying Gauthier boy was offering his life to expiate the sins of La Buche, to say that he had just predicted the hour of his death and suggest that it would coincide with some important event, probably the shutting down of the brothel, to indicate further that if this prediction came true the people of La Buche would then have proof that their Little Saint had gone straight to Heaven—why, it amounted to forecasting a miracle! This was a spectacular bid for power; should today's events substantiate the predictions, the women would shift their allegiance instantly from their Curé to the old Jesuit, who could then influence them all to petitioning the bishop for a new priest in the presbytery.

It was a move of the greatest cunning, if only by virtue of its being so simple: the old Jesuit was well aware that once the women had called for a charivari they seldom failed to pass swiftly to action, and he knew, as everybody did, that the Gauthier boy had only a few days left to live, so that to link these two events in the minds of the women was easy enough. Nevertheless, the daring of it was extreme. Would the women take the predictions seriously? Would they believe a tale of that sort? Miracles did not happen any more, at least not in

La Buche in the middle of the twentieth century! But even so, assuming that the women believed him, what if the Gauthier boy lasted another couple of days, or weeks, and what if there were no charivari, not even an orderly demonstration? What then? Ah, the old fox had gone too far this time. He was really digging his own grave!

"And, by green horse, I'm going to give him a hand," Monsieur le Curé reflected, chuckling over his breviary.

He was strolling the length of the back porch, where patches of sunlight between the columns struck his bushy red hair. The little book was held perpendicular to the upper slope of his belly, resting there as upon a stand, and at every tenth step his left hand would rise in a wide arc to turn another page. Years of reading these canonical prayers had erased all meaning from the fine print, so that he now performed the ritual with that same absent-mindedness with which he dressed in the morning or shaved before Sunday High Mass. Just as some of his best sermons had come to him in the bathroom, so now, while his eyes raced over the Latin words, his thoughts converged upon finding a way to outwit Father Boulanger. It seemed an easier thing to do now than before the sermon; at least he knew exactly what the old Jesuit was up to.

Therefore, he began by assuming that the worst would come to pass: both the charivari and the death of the Gauthier boy would take place before the end of the day. Since he stood alone against the restless crowd of women, it would be futile to try to prevent their uprising, and since he was not a doctor, and did not believe in miracles, there was little that he could do to keep the Gauthier boy alive. This, he reasoned, was the realistic approach. It was useless to oppose the course of events. He assumed, further, that in the conjunction of these two events the women of La Buche would find proof that their Little Saint's predictions had come true. And he

271

concluded that this was the point on which he must seek to defeat the old Jesuit. His own objective, then, would be to make sure that these two events would not be linked in the minds of the women. If he could not prevent a charivari, he could at least maneuver in such a way that it would be raised on his own terms.

Now, there were ways of controlling a charivari. It had been done before. Not all charivaris had ended in disaster and loss of life. Why should this one be different? Planned carefully, it could bring happy results. The old Jesuit's bid to power and glory could be turned into defeat and ridicule, the brothel shut down for good, the women appeased.

"But how?"

As he pondered this, weighing one course of action after another, and seeking to match the old Jesuit's cunning and boldness with even more daring strategies, Monsieur le Curé grew excited and walked at a quicker pace. He was living the very essence of his Curé's life, and he relished it. No spiritual matter engaged his convictions and energies and talents so keenly as did this struggle for secular and ecclesiastical supremacy in this spot of timberland he called "his parish." He, not the Jesuit, had built this parish; he, not the Jesuit, knew what was good for these lumberjacks; he, not the Jesuit, was the boss here. And under the category of Jesuit came all the bishops, cardinals, the Pope himself, the saint-makers, all those who knew more Latin than French and felt naked without a soutane on. To fight them all was a matter of survival. To beat the Jesuit to the punch was to give a braggart city jack a case of calk-pox. It was not pretty, but such was the law of Timberland. And Monsieur le Curé had too much lumberjack's blood in his veins to pack up his bags and run away. Just as the robe failed to reduce the thickness of his neck or hide the raw strength of his large frame, so the many years of Mass celebrating and breviary reading had not smothered in him an atavistic propensity to enjoy a rough battle.

The nearness of a showdown with Father Boulanger, then, kindled his imagination to think up schemes no less dangerous than the one they were meant to outdo. No matter. The time for caution was past. He would be bold, would call a charivari himself, order the women to march on the brothel. This was the only way to control the uprising so that there might be no violence and disastrous consequences, the only way to make sure the event would serve his own ends. However, there was Maurice to contend with, and La Dupré, and La Pitoune. There was also the problem of Mademoiselle Serval's disappearance. If it turned out that she had been killed, and her body were found, then the women's vengeance might be difficult to hold back.

"Fulgence!" Monsieur le Curé called at the kitchen door. The echo of his voice rang up and down the empty corridors, deepening the silence of the house. "Hey, Fulgence, aren't you back yet?" he called again.

The silence was suddenly broken by the sound of an old woman wailing: "The Good Lord is mad at us."

Monsieur le Curé listened closely.

"Mad at us, mad at us, mad at us," came the weird litany.

Grumbling at the disturbing intrusion, he stepped inside and headed for his office, where the wailings seemed to be coming from.

The Bureau sisters were sitting on the bench near the door. They wore their usual black frocks and shawls. The younger one, who was about eighty, greeted the priest with a look of reproach. The other stared vacantly into his face. Her crooked old fingers were wrapped in a giant-size rosary, whose beads she rolled past at a ravenous speed, substituting the *Aves* and the *Paters* with, "Mad at us, mad at us, mad at us. The Good Lord is mad."

Monsieur le Curé decided instantly that this senile litany was an act, put on to touch his sympathy. As he suspected the purpose of their visit, he went straight to the point: "What have I done wrong this time?"

The younger sister shook her head to show how strongly she disapproved of Monsieur le Curé's alleged misconduct.

"Well, speak up."

The younger one nodded sadly toward her wretched sister, then looked up at the priest: "See what you have done, Monsieur le Curé. It's all your fault."

He breathed a sigh of impatience, at which she answered, in a shrill voice: "We are going to make changes in our will, Monsieur le Curé. Unless . . ."

Countless times in the last few years the Bureau sisters had threatened to write Monsieur le Curé out of their will. Some of these threats had been means of getting help for which they might have had to disburse large sums in professional fees: collecting rent moneys, for instance, had often been much easier during the days that followed a stiff sermon on the Christian's solemn duty to honor his debts. Other threats had turned out to have been mere pretexts to force Monsieur le Curé to listen to the sisters' shrill prattling during a long summer afternoon. If it was cold in church, or tavern noises spoiled the sisters' sleep at night, if Monsieur le Curé snubbed them by starting Communion from the left end of the balustrade while they knelt at the right end of it, or if he happened to be out fishing when they knocked at his door for a friendly chat after going around the stations of the Cross, they would make sure to inform him of the gravity of the outrage, hinting at how much it was likely to cost the parish. And Monsieur le Curé would invariably show himself most patient and helpful and apologetic, assuring

274

them of his deep concern with making them happy in their lonely old days. Having repeatedly inquired about the exact details of the will, which, he was told, bequeathed the Red House to the parish, he knew what benefits to the community could be reaped by an extra dose of Christian tolerance.

This morning, however, he found it extremely difficult to remain patient. Bluntly, he asked: "Unless what?"

"Unless you do something about our new tenants in the Red House," the younger sister replied.

"But what can I do? I'm not their landlord. You rented to them. I didn't."

"But don't you remember, Monsieur le Curé? When we asked for references, you yourself said it would be a good deed to rent the house for a rosary factory, and you even suggested cutting down the rent a little."

The priest cleared his throat.

"I don't mean to blame you, Monsieur le Curé," she went on. "Of course you did not know these men were so evil. But now you know, as everybody in town does. So they must be evicted at once. There will be charivari if they stay one more day. Then what will happen to our property? Our poor red house, just painted all anew last year. They will set fire to it, I'm sure."

"Fine," exclaimed the priest. "In that case you won't need to make any more changes in your will. Good riddance." And he walked up to the front door to see if Alice or the beadle were coming back.

"But you must do something, Monsieur le Curé," the younger sister pleaded. "It is in your interest, after all."

"The Good Lord is mad at us," the other went on.

"Please, save the house, Monsieur le Curé."

"Yes, save the house," he snapped, "so that you can turn round and give it to Father Boulanger, I suppose."

"That is what we will do, if you don't help us."

"Go ahead. What would I want to do with a pile of ashes, anyway?"

"Please, save the house."

Monsieur le Curé turned back. "But I can't work miracles, my good woman."

"Oh, yes, you can, if you try hard enough."

Resolved to put a quick end to this litany, Monsieur le Curé rapped out in tones of severe reprimand: "If you had given the house to the parish, as I advised you to do, last year, we would not be having all this trouble today. Instead of a house of sin there, we would have our headquarters for the Virgins of Mary. Now, wouldn't that be much more to God's liking?"

"But it's such a good source of income."

Monsieur le Curé threw up his hands. "That's just the point. Money, money, money! It's the only thing you worry about. You lie for money, you turn your property into a house of sin for money, you get in trouble because of money; then you come here and throw the blame on Monsieur le Curé."

"The Good Lord is mad, mad."

"Yes, the Good Lord is mad. And so is your Curé."

The younger sister crossed herself.

"Why, even the Protestants have more sense than you. If I were you, my good woman, I would waste no time. Instead of coming here to threaten your Curé, I would go to church right now and drop to my knees and ask God forgiveness. And I would ask God to help your Curé straighten out this awful, awful mess you've made. Go now, right this minute. In the meantime, I'll see what can be done."

The younger sister helped the other to her feet, and they started to leave, while Monsieur le Curé held the door open. Pointing solemnly toward the church, he added: "Go in there now, and make a promise. Promise to God that if your Curé can help you out, you will put your property to more Christian uses from now on. Understand?"

"Thank you, Monsieur le Curé. We will pray for you."

"And for yourself."

"Yes. For ourselves, too."

Monsieur le Curé let out a deep sigh of relief. He wiped the sweat off his forehead and the back of his neck, and stood leaning against the pillar of the porch a moment.

All was quiet on the Place de l'Eglise. A handful of children were playing tag in the center. At the door of the Police-and-Fire House a fireman sat on the bumper of the truck, drowsing in the sun. A few women, arms full of parcels, were resting their legs on the steps of the church. A curly-headed boy was floating a toy canoe in one of the Holy Water fonts. The only note of disquiet in the air was a faint noise coming from the crowd on the Rue des Erables, where the sidewalks were full of women going in and out of the shops in a bustle of agitation.

This contrast gradually moved Monsieur le Curé to a feeling of alarm and distress. The serene quiet of the Place, under this bright sun, was shattered with scenes of imagined violence. He saw the angry crowd of women rushing past, just as he had seen them thirteen years before. He saw the wretched girls being dragged out of the brothel and stripped naked and burned alive, strangled, trampled to death under the pouncing mob. He saw the flames soaring wild into the evening sky, high above the cross on top of the belfry, which tumbled down to ruin in a final picture of total destruction. And in his imagination the happy laughter of children at play was buried under an uproar of savage cries that mingled with moans of agony rising from the victims.

Abruptly, Monsieur le Curé turned away, and took refuge in his office. Here he sat down to one, then another, bottle of ale. He felt that he would need a lot of it before this day was over.

*   *   *

At the same time that Monsieur le Curé imagined La Buche being turned into a holocaust, Father Boulanger visualized it as a sanctuary.

Looking out the window of his office on the third floor of the seminary, he saw the town as it would be in the future, a haven for prayers to the Saint of Timberland. The crowd of women shopping on the Rue des Erables became a procession of pilgrims, and the signs advertising "Charivari Specials" dissolved into religious banners that waved gently over the faithful heads lowered in prayer. There were people from all parts of the Province: women and children and old folks, city-dressed people and loggers, some on crutches or walking with canes or wearing steel braces, others in wheelchairs, on stretchers. Their praying and chanting silenced the rumblings of the rapids, and the sharp smell of wet bark in the air was replaced by the soul-pleasing perfume of Blessed Incense. The black of the asphalt pavement, mingled with the muddy brown of dirt roads, wove a broad canvas upon which thousands and thousands of feet shuffled piously. He followed them into the house where the Saint was born, to the Haymarket where he played as a boy, to the Convent classroom where he learned to shape the letters Jesus, to the chapel in the Seminary where he heard the Divine Call and to the garden where, at the intersection of the two gravel paths now immortalized by a stone inscribed with the details of the event, he had answered the Divine Call by vowing his life to the services of God among his people in La Buche. From here the procession cut across town to the river, where part of the wild waters were detoured into a small pond tree-shaded and ringed with

278

benches to commemorate the Saint's poetry-reading after-
noons in the simple quiet by the rapids. And then the faithful went on to the last stretch of the pilgrimage, up the slope
of La Colline Sainte-Marie, where a splendid Basilica dom-
inated the countryside. It could be reached through a wide
curving stairway made of five hundred steps, and among those
who were able to walk there were many who climbed them,
stopping at every hundred steps to recite one decade of the
chaplet. The others formed an endless serpentine of human
suffering that went inching up the side ramps to the shrine,
where they prayed that a miracle might enable them to leave
behind their crutches, canes, stretchers, braces.

Vivid was this vision of tomorrow's La Buche in the mind
of Father Boulanger. And complete. Sketched upon immediate reality by the broad lines of the sermon still in his head,
it was reinforced by his determination to surmount the ob-
stacles now being raised by Paul Gauthier. He sensed that he
had spoken the words of God's will. Faith sustained his
certitude that the Good Lord would give him strength to
carry it out.

Turning away from the window, he said: "No. I can't do
what you demand of me."

"Why?" asked Paul.

"Because Claude's life is in the hands of God," replied
the old priest. "And it would be an act of evil pride to inter-
fere with His Divine Will. Besides, it is Claude's own wish
that things should be so. He has offered his suffering, his
young life, to expiate the sins of his people, including your
own. And now, you, his brother, ask me to stand in the way
of that sublime sacrifice? Why, young man, you don't seem
to realize how evil, how cruel, that would be. Did it ever oc-
cur to you to consider this aspect of what you propose to do?"

"The only thing I consider is my duty," Paul replied, stand-

279

ing on the other side of the desk. "The boy is sick, he needs an operation, and it is my duty to make sure he gets one."

Father Boulanger sat down and crossed his hands. "It seems to me rather that your duty is to pray for your poor brother."

"As I told you before, I did not come here to listen to a sermon."

"You are still very rebellious, young man."

"Yes. And I will become even more so, if you don't make my mother sign for that operation."

Not accustomed to such open defiance and lack of respect for the soutane, Father Boulanger lit his pipe to smoke away his disquiet. And for the second time he invited Paul to sit down.

Paul remained standing. "So what's your answer?"

Father Boulanger let out a puff of smoke, and through it he stared ponderously up and down the giant body.

This added a tinge of self-consciousness to Paul's irritation. He could not repress a sudden urge to ridicule the preposterous schemes which he knew were brewing inside the Jesuit's head. "You have been whacking at the wrong tree, sir," he began. "I'm only trying to do you a favor by stopping you before you go too far. You know very well that people don't believe in miracles any more, at least not around here."

The old priest interrupted: "But you must not assume that because you lack faith everybody else does. If it is true that people do not believe in a miracle at the time it take places, it is nevertheless a fact that they do believe in it afterwards, when the irrefutable proofs are shown them. We all know it is not in heaven that saints are made, but right here on earth, among us. Only, we must not be blind. We must learn to recognize an act of God. Now, I don't suppose you have ever stopped to consider how good, and pure, and simple, and saintly, our little Claude is, and has been all his life.

280

Your sinfulness prevents you from seeing him that way, no doubt, just as it blinds you to the obvious fact that this corner of Timberland, this small town of ours, provides a perfect setting for public devotions and pilgrimages. Look at that magnificent forest! See how warmly, how protectively it hugs the contours of our village. And why? Why has this splendid forest been preserved all these years, why has it not been felled by the logger's axe? Because it was meant to frame a future sanctuary, dedicated to the worship of the Saint of Timberland. This is the reason. Only an act of Providence could have made it stand here until now. For it is also written that the loggers shall have their saint. The musicians have Saint Cecilia, the carpenters have Saint Joseph, the chaste maidens have the Holy Virgin Mary, even the truck drivers have their Saint Christopher; why, therefore, should not the loggers have their own patron saint, their Saint Claude? Furthermore, since the people of this Province either come from, or are still, men of the woods, is it not natural, that their patron saint be the Saint of Timberland? Don't you see, young man, how wise the ways of Providence can be? And don't you realize how grateful you should feel that God has chosen your family for such a great role in the religious life of your people? Or will you be a Thomas all your life?"

"But who in the world is going to believe that my kid brother is a saint?" Paul said. "You are going too far. Or maybe you ought to pick somebody else for the job. Just last night, for instance, the boy told me he was in love, gave up the idea of becoming a priest; he wants to go away with his girl right now. How about that?"

"I know," said Father Boulanger. "He told me the same thing this morning. However, you obviously did not understand what your brother means, again because of your stubborn pride. When our little Claude speaks of seeing his girl

281

very soon, it is the Virgin Mary whom he contemplates. In his last moments he is rewarded with visions of her as real as if he were actually in Paradise. And naturally he longs, he yearns, to be Up There, with her."

"Like hell," Paul snapped.

Father Boulanger puffed away the disrespectful remark. "Such a beautiful death, peaceful and happy, is what you want to deprive your brother of, after all that he has gone through! And you still insist that you are only trying to do your duty? My dear young man, how far gone you are on the road to damnation! Your hatred of the priest and of your Mother the Church is blinding you. The fate that you suffer is the lot of all renegades. Pride confuses your emotions and your motives. It is not your dear brother that you think about at this point. You think only of rising against God's Divine Will. You seek to destroy the word of God as it is pronounced by us, His representatives on earth. You wish to make certain that His Kingdom will not come. If you only knew how vain your rebellion is."

Paul stepped up to the edge of the desk, arms akimbo. "Look here, sir," he said, "I don't like to show disrespect for old folks and to talk rough to them. But if you go on giving me a sweet sermon instead of action, you'll end up driving me to do something rash. Now, I'm telling you in a nice way."

"Let me assure you of one thing," said the old priest, who was becoming calm and self-confident in the exact measure in which Paul was growing aroused and indignant. "God's will has defeated more formidable enemies than you. And your Mother the Holy Church has taken back in her fold many prodigal sons who strayed even further than you have. Don't you see, then, how futile it is to behave as you do? Do you realize how hard I am trying to help you?"

"Ah," Paul exclaimed, "so now you are trying to help me by murdering my brother, is that it?"

282

Father Boulanger lowered his gaze to the folds of his soutane. He said nothing. He could only shake his head in sorrow.

Paul rapped out: "Do you know what it means to have worked all your life for your brother as I have, and to feel that your whole life depends on whether or not he is going to pull through? Yes, it may be that I need help. But then the help I need has got to come from seeing the boy live. He's all I have."

Father Boulanger nodded in slow affirmation. "That is what I was trying to tell you before. But you would not let me go on. As you said so well just now, your motives are pure selfishness. You are trying to find in your poor brother a reason for living, a purpose in life, a meaning, something to believe in. And why? Because you have given up your faith. Outside the great family of your Mother the Holy Church, you are a lost wanderer. And you will fail utterly. You must never forget that man must live for his soul, by his soul, in his soul, alone. No other human being, mother, father, sister, brother, or friend, can give real purpose and meaning to your existence. Your soul, in the image of God, is central to your being. The essence of Him is in you. Cast It out, and you are lost."

The old priest paused for breath. He was on the point of going on when Paul, clenching his fists tight to control his agitation, declared in tones of deep feeling: "Now let me tell you something once and for all. You and I, sir, don't happen to believe in the same God. Well, that's just too bad, I suppose. But the sooner you accept this as a fact the better it will be for both of us. You had better forget that I once served Mass for you for a nickel. There's been a lot of water and timber down the rapids since then. Now, I know nothing about religion, I'm not an educated man. A lumberjack is what I am, and

283

lumberjacks, poor bastards, don't have the brains to understand all that goes on in that head of your Mother the Church. But this much I know just the same: Your religion is rotten; it makes people cruel so that they turn against one another and kill one another, and all for a pack of lies, lies, lies. And I want no part of your God either, because your God makes people feel like worms, and that's no good for people. Your God is cruel, sir. I don't know what river you fished Him out of, but I know it isn't the same God that Jesus talked about. No, sir. I've been doing some reading of my own out there at camp. And I know that your God isn't the same God that Jesus had in mind. Anyway, I want no part of Him. Find me a God that's good for the people, and kind, and gentle, and I'll say yes, I want to believe in him. Find me a God that lets a man feel like there is an ounce of dignity in him, and I'll do anything for this God. But let me tell you: You are not going to find this kind of God under your skirts, that much I know for sure. You priests, and God who is good and kind, could never exist together at the same time. You teach that suffering is a virtue and that man is low and sinful and vile, and this keeps you in business and fat like a gang of jacks fed on beans and thick cream. That's the whole point. You don't give a damn about the people, so long as they believe what you tell them. That's the way you are. You even kill in the name of your God, just to stay in business. And on top of it all we are supposed to thank you for doing a thing like that. For God's sake, sir, what are you trying to do to us poor lumberjacks?"

Paul expected a reply from the old priest, but the latter said nothing. He kept his head lowered in meditation. After a while Paul went on: "Now, I'm not the kind of a guy who goes around telling people what to do and what to believe in. I have never talked to anybody before the way I am talking now. And I have to step on my pride to do it, you may be sure of that. All I want to come out of this is a clear understanding between us. You stick to your beads, and I take care of my brother. Clear?"

Father Boulanger remained silent.

"All right, then" Paul cried. "Have it your own way for now. But, by God, don't say I didn't warn you."

Father Boulanger did not look up, said nothing.

"I wish that I didn't have to talk this way to an old man," Paul said. "But when I think of the low rotten scheme that's on your mind I can't help feeling the way I do. Wickedness and white hair don't go well together; and when there is a black robe down below it's even uglier to look at. But never mind. I suppose your God will forgive you in the end. A couple of words in Latin, and the sign of the cross, and there you are, clean as an angel. And all this time the blood of my brother is dripping hot from your hands."

"Please. You have said enough."

"So now you pretend to feel human inside?"

Father Boulanger shook his head in deep sorrow. "What evil, what hatred, my child!"

"I wasn't born with it."

"Don't you respect anything?"

"Yes. I respect life."

Father Boulanger crossed and uncrossed his hands. Finally he stood up and said: "Tell your mother I wish to talk to her. I shall see what can be done."

A faint ray of hope appeared on Paul's face.

"But I can promise nothing," the old priest added. "I am not the master of my own destiny. Nor am I your mother's conscience, or our little Claude's creator. God has the last word. Whatever fate he has in store for me, I am ready to accept it."

Paul turned abruptly and walked out.

fourteen

Madame Gauthier was kept busy
answering the telephone and the front door. There were inquiries concerning the great event predicted in Father Boulanger's sermon. "Could it possibly mean the Charivari?"

Madame Gauthier's reply, vague but uttered in a tone of oracular solemnity, soon convinced the doubting ones that it meant exactly that. The truly pious women offered congratulations. "Just think of it: to be chosen the mother of a saint!" Sentiments of profound sympathy were expressed in Sunday phrases, or in the simple words of Timberland spoken in painful awareness of their inadequacy to convey all that one feels in the presence of death.

Among those who presented their most sincere condolences, there were some who brought rosaries that they wanted spread on the coffin; others had flower pots, jars of Holy Water, candles blessed by the Bishop of Trois-Rivières. Several women wanted to help with the housework, now, or in the hard days ahead. Between stifled sobs and sighs of mournful resignation a few mothers managed to put in a hesitant question about the wake. By mid-morning several patches of material had been clipped off from the curtains where the relic-hunters had seen the Little Saint stand so often.

Alice called and asked if the sick boy was strong enough to travel to a hospital in Grand-Mère; Monsieur le Curé, she explained, had just learned of the sudden turn for the worse and would be very glad to recommend a specialist and lend his car—"What? Go and ask Father Boulanger?" Very well, she would give him that message, though she couldn't guarantee the Curé would like the rude way his offer of help was being received! Then the superior of the convent appeared at the door; she embraced Madame Gauthier and called her "sister," which left Claude's mother utterly speechless with beatitude. On her way out the thoughtful nun promised that in another hour or so there would be "a little surprise that will gladden your heart, my dear." The phone rang again. It was Monsieur De Blois, to announce that he and his wife had just decided that their newborn baby would be baptized Claude. After that it was the doorbell, and the phone again, and again a host of kind souls at the door. And there was the sound of Claude's respiration, his footsteps, that she must remain attentive to all the while.

However distracting, all this activity did not relieve Claude's mother of the problem uppermost in her mind. Her powers of invention, now that they were being put to sinful aims, failed to produce the lie that she needed to tell her confessor

288

when she would give him the money. Each time she found herself alone for a moment between the telephone and the front door the thought of it struck with renewed urgency. Toward the end of the morning she was so overwrought with helplessness that she headed for the kitchen with the set intention of throwing the money in the garbage pail. But fortunately for the cause of the Little Saint of Timberland, Madame Dupré came in at that moment, so that Claude's mother was given the birth of an idea as to putting it to better use.

The stationmaster's wife first made it plain that she was here in her official capacity of Présidente des Dames de la Grâce. She recited a formal expression of condolences. Then there was a full report on last night's meeting, with emphasis on the fact that never in the history of Les Dames de la Grâce had their leader been elected by so unanimous a vote.

"I am *so* glad for you," said Claude's mother.

And now Madame Dupré announced that she was going to organize a general collection for Masses. And she hastened to add: "If everybody gives as much as they ought to, very generously, there might be enough to help with the cost of the funeral."

"Contributions!" Madame Gauthier exclaimed, her hands closing over the money in the parting of her breasts.

"Are you not feeling well?"

"I am all right, thank you," said Madame Gauthier, absently. She went to the door and opened it, inviting her guest to leave.

This sudden change of countenance made the stationmaster's wife feel she was being snubbed again. "That's what you get when you try to help people," she muttered. "I should have known better. She'll be stuck up even in her own grave, that one." Then, at the door, her wounded vanity came out in bitter words wrapped up in an outpouring of sisterly tenderness: "My poor dear," she said: "Your little one did not have to offer his young life as he did, really. We are going to shut down that place, anyway."

Meanwhile, the Daughters of Mercy appeared outside. There were about ten of them, dressed in black frocks and carrying giant chaplets with beads the size of French cherries and the color of coal. They formed a picket line in front of the Gauthier house, and began reciting the *Aves* in high fragile voices as they shuffled piously on the heels of one another, their old wrinkled heads lowered in a formal expression of grief. Women passing by with arms full of shopping bags stopped and joined them for one decade or two. Children were told to go on home; they could not be relied upon to maintain an air serious enough for the occasion. Tavern noises came from down the street. A succession of signals, originating from the mourners, soon went traveling from woman to woman and group to group until, finally, the doors of Lambert's were slammed shut. Now, in spite of the large number of people on the sidewalks, the sound of praying could be heard clearly all the way to the church. Inside the presbytery, Alice hastened to alert Monsieur le Curé, who was talking with the beadle on the back porch. "Yes. That looks like one of his tricks, the old fox," he commented. And he ordered Fulgence to go and look for Paul everywhere in town and send him to the presbytery right away.

Moments later, a note of profane disquiet suddenly descended upon the pious recitation of the rosary. It came from La Sauvageau, a little woman with round shoulders and a worn look, who, standing across the street from the mourners, shouted at the top of her voice: "What's the use of praying? He is much better off dead, the poor lad. There won't be no more misery for him now that the Lord is calling him back.

Pray for the living instead, if you think it will do any good; for it's us that need it, all of us that have to go on with this rotten life 'till the Lord takes it into his fancy to do us a favor and let us drop dead. Ah, if I had known what I know now, when I was his age, I would have quit, too."

Piercing glances flashed toward her from the mourners and from the women who had joined them. The sound of the recitation suddenly grew quite loud, for they all knew that she would become silent the moment nobody listened to her wailings. It was always that way with her.

But this time they were wrong, obviously, for she went on shouting and cursing and blaming the whole world for the terrible tragedies that filled her heart with so much bitterness. True enough, the poor creature had had a fair share of misfortunes. Her husband had died of gangrene from an axe wound at Bechard; her son had been shot down by the Mounties while hiding in the woods to evade the draft; her daughter, the one with the pretty blue eyes, had run away to Montreal and married a Jew. And now, just last night, another tragedy: Minouche, her only child left, had come home late with her skirts full of ravine-mud and no panties on. Ah, they could pray all they wanted, it would change nothing in this world that was so rotten; the ones who were smart gave up the ghost while they were still young. The innocent ones, were not innocent anymore; now they went around showing their bare ass to the moon like a bunch of dirty Protestants! "A fine world to bring children into!"

A group of schoolboys could be seen coming down the Rue des Pins toward the Gauthier house. Anxious that the innocent be spared the shock of such scandalous wailings, two mourners started across to where La Sauvageau was still shouting. They grabbed their giant-size rosaries and swung

291

them with threatening intent. She became silent at once, then took to her legs down the street like a hunted dog.

Fortunately, her shocking utterances did not reach the ears of the schoolboys. And a good thing it was indeed, considering the beautiful thought of brotherly kindness that dwelled in their innocent souls at that moment. The youngsters, twelve of them representing the twelve grades at the convent school, carried small envelopes that contained one dollar each. The collection has been organized by Mother Superior, who had also instructed the delegates to ring the bell, give the money, not ask to see the Little Saint, and then go on home directly.

Madame Gauthier opened the door in answer to a shy knock from the oldest boy who acted as leader of the delegation. In a voice shaking from self-conscious solemnity, he recited: "For Our Little Saint, Madame; one High Mass, and two Low Masses." And at the same time each child handed over his envelope.

"So *this* was the little surprise!" Tears of tender joy filled the eyes of Claude's mother. She gathered the children under outspread arms, and raising her eyes to heaven she sighed: "Oh, dear Lord. Thank you. Thank you so much!"

The youngest one, a little curly-haired fellow with holes in his pants, cried out suddenly: "When's the miracle?"

The others poked him to quiet with elbows and fingers. He began to cry. Claude's mother picked him up and hugged him, she dried his tears with her fingertips and consoled him: "It is by little children like you that the world will be saved."

Such affectionate praise caused a broad grin of pride to flash on the little fellow's face. The others gazed gravely at their feet, forced to listen to Madame Gauthier's sermon on the virtues of hard work, piety, as exemplified by Claude when he was their age. Then she told them to go home, and be

292

good, and they marched away in single file, like a group of first communicants, while the mourners nodded in admiration. Trailing behind the rest was the curly-haired boy who had stolen the show from the head of the delegation. At the next corner his companions gathered quickly around him before he could escape. He was tagged "It" in a game of hide-and-seek, and they all ran off to the Haymarket.

Inside the Gauthier house, meanwhile, the phone was ringing again. But Claude's mother would not answer. Sitting at the kitchen table with the money in front of her, she was trying to divide it into two contributions in amounts proportionately acceptable to Father Boulanger. But each sum was still considerable. A lie remained a lie no matter how good her intentions might be. Madame Gauthier sighed. She put part of the money in an old shoe-box, and the rest in a wooden box in which she used to keep her chaplets and jewelry crosses. She was just closing the boxes when the front door opened and Paul walked in. Hurriedly she covered the boxes with a towel.

"Father Boulanger wants to talk to you," Paul said gently.

Startled, she stood up. "Have you been to see him?"

"Yes," he replied, going up the stairs.

She hurried after him. "Paul."

"Yes?" He turned. "What is it?"

"Did you . . . I mean, what did you go and see him about?"

"You will find out when you talk with him."

The look in his eyes as he said this shattered her sudden hope that perhaps he had had a change of soul, at last, and confessed to Father Boulanger.

"But you had better go now," Paul said. "He is expecting you."

His mother returned to the kitchen and picked up the boxes of money. What had he seen Father Boulanger about, she wondered. A prey to growing suspicion, she left the house.

Then on the sidewalk, she asked the mourners if they would please recite the next Mystery for the salvation of Paul's soul. "Yes, indeed," all of them bowed respectfully; so that she was now able to go to her confessor with a hopeful heart. Her hands were trembling as they held the boxes containing her contributions.

* * *

"It's all set. We are leaving," Paul announced cheerfully on entering his brother's room.

From the floor where he was putting on his boots, Claude exclaimed: "Wonderful!"

"As soon as I can get Lambert's car, which should be around four, maybe five."

"I'm ready to go right now," Claude said. And he got up to his feet to show that he would be able to make it. "I have been exercising all morning long. Fifty-three steps without my cane just now. Watch. I'll bet I can double, even triple that, so you won't have to carry me on the portage stretch to the shack. Look."

"But we are not going to the lake," Paul said.

Claude came to a standstill.

"I am taking you to a hospital in Montreal."

His face dropped. He became unsteady on his legs.

"Don't be upset, boy. I have good news for you," Paul said. And he helped him to the chair near the foot of the bed. Then lacing up Claude's boots he told him about his conversations with Doctor Gendron and with Father Boulanger. After leaving the Seminary, he had gone back to the doctor's office, and reported that the priest seemed willing to let Claude undergo the operation. Doctor Gendron had immediately telephoned Montreal, to make the necessary arrangements, then he had given Paul a typewritten release which Madame Gauthier would have to sign. "In case she doesn't want to take the trip to the hospital, where she would normally be asked to sign it," Paul explained, and he went on to declare enthusiastically: "And I know she will sign it when Father Boulanger has talked to her. So you see, we are all set."

Claude went over to the window leaning heavily on his cane. A breath of sun-filled air greeted him, but he made no effort to take it into his lungs.

"I suppose it's a bit of a shock," Paul said. "But cheer up, boy. Now you have to get used to the idea of being well again."

"I was ready, had everything figured out."

"I know what you mean. You were desperate and you had lost hope. You were afraid to think of the future. I know. I've been through the same thing. But believe me, it's not too hard to learn again how to hope, once you set your mind to it."

"No. Not after you have resigned yourself to death."

"But you have no right to give up."

Claude turned and faced his brother. "Why pretend? You and I know what is going to happen. It's only a matter of time. So let's not fool ourselves, Paul. I don't want to start all over again, just to end up facing another deception. No. No. Let's go to the lake, as we had planned. You promised we would."

"I'm taking you to the hospital," Paul countered in a firm voice. "There is still a chance, and I'm going to make sure you get the benefit of it."

"Why are you so hard, all of a sudden?"

"It's my duty."

"If only you knew what I have gone through! Have pity. Don't force me to build a lot of false hope again."

"If father were alive today, he would do exactly what I'm doing."

Claude sat down again, sighing in pained perplexity, while Paul began pacing up and down the length of the room. A long silence descended between them. The phone rang; they paid no attention to it. Claude's respiration, rapid and hoarse, sounded in counterpoint to Paul's footsteps that told of the nervous anxiety now besetting him.

After a while, Paul stopped suddenly, and said: "Do it for me, boy."

"I suppose I'll have to," Claude said resignedly.

"I don't mean it that way," Paul retorted. Then in a voice of passionate conviction he added: "What I mean is . . . By Christ, you've got to keep going. Don't ask me why, I don't know. You're the one who's got all the brains and the schooling so maybe you know the real reason. It's just wrong somehow to give up. Come on, pull yourself together."

"And what about my girl? I'll never see her again."

"You will," Paul said. And as an afterthought he added, "that is, if there is really a girl."

"What do you mean?"

Paul hesitated a moment. Then with his back turned to his brother, he said: "The doctor said you might be imagining things, at this stage."

"Don't tell me you think I am delirious, too, like Father Boulanger and mother, who talk to me as if I were out of my mind?"

"Tell me about her," Paul said.

It was some moments before Claude could muster up enough courage to try and prove that Lise did exist. Pointing his cane at the rooftops beyond the window, he said: "See that red house over there, the one that belongs to the Bureau sisters? That's where she works. I've been watching her go into that house every night in the last few weeks. She came here last night while mother was out at the meeting. And around six o'clock tonight she'll be standing there to wait for my signal. Don't you believe me now?"

Paul let out a long sigh of relief. "It's all in your imagination. Standing here at the window and watching these girls go to work is what did it. You see, as the doctor explained to me, the fever . . ."

"Please," Claude interrupted. "Look under the mattress, there. You'll find the book she brought me last night. Look."

Paul turned from the window. His face was drawn in an expression of pained surprise.

"Well, look," Claude urged him. He got up and limped toward the bed. "I'm going to prove it to you."

"Never mind," Paul said.

On lifting the mattress Claude let out a cry.

"Never mind," Paul repeated. "I believe you, boy." Then he explained what had happened to the book.

"But there was money in it," Claude said, almost crying with vexation, "two hundred dollars. *Her* money."

"Don't worry about it," said Paul. "I have enough on me." He was gazing blindly through the window over the rooftops that glinted in the sun. How desperate he must have been. How desperate! he thought. He almost wished that he had not insisted on the trip to the hospital. Remembering what the doctor had said about the chances being very slim, he knew that sharp pang of helplessness people feel when they become aware that in trying to do what they think is their duty they are only being cruel to someone dear.

"Would she come with us?" Claude asked, after a while.

Paul nodded yes.

297

"She is a good girl, Paul. You will like her."

"Sure. Of course I will."

Claude explained where she lived, and spoke rapturously of her. "Lise . . ."

"I'll find her," Paul interrupted.

The phone was ringing again. There were knocks at the front door, and the muffled sounds of praying from outside. Finally Claude asked: "What did the doctor say the chances are?"

"Very good."

Chuckling in disbelief, Claude picked up his cane and resumed his exercise, as Paul, distressed by what he had just heard, left to go and look for Lise.

* * *

The arrival of the schoolboys at the Haymarket brought a moment of relief and hope to Lise. Hiding in a horse-stall at the sidewalk end of one of the three stables that bounded the square, she watched the gay youngsters burst noisily onto the place. They went running in and out of the open-front stables, chased one another with handfuls of dung-soiled straw; they jumped and rolled in the haylofts and then scurried among the stalls, looking for a good spot to hide. "GO!" they shouted to the blindfolded little fellow in the center of the square, who set out to seek them in their hiding places. With one hand groping the sunny air, the curly-haired "it" started vaguely toward the main building. But halfway there he stopped, stood still a moment listening for clues. "Pst! Pst!" Lise whispered to attract him. "Pst! Pst! Pst!" In quick response he began to zigzag in the direction of the stall, where she now got up and, after furtive glances up and down the street, felt safe enough to step out into the open of the sill. The boy was no more than fifteen feet away from her when a sudden burst of giggles made him stop and turn sharply to the right toward the other end of the stable. Lise went back into the dark corner of the horse-stall, to wait anxiously for the next chance.

She had spent the night here on a bed of straw. Mice and the cold had kept her awake shivering under Monsieur le Curé's soutane. Only at sunrise had she been able to sleep at last, when the sun poured bright and hot through the open front of the stall, chasing the rodents away and warming up her legs and shoulders. Late in the morning, she had been frightened awake by shrill voices of women nearby. What she then witnessed filled her with terror. A mass cleanup drive of the rooming houses was in progress under the leadership of Lise's landlady, who headed a platoon of indignant women going from door to door in search of whores. Shouts of violent wrath, cries of charivari, mingled with shrieks of horror and hysterical screams of fear as the girls were dragged out by the hair, kicked, spat upon and chased down the street at the end of broomsticks that cut the air with murderous intent.

The tumult brought a score of women and children out of the houses across the Haymarket to join the chase. One girl, who had been pulled out of bed half-asleep, suddenly found herself trapped between two advancing fronts of threatening females. They jumped on her, tore at her underclothes; some of them dug their nails into her bare flesh, and as she stood there too frightened to move, they burst out laughing, jeering and cursing, urged her to run for her life, which she did, like a hunted deer. They gave her a good chase toward the Haymarket and across the square into a horse-stall where she stumbled, picked herself up and, climbing on top of the manger, jumped through the window and landed with a dull crash on the sidewalk planks. Some of the women rounded the end of the stable and continued to chase her up the Rue des

299

Sapins all the way to the brothel, while the others went back in the direction of the rooming houses.

Gradually the crowd began to disperse, with a steady lowering of voices amidst nods of approval, promises of more effective action tonight. Lise, crawling to a dark corner of the horsestall, buried herself in the straw. The wall that protected her from passers-by was full of vertical slits, knotholes and broken boards, and she hardly dared breathe until all was quiet again. She decided to seek refuge in the presbytery or at the train depot. But on peeping through a knothole she felt a sudden sharpening of dread. Groups of women were still about, chatting on the steps of the rooming houses, and walking home with arms full of groceries; it would be impossible for her to escape their attention. Lise shivered in the dung-stinking heat of the stall. Her only chance of getting away was this blindfolded little fellow with the curly hair and the holes in his pants, who was coming close to her again.

"Here, sweetie," Lise called him softly.

He went toward her, groping with one hand as through a thick underbrush, while his playmates giggled and whistled louder in expressions of sheer delight at seeing him go where they were sure nobody was hiding.

"Here, sweetie, right here. That's it."

Lise was now able to pull him by the hand to the dark corner. She made him sit down on the straw. Then she removed the woolen sock they had used as a blindfold.

His young eyes brightened in happy surprise. "Let's go hide together," he said.

"No, no. We stay right here," she whispered.

His face dropped. Why wouldn't she come and hide with him, out there in the last hayloft? It would be so much fun to surprise the others.

300

Lise pulled out of her handbag a piece of paper and a pencil, and scribbled a short note asking for help. She put the note in a pocket of the soutane, made a bundle, then gave it to him with a dime.

"Take this to Monsieur le Curé right away." She pushed him gently. "Go. Run before the others can catch up with you."

He gazed happily at the dime in his hand. But there was the game. He did not want to leave his playmates, because he feared that without them he might not be able to witness the great event that was promised. "Couldn't I go after the miracle?" he said.

"What miracle?"

"The miracle. You know, the miracle."

The clear look of innocent wonder in his eyes, as he said this, went to Lise's heart. She wrapped her arms around his delicate body and hugged him with all the passionate yearning of her frustrated womanhood. Holding the little fellow in the cradle of her arms, she said with tears in her eyes: "Oh, but it's you, my sweet, it's you who are the miracle."

"Me?" He grinned with delight.

"Of course, my sweet. Now go, hurry. In my heart you will always be my little miracle."

A long sigh of pride and contentment. Then he darted out of the stall, and across the square. But he was not fast enough to escape his playmates, who came out of hiding in protest against his breaking the rules of the game. From the four corners of the square they converged upon him. He tried to break through the circle, but they closed in around him.

Where was he going? What did he have there? What did he find in that stall?

Frightened, he held the bundle tight, began to scream as the others tore at him to pry the bundle loose from his grasp.

The noise attracted women from the houses across the street. Now what were they trying to do: strangle the little one? Couldn't they go and fight with boys their own size! Much good it did to send those brats to the nuns for schooling! Look at that, carrying on like a bunch of throat-cutting Protestants!

The women hurried to separate the schoolboys and a small-scale brawl ensued. The older boys, resenting interference from women who were not their mothers, used words that belonged to the vocabulary of their lumberjack fathers and that their own mothers had often warned them never, never to repeat. Cheeks were slapped hard, ears were pulled. Taking advantage of the excitement the curly-haired little fellow managed to get away.

He came running back to Lise, still clutching the precious bundle that she had entrusted him with. Lise motioned him away; the women and childrn were coming after him. But he was too frightened to heed her; frantic he flung himself in her arms amidst tearful assertions that he had done his best.

"Of course, my sweet," she consoled him. "Of course, you did your best." She gave him a last quick hug, aware of the women shouting: "That's one of them. She's a whore."

"Let's get her!" They cried, making for the stall. "Get the whore!"

Lise dashed out, rounded the corner of the stable and ran in the direction of the Rue des Sapins, followed by the ravenous pack of women and schoolboys screaming with charivari-hunger. More women came out of the houses, armed with broomsticks to join the crowd of pursuers.

Lise dared not look back. A short distance ahead was the ravine, at the end of the road, where the Rue des Sapins began. To the right, several blocks up, stood the train depot. Wild with terror she raced on. A broomstick hit her left ankle. A shower of pebbles struck her in the back.

"Down with the whore!"

"Stop her!"

"Get the whore!"

The front lines of the mob now consisted mostly of children. They were yelling louder than the women, many of whom had dropped to the sides out of breath and wiping their brows. The boys charged forward, holding their schoolbags poised to strike. In their mouths the word whore was the primitive call of the jungle. Oh, to catch this whore with the long black hair flying in the wind, to bring her down.

Their cries and sheer animal frenzy frightened Lise even more than did the women. She expected to be felled any moment. Every muscle of her body was tight in agonizing anticipation of a blow. Hunching her shoulders and lowering her head, her lungs bursting for air, she made a last desperate sprint for the depot and safety.

At that moment Monsieur Dupré, drawn to the window by the noise of the chase, recognized Lise. He made a quick about-face. "Lock the doors, Arthur," he shouted. "I'm not here!" And he ran to hide inside the ladies' room. From the rear platform where he was unloading one of the kerosene drums taken out of the coal shack, Arthur hurried on his long unsteady legs into the waiting-room and to the front door to see what the racket was all about. He stepped out on the platform just as Lise ran onto it at the right-hand side.

"Hah, here's one! You, slut," exclaimed Arthur, his blood-shot eyes glowering at her. Wild with revenge for the treatment Paula had given him, he moved toward her menacingly with clenched fist.

Lise found herself trapped on the platform between him and the mob now gathering at her feet. The shouts began to subside. A tense hesitation stilled the crowd. All eyes shifted back and forth from Lise to Arthur, who was advancing steadily toward the terrified girl. The silence was deepened by clamoring voices coming from the center of town. The man was advancing more slowly now, relishing his role of public executioner, as Lise, inching away from him, watched his feet with the cornered look of a trapped animal. Arthur undid his belt, and winking at the mob, he braced himself to strike. A cry that was almost a moan rose from the women, and there were half-suppressed cries of pain from many of the children, as the belt cut a wide arc through the air and swung downward for Lise's legs.

She skipped. The buckle of the belt hit the boards, bounced, and the belt completed the circle, throwing her assailant off balance. Furious, he tried to strike again, but Lise caught the belt in mid-air and jerked it out of his hands. The next second she struck him across the face with all her strength. Arthur fell to the ground uttering a piercing howl of pain, and as the mob stood gazing with unbelieving eyes, Lise leaped down from the platform. Swinging the belt with savage fury, striking women and children alike, she made for the tracks that led to the forest between the rapids and the southern end of the Rue des Sapins. Sobbing, her last strength ebbing away, she pushed on, until suddenly she grew aware that the cries, the pounding of footsteps, were no longer behind her. But she did not slow down until she reached the first cluster of pines, where panting and spent she took cover in the underbrush.

What had happened was that another distraction had drawn her pursuers off her trail. For now rounding the corner of the Rue des Erables and the Rue des Pins another mob could be seen headed by a blond-haired woman who was running for her life. Screaming, the two mobs merged into one. But where was she? Where was the quarry? Above the tumult rose the voice of Arthur.

"Over there! There she goes! Over there!" He was pointing to the corner house, where he could see Paula trying to make her escape. She was running down the Rue des Sapins in the opposite direction to that in which Lise had been pursued a moment ago. The mob joined the chase in one great rush forward, everybody running, shouting, mad for blood.

The deafening uproar sent Paula's heart racing wildly. It was hopeless; she would never make the distance of all those blocks stretching ahead before she could reach the brothel. On her right was the ravine. But the footbridge leading to it seemed miles away, although actually it was only a few hundred feet. She had lost her shoes, the pebbles were cutting sharply into her feet. Unconsciously she clung to the torn paper bag she was holding. It was now empty of the food which she had gone out to buy at Ti-Pit's for the girls who did not dare leave the house after being chased out of their rooms near the Haymarket.

"The whore! Whore! Get the whore!"

Now the shouts were coming from ahead of Paula as well as from behind her, for there had just appeared up the street another band of women and children, led by La Pitoune, who were setting out to comb the woods for Mademoiselle Serval's body.

Her escape cut off, Paula knew that the ravine was her only hope. She veered toward the path that led to the footbridge. But some of the boys closing in on her had anticipated her move; they had jumped the ditch on the right and after cutting across the brush emerged at the other end of the path. Locking arms across the path they barred her approach to the bridge. Desperate, with lowered head, Paula bore down on them, punching and kicking her way through the cordon. Her torn dress hanging from her, her hair in wild disarray, she ran across the bridge and into the ravine where she finally took cover in the thick brush.

"Where did she go? The bitch! She got away."

Frustrated, the mob milled around the footbridge, and gradually began to disperse. La Pitoune rounded her people up to lead them on the search for Mademoiselle Serval's body in the woods. There were shrugs of failure, exclamations of "we'll get her later with the others," as the women shuffled slowly back to the street. They had done their duty; it had been a good chase. Energy must be spared for tonight. As for the youngsters who still wanted to hunt for their quarry in the ravine, "Sure. Go ahead," they said. The children had their blessings.

The youngsters stamped across the footbridge, invading the ravine with leaps of joy and the gay noises of play. Here, at last, was a real game of hide-and-seek. And what a prize! To catch a whore! They filled their pockets with stones and scattered into the brush, some crawling like soldiers in the line of fire, others gliding in emulation of Indians stalking their prey. Currents of rustling leaves furrowed the brush from one end of the ravine to the other. Here and there a young head emerged for a peep around. The suspense of the hunt was deepened by the low rumble of the rapids, the beat of the logs cascading down the chute.

Crouching, Paula moved toward the path that cut through the middle of the ravine from the footbridge to the wall of boulders. Her clothes were in rags. There were bruises on her face, arms, legs, and her knees and feet were bleeding. But the pains were numbed by the strain of her efforts to get to the rocky beach along which she might flee into the woods to hide until dark. Whispers nearby suddenly made her throw herself to the ground.

"Hey, what's a whore?"

"It's a woman who's married to the devil."

"Is that right?"

"Sure. And when we catch her, you'd better be careful not to touch her skin. Could burn you to death."

"I don't believe it."

"That's what Ma says."

"Give me some of your stones."

As soon as the whispers had died away, Paula resumed her creeping toward the path. Light running on the bridge told her that more children were joining the hunt. Waves of crackling branches swept through the brush. The hunters were everywhere. The path came into view beyond a sun-drenched glade ahead. She straightened up and made for it.

The sight of her blond head cutting through the branches was greeted by shouts from the children standing watch on the footbridge.

"There she goes!"

"To the bank!"

And the next second Paula was running toward the rapids under a rain of stones. The boys leaped out of the brush, converging upon the path in a rush that drove her to seek refuge between two large boulders. Stones were flying into the water behind her. A shower of rocks and earth poured down on her head, her shoulders and back. Having found her hiding spot, the youths aimed their volleys in a concentrated attack to force her out in the open again. Some of the older boys started climbing the bank with short branches and knife-like sticks between their teeth. Paula's head suddenly appeared against the sky. And now her shoulders, and the rest of her, rising from behind a large rock, became an open target, as she moved from boulder to boulder in an attempt to climb down onto the beach. A large stone struck her in the chest. She stumbled, her hands shot up to protect her face, and then she screamed in pain as another struck her full in the throat, knocking her off balance. The blow sent her reeling to the edge of the water, where she slumped down in agony and rolled over into the current. A last yell of despair, and she was swept away into the silver-green foam.

Not a sound was heard from the children gathered on the bank to watch the end of their hunt. They stared in horror, their mouths opened wide at the spectacle of those terrible rapids unleashing their fury upon the body of their victim. Like a log fallen from the chute, the body was dipped, pulled out, and dipped again, floating now gently on a pool of foam and then wheeled violently down a black-silked eddy, to disappear among spray-spitting rocks and, downstream, to come out again carried by a deeper, faster current. Now the body was wrapped around a steeple-shaped rock jutting out from the heart of the rapids. The legs and arms pointed downstream, while the current lifted the head to float unmoving. The neck was twisted, the eyes stared blindly at the sky, and two gold teeth could be seen sparkling in the sun.

The children took to their legs across the ravine, fleeing in panic with shoulders hunched as though before the first rushing waves of a flash flood. And each one of them uttered to himself in feverish trepidation: "I didn't do it. It was *his* stone that did it, not mine."

*   *   *

The sunlight and the tumult did not reach Father Boulanger's office overlooking the town from the second floor of the seminary building. The windows were shut and curtained behind the old priest, who sat at his desk in the dark, absorbed in meditation to calm the storm of disquiet which Paul's visit had raised within the usually peaceful confines of his soul.

"Have I gone too far? Am I forcing the Hand of God? Is there vanity in my heart?" he asked himself. But only to hear

308

an inner voice reply: "You are doing the right thing. In your heart there is no motive other than love for God. Your entire life has been devoted to the Greater Glory of God on earth. You must trust in the purity of your heart."

Translated into these terms, the question of right or wrong posed by his part in the death of the Gauthier boy seemed to call for one answer only, and a simple one at that. He was doing right, for how could he possibly do wrong after a lifetime of virtue? To regard his deed as evil would be equal to admitting that all his life of priesthood had been evil, since this one deed was the end result of it. And this, Jesuit-logically speaking, was impossible, just as, humanly speaking, it would be intolerable. It was sufficient to know and to believe that in his heart there was no evil design, and that there could never be such a thing, just as, according to what he had preached all these years, the Good Lord, since He was good, could do no evil.

Yet Father Boulanger was not at peace with himself. Paul's words had profoundly disquieted him. It was as though he were looking for a means of giving up his plans, a justification for retreat before the last stage of the battle. In truth, the very grandiosity of his dream of a Little Saint of Timberland was beginning to frighten him, as the hour for the predicted miracle drew near. Hesitation, the wish to transfer the burden of decision onto somebody else, had fully mastered him by the time Madame Gauthier walked in.

His greeting to her was a question asked in a voice weakened by anxiety: "Did your son tell you about the operation? What have you decided?"

Claude's mother came to a standstill. Her fingers tightened their hold on the boxes of money.

"Come, my good mother," he said, inviting her to sit in her usual chair in front of his desk.

"An operation?" she said, astonished.

Father Boulanger gave a brief account of Paul's visit, although he was thoughtful enough to spare her the pain of hearing the blasphemous accusation that her son had voiced. He mentioned that he had telephoned Doctor Gendron who confirmed everything about the trip to the hospital. Then he hastened to repeat his question, "What do you wish to do?"

"An operation?" Madame Gauthier exclaimed again, unbelieving.

Avoiding her troubled eyes, he said: "You must decide."

"I don't know, Father," she moaned. "I just don't know."

He nodded gravely, as a doctor would.

"I will do anything you say," she pleaded.

"The decision must be left entirely up to you, my good woman."

"But you must help me, Father."

He remained silent.

Frantic, she blurted out: "This is so unexpected. I was coming here to give you all this money. Here. This box from the children, and that one from the mothers of La Buche. For their Little Saint, just as it says here on the labels. Now, I don't know what to do." Then as the old priest hurriedly opened the curtains and sat down to count the money in a pool of sunlight on his desk, she went on: "If only I were certain that he would recover."

"From what the doctor tells me," he said, obviously astonished to find the sum so considerable, "the chances are not in his favor."

Madame Gauthier sighed: "A priest alive might well be worth a saint in heaven?"

"Perhaps. But who are we to judge? It is now evident that the Good Lord's word has been spoken to us once again. Look at all this money, hours only after my sermon, and at a time

310

like this, when our poor families have hardly enough to eat!
What else could this mean, but that the Good Lord expects us
to carry out our duty to the very end? Indeed, my good
woman, we have no choice. This is clearly an act of Divine
Providence. A moment ago I wished not to influence your
decision. But now I must impress upon you that to allow this
operation would only mean standing in the way of God's will."

"If you say so, Father."

"Besides," he went on, "it would be cruel to subject our
little Claude to a hopeless treatment."

Fingering her collar nervously, Madame Gauthier rose from
her chair.

"He is so resigned, so much at peace now," said Father
Boulanger, escorting her to the door. "Do not be alarmed.
This evening I shall send a group of seminarians to pray at his
bedside."

"That would be a great help, Father," she said.

The old Jesuit shook his head in sadness when she had left,
as some priests do at the sight of human suffering which they
know is absolutely necessary for the establishment of God's
Kingdom on earth. But the next moment he found cause for
consolation and hope, when he counted the money again and
made note of the contributions in the ledger that contained
everything about the Little Saint of Timberland.

Downstairs, Madame Gauthier went to the chapel, where
she hoped to find a priest ready to hear her confession. She
walked quickly and as though pursued by the sound of her
footsteps reverberating from the bare stately walls. The
thought of confessing to a priest other than Father Boulanger
filled her with dread, a sense of being unfaithful, which turned
the venial sin of her lie about the money into a mortal one
that loomed beyond remission. Not unlike the wife whose
first fall is sought under cover of darkness and in the arms of

311

an imagined anonymity, she entered the rear of the chapel without lifting her eyes to the altar, then walked swiftly into the confessional, hoping to find a priest she had never seen before, would never see again.

But the wicket did not open. There was no priest in the dark of the other side. She waited, hoping that another in the chapel might have seen her. But nobody came. The heavy stillness of the box closed in on her. Quivering, she groped her way out through the folds of the curtain.

On coming out of the chapel she heard footsteps down the corridor. Her heart fluttered with hope. It *was* a priest. And they had never met before. His arms were full of books and papers and he seemed in a hurry. She walked up to him. "Please, Father, would you hear my confession?"

"What?" he grumbled. At this hour of the afternoon! He would be late for his class. Perhaps she might try the presbytery.

But humbly she begged him to hear her. "Very well, come," he said with a shrug of annoyance. And he preceded her into the confessional, still grumbling.

There was the tense murmur of her confession. Then a pause.

"Is that all?" the voice of the priest could be heard asking sharply.

And after another pause, followed by more intense whispering, he stepped out of the confessional and let the door close with a bang.

Madame Gauthier remained in the dark of the box. He had given her the stiff penance usually handed out for mortal sins: one full rosary. She would stay here and say it all, at peace now in the knowledge that she had done her duty.

fifteen

News of Paula's death traveled
quickly through the town and soon there was a steady stream
of the curious making a pilgrimage to the footbridge, where
they might observe with satisfaction the vengeance meted out
by the Good Lord.

All kinds of rumors were abroad, collecting women and
children on doorsteps, sending them along roads and alleys to
swell the crowd in the center of town. Some said that Mademoiselle Serval's body had been found in the woods, no, not
in the woods but in a horse-stall at the Haymarket, while
others said that it had not been found at all. Monsieur le
Curé was right, she was in a Grand-Mère hospital getting her

313

insides straightened out. Lowered voices told stories about Monsieur le Curé's soutane and the whore's note in it. "How about that!" And harsh words were exchanged over the question of whom that soutane belonged to: Monsieur le Curé, or Monsieur le Vicaire? News went around that one of the firemen had just drowned while trying to pick up the whore's body with a hook. There was talk of the Little Saint of La Buche—he was dead, he was not dead yet, he would give up the ghost before, no, after the charivari. And there were rumors about all of this being only a lot of rumors. The animated sounds of the crowd forced the Daughters of Mercy to raise the tone of their recitation. Sidewalks on both the Rue des Erables and the Rue des Pins were crammed with women and children. Ti-Pit shut the door of his store. The clerk at the Liquor Commission Store decided it was time to lower the protective iron grill across the windows already showing obscene words soap-written by the more daring among the schoolboys.

"Look at them bitches. Man, they're hot and ready!" Red Mallet remarked to a half dozen jacks who were watching the scene from a table at Lambert's. "Mark my word, they're not going to stop until they can stew a couple of them girls for tomorrow's breakfast."

"I never seen the likes of it where I come from," said one of the jacks, shaking his head.

And another one declared: "In my neck of the woods we beat the hell out of them in the fall, so they keep quiet 'till we come back in the spring."

"A good stuffing is what they need."

"Sure."

"You know what happened back home a couple of years ago, when they caught the Curé on top of the mayor's wife in the hayloft?" said one jack, who came from a small village near

Quebec city. And as the men focused their beer-veiled eyes upon him, he went on: "The women raised a hell of a charivari, lasted two full days and two full nights it did, right in front of the mayor's house, and they didn't let off until the mayor himself dished out a hundred bucks to buy his peace and make sure his wife wouldn't get shaved like they threatened to do."

"But what about Monsieur le Curé?"

"Bah! They gave him the hundred bucks, to say Masses for his sin."

The men burst laughing. But Red quickly brought them back to the gravity of the present situation. "Now, seriously, men," he declared, "I think we ought to do something about this mess. Hell, you know damn well this sort of monkey business would never happen if the local boys were back home today. Let's stick together, us jacks. Sweet Jesus, the time hasn't come yet when jacks are ready to take this kind of licking from women. What do you say we all get down there and give the poor girls a bit of protection?"

Their response was silence. All as one they shifted their gaze onto the noisy crowd moving past the windows of the tavern. Nobody wanted to be the first to declare that the lot of them didn't stand a chance against such a horde of wild females.

"After all," Red insisted, "it's in our interest. What if every village down the line decides to do like here and drown our little sweeties." He appealed to their sense of adventure— this town was dull, nothing to do 'till tomorrow's train, so why not get a bit of excitement out of it; and besides, there was a good chance of being paid in goods. After all, they weren't going to save the girls' skin for nothing! Still the men remained silent, unmoved. Red raised his voice to reach the few dozen men in the rest of the room. He waved his arms to attract the attention of Lambert, but the latter was talking

315

with his three waiters at the bar, giving them instructions to barricade the front windows with tables and chairs. Red ordered another round of beer for everybody, and tried once again to rouse the men, but the jacks told him to cut out the sermonizing.

Paul Gauthier entered and went over to the bar. In the last few hours he had looked for Lise all over town. Hints and rumors had sent him to the rooming houses, the Haymarket stables, the ravine, the yard of the depot and the outskirts of the forest. Darkness was approaching. He was giving up hope of finding her. "Have you got the car?" he asked Lambert.

"No," the other replied. He explained that Maurice and Altar Boy wanted to keep it overnight in case things got rough and they needed to get away fast.

A look of disappointment broke out on Paul's face.

"But I'll tell you what," Lambert added; "the beadle was here looking for you a while ago. He says the Curé wants to see you right away. I think he might be able to help you out."

"Thanks," said Paul. And he left the tavern at once, by the back door. It opened onto an alley that would enable him to avoid the crowded Rue des Erables. On the run, he headed for the presbytery.

On the front porch, at that moment, Monsieur le Curé was briefing Madame Dupré on what to do when the charivari began. These last-minute instructions were the result of careful planning that had kept the priest busy all afternoon. After putting together the various reports from Alice and Fulgence, he had paid a visit to Maurice and talked him into giving the crowd two hundred dollars in order to avoid violence. Maurice did not need much convincing; he was too shaken up by Paula's tragic end. Monsieur le Curé had also persuaded him to pack up and leave town in the morning. He had then summoned help from the Provincial Police Headquarters in Trois-

Rivières, telling them about the murder of Mademoiselle Serval which he did not want the local authorities to handle lest the women, on hearing of the arrest of Maurice and Altar Boy, get beyond control. And finally he had written words to be sung to the tune of *Alouette*. Giving a copy to Madame Dupré, he now said: "I will start them off with the first two or three couplets. Then you take over. Make it gay, light, give it pep and the spirit of good clean fun. And make sure they keep singing all the time, even after you have collected the money."

Madame Dupré shrugged that she would try, do her best, though she could not promise it would work out.

"Just do as I say," Monsieur le Curé insisted. "Now go and spread word around that they'll pay two hundred dollars and get out in the morning. Go."

She hesitated.

"Yes, yes, Madame la Présidente. I'll give you a chance to make a speech. But by green horse go, they're waiting for you."

Madame Dupré took a deep breath, smoothed down the lapels of her coat. Then she started across the Place de l'Eglise, walking at a quick pace and waving to the crowd to pay attention. "News! News! Women of La Buche. I have news for you!"

Monsieur le Curé wiped his forehead in a gesture of relief. He sighed as people do when they decide to keep their fingers crossed. Seeing the crowd gather rapidly around Madame la Présidente increased his hopes that she might yet be able to control the women. And as his gaze wandered across the square, what he saw there pleased him also: the police-firemen, following his instructions, were preparing the truck as for a major fire. Fulgence, too, was at his post, smoking soberly near the bell ropes. Monsieur le Curé checked his watch. Time

317

was running short. Now he would go into the kitchen and see how Alice was getting along with that girl Lise, who had sought refuge here after crawling through the forest. It might be wise to move her down to the cellar, just in case. He was about to step inside the presbytery, when Paul Gauthier appeared around the corner of the building.

"Am I glad to see you!" the priest exclaimed. "Come in, son."

On the porch, Paul said: "What is it?"

Monsieur le Curé put one hand on his shoulder. "I talked to Doctor Gendron . . ." he began.

But he was interrupted by a shrill blast. It was the steam whistle at the shirt factory. Five times it blew, proclaiming the end of another day of work. Now the factory girls were coming out to join the crowd.

And at that moment the tocsin tolled its first call, a clear, high-pitched peal that made every woman and child downtown look at the belfry.

"Louder, you, idiot. Louder," Monsieur le Curé shouted at his beadle across the square. This was the time he had planned on getting the crowd to assemble before they could drift on their own toward the brothel. Fulgence dropped his cigarette, and using his two arms he pulled harder, faster. The peals rang sharp through the crowd. There was confusion. Some women wanted to head directly for the brothel, others shoved and pushed to move on toward the Place de l'Eglise. Madame Dupré beat the air with her arms, enjoining the women to follow her to the presbytery.

*   *   *

Late afternoon was darkening above the forest of pines east of the rapids. The sun, a great disc of fire sinking behind the Colline Saint-Marie, turned the western heavens into a blood-

318

red tapestry against which loomed the Seminary's massive silhouette. Long streaks of crimson cloud spanned the sky from the belfry to the shacks scattered on the nothern limits of town beyond the shirt factory. Farmers from nearby could be seen hurrying down the road to town from the hills. The air was full of the loud tolling of the tocsin.

The peals of alarm, repeated on and on, emptied the houses of men and women and children. Those too old to get out insisted on being moved to windows or porches where they might catch at least a murmur of the charivari-bound community. Families within seeing distance of the brothel lined their front porches with chairs to be rented at fifteen and twenty-five cents for the night. Children went rummaging in back yards and coalbins for noise-makers and things to throw at the whores, while mothers who had gone to street corners for the latest rumors ran back home to pick up babies, shawls, broomsticks, and lock the doors. Not one soul was left on the rocky beach by the rapids or in the ravine; Paula's death had already become tomorrow's tale. What mattered now was to join the crowd downtown.

The factory girls did not even bother going home for a quick bite to eat or a change of clothes. They came resolutely marching down the Rue des Sapins, shouting what they would do to the whores whom they expected to find already dragged out into the open of the Place de l'Eglise. As they reached the corner of the Rue des Pins and the Rue des Erables, the scene became one of confusion. The throng heading for the square did not move fast enough for the rushing factory girls, whose blood-thirst was more intense than that of the rest because it had not been partially satisfied by the excitement of the morning and afternoon chases. And when word got around that this was only a rally, there swept over the rear of the crowd a wave of frustration that sparked hoots and catcalls, cries of indignation. The Daughters of Mercy were driven off the sidewalk and onto the doorsteps of the Gauthier house. A group of factory girls gathered in the nearby alley and waited there for the rest to join them in an immediate march on the brothel. But the others were engulfed in the crowd that continued down the Rue des Erables toward the Place de l'Eglise, where Madame la Présidente could be seen waving importantly at the multitude from the steps of the church.

The women nearly had their first mob casualty when Ti-Pit, having locked his front door for the day, tried to cross over to Lambert's. The dense throng carried him half a block down the street, and as he struggled back against the rushing stream, threatening them all with loss of credit and sure starvation, they shoved and pushed and squeezed him against the windows of the tavern and held him there, until a gang of jacks headed by Red came out to his rescue. La Pitoune was watching the scene from her bathroom window above the store. She remained there long after her husband had been pulled inside the safety of the tavern, and her expression then was that of a person who has been stunned by a violent evil wish. More and more women and children and factory girls kept pushing and shoving down the street, so that there was a perceptible stepping up of the advance to the square. A handful of schoolboys made their way to a spot of clear ground near the Police-and-Fire House, where they huddled quickly to work out arrangements for a noise-band to lead the women to the brothel; straps had been fitted to a large washtub that would be the drum, and there were pie tins for all to serve as noisemakers. The women shifted their gaze back and forth between the steps of the church and the porch of the presbytery. The clamor was gradually subsiding, as the Place de l'Eglise filled up. And still the peals of the tocsin went on ringing.

Monsieur le Curé, meanwhile, had drawn Paul inside the

320

presbytery and told him of his wish to help Claude undergo the operation Doctor Gendron had talked about. He offered his car, insisted that Paul drive his brother to the hospital at once. "But don't ask me to explain everything at this time," he added. "I will tell you all about it when this trouble is over."

"You won't need to," said Paul. "I had a long talk with Father Boulanger this morning."

"My car is in the garage. Come, I will give you the keys."

Then as they walked down the corridor leading to the back of the house, Paul said: "I guess my brother and I are lucky you don't believe in saints, and miracles."

"Tsut. Don't say that."

"Anyway. Thank you very much for the help."

"Remember one thing," said Monsieur le Curé. "There are two kinds of men who wear the soutane; the Jesuit, and priests like me."

They had reached the entrance to the kitchen. Monsieur le Curé went on ahead to get the keys hanging from a nail at the door. Paul came to a sudden stop.

Lise, seated at the table with an untouched glass of milk in front of her, was staring down at her lap in abject misery, while the maid Alice lectured her on the evil of prostitution and the virtue of clean living—sin didn't pay, that was easy to see, it was much better in the long run to . . .

"That's enough, Alice," said the priest. "Now you two go downstairs and stay there until the crowd leaves the square. Some of those women are liable to burst in here and find you, and that could mean serious trouble for all of us. But don't worry, daughter, we will find a way to get you out of town safely in the morning."

Paul said: "You come with me now. I will take you as far as Montreal, if that is any help."

321

Lise stood up, uttering a word of surprise, but Paul acted as if he had never seen her before. Of Monsieur le Curé he asked: "There is enough room in your car for all of us, isn't there?"

"Sure," the priest mumbled, somewhat puzzled by this sudden offer to help, yet greatly relieved that Lise would be taken off his hands. And before he had time to say another word, Paul took the keys from his hands and walked quickly out to the back porch with Lise.

"Well," Alice exclaimed, eyebrows rising and lips tightening. "Let us pray she doesn't try to carry on with her filthy business in *your* car!" She was winding herself up for more, but Monsieur le Curé cut her short: "Go and see what's happening out there. Find out what the women are saying."

On the back porch, Lise seemed suddenly frightened. She withdrew her hand from Paul's.

"I am Claude's brother," he said. "Come." And he pulled her swiftly by the hand toward the garage that stood beyond the vegetable garden some twenty yards away. The driveway faced the side of the church across the narrow street which led into the Place de l'Eglise. They ran as fast as they could, in full view of the gathering crowd.

"It will be impossible to drive through," Paul said, on reaching the garage. "We'll have to wait here until they go." He left the doors open wide enough to watch the goings-on.

Lise asked: "Are you really Claude's brother?"

"Yes," he replied coldly, sitting down on the rear bumper of the car. Feeling rebuffed, Lise stood nearby in silence.

The tocsin had stopped tolling the call to rally. The Place de l'Eglise was a seething mass of people. The air vibrated with tense murmuring as news of all sorts circulated freely among the women—there would be no charivari after all, they would have a speech and a sermon instead. There would

322

be no miracle; the little Saint of La Buche was feeling better, he was being taken to a hospital in Montreal. The men were rushing down from Bechard to save the brothel. Lambert was rounding up loggers to break this rally and drive everybody home with beer bottles. The brothel was shut down already and the owners leaving town, scared to death.

This last rumor had reached the square by way of the Rue des Erables, where several women swore that they had seen the two city-slickers arrive at the depot in Lambert's car now parked along the rear platform. A cry of protest rose from the crowd. Factory girls burst out with shouts: "To the depot! Don't let them get away! To the depot!" Madame la Présidente, yelling for silence from the steps of the church, began to despair of obtaining even a semblance of order. Her disquiet was intensified by the dread of what might happen to her poor Louis, should the crowd suddenly move to assault the depot. Where was Monsieur le Curé? What was delaying him? The crowd was spreading around the presbytery on three sides, and now the overflow began streaming onto the driveway of the garage.

Paul closed the doors completely, and stood watching at a knothole in the side wall.

Lise asked: "How is he?"

"I'm taking him to the hospital for an operation," he replied.

"Oh!"

"What's wrong?"

"Nothing. Nothing."

"It's risky. But so long as there is one chance left, we must try."

"Does he really want to go?"

"Yes. Provided you come along."

"Did he say that?"

"He sent me out to look for you."

Lise fell to gazing at her feet in wide-eyed amazement that drew a faint smile on her lips. And she said, softly: "To think that I was giving up hope of ever seeing him again."

"I'm not so sure it's the best thing for him now," Paul snapped.

"Why?" said Lise. "Why do you say that?"

But Paul, suddenly aware of an abrupt hush in the crowd, did not answer.

All heads were turned toward the steps of the church where Madame la Présidente was finally getting everybody's attention. The beadle had brought her a chair on which she stood in the center of the opened doors, with the Sanctuary lamp burning dim in the background. Throwing her arms wide apart she commanded absolute silence. "Women of La Buche!"

And now she began at last, declaiming in high tones of formal oratory: "Women of La Buche; it is with a sense of duty, it is with a sense of honor and pride, it is with joy in my heart, indeed, women of La Buche, it is also with a deep, deep sense of great, may I say, historical consciousness, that I stand here before all of you, to report on the grave situation which an All-wise Providence has entrusted me to handle on this day, this very first day as your duly elected Présidente. And let me say to you all right now: no, women of La Buche, you shall have no cause for disappointment in your *present* leader. For what I have to announce at this moment will prove beyond doubt that my devotion to Les Dames de la Grâce, my firm policy of immediate and forceful action, can be matched only by this wonderful, heart-warming, inspiring, and let me say, rewarding, sight of so many of us gathered here under the banner of vigilant chastity, eternal virtue."

Such an opening statement, much as she had expected from it at the time of preparing it, drew only a mass expression of restlessness from the crowd. She was quick to change her tone

324

of pompous rhetoric to one of gay folksiness, as she went on to announce: "They are leaving tomorrow. And they are paying us two hundred dollars for the damages. Yes, women of La Buche, TWO HUNDRED DOLLARS IN COLD CASH," she repeated at the top of her voice. And now she paused, expecting a great burst of hand clapping.

But instead of handclaps her announcement released a current of agitation through the crowd. "Only two hundred dollars!" The word jumped from mouth to mouth, whispered and shouted, giving rise to exclamations of disappointment, utterances of wrathful indignation. By the strange mechanics of crowd psychology the amount increased as it traveled, so that the women jamming the Rue des Erables heard it as five hundred, and it re-entered the square growing to six, to seven, and these amounts, jolting against the original two hundred, created such confusion that Madame Dupré was forced once again to shout for order, only to be greeted by calls to charivari. Madame Dupré yelled for silence and threw her arms in the air to hold the crowd. But impatience, anger and protest were visible on all faces. Everybody itched to get moving toward the brothel. Small groups gathered at the end of the Rue des Erables. The fringes of the crowd began dispersing.

Inside the garage, meanwhile, Lise was again asking Paul why it wasn't good for Claude to see her again, why, suddenly, she was supposed to be bad for him, when until now she had been the only thing that truly mattered in his life, as Claude himself had told her so often. Paul tried to quiet her, explaining that he had not meant to condemn her, but rather that he worried over how Claude would react when he found out the truth about her.

"But he won't," she cried. "He won't live that long—Oh, why do you have to take him away now?"

"He has a right to live."

325

"But we are happy like this, with the little time there is left. Can't you understand that?"

"He is just a kid," Paul said. "A thing like this would break him for life. With you it's different. There really isn't much ahead."

"There was this, at least," she said brokenly, tears in her eyes.

"But at what cost?"

"So I have no right to happiness?" she asked, a fierce look flashing through her tears. "Is that it?"

"I wouldn't want to be the judge of that. All I want is for him to get well again, and I'm afraid he won't if he has to face this kind of deception. Now, if you really love him . . ."

"Oh, it's all so rotten," she wailed.

"Now, now."

"I knew something would go wrong. It was too good, would have been too beautiful. A girl like me has no business wanting love," she cried, surrendering to her wretchedness.

Paul put his arms around her shoulders and drew her to his chest in an embrace that he yearned to make tender, soothing. Then in a gentle voice he began to tell her: "You come to the hospital with us now . . ." But the rest was drowned under a tremendous ovation sounding from the Place de l'Eglise.

"Vive Monsieur le Curé!" mothers and children and factory girls were shouting all as one. The few who had set out for the brothel turned back. A regrouping movement swiftly gathered up the stray fringes of the crowd. Madame Dupré stepped down from her chair heaving a sigh of defeat. All eyes focused on the presbytery.

The rotund figure of the priest had just appeared on the balcony overlooking the square. His bushy red head emerging in the blue-gray twilight drew wave after wave of hurrahs, and this was followed by shrill pleas for blessings. Never had

Monsieur le Curé been gratified with so great a display of
enthusiasm. Never had he been made to feel so acutely how
much his parishioners needed him. And if it pained him to
sense that the sanction of his cloth was being sought for an
act contrary to the dictates of his conscience and the desires
of his heart, he did not show it: a radiant glow of good humor
brightened up his puffy face, he waved and nodded approvingly
at the cheering multitude, fully aware that he must promote
them to an even higher pitch of gay spirit if their charivari
was to be kept at a minimum of violence. The beginning of the
rally he had watched from the window of his office; La Dupré
had made a mess of it with her pompous speech-making. It
was now up to him to save the situation. A sweeping gesture
of the arms brought him immediate silence. "Now you all
heard what your Présidente had to say," he began.

"And then?" asked Lise, drying her tears.

"We'll see," Paul said. "The important thing right now is
to make sure he doesn't learn the truth until he is well enough
to take it."

"There is *that* truth," Lise said. "But there is also the truth
of what I am when the two of us are together. Isn't this the
one that really matters?"

"It'll be for him to decide."

"I will make him happy."

"You were counting on a few days only. And he was desperate. But now, you might have a whole lifetime together, and
that makes a big difference."

"I will change."

"But will it make the deception easier to take?"

"It will. I know it will."

"Let's hope so," Paul sighed. "At any rate, it's too late
now to change anything. And as far as I'm concerned, you
might yet turn out to be a good woman for him; who knows?

327

For the time being, though, let's be careful what we say in front of him. You might have to invent some kind of story about your going in and out of that place at night."

"There is not much I will add to it," Monsieur le Curé was declaring; "except that I want this charivari to be remembered as a great demonstration of thanksgiving and joy." His powerful voice tearing through the silence-filled air carried clear to the four corners of the crowded square, sounding in jovial intonations a message of holiday spirit. He mentioned that the money which the men had agreed to pay in return for their peace should be received as a token of La Buche's victory over sin. Then he went on to announce that the parish didn't want a cent of it; he, in fact, would like to see it used according to their best wishes—for a bingo, perhaps?

"Yes. Yes."

"A bingo."

"Let's have a bingo."

"Bingo. Bingo," everybody shouted. Nods of approval were exchanged. Eyebrows were raised in appreciation—Ah, he was all right, that Curé of theirs. And they all told him so in one great burst of applause.

Paul said: "If only we could get to Claude before he sees this crowd reach the brothel!"

"But what about your mother?" asked Lise.

"If she comes along we will have to say you are a friend of the Curé or of his maid, maybe."

"So we will celebrate with a bingo," cried Monsieur le Curé. "I want to see every one of you at the auditorium of the Seminary in two hours from now. There will be lots of prizes, in cash. And your chaplain Father Boulanger will be there in person to call the numbers. I'll see to that."

The crowd cheered.

"They frighten me," Lise said.

"They will start moving soon," said Paul. "Then we'll try to get out of here."

His arms poised for a general benediction, Monsieur le Curé demanded: "Now everybody on your knees, please." And as women and children pushed and shoved for a spot to kneel down, Madame Dupré moved swiftly along the edges of the crowd toward the Rue des Erables, so that she might be at the head of the throng when the signal to go was sounded. The priest drew the sign of benediction three times over the multitude of heads lowered in pious respect. And at the same time he intoned: "The spirit of God is now in every one of you. Let there be no violence. Let there be joy in your hearts . . ."

"How can he tell them a thing like that, just when they are setting out to kill people?" Lise said, with a shudder of indignation.

"What else can he do?" Paul replied. "He is only trying to get them to kill a little less. When people are thirsty for blood, they prefer to do their killing in the name of God. It's easier that way. They want the priest to remind them that they are right. That's what they have priests for in the first place."

"For this is indeed a day of grace, a day of joy." Monsieur le Curé was saying. "Not only is the house of sin being shut down for good, but there is also the fact that our Gauthier boy is now feeling much better."

This was greeted by exclamations of surprise. Children gazed at the priest with open mouths; their young faces showed disappointment—would there be no miracle after all? Mothers crossed themselves, either in the belief that the miracle had just taken place or in sudden dread that it was being called off by Heaven in retaliation for the murder of Paula.

"Yes, dear mothers and children," the priest went on. "This

wonderful news has just reached us a moment ago. The Gauthier child is now on his way to a hospital in Montreal, with Father Boulanger's blessings, of course, and with our prayers for a full and prompt recovery. Now, is this not an occasion for rejoicing?"

"Yes, yes," the crowd cheered.

Paul said dryly: "The Indians used to cheer and dance before they burned their victims. Always did it in the name of the Grand Manitou. No, we haven't changed much. Timberland is still Timberland."

"Listen," said Lise.

Monsieur le Curé was piping up the refrain of his charivari marched on the air of the folksong *Alouette*:

> "CHAAArivari, women of La Buche.
> CHAAArivari, charivari Now-ow!"

and at the same time he waved at the crowd that they could go now, with his blessings. Everybody stood up amidst a rising of voices that delayed the start of mass singing. Bits of the refrain echoed tentatively here and there. The priest called the refrain once more and beat the air to enjoin the crowd to sing out. The gay tune spread, releasing currents of pent-up eagerness among the women and children. There was a moment of confusion; some girls yelled for Madame la Présidente, mothers grabbed their children by the hand and told them to hold on tight, shouts of charivari blended with the lively singing. But in a short while Monsieur le Curé had them all chanting merrily at the top of their lungs:

> "CHAAArivari, women of La Buche.
> CHAAArivari, charivari Now-ow!"

Paul told Lise to lie down on the floor of the car behind the front seat, to avoid being seen. Then he opened the garage

330

doors all the way, and tried to guess what direction the crowd would start moving in.

But no sign of marching out was yet perceptible from the square. Everybody was singing gaily and marking time, waiting for everybody else to lead the way. Madame Dupré had rounded up a handful of assistants in the middle of the Rue des Erables; this would be the head of the march, she declared, all of them must stay close to her under the banner of Les Dames de la Grâce which was now being raised overhead by two schoolboys sporting broad grins of pride. Struggling for a path through the crowd were the members of the noise band, with their washtub-drum and pie-plates sounding out for space; they, too, wanted to reach the head where the banner was. Several women had climbed on the steps of the church where they screamed to the four corners of the square: "Get going. Start moving. Charivari!"

> "No more house of sin in town.
> No more house of sin in town."
> "House of Sin?"

called the priest. And the crowd picked up the incantation,

> "House of Sin!"

followed by a rapid exchange between the priest and the crowd:

> "Charivari?"
> "Charivari!"
> "Now?"
> "Now!"
> "Now-ow-ow!"

And then altogether:

> "CHAAArivari, women of La Buche.
> CHAAArivari, charivari Now-ow!"

The next incantation was called out by Madame la Présidente on the other side of the square. There was a lull in the singing, as all heads turned toward her. She sang out the couplet once again. The response was a great swelling wave of joyful singing that could be heard miles away.

And now the march began. It was slow and orderly, much like a formal procession except for the charivari-song. The blood thirst, the frenzy, the urge to chase and beat the whores were mastered, converted into cries of joy, outbursts of merrymaking, a mass celebration of triumph, the sight of which filled Monsieur le Curé's heart with gratitude, hope. He stayed at the railing of the balcony as the women evacuated the square, and he prayed silently that nothing would happen to throw the crowd suddenly back into the grips of its earlier hysteria. Down the Rue des Erables the throng moved steadily, keeping off the sidewalks and marching in tight formation; broomsticks hit the pavement in rhythm with the singing, the noise of kitchen utensils rose to accentuate each response to the call "Now-ow-ow!" and women gazed proudly at the banner on which the words LES DAMES DE LA GRÂCE, imprinted in large letters vigilant-red, stood out fierce and eternal against a waving cloth of chastity-white silk. And Madame la Présidente was in top form; she called out the tune in tones of boisterous leadership, punching the air in emphasis.

At the corner of the Rue des Pins there suddenly appeared a gang of fifty-odd loggers with bags and rolled-up blankets. Bernard Toupin had let them off at the Haymarket and parked his bus there, refusing to drive further into town, from fear of damages to the bus in the midst of the tumultuous demonstration. A head-on clash now seemed imminent between the loggers and the crowd. But Madame la Présidente showed enough presence of mind to call the march to a quick halt. There were a few exchanges of obscenities between the jacks

332

and the factory girls. Bernard headed for an alley on the right side of the street and disappeared toward the rear entrance to Ti-Pit's store. All of the jacks were finally able to reach Lambert's tavern unharmed. And now Madame la Présidente ordered the crowd forward. The singing was resumed.

It was good to hear. So thought Monsieur le Curé, as he went back inside the presbytery rubbing his hands in satisfaction. His maid Alice was standing at the door.

"There they go," she said, pointing to the car now driving out of the garage. It made a right turn into the road that ran back of the church toward the southern end of the Rue des Sapins. Obviously, Paul intended to reach home the roundabout way, coming up from the depot and behind the crowd which would head for the brothel by turning left on the Rue des Pins and then right into the alleys and dirt roads that were the short cuts to it from the center of town.

Nodding approval, Monsieur le Curé sighed: "Well, our troubles are over. Let's hope."

"But look!" Alice suddenly exclaimed, her eyes widening in dread, as she gazed at the sky across the roofs.

There, in the darkening night above the rapids, a thin column of smoke was rising. It seemed to come from the yard of the depot. Deep-red flames began to color the smoke. In a moment the fire brightened up the brush around the coalshack. The lively singing of the crowd grew confused. The march slowed to a stop at the corner of the Rue des Pins and the Rue des Erables. The sky was rapidly becoming fire-red.

"By green horse," Monsieur le Curé cried out in sudden rage. "The devil's got a hand in this!"

sixteen

Of all the rumors circulated among
the women a while before, at least one was founded on fact:
Maurice and Altar Boy were indeed arriving at the train depot
in Lambert's car just then. They parked along the rear platform, to avoid further exposure to the crowd, and then they
hurried inside, Maurice cursing at Altar Boy as he had done all
day long, and the latter swearing to do his best to fix up the
mess. Both men were unshaved, and though the evening air
was mild, they wore coats over their city suits.

The waiting room was dark, silent. In the cage, an electric
bulb burning under a porcelain-green shade poured a full cone
of yellow light upon a desk littered with papers and parcels.
The stationmaster was not there.

"Louis," Maurice called out. And Altar Boy hastened to echo: "Where the hell are you, Louis?"

After a moment's silence, deepened by the rising cheers of the crowd in the center of town, they heard the baggage-room door open. Arthur appeared, grumbling: "What you want?"

Maurice walked up to him while Altar Boy went searching the four corners of the room. "Where is Louis?"

"Gone home," cried Arthur, reeling and rocking on his long legs in an attempt to appear twice as drunk as he was.

"What are *you* doing here?"

"Helping him out for a couple of days. And getting paid for it, too."

Maurice's manner became suddenly affable. "Good for you," he exclaimed. And pretending to know nothing of what had taken place between Paula and Arthur the previous night, he added: "But if you ever want your old job back . . ."

"Like hell, you bums," Arthur cut him short. He let out a string of obscenities that held Maurice's attention while he drew him away from the baggage-room door to the center of the room.

Here, the faint light from the cage showed up the one side of his face that was swollen and cut.

"But what happened?" Maurice asked with a great show of concern.

"It's one of them bitches of yours," Arthur snapped. "But wait 'till I get my hands on her. Anyway, what do you want?"

"We're looking for a trunk."

"A trunk!" Arthur echoed, staring at the floor in a pose of hard pondering. "What kind?"

Altar Boy joined them. "A black one, the steamer kind."

"Where's it going?"

"Nowhere."

Maurice promptly put in: "One of our girls had it delivered here last night. She had a fit and was in a hurry to leave, so I wouldn't be surprised if she didn't put a tag on it. But now she's changed her mind, wants to stay."

"Hum!" Arthur mumbled, "let me think." And after a long pause designed to convince them that he was doing his best to trace that trunk among all the shipments he had handled that day, he asked: "Did you say there was no tag on it?"

"That's right."

"And it's black, you said, the steamer kind?"

"Yes."

"Well, there was one like that standing on the front platform this morning. I remember now. We put it out there, in the coal shack."

Maurice and Altar Boy exchanged a look of alertness.

"That's where we put all of them trunks that don't have tags on," Arthur hastily explained, leading them out to the rear platform. And he went on, in a further attempt to dispel the doubt that he could see on their faces: "The baggage room was full up, anyway. See them cartons of cotton out here? We didn't even have enough room for all of them inside. Come along."

Maurice said: "I'll wait in the car."

"You want that trunk, or don't you?"

As Altar Boy fetched the dolly at the other end of the platform, Arthur pulled a flashlight out of his pocket and said: "I can't let you have that trunk unless you tell me what's in it, so I can check. That's what the boss said. And the two of you have got to be there, 'cause there must be a witness. That's the law."

"All right then," Maurice consented grumpily.

Pushing the dolly past him, Altar Boy muttered between his teeth: "Hey, boss. That son of a bitch is faking."

Maurice shrugged. They followed Arthur down the path that led to the coal shack on the other side of the tracks.

Confident that his scheme was working out, Arthur flashed his light into the sky twice. The signal was picked up by Monsieur Dupré at the window of the ladies' room; he immediately stepped down from the seat and ran along the wall of the waiting room to his desk where he picked up the phone and called the police-firemen to hurry over and arrest the murderers. Arthur went on making an elaborate show of drunkenness, as though this might convince the men that he knew nothing about the contents of the trunk, or that, if he did know, he did not give a damn about it anyway. Moreover, it helped disguise the nervousness which he began to feel as they moved nearer the shack. About halfway there he stopped suddenly and declared that he was too drunk to go any further —would they be gentlemen enough to give him a ride in the dolly for the rest of the distance?

"Sure," said Altar Boy, glad to oblige. He winked at his boss in a way that meant: "Don't worry. He ain't fooling me."

Arthur sat on the dolly and lighted the path with the flashlight held between his knees, whistling softly to himself. As he pushed the dolly, Altar Boy toyed with the idea of hitting the drunk on the head and getting it over with, while Maurice followed a few paces behind, swearing under his breath. This dumb henchman of his had made a mess of the whole thing. He was on the murder path again. It was high time to get rid of him.

When they had picked up Mademoiselle Serval last night, Maurice had intended to drive to Grand-Mère and leave her there in the hands of associates on whom he could rely to keep her away from La Buche a few weeks, at least until the rush was over. But in the struggle that she put up for her life, Altar Boy, though he had only meant to silence her screams, had gripped her neck too tightly with his powerful hands. Then he had shaken her so violently that her head had hit the doorport of the car and split open. Driving down the Rue des Erables, the two men had wrangled over what to do with the body. Maurice wanted to drive north into the woods and bury it there. Altar Boy insisted on throwing it in the river. It was the latter's move that was finally decided upon, for the murder, coming as it did minutes after the fight with Paul, was arousing Altar Boy to such a pitch of violence that Maurice, in fear for his own life, ceased contradicting him and drove obediently up the Rue des Sapins toward the footbridge beyond the train depot. The sight of Lise with her trunk, just then, inspired Altar Boy with the idea of putting the body inside the trunk so that she might get caught with it and take the rap, which, he declared, was what the little bitch deserved anyway for walking out on them as she did. And he swiftly executed his scheme, in spite of Maurice's objections that it would be much safer to get rid of the body for good by either burying it in the woods or throwing it in the river. "You let me handle this," Altar Boy said, confident that once the panic was gone his boss would really appreciate the cunning of his right-hand man.

"A bloody mess you made of it," Maurice said later. Now the whole town was aroused; those women could smell the blood. Instead of a regular charivari raised against them now they would be stormed out of town with nothing on their backs. News of Paula's death and of Lise's being chased by the mob did not help matters. Even Monsieur le Curé's assurances of a peaceful demonstration in return for two hundred dollars handed out to the leaders of the crowd did not relieve Maurice of the dread of coming violence. He felt certain that the trunk would be opened; Lise was too frightened to show up on the streets again and go to the depot to claim it.

He decided to drive out of town at once, and return in a few days to pick up the equipment in the back room. To the girls he said that he was only stepping out to get them some food, would come right back and face the crowd with them, business as usual in the meantime. And to Altar Boy he made it plain that he wanted no more argument about what to do with the body: they would go to the depot and get the trunk and then bury it in the woods somewhere on the way to Grand-Mère. "Sure, boss, sure; anything you say, boss," Altar Boy dutifully agreed, swearing to himself to do his best to repair the damage he had done.

But now, as they reached the coal shack, it was with a broad grin of delight that Altar Boy reacted to the sight of the kerosene drum standing nearby. "Holy Spirit," he thought to himself, "that'll do it nicely." In one stroke he could get rid of the body and of Arthur. What a fire! That was neat. What luck!

And Maurice, for once, contemplated the same move as Altar Boy's. With this variation, however: if he could get his dumb henchman inside that shack he could get rid of both of them at the same time.

As for Arthur, he took his time getting up on his legs. He had opened his penknife and hidden it inside his sleeve, at the ready. He thanked Altar Boy for the ride.

"Don't mention it," said the other, moving slowly toward the drum in the dark. Maurice stepped off in the opposite direction, to urinate, he announced.

Arthur then began lifting the door of the shack, lifting it slowly as though it weighed a ton; the counterweight, if jerked, might snap the rope which he had already knifed down to a few strands. He watched Altar Boy from the corner of one eye. The baby-faced giant with the boxer's nose was noiselessly tipping the drum over after he had unscrewed the cap. The thin oil came gurgling out onto the ground, soaking it and trickling to the foot of the shack on three sides, filling the air with the throat-gripping smell of kerosene. At the same time he was making head-signals at Maurice, meaning: "Come on, boss. Shove him in there." But Maurice was waving: "No, no. You go ahead. Give him a good push." And he held up a match to indicate that he was ready.

"Here you are," exclaimed Arthur, flashing his light on the trunk. He stepped inside the shack and stood along the rope, calling out: "Is this the one?"

The two men approached the door suspiciously.

"Now suppose you start telling me what's in it, so I can check if you're telling the truth."

"That's the one," Maurice said.

Altar Boy took a few steps forward, staring fixedly at the trunk to disguise his intention to reach for the door and pull it down shut, with Arthur inside. Maurice was quick to guess his next move, and this provided him with the opportunity he was waiting for. In a sudden leap he threw all his weight upon Altar Boy's back, sending him tumbling forward to land on his knees beside the trunk. Maurice reached for the door, but Arthur pulled at the rope, raising the door a few inches above Maurice's outstretched arms. Altar Boy had jumped to his feet and now he grabbed Maurice by the neck and the two of them rolled to the ground inside the shack. And as they went at each other Arthur cut the last strings of the rope and the door came sliding down shut with a loud bang. Then he climbed on top of the trunk and from there jumped over the partition, landing on the coal pile down which he let himself slide feet first toward the wicket. He wiggled through it in no time, shut and locked it on the outside. He was picking chunks of coal out of his pockets and wiping the coal dust off his face, when the men inside burst out:

"That son-of-a-bitch."

"Now you get us out of here, bright boy."

Arthur chuckled. He walked around the shack to the main door and made sure it was locked. Yelling and cursing, the two imprisoned men were throwing their weight against the door. They began kicking at the planks.

"Now, now, don't be nasty," Arthur told them in the manner of nuns reprimanding schoolboys. "You're going to burn for this."

"Open that door, you bum," they screamed.

He flashed his light into a knothole and demanded: "How about my fifteen bucks, now?"

The two men quieted down. A tense whispering followed, over which rose a burst of singing voices from the streets beyond the depot. A moment later Arthur caught sight of rolled-up dollar bills being squeezed to him through the knothole in the beam of his flashlight. He took the money but did not even bother to count it. "More," he ordered. "Come on. That's not enough."

This second request was greeted by an outburst of renewed cursing and violent kicks at the planks. One board, Arthur saw, was already giving way. Quickly he struck a match, threw it on the oil-soaked ground, and started running.

First there was a flicker, a wink of brightness, a puff of smoke, as if the kerosene seemed unlikely to ignite. Then suddenly there was a burst of flame. It went running a lace of tongue-like fire all around the shack, hugging the foundation and licking the walls, topping the roof with a volume of black smoke that blended with the night until the heart of it burst open with a blazing roar that smothered the screams of the men inside."

"Arthur," Monsieur Dupré was heard calling from the rear platform of the depot. "Oh, Arthur. What have you done?"

The singing came to an abrupt end in the center of town. The two men in the burning shack were silent now. There was only the sound of Arthur's thin, weird laughter haunting the brush, as he ran into the woods along the rapids.

Then as the flames penetrated to the other drums in the bin, there came an explosion that sent a flash of hell-light over the whole town. The shack flew off the ground in pieces of burning timber mingled with chunks of coal scattering all over the brush, some of them dropping in the rapids. One splinter shot a blazing trail above the tracks and landed on the rear platform of the depot, where Monsieur Dupré kicked it off to the ground just in time to prevent its contact with the kerosene drum standing there.

From noon-bright the sky turned deep red, pouring blood rays over the gabled roofs, into the streets. The crowd appeared stilled in an incandescent pool of unearthly radiance, all mouths gaping, all eyes staring above as though to an apocalyptic vision of the Last Day. For a moment it was possible to hear the rumble of the rapids again and the beat of the logs in the slide. But not for long. The crackling and the splitting of wood and the silken whispers of flames rose to awaken the women and children out of shock. What had been a singing purposeful crowd a moment ago now became a confused mob, as everybody burst out screaming: "Fire!"

"To the depot!"

"Fire!"

Thus the course of the charivari was changed as surely and efficiently as if, according to Monsieur le Curé, the devil himself had had a hand in it. Instead of heading for the brothel, the crowd, no longer orderly but a mob once again, rushed for the depot, shouting hysterically. Running, panting, pulling and shoving, everybody gazed into the red sky above the depot, as though the devil himself had risen out of the flames

343

to beckon them all to come, hurry, help themselves to this good fire that was the only way to kill sin. The banner of Les Dames de la Grâce was mowed down and trampled to pieces. Madame la Présidente was still in the vanguard, but she was no longer leading; rather she was being pushed ahead by the mob. And as she ran she kept staring in alarm at the depot—Louis, poor Louis, he was in that fire, she was sure of it; burned to death he would be by the time she could get to him. There would be no last word, not a chance to ask forgiveness for all the times she had boxed his ears, all the times she had raised her voice at him; no, no, the Good Lord must not make him die without a last word of forgiveness for his wife; he must not leave her that way.

"Wait, Louis. Wait," she cried, as the rushing mob bore to the right and headed for the yard behind the depot. Panting, she climbed onto the front platform. A handful of tenderhearted wives hurried to comfort her. Yes, poor Louis, he had been a good family man! Her right hand pressed her heart in solemn confirmation of their praise. Fortified by so much sympathy, she summoned her courage and walked into the waiting room, expecting to find an empty cage.

But there was Louis, seated diminutive and helpless on a bench against the wall, his back turned to the blazing coal shack, his chin on his chest, his hands crossed on his lap and his pale eyes fixed in anguish on his toes.

Such a sight caused his wife to undergo a sudden reversal of feelings. As ardently as she had cried for his safety and forgiveness a moment ago, she now pounced on him fierce and terrifying as ever. "You coward, get up from there."

The little stationmaster sprang to his feet, uttering incoherent phrases of despair and apology.

"What's the idea? Sucking your thumbs while the whole place is burning down! What happened?"

344

"I, I don't know. Please. It wasn't my fault."

"But what happened?" she demanded, moving up to him menacingly, which sent an exchange of appreciative nods among the women who had followed her in. See, that's the way to handle a husband!

Wringing his hands in distress, Monsieur Dupré moaned: "Please, dearie, don't accuse me. What will they say at the head office? My job!" And frightened out of his wits he blurted out that Arthur had started the fire; Maurice and Altar Boy were in the shack, burned to death by now, he was sure. "But the firemen are coming," he added. "I called them."

This was all the women needed to hear. Leaving their Présidente to do as she liked with her subdued husband, they dashed out of the waiting room to spread the news around.

The mob was all over the place, pouring into the yard and surrounding the depot on all sides. And there were more coming down the Rue des Pins. The clamor was deafening, as everybody drank the red heat of the fire that saturated the air and distilled into their panting breasts the fever of Timberland delirium. The vanguard of the crowd had come to a halt about thirty yards from the fire. But the pressure from behind forced them to move closer until the heat stung their faces and the sharp smell of burnt kerosene gripped their throats. Yet in spite of the discomfort and the danger, no one wanted to turn back, while those in the rear yelled for a chance to get up front. Few bothered to ask what had caused the fire; most seemed not to care. What mattered was that the fire was here, raging, real. All as one, they surrendered to the spell of it, as the confusion and the clamor subsided, and a great sigh rose from the crowd.

The whole place had become the stage for a ritual perhaps as ancient as the roots of the dark silent trees that enclosed it. During a long moment, now, the crowd expressed its primi-

345

tive veneration for those flames which cast upon all faces a glow of inner contentment, as though in the depth of each soul a promise were being fulfilled, a pardon granted. Indeed, the soul that united them all just now was the soul that needs fire, violence, and blood in order to go on dreaming of dignity and virtue. No outburst of joyful singing, no prayers in common, no priest-ordered celebration could satisfy it. The soul that had needed the Holy Host this morning was the same soul that needed the fire and the blood tonight, the same soul that would need the Holy Host again tomorrow morning. And with nearly as much reverence as for communion at the balustrade it now remained still, silent, piously partaking of the good fire. The elbow-rubbing that went on everywhere was friendly now, as in crowded churches. Everybody was groping for everybody else's presence in a mass expression of solidarity.

It was this dense, hushed crowd which Paul came upon at the corner of the Rue des Sapins. He had planned on turning left in front of the depot. The car headlights revealed a Rue des Pins packed solid with people who did not seem to want to do anything but stand there and gaze at the flames. He stopped, turned off the lights.

"What are you going to do?" asked Lise, who did not dare raise her head above the back of the front seat.

"Check the doors."

From the floor where she was sitting Lise made sure they were locked.

"You wait here while I go and pick him up," Paul said.

"Please don't."

"It's only a few blocks away."

"Don't leave me here all alone," she pleaded.

"This crowd is going to stay here all night."

"They'll start moving soon, you'll see."

And, in effect, Lise had hardly said this when Paul noticed a current of agitation running through the crowd. Women cupped their hands to their ears to catch a word, then quickly turned around to pass it on. Mothers picked up their little ones in their arms once again.

"Maybe you are right," Paul said to Lise. "Let's wait a while."

The crowd was indeed coming out of its fire-gazing spell, as word finally circulated that the two brothel-keepers were being burned to death in that blaze. First there were muffled cries of horror, but the next moment there were sighs of relief. Hands drew the sign of the cross; faces raised expressions of gratitude to heaven; even the children understood that an act of Divine Providence had just been performed for the good of everyone. This was followed by a quick return of the excitement and charivari-hunger that could not be satisfied with one holocaustic feast alone. In fact, as the significance of the men's death sank home, it rekindled their passion for brothel-burning which demanded gratification more fiercely than ever, now that the smell of burned flesh was in the air, now that the blood in their veins streamed hot with the rays of the good fire that kills all sins. From looks of gratitude for the death of these two merchants of sin they passed on to imploring glances at the flames beyond which they beheld visions of whores roasting alive. From words of relief they passed on to calls to violence uttered in voices strained by the frustration of their not having had the chance, at least, to shove the two sinners into the shack and put the match to it. From signs of the cross they passed on to obscene gestures; those whores would not get off so easily as their whoremasters had. "Quick! To the brothel!"

A clamor arose from the crowd as the excitement spread rapidly. "To the brothel! Get the whores!" A drum of kerosene was hoisted onto a baggage wagon and its contents poured into the boys' washtub-drum to provide fuel for torches. Girls sacrificed their kerchiefs, women their aprons, which they wrapped around the end of broomsticks and then passed on to the youngsters on the wagon for a dip in oil. Madame la Présidente stood on the platform shouting for order, but the women only booed. She stepped down at once, determined to remain their leader at all costs. She posted herself at the handle-bar of the wagon and called for a few stocky wives to help her pull on ahead. The spark of a first torch being lit, just then, drew cheers from the mass. Everybody burst out shouting:

"Down with the brothel."

"Let's go."

"Down with the brothel!"

Then against this clamor which filled the violent night, there now sounded a loud chorus of male voices bursting out of Lambert's back door:

"To the brothel."

"Hurry up, men. Let's save the girls."

There was no confusion here. Nearly two hundred loggers marched out of the tavern and up the alley that would lead them to the brothel by the back roads, thus avoiding the danger of an early clash with the mob of women. And though most of them had rubber-like knees and bellies full of beer, they wore on their faces the sullen look of men setting out to perform a duty which they could no longer shirk, however grim it might turn out. They had listened to a lot of speech-making by Red Mallet; Monsieur Dupré, coming in just then, had hastened to put in his own word, after quickly swallowing two pints of ale for courage. It was time, he proclaimed, it was high time for all honest men to set their foot down. And then Ti-Pit had erupted in support of this view. Nowadays it was the women who wore the pants in the house, whereas in the old days . . . why, a jack didn't lose his pants to his woman just because he had to swing an axe at camp nine months out of the year. "Holy sacraments, what's needed now is guts, men, balls!" To all of this the loggers had listened drowsily; most of them were only passing through on their way home, they didn't really care what happened in this town. But when Monsieur le Curé had burst into the smoke-filled room, sounding out an urgent appeal for help to guard the Red House against possible fire and destruction, using, as he did, the language of his blood rather than that of the pulpit, they all responded at once, and without reservation, for there was not one among them who did not feel a bond of sympathy between himself and any man who was a true jack under the cloth. And so they followed this Curé, as they would have rallied to the help of another jack.

Ti-Pit was delighted. He itched to be in the thick of the fight, swinging left and right—but not with his fists; as far as he was concerned, there was only one thing to beat women with; a strong whip. While the rest of the loggers left by the back, he walked out the front and headed for his store.

Crossing the street, he noticed that there was no light in the bedroom window upstairs. "So she's asleep," he thought. And for once he felt truly proud of his Pitoune. At last, she was beginning to behave like a decent wife. On coming back from the woods this afternoon she had complained of a headache, and he had made her understand that it would be better for her to go to bed for the rest of the day, take no part in this nonsense of charivari. She had followed her husband's advice for once. It was with a sweet feeling of gratification that he now conjured up the sight of her getting up tomorrow morning, prim and pretty and all smiles after a long night of rest, eager to give him a hand behind the counter.

Carefully he unlocked the door, and stepped inside, avoiding the few spots in the floor where an odd board might creak and wake her. From the ceiling at the other end of the room hung all kinds of harnessry: breastbands, hip straps, short and long reins, blinds, saddles and cheek-pieces. He pulled down a pair of short reins, from which he removed the buckles. He was folding them in two, for easier whipping, when he thought he heard strange sounds coming from the back room. Alert, he listened closely. The sounds now became louder, more distinct—full-throated noises, half sighs and half moans, mingled with the rapid breathing of a man. Never having heard such sounds from his wife, Ti-Pit concluded that some hot-blooded factory girl was being given a tumble by his delivery boy back there. But how? The key? Trying to make as little noise as possible, he picked up a flashlight from the counter, tip-toed into the back room and cast a beam of light where all this dirty noise was coming from.

There she was, La Pitoune, with Bernard, and both of them going at it a mile a minute.

"Holy Sacraments!" Ti-Pit dropped the flashlight and stood there frozen, too stiff with shock to stop Bernard who got away by the trap door in the center of the room.

"Jesus-Mary!" cried La Pitoune, pulling down her skirt. "He's gonna kill me."

And this was exactly what Ti-Pit meant to do as the shock left him. He leaped forward and swung the reins with such force that it would certainly have killed her on the spot if she had not been nimble enough to jump down from the pile of pea bags and dash to one side. The blow struck the top bag and split it open; a torrent of peas came pouring down on the floor between them. She ran to the back of the room and around a stack of cartons, trying to reach the door in the opposite wall, only to bump into her husband at the doorway.

350

Ti-Pit swung again and again but missed her as she made for the front room. Panting, he swung at her once more, and hit the counter with a loud cutting slap.

"You rotten bitch!" he cried, chasing after her in the semi-darkness. Unfolding the reins to lengthen the whip, he swung furiously but the reins, wrapping themselves around a box at the foot of the counter, jerked him to a sudden stop. By the time he pulled the whip free she had dashed out the front door.

"You bitch. You whore," he cursed at the top of his voice, chasing after her on the sidewalk in the direction of the Rue des Pins, the tails of his shirt streaming behind him.

But she was rapidly outrunning him. A group of women carrying lighted torches could be seen entering the alley to the right of the Gauthier house. The rest of the crowd was still swarming around the depot and the bottom half of the street. La Pitoune sprinted toward the alley, hoping to escape into the thick of the throng.

At the corner of the street stood Monsieur Dupré, waiting for the last of the mob to leave the depot so that he might return there unharmed and lock the doors. As La Pitoune came running toward him, he heard Ti-Pit shout: "Stop that whore. Grab her, Louis." In a burst of unusual courage, the little stationmaster reached across the sidewalk and caught La Pitoune's skirt, pulling her to a stop. She turned, and when he would not let go, she kicked him hard between the legs and raced on. Monsieur Dupré folded at the waist with a shrill cry of agony. Cupping his hands over his wounded sex, he fell to nursing it tenderly as Ti-Pit came storming past with his whip cutting the air. Furiously he swung with the reins at full length, but the blows were wild, and he was tiring. Once again she was able to stretch her lead over him. "Stop her. Stop that whore," Ti-Pit screamed impotently to the crowd in the alley.

La Pitoune, bursting into the midst of them, echoed her husband's call. The whores. "Come on, everybody," she cried. "Let's get those whores." And before anyone knew quite what had happened the lot of them were carried forward in a sudden rush toward the brothel. In the rear came Ti-Pit, urging them on ahead with his shouts. "Get her. Get that whore!" while in front La Pitoune went on leading them with her own: "Those whores. Come on, everybody. Let's get those whores." A short distance further, the throng picked up La Pitoune's call and repeated it in growing excitement, oblivious to the demands of Ti-Pit, who kept running and shouting vainly behind them.

Nearly half the mob had left the scene of the fire by this time. Hundreds of women and children were now marching behind the baggage wagon up the Rue des Sapins. Their lighted torches cast along the fronts of the houses enormous shadows that danced in sinister patterns. The rest of the mob was coming up behind, still pouring out of the yard of the depot, when the firetruck finally appeared down the Rue des Pins, and drove into the yard by the left side of the depot, dividing the crowd into two. The overflow began spreading into the Rue des Sapins where Paul was still waiting.

"Now they're coming this way," he sighed in growing despair.

Lise risked a glance above the front seat. But she quickly crouched back on the floor at the sight of dozens of women marching toward them.

"Let's drive off, please," she cried.

Paul turned on the engine and started to back up. "We'll try in here," he said, nodding toward a narrow road that led to the rapids on the right.

They turned into what had been a towpath in the days when La Buche was a logging camp and timber was hauled from

La Colline Sainte-Marie down
across the forest through which
bytery in the afternoon. The trees
way, a distance of about one hund
look like a narrow gutter for ston
bottom of the car scratched the ea
drove very slowly.

"You needn't be afraid out here," he
"You will hurry," she pleaded.
"I will carry him. It won't take long.
A clearing came into view, with the
the edge of it. There was just enough s
around. When Paul had parked, with the
into the road, he turned off the engine a
the lights on."

She got up on her knees and tried to look
"Don't worry," he said. "It's often a lot safe
the woods than out there in the open."
"Please hurry back," she urged.
Lise kept her eyes on Paul until he had disapp
the end of the path into the Rue des Sapins. 7
back on the seat. The rear-view mirror framed a be
that were the foot of the rapids no longer violent
and dormant. A sigh of yearning escaped her, and t
her eyes. Claude would be here presently. She was n
anymore. Yet there was anguish in her heart, a sort of
that was new, which she had never felt when they were
would not last. Was this the price she must pay for havin
beyond tomorrow?

"Oh," she moaned softly, why must she feel so sad
time like this? And she began to speak to Claude in her hea
asking him to come now, hurry, there was so little time left. .

Along the edge of the rapids, at that moment, Arthur wa

toward the car whose arrival had interrupted his flight
the woods. "What the hell is going on?" he exclaimed.
uré's car!"

*　　*　　*

ıde had just awakened from a brief rest after so much
ıg exercise earlier. All he could hear now was a clamor
from the streets. The dark above his bed was ceilinged
reddish forms that danced weirdly. The air that he tried
ıke into his lungs nearly choked him with its acrid taste
ıurning coal oil. All of his senses quickened, as did his
ıthing once again and the beat of his heart. He got up,
ımbled over to the window and flung the shutters open.
He saw throngs of people rushing out of alleys and roads
erywhere. The intersection in front of the Red House was
ımmed with women and children. Some of them were armed
ıith burning torches that let out a heavy black smoke, others
ıere bombarding the front of the house with kitchen utensils
ınd rotten vegetables, all of them were shouting at the top
of their voices in shrill bloodthirsty tones. Though unable to
hear distinctly what they were shouting, Claude guessed from
their gestures that they were calling for whoever hid in that
house to come out at once. Now joining the mob, was a long
serpentine of torch-wielding women marching behind a baggage wagon on which several youths were preparing torches
and distributing them left and right. Wave after wave of
frenzied confusion rose from the nearby alley, as one throng
on the heels of the other came rushing by in a wild stampede
to join the mob in front of the Red House. And all of this,
under a sky fire-bright from the blaze that went on raging behind the depot.

The terror of it was such that Claude at first supposed
himself in the throes of some hell-haunted nightmare. He

354

looked away shaking his head. But the next moment he realized that he was fully awake, when he saw his mother enter the room.

In a voice that rang strained from her effort to disguise the surprise and irritation at finding him up on his feet, she said: "Come back to bed, Claude."

He looked out the window once again hoping against hope to see Lise, or his brother. But all he could see was a multitude of heads and faces and now a volley of burning torches being hurled at the Red House. A burst of mad cheers rent the air, making the windowpane vibrate against the palm of his hand that was resting there for support.

His mother slowly came up to him, with that same look of overly tender care with which she had repeatedly approached him ever since she had determined that he was delirious. Pulling gently at his sleeve, she said: "Come, my little one. Your fellow seminarians will be here any minute."

He could see one side of the Red House grow bright from the flames that licked the foundation. And he could hear now clearly the word sounding out of every throat down there: "Whores!"

"Don't look at all that violence."

"Whores!" the crowd hollered.

He turned upon his mother a look wild with the need to know what was happening, but she was afraid to scandalize his innocent soul.

"Tell me," he pleaded.

In a tone of pious solemnity, as though reporting officially to God on a public achievement that ought to please Him greatly, she declared: "That is a house of evil, over there. Terrible sins have been committed behind those walls, the worst sins imaginable. But we are finally putting an end to it all, dear God."

"A house of sin!"

"It's not that we didn't pray and do all we could. Even Monsieur le Curé tried to chase them out the peaceful way. But when the devil decides to take over a town, and uses bad women to do it . . ."

"Bad women!" Claude echoed in an agony of disbelief.

"The devil's own wives, all of them," his mother went on. "Ah, when something like that happens, it almost takes a miracle to get the Lord to come back to us, poor folks . . ." Her words were drowned under a rising wave of voices screaming. "WHORES. COME ON OUT, WHORES!"

"No," Claude moaned. "No. No."

His mother said no more. She stared at him in pained perplexity, as his eyes, wild with anguish, shifted from the mob outside to his bed, and back again. She sensed that she had said too much, and remorseful, she picked up his cane and put it in his right hand, trying to lead him away from the window to his bed.

As he turned, he cast upon her a look of such infinite sadness that it pierced her to the heart. But smothering her emotions, she quickly rallied to the call of duty. "Come now," she said. "You must rest."

He let her pull him gently toward the bed, but once there he refused to lie down, saying that he could breathe more easily sitting up. She led him to the chair, which she turned at such an angle that he would not be able to look out the window. When she had made sure he was comfortable, she tiptoed toward the door, where she stopped, remembered something.

The golden crucifix! She fetched it from the wall at the head of the bed and put it in his hands on his lap. "Wait, my little one, wait," she whispered and hurried out of the room in search of Father Boulanger.

356

Claude did not hear her. He sat rigid in his chair, unseeing, lost in a whirl of conflicting thoughts and emotions, while the four walls of his room echoed the terrible word which the mob now chanted in alternation with handclaps as a command to come out of that house and surrender.

WHORE. The word flooded his mind with visions of Lise in sexual intimacy with a host of strangers. He could see her white shoulders yielding to caresses from the lips of others, could follow the play of alien fingers curling her long black hair while she nodded languidly. Her lovely visage was all aglow with ecstacy, and he could hear faintly, could feel on his throat, the warm sigh of passion with which she always gave the last remnant of herself. He dwelled upon these visions of Lise with that strange mixture of delight and torment which often haunts a jealous heart. Giving in to the perversion of this new passion in him, he longed to know the identity of all those strangers in whose arms his Lise had lain. He tried to substitute for those alien, impersonal faces, those familiar to him, faces drawn from among his fellow seminarians, and murmured the words of sweet love-play whispered between them and Lise—until he thought his unhappy heart would burst, and going over to the bed he fell upon it sobbing out his anguish and his grief.

"Oh God! Oh my God!" he moaned, seeing Lise, feeling her as she was in his arms on this very bed the night before, Lise the tender friend and lover, Lise drinking from his lips the words of their Baudelaire, Lise by the rapids of an afternoon in spring. "Lise, Lise," again and again he whispered her name like an incantation, as if it were the very life-giving air that he needed so frantically to live. But even as he clung to her so desperately in his thoughts, he heard the terrible word "whore," and she was lost to him again.

Like a child stranded in the wilderness, who cries out for

someone to lead him back home, Claude turned to the Crucifix in his hands, and weeping for his lost illusion he begged from It a word, a sign of mercy. "Oh, Lord, have pity on me." He whispered of the years spent in humble prayer and adoration at the feet of that same Christ on the Cross, as though the memory of his past love and servitude might move the Golden Figure on his behalf. Unaware that he was praying, he uttered the old invocations of consolation and strength for those last-moment pangs of anguish, when man must stand naked in his ultimate aloneness on the threshold of the hereafter. But the words brought no consolation now, no renewed strength. There had been a time when the very saying of these words made him feel a blissful communion with his Creator, brought him strength and solace and hope. But now he felt nothing, only the hollowness of his own despair. He stared at the Golden Christ upon which the fire from outside cast a soft reddish glow, felt hard metal on his fingertips. The Crucifix had grown heavy, so terribly heavy.

He was about to let it drop hopelessly from his hands, when with his last strength he grasped the Crucifix fiercely once again, and pressed it against his breast, in what must have been his only true moment of prayer since giving up his calling for Lise. Yet not one word came from his lips. All of him seemed to have concentrated itself within the thin frame of his hands gripping the metallic limbs of the Christ. It was as if he were spending his last breath in this effort to extract one quiver of life from the Golden Figure on the Cross, one drop of blood, only one drop, that an old illusion might be reborn to take the place of the one he had just lost. In that trance he did not feel the pain in his fingers that were too fragile for the sturdy Golden Figure. But when he looked at it again, he saw a trickle of blood on the breast of the Christ, the blood from his own fingers.

A few minutes later, still in a daze, he was struggling down the stairs, guiding himself with one hand on the wall and with his cane sliding down the railing. The kitchen door was the nearest way out. He stopped a second to catch his breath, then went across the yard, groping with his cane in the darkness and praying for enough strength to find Lise. A short distance ahead ran the alley that led to the Red House.

It might have been a corridor in Hell. Swarms of people ran wildly toward the house on fire. The air was vibrant with red heat. A storm of feet shook the earth. The clamor rang infernal, shrill with hysterical cries of women and children running into one another.

Claude tried to enter the flow of people. But a rush of elbows and shoulders and knees sent him reeling back against the fence. He stood there a moment shaking his head in an effort to dispel the fog of dizziness that blurred his sight. Suddenly, he thought that he could hear his name being called out somewhere in the mob.

It was his brother Paul, whose blond head towered above the seething mass. Again and again he called out Claude's name, looking all around for him while cutting a path for himself through the mob with his long sweeping arms and legs.

Claude, who could now see him, wanted to shout that he was here, against the fence on his left. But he was too weak to raise his voice above the clamor. He raised his cane to signal his brother. At that moment a group of schoolboys came storming by: failing to recognize their little saint in this tumult, they jostled him violently back against the fence.

"Get out of the way, drunk!"

On his knees, bent in two, he struggled to breathe, clutching at the foot of the fence. He tasted dust, and he could feel the pounding of a thousand feet in his ears. Just as he was lifting his head again, an old woman stumbled over him.

"What! Puking all over!" she screamed, furious at being delayed. "Get back to the tavern, you," driving home her command with a good poke in his ribs with her broomstick.

The blow sent Claude flat on his face. He had fainted.

When he came to, moments later, the rear end of the alley was deserted. At the other end, through a cloud of dust, he could make out the fringes of the mob that loomed immense and hysterical in front of the Red House. It was not too far from here, he thought. Yet he despaired of making it, when, on picking himself up, he had such a sensation of whirling in his head that he would have fallen back to the ground if the fence had not been there to support him. It took all his fast-ebbing strength to drag his weary feet a few steps at a time toward the burning house, which now seemed to him as awesome as the gates of Hell.

seventeen

Panic had gripped the girls inside the Red House at the approach of the mob. To run out was unthinkable; they had heard of Paula's death, and they knew they would fare the same way at the hands of the crowds. Now they were huddled together in the front room, near the couch and the jukebox, as if to draw comfort from their nearness to one another. They had locked up one of their number, Marie, in her room upstairs, to keep her from running out to her death in her anxiety to escape.

Israel was at the front-door curtain, watching in horrified fascination the mob milling about outside. He had come single-handed to help the girls, and, if need be, to lead them

361

to safety. Nothing in his limited experience permitted him to believe that the people of La Buche were actually bent on a mission of death. These good people in whose primitive virtues he had believed with such passionate conviction! At the same time, memories of pogroms against his own people came back to him. A pogrom in La Buche! But how could such things be?

Now the front ranks of the mob, getting little satisfaction out of shouting vainly for the whores to come out, were going to try to force their way in through the front door. They rounded up a lot of broomsticks and tied them in a solid beam. Then four stocky women took hold of it, cocked it at the waist-high position and crying "One, two, three, all together!" they dashed with their improvised battering ram toward the door.

The door received the blow with a deep thud and the brittle sound of cracking wood. But it remained shut. The two panes of glass in the upper part of the door had shattered under the impact, which sent Israel reeling back in surprise and fear, his hands raised to shield his face. Now they were throwing rotten vegetables and stones, at the window. With broken glass flying everywhere, the women holding the battering ram had to step back for safety before another assault could be launched.

"Come on out, whores!" the mob yelled, stamping the wooden sidewalks with feet and broomsticks in impatient insistent rhythm. It soon became the steady beat which everybody picked up as an accompaniment to the call, "Come-on-out, whores! Come-on-out, whores! Come-on-out, whores!"

For a moment, after the assault on the door, Israel had stood back in shock, surprised to find he was unhurt. But now the cries of the girls in the parlor brought him to their rescue.

One girl was screaming in pain and terror. She was holding

her face in her hands and blood was trickling down her wrists from between her fingers, while another, in feverish haste, was tearing off pieces of her petticoat with which to administer first aid. Two girls, frozen in panic, stood holding each other like lovers in the opposite corner, their hands spread out protectively over the back of each other's head. Another had been hit by a rotten tomato, and now she was wiping her face and her throat with the hem of her skirt while tears of rage streamed down her make-up. Still another had jumped on the top of the music machine, where she was now shouting encouragement to the rest. They were rushing about wildly picking up the stones and rotten vegetables that littered the carpet and pitching them back at the mob through the broken window, returning, at the same time, the insults and the threats that now sounded as though uttered at the very edge of the sill. The gaping hole that had been the window moments before, revealed the seething body of the mob, a host of faces and arms moving in gesticulations of madness under the reddish glow of burning torches.

"Come on, girls," Israel shouted. "Let's block that hole. Here, give me a hand with the couch."

Maurice himself could not have had a quicker or more obedient response. In seconds Israel found himself surrounded by the girls, who flocked to him in feverish need of protection. The realization that they depended on him for their lives gave him a new strength and courage. To protect one of the girls he threw himself in the path of a burning torch; it landed on his legs and he picked it up and threw it back at the mob. A burst of indignation filled the air, followed immediately by a volley of kitchen ammunition striking the façade of the house. But Israel had no eyes or ears for what was going on outside any more. His fate had become inextricably bound up with that of the doomed girls.

363

When the couch had been moved into position blocking the window, he told them to fetch chairs and bureaus from the other rooms to barricade the front door. In the thick of the confusion with the girls running back and forth upstairs and pushing what furniture they could find down the staircase, suddenly he remembered Marie, imprisoned in her room. It was at that moment, as he was about to go up to get her, that someone shouted "Fire!"

"Fire!" others echoed, stampeding down the stairs, while those in the front room stood rooted in terror at the smell of smoke. Already there was a low wall of flame encircling the porch, and now smoke was billowing into the house and up the stairway as Israel fought his way up through the litter of furniture and the girls descending in panic. It was only when he reached Marie's room that he realized the door was locked and the key was downstairs. Desperate, he hurled himself against the door, his ears ringing with the shrieks of the girl inside, his lungs filling with the acrid smoke enveloping the corridor. When at last the door gave way to his frenzied thrusts, a scene of horror greeted him. A flaming torch had crashed through the window and now Marie, her clothes on fire, was trying to escape through the opening. A roar arose from the crowd below as they saw the head and shoulders of the girl emerge in a shroud of smoke. In vain Israel tried to pull her back inside. The girl held on to the window pane with the grip of one demented, as screaming and kicking she fought her rescuer off.

*   *   *

It was at that moment that La Pitoune joined the mob. Or, more precisely, she bored a path for herself into the thick of it, while Ti-Pit, in the rear, panting from the chase but still swinging his whip, kept shouting in wild rage: "Get that whore.

That one over there. My wife!" But "my wife" got lost, buried under La Pitoune's own exhortations, which the mob readily picked up as her followers had a moment before. People shouted at him: "Not that way, you big fool!" and pointing to the flaming brothel behind him, "Over there. Over there!" But his attention was on La Pitoune alone, and he ploughed on swinging the whip careless of where it might strike, throwing his enormous frame left and right to knock down those who crowded him. Cries of anger and of pain rose around him as people struggled to get out of the way of the flaying whip.

"He's gone nuts."

"Stop him, before he kills somebody."

The main body of the crowd seethed with movement as some tried to get away from the madman, while others pressed forward for a closer view. This movement was intensified by the pressure of another group moving in from the opposite direction. It was made up mostly of youths bent on wheeling the baggage-wagon through the crowd, to be used as a speaker's platform for Father Boulanger, who had made them get rid of their makeshift torch factory and said he wanted to address the women. The venerable white head of the old Jesuit could be seen as he pulled and pushed with the youths, and then quickly accepted a hand here, two pairs of shoulders there, with which to help himself climb onto the wagon as soon as it was wheeled to the position he wanted, right in the center of the place. Only a few feet away was La Pitoune. In mortal fear that Ti-Pit might break through the crowd and finally get to her, she had wriggled herself through the maze of legs and was about to crawl to safety under the wagon-platform, when a bold youth, unable to resist the view of her behind, gave it a vigorous pinch.

"Jesus-Mary," she screamed, in pain and wounded dignity,

which caused Father Boulanger to start in shock, and look around over the edges of the platform, wondering what the devil himself was up to now.

"The bitch! Let me get to her. The bitch. The whore! Get out of my way, all of you. Let me pass!" Ti-Pit was shouting, not far away.

The solid mass of women all around him had finally brought him to a stop. But this did not bring him to his senses. He was still yelling and struggling to break through, when a large firm tomato hit him square in the face.

Ti-Pit stopped shouting, and looked about him with that glazed look of incomprehension seen on a trapped beast. His large frame was a panting mass of beer-blown flesh, hairy patches of which were exposed around the belly where his shirt had come out of his trousers during the wild chase. Big drops of sweat ran down the sides of his flushed face. His bald dome gleamed yellow in the light of the blaze from the brothel, which was now lighting up all the faces.

"Why don't you go home, Pit," someone suggested.

"Go on home, before anything happens to you."

But his only reaction was to burst out shouting again after "That whore," and he recommenced flailing with his whip. Screams of pain followed by a tremendous burst of anger and indignation erupted everywhere. Then the ring closed in on Ti-Pit, smothering his movements under a shower of kicks and blows. He soon went down under the onslaught of the infuriated women who in turn had to shove and kick their way out of the melee as the rest of the mob pressed in for a closer view. Father Boulanger tried to quiet the crowd but his voice could not be heard above the tumult of the screaming, churning mass below him.

Now a great cry of excitement rose from the front of the mob. All heads turned instantly to see the cause of it. There, half hanging from the second-floor window of the brothel, was a real live whore wrapped in a bedsheet, struggling to get out.

The melee quieted instantly, as the women at the core of it scrambled back to their feet. The last one to rise from the ground, where Ti-Pit could now be seen sprawled motionless and almost naked, kept complaining that her shoe was stuck in something.

"Oh, my God!" she screamed, suddenly realizing, on looking down more closely, that the heel of her shoe was stuck deep in Ti-Pit's mouth, rammed down his throat. His eyes, open wide in death, were staring straight up at her. Uttering a second scream of horror, she wrenched her foot free and pushed her way into the thick of the mob; while a handful of women began gathering over the grocer's body.

The rest of them, however, would not be distracted from the spectacle now offered at the second-floor window, where the poor woman was hanging from the sill, screaming and staring in terror at the flames below. Look! The bedsheet was slipping down, exposing the girl's naked body and quickening the blood lust of the mob. What was the good of a fire, if it didn't drive the dirty whores out of the house and into their hands? the women asked, twisting their apron strings and stamping the ground in impatience and frustration. Oh! if only they could lay their hands on that one!

They saw the smoke from below meet with the smoke now puffing out of the window. Father Boulanger ceased waving his arms for attention, and stood staring at the girl with eyes filmed with horror. Now a large tongue of flame shot upward and curled into the window, wrapping her completely. There was a last piercing scream, and then, when the flame receded and exposed the window once again, she was no longer there. She had apparently dropped back into the inferno that the house had now become.

The mob let out exclamations of disappointment, horror

367

and indignation. But these gradually died away as the flames, magnetic in their tremendous bright upward devouring leap, held everybody's attention in a moment of suspended breathing. Father Boulanger, standing with head lowered on the wagon-platform in the heart of the crowd, his shoulders sagging as if under an intolerable burden, drew a solemn sign of the cross over all those wretched sinners, both inside the house and out.

And now could be heard, as though rising from the earth itself, a low, haunting chorus of lament, the last moaning sounds of the luckless girls trapped in the blazing pyre. Nobody was shouting anymore. If there was movement, it was a kind of slow hesitant shoving back from the fire, for the heat in front was intolerable. Above, and only a few feet from Father Boulanger's white head, hung an enormous rolling cloud of black smoke, blanketing the hushed crowd below. Like a huge multi-headed monster whose first pangs of hunger were now relieved, the mob took in with mouths and eyes open wide the soothing spectacle of the flames, the crackling of which told every wife and mother and factory girl in the lot that all danger was now past, their jacks would be theirs, and theirs alone.

On the fringes of the crowd, meanwhile, there was increasing agitation. The firemen were trying to drive their engine through, but a solid wall of indignant women barred the way, shouting: "No, sir. Over our dead bodies you will!" These were led by Lise's landlady, who had gained considerable power with the women of the town since her bold raid on the boarding houses in the morning. Arms akimbo, she stood with her legs almost touching the bumper of the truck in fierce defiance.

"Just you try," she hollered, when they threatened to cut a path for themselves with their hoses. Fusillades of threats and obscenities were exchanged, during which several of the firemen went around to the back and connected one hose, so that they could spray the houses on either side of the brothel and at least prevent the fire from spreading. The lowering smoke was finally pierced by a long, arching jet of white, which caused the group of obstructionists to give up, but not without their leader's expressing her utter contempt by spitting out:

"All right. Let them amuse themselves, the pissers."

Meanwhile, on the other side of the place, the gang of loggers headed by Red Mallet and Monsieur le Curé were trying to penetrate the mob in a belated attempt to reach the blaze and perhaps save some of the girls. They had just carried Ti-Pit's body onto the porch of the nearest house and left it there, covered with Monsieur le Curé's soutane, to be wept over by Monsieur Dupré. His wife, who was standing nearby, was about to pull him away when she heard a familiar voice calling her.

"Help me, please, Madame Dupré. Help me find Father Boulanger."

It was Madame Gauthier. Hysterical since leaving the Seminary, where they had told her that her confessor was at the Red House, she was in despair of ever finding him in such a crowd.

"You come right with me," said Madame Dupré, taking her hand. Glad to get a bit of attention after all the failures she had suffered in the first part of the charivari, she shouted for everybody to clear the way, so that they were soon able to reach the wagon-platform, where she delivered the distressed mother into the hands of her confessor.

"You must come now," Claude's mother pleaded. "He is asking for you. I am afraid this is the end, dear Father. Please won't you come?"

He offered his hand to help her climb onto the platform.

"It will not be necessary. Look!" he said, pointing toward the alley.

Madame Gauthier scanned the fire-lit distance over the mass of heads at their feet. Her hands clutched at her heart, and an expression of painful alarm came over her worn face. "Claude!" she cried. "Oh, my God."

He was there, coming out of the alley to the right of the blaze. Two youngsters on each side of him were pointing him to the front ranks of the crowd. The women stepped back, staring open-mouthed, as if they were seeing a vision. Now rose from the thick of the mob a man's piercing cry. "Claude!"

It was Paul, who was struggling to break through the wall of human flesh separating him from his brother.

"My poor baby," Madame Gauthier wailed.

Gently pressing her elbows, Father Boulanger made her kneel down next to him on the platform. "Have courage, my good mother. Have courage," he whispered.

Nothing that had happened so far in the charivari had upon the women an effect so profound, so immediate, so shattering, as their sudden realization that the Little Saint of La Buche was here among them. In a matter of seconds after Paul had called out for his brother, and Madame Gauthier and Father Boulanger had knelt down, the whole mass of them were on their knees, crossing themselves, and praying. Paul, calling out his brother's name again and again, now was able to advance much faster in his desperate effort to save Claude.

But he, deaf to the heart-rending cries of "Wait, Claude. Wait!" from his brother, and blind to the blaze that raged increasingly near, uttering in yearning tenderness the name of his one last illusion whom he believed still in the heart of the fire, walked unhesitatingly into the pit of the inferno.

They saw him disappear under the crumbling roof of the porch. Then they saw his brother follow him like a madman.

370

Father Boulanger, his arms stretched to heaven, cried out: "Thy Will be done, Oh Lord!"

And they all prayed in loud voices now, trembling, many of them, as before a sudden vision of Heaven or Hell. Their promised Miracle had been granted.

"Thy Kingdom come!"

"Thy Will be done!"

Paul, in one great leap, crossed the wall of flame to find his brother lying face down across a pile of burning debris. He picked him up and threw him over his shoulders. A smoldering beam lay along the front of the house, at the foot of the window that let out twisted tongues of fire. Relying on the calks of his boots, he walked on it as he would on a log driving down the river. It led him to a small opening where a section of the roof of the porch hung at an angle from the wall, making a sort of overhang beneath which the flames could not reach. Through this, he was able to jump clear of the blaze, seconds only after he had last been seen by the crowd.

"Thy Kingdom come!"

"Thy Will be done!" the women were chanting in chorus to Father Boulanger's incantations.

When he reached the alley, Paul stopped a moment to catch his breath, and steady Claude's body over his shoulders. "It's all right, boy," he panted. "She's waiting for you."

"Thy Will be done!" he heard the crowd chant, as he resumed carrying Claude's body down the alley, toward the river. He continued to speak to him encouragingly, as to a child, although he knew with crushing certainty that his brother was dead, had been dead even before he was snatched from the fire. Now he was going to carry Claude away and put him to rest in a little corner of their past where nobody would ever have access. Only Lise would know about it, for she, too, loved Claude as he was. Nobody else would ever know. The fools! They would lose their saint. But that was what they deserved, the murderous fools. He would never let them have his brother.

Paul glanced left and right in fear of being seen. But there was not a soul anywhere, even on the Rue des Pins which he crossed on the double, and left as soon as the entrance to another alley appeared on the right. This would take him to the river by way of a detour around the depot which he wanted to avoid in case there were people still watching the smoldering shack behind it. A short distance ahead, he saw light at the kitchen window of the De Blois house; two women were cooking in preparation for the feast that would celebrate the baptism of the little boy next morning. He ran past, then turned left to cross the Rue des Cèdres and enter the path that led to the river. The foot of the rapids came into view at the end of the wall of trees on either side of him. He saw Monsieur le Curé's car. A woman was lying next to it on the ground.

It was Lise. The sight of her sent a pang to his heart. He placed Claude's body near her and dropped to his knees between them.

Lise lay on her back with legs spread apart and arms outstretched, and her fingers curled up like claws as if in a last desperate effort to fight off an assailant. There was blood streaking down her face from a large wound, possibly inflicted with a stone, on her forehead, and Paul saw that already her eyes were glazed with Death.

"What happened!" Paul cried. "For God's sake, who did this to you?"

She moaned weakly. He took her cold hands in his. "Tell me, Lise," he said, bending close to her.

A flash of recognition cleared her eyes for a moment. She

372

tried to smile, as though to tell him: "What's the use? No matter." Then her eyes closed in infinite weariness and her whole body was shaken with a fit of trembling. Paul placed her hand on Claude's body so that she might feel her beloved was near her. As he helped her feel his brother's chest, his shoulders, his face, his hair, he nodded yes to the questions in her look. Tears rolled down her cheeks.

"I did all I could," he tried to explain.

She heaved a long sigh of acceptance. Paul helped her as she made an effort to raise herself on her elbows and lean toward Claude. But before she could bring her lips to kiss his dead, peaceful face, her breath was spent. Paul felt her death suddenly filling his hands.

For a long moment he remained on his knees between the two departed lovers, his body bent with grief. An observer might have thought he was praying. But all that was in his mind and in his heart was the baffling, unanswered question: Why? "Why?" he asked the trees, the stars, the silent, omnipresent night. So young, so gentle. Why should they die, he asked, while those cannibals of destruction and prayer remained alive in their wickedness? Until at last the dam of rage and bitterness in him broke, and his eyes were blinded with tears.

eighteen

And now it was dawn again. Dark-ness had drifted off to dissolve beyond La Colline Sainte-Marie, leaving La Buche clothed in a gray shroud. The morning fog, rising from the rapids in large puffs of vapor, spread a gauze of dew over the shack-quilted slope of the hill. But as yet, no sun behind the wall of pines across the river.

Paul, using his hands, finished spreading the pebbles evenly over the two mounds of earth on the bank of the river. He had washed the bodies in the foaming waters of the rapids, laid them naked on beds of pine needles and soft ferns, their faces turned toward each other. Then he stood in the first light

375

of day beside the double grave, gazing for the last time at the two lovers, before covering their last resting place.

The fog was growing denser, hiding the belfry, the cross on top of the convent, the chimney above the shirt factory. It rolled in broad waves of mist into the narrow dirt roads and alleys, dissolving as it touched the ground, so that the sidewalks on both the Rue des Erables and the Rue des Pins began to look as if they had been washed thoroughly clean. The fog now seemed to hang still, dense, in a last massive penetration into the walls of the houses, which received it through the scanty weather-strippings between the logs and around the door and window frames.

Here and there a light was switched on, then all the lights came on inside the De Blois' house: it was time to get up and get ready for the baptism of the little one.

But most of the people had not yet returned to their homes from the charivari, where they dug for bones among the still-smoking ruins of the brothel, while Monsieur le Curé rushed about administering last rites to each human frame as soon as it was pieced together.

Paul drove in the direction of the presbytery garage, to return the Curé's car. He did not look back between the columns of stately pines moving past on each side of him. His eyes seemed to be fixed not so much on the road ahead as within himself, fixed upon some inner contemplation of a knowledge all-embracing and infinitely sad. His sorrow was of the kind that is host no more to sentimentality than it is to revenge. It held him in a state of painful awe, which is seldom known so acutely to man after childhood. And if he could bear it, it was only because the night that was deserted of people, and the forest that was his home, gave his soul that solitude within which it is sometimes possible to suffer a great tragedy without asking what are the causes of it, who is to blame. The hurt was too great. It could not possibly have been inflicted by the conscience of man; only Fate could have willed it, whatever Fate might be.

Now the sun, in its impersonal round of life-giving, shot a first beam of light that darted through the slumbering leaves and went ricocheting among the tree trunks, leaving in its path a million little sparks of brightness where the bark was streaked with pine gum. Seconds later it shot across the gray sky a broader, steadier beam of vibrant light, then another, and another, until they united in a fanlike illumination towards which the fog, at its crest, began to rise in aspiring sighs of mist. Soon the top of La Colline Sainte-Marie was visible, with its asphalt road shining along its lazy curvatures through the forest morning green. The cloud above the rapids grew lively with brightness, regained its silver-green hue of the spring dawn. The windows of the shirt factory seemed suddenly to have been painted bright yellow during the night. The belfry, able once again to boast of its proud cock, received the bright darts from the sun and reflected them over the roofs down below. The disc of fire was rising from behind the trees across the river, climbing from crest to crest of pines that layered the horizon. From one end of town to the other the fog dissolved to a thin curtain of radiant mist. Stray shafts of light hit the gabled roofs in a lively erratic invasion of brightness that made the shingles release large drops of dew onto the wooden sidewalks. It was a beautiful, splendid morning of April, perhaps the most breath-taking of all the beauties of Timberland.

Only the air was foul with the smell of burned human flesh.

The acrid taste of it gripped Paul's throat, as soon as he left Monsieur le Curé's garage and started across the Place de l'Eglise. It permeated the air with an intensity equalled only by that of the fiery splendor of this April morning. So it seemed to him, for whom the conflicting duality of murder and beauty now seemed to be the very essence of existence. And understanding this, there came to his soul an overwhelming sense of tenderness and anguish, for knowledge alone could not banish the grief that tore at his heart.

The doors of the church were open. He was seized with a sudden impulse to go in, if only for a brief moment of peace in that sweet incensed twilight of consciousness. Except for the black figures of the two Bureau sisters bent in prayer in a rear pew, and the small De Blois party gathered around Monsieur le Vicaire at the font, the House of God was empty, infinitely beckoning with its gentle secure quiet that seemed to promise everything. But Paul checked himself on the top step. To go in there now and drop on his knees would change nothing, would not move the clock back to the day before yesterday. He could see on the faces of the De Blois party a tense expression of joy which disguised a deeper concern lest the newborn die without benefit of the blessed water on his head, the grain of salt on his tongue. He heard the priest enumerate in Latin the names: "Joseph, CLAUDE," and at the same time he saw the infant's father smile with pride that his son was being named in honor of the Little Saint of La Buche, as Madame De Blois wanted it.

"Poor fools," Paul muttered between his teeth, torn by conflicting emotions of compassionate understanding and rebellious condemnation. "Poor, murderous fools!" He turned away.

The Place de l'Eglise was rapidly filling up with people. They were bringing the bodies here through the Rue des Erables.

At the head of the cortege were Monsieur le Curé and Red Mallet, both in shirt sleeves, carrying Ti-Pit's body on a stretcher, covered by the priest's soutane. The grocer's face was uncovered; the broken jaw was held in place by a logger's belt tied around his chin and the top of his head, and his sightless eyes stared up into the bright heaven. Then came team after team of stern, sober-faced loggers with tanned backs and hairy chests exposed to the bright sun, each team carrying a couple of boards on top of which the remains of some luckless girl lay hidden beneath a checkered shirt. Now and again a team would stop for a better grip, or to rearrange a shirt that kept sliding off, uncovering a chunk of charred flesh or bits of bones the color of rotting bark. Women held their breath in horror, while children stared with big eyes full of curiosity. One, two, three, four! the children counted with fingers pointed at the corpses, until more than a dozen had been carried past toward the steps of the church. Behind marched a solid line of women, serving as a barrier between the first part of the cortege and the last, which was headed by Madame Dupré and Lise's landlady. High on their shoulders they bore what they thought were the remains of the Little Saint of La Buche wrapped in the banner of Les Dames de la Grâce. Father Boulanger walked behind them, distributing signs of benediction left and right over women and children dropping to their knees and crossing themselves along the way. And at the rear of the procession, coming down the Rue des Pins and pouring from everywhere between the houses and out of alleys, appeared the remnants of the mob, rosaries in hand, pushing and shoving while the sound of their prayers spread to every corner of the square. The bodies were placed on the steps of the church, and soon there rose above the clamor the deep-sounding toll of the funeral bell, calling one and all to a mass funeral service that would be held as soon as the baptism was over.

Paul could not take his eyes off the body whose contours

were discernible beneath the banner, as it was carried above the mass of heads bent in reverence. It occurred to him with sudden alarm that perhaps someone had followed him to the river and gone there afterwards to disinter his brother. He stepped forward as soon as the body was laid on the top step. But he was unable to see a thing, for at that moment a most disrespectful scene exploded around him.

"What's the idea, ringing the funeral bells at a time like this?" Monsieur De Blois was shouting at the beadle. "I paid you fifteen dollars for ringing the bells of joy, clear and loud. What's the matter with you?"

Monsieur le Curé intervened, trying to make the little clerk understand the solemnity of the occasion. But to no avail. Monsieur De Blois shoved the beadle aside, and started furiously jerking the other rope himself, while the beadle continued to pull at his own. All heads on the square turned to look up at the belfry. Had the devil himself climbed up there to mess up things? And to make the scene worse, though this was far from his intention, Father Boulanger stepped into it, and took the side of Monsieur De Blois against Monsieur le Curé. This was indeed a day of joy. Let the world know about it. Ring the bells of resurrection. "Beadle!"

"This is *my* parish," Monsieur le Curé said emphatically, throwing his arms in the air to drive the others away. "Nobody is going to tell me how to run it."

Madame Dupré and Lise's landlady joined the argument. Insults and threats flew everywhere, punctuated by fists and finger-shaking, as the bells went on ringing their discordantly weird call for funeral and for joy.

Taking advantage of the confusion, Paul went over to where the Little Saint lay. From the folds of the banner boots emerged. Only the soles were visible, but twisted and burnt though they were, enough remained of them to tell they could

380

not have belonged to Claude. The calks were still hanging on. Claude never had had such hunting boots. Paul lifted the banner enough to look at the charred head and drew back in horror.

Poor Israel! he thought. Poor fool! If you only knew . . . Or is this what you really wanted to know? They'll quiet down for a while now. Then they'll start the whole business all over again. They won't stop 'till everybody in Timberland has given some of his blood to make another saint. That's the way things go, out here, Israel. You should have stayed where you were.

His thoughts were interrupted by the demented Bureau sister. She had caught sight of Paul standing there, tall and imposing, by Israel's remains, his bushy blond head glowing in the sun. And now suddenly she stopped repeating: "The Good Lord is mad at us. Saint Peter won't give us the key." And rushing up to Paul, she pulled at his sleeve and said in feverish urgency: "Oh, here you are, dear Saint Peter! Have you found the key yet? Do you have it? Give it, Saint Peter. Give us the key now."

Paul just stood there looking at her with an expression of bewilderment as great as her own, until her sister came and pulled her away.

It took Paul a long moment to recover his senses, so weirdly disquieting was this sudden appearance. He could not shake off the growing sense that the old lady's words had a special meaning for him. He was tempted to turn back and tell her: "Yes, I have found the key. Follow me. I will show you." Carried away by his emotions, he walked quickly away from the church through the crowd, toward his mother's house.

Expressions of surprise, angry protests rose from the women and children on finding him here when everybody was certain he had died in the fire. But he went on through them, hearing nothing, seeing no one. They pointed at him:

"The Devil himself, in person!"

"He's got fire in his guts. That's why he's still alive."

"That's it."

"It's always the good ones who die."

"Hey there. Where do you think you're going?"

These remarks, and many more, trailed him all the way to his mother's house, where, opening the door, he came face to face with her.

"Where are you going?" she asked.

"To get my bag."

She stepped aside to let him in. Their eyes did not meet; or if they did, neither was aware of the fact. His stared ahead unseeing from the strength of his decision; hers were lowered on Claude's special nightshirt freshly ironed and folded neatly in her hands. When he came down from his room with his bag over his shoulder, she was on the sidewalk waiting for him.

"Paul."

"Yes, mother."

"You're sure you want to go back there now?"

"What is there left?" he said. Their eyes met and what she saw in his clear gaze left no room for doubt.

And so they parted. Madame Gauthier walked slowly toward the steps of the church where she would wrap the remains of her Little Saint in the special nightshirt that his fellow seminarians had given him. Paul headed for the depot, where Bernard would drive off to Camp Bechard.

On La Place de l'Eglise, the women of La Buche were still on their knees. The loggers stood by watching with stern faces the argument between Monsieur le Curé and Father Boulanger as to whether or not the dead ought to be given an official service inside the church.

The whole of Timberland, basking in splendid sunlight, reverberated with the jarring toll of the funeral bells mingling with the peals of joyful resurrection. Only one voice remained ever harmonious, that of the beat of the logs in the chute blending with the now gentle, now fierce, lapping of foamy waters over the rocks in the rapids.